Drapetomania

Or,

The Narrative of Cyrus Tyler

& Abednego Tyler, lovers

TEAM
ANGELICA

Published May 2018 by Team Angelica Publishing,
an imprint of Angelica Entertainments Ltd

Team Angelica Publishing
51 Coningham Road
London W12 8BS

TEAM
ANGELICA

www.teamangelica.com

A CIP catalogue record for this book is available from
the British Library

ISBN 978-0-9955162-7-4

Printed and bound by Lightning Source

*Cover photograph by Jaroslav Scholtz; a special thank you
to Taofique Folarin and Urbain Hayo, and to Kate
Farquharson. Huge thanks and hugs to Diriye Osman.*

Drapetomania

Or,
The Narrative of Cyrus Tyler
& Abednego Tyler, lovers

- A Novel -

John R Gordon

Drapetomania *n. (obs): the pathological psychological condition wherein a slave feels compelled to escape his master, however well that master treats him. Recommended treatment for this condition: firm discipline.*

Book One

Chapter One

A door opened with no light behind it and, unseeable yet nonetheless obscurely detectable, a man stepped down into the darkness outside, a shadow within a larger shadow, and neither the door opening nor the man stepping down made any sound. For a time he stood there before the cabin, neither moving forward nor turning and going back in, existing in a quantum indeterminacy it seemed, restless in every part of his being but immobile as a stump. His name was Cyrus, Tyler's Negro, and this was the Tyler estate. He looked up at the black, flint, star-chipped sky: hard as destiny and as mechanically preordained, so vast it was as if nothing ever ended or could end; no journey be completed, no destination reached. Cyrus, field hand on the Tyler estate, felt an iron weight set heavy in his chest.

Don't change nothin though, he thought. Hope or none. Don't change nothin.

A shudder ran through him then: no, he would not turn back, though the night was bitter cold, and the pitiless air gripped his face tight and made his eyes ache and the rims of his nostrils burn. It clamped the oblong of bare brown skin at the back of his skull where it showed above a ruck of scarf and below the brim of the worn felt hat he kept pulled down low on his shaved head, and made him hunch his shoulders; it penetrated the gaps in the rough stitching of the coat Bella had made him from old scraps of felt and discarded horse-blanket, and slid in through the folds of the coarse cotton shirt he wore beneath it, prickling his chest and belly and sides. Sense-memories trickled into his lower brain then from the cabin behind him, weakening his resolve: the proximity of warm bodies huddled under blankets; familiar breath, familiar smells; reassuring; and if not safe, no, never that, not when senseless violence might manifest itself at any moment, safer at least than the unknown, unknowable road before him. But being drawn back to what was easier fired sudden rage in him, and resolved him to go on.

Comfort ain't nothin to me.

The moon slashed his blackness with the whiteness of bones and ivory as he crossed the yard, his shadow tagging along behind him like a hound, sharp-etched against the limewashed shingles of the cabins as he passed them by, cabin after cabin, to the end of the row. His mouth was dry and he was sweating despite having made no substantial physical exertion. So far.

Had he been given a choice he would not have chosen this bitter night to run; nor this bitter season, when the raw air seared shrinking lung-linings with each inhalation, stripped heat from a body faster than a skilled butcher cut bacon from a hog-back; when the frozen mud jutted up beneath his shoddily-booted feet like rusted hoe-blades, as if the land itself was working against him and in service of those who claimed to own him as they owned a mule, a plowshare, a beer-barrel, a stretch of tilled or untilled earth; would not have chosen this time of year, when the bared branches offered a running man the least cover they could from pursuers who maybe might – though how he hoped it would not be so – detect his flight even before the dawn; no clouds in the sky, and a bright moon that would not merely reveal him as a fugitive, but would lay him bare to those pursuers in some larger stripping and revelation. No, this night he would not have chosen. But running is never a choice: the moment arrives and you seize it and go, or you fail and remain. You go on and risk all, you honour every part of your being that cries out for this: muscle, sinew, brain and bone and heart; or you return, diminished, to where you were and what you were, knowing that each chance not taken graphs, regardless of the survival of the housing flesh, that slow, remorseless dwindling towards a final point of absolute extinction of the soul.

And so for Cyrus the particular moment of his running was spontaneous: from the gut and not the head, and in that sense unplanned. Yet on another level it had very much been planned for: not the exact time; not the day, nor even the season, but for all that, deep in that part of himself he showed nothing of to any other man or woman save perhaps one – yes, there had been one, but he was gone now – that part of him that was concealed like the light of a lamp when you blind it on the hunt

– it had indeed been planned for.

Such an act of deep concealment came naturally to Cyrus, as did other, stranger concealments, and was as necessary, for from his earliest years he had seen others – young men, mostly – who let the need to run shine out from them; and had seen those same young men betrayed by their own kin and kind from fear of the chastisements meted out to those who remained behind, chastisements that were a double rebuke, for both bravado and its lack, and the more mortifying as a consequence. He had watched as those as-yet-unbroken men and sometimes women were betrayed in a betrayal that for all its sting had nothing of morality about it, but was rather the result of those bitterest pragmatic psychological calculations made by each as to what he or she must do in order to survive: just that, because without survival there can be nothing.

And Cyrus felt the trap in the marrow of his bones: to be forever docile so as to do no harm to those he lived among, above all those he shared the cabin with, and with whom he worked the fields; those who were his whole world, and if not his blood then a contiguity of muscle and flesh so close as to stand for kin in every sense save birthing. A family of men: his team.

Solomon was the tallest, oldest and strongest of them, their captain. Then came Cyrus himself, for he was heavy-muscled and broad-shouldered, and could tote a bale with the best, and was in addition a fast picker. Then Zeke, shorter, leaner, quick in his movements, sleeping with the banjo he had made from board, screws and cat-gut cradled to his breast, a ladies' man when he had the chance; long-faced, cinnamon-brown Samuel who preached on Sundays; and until that summer there had been Nate, who whittled wood, freeing from its confines with his blade little figures that some said were like to things from back in blackest Africa, but who could know for sure these many generations hence and begat here? Then there was sad-eyed, gray-eyed Joseph; and Lil Joe, with his cheeky grin and straw-brim hat wide as a lady's, a discard rescued from the rubbish heap with its crown punched out.

Along with the ninety-something other hands on the Tyler estate, beneath the unforgiving eyes of the overseers they worked the fields in teams, plowing, planting, picking from dawn to dusk, Solomon leading the hollers; and come baling time they worked on into the night as well, and sleep was in short supply. When the work-day was done, and their other chores completed, the team slept all together in the same cabin, Cyrus, Solomon, Zeke, Samuel, Joseph and Lil Joe, under rough blankets on straw pallets, in the winter months packed close about a small pot-bellied stove, waiting on the rooster's call, the first flare of sunrise, the pitiless turn of the seasons.

Maybe half the hands were born, as Cyrus had been, on the estate, and had never been beyond its bounds. The other half, imports as it were, mostly knew nothing more than a single other estate, an auction-block, a long dirt road along which they rattled but a single time in a caged wagon beneath a burdensome sky, for knowledge of geography was at all times kept from them. Cyrus often suspected that those he shared the cabin with dreamed the same dreams, though they never spoke of them, as he did not. And of his plan too he never spoke, because he knew what they would say if he gave utterance to it, if he no more than confessed to the thought of running: They'll catch you, fool. You gon die. Die ugly, and make it the worser fo the rest of us you leaves behind. You gots a duty to make the best of it wherever you is, like the Good Book says. Gots to wait on God's good time, like Moses waited in Egypt land.

He had no blood kin. His mother had died giving birth to him, round corn-shucking time they said, bled out and died like a beast with its throat cut, and he was raised passed round the other women in the cabins, a closed, silent child from the beginning. His father, also a field-hand, got bit by a cotton-mouth one broiling summer day, bit on the ankle while he and his gang were digging a ditch to drain the swamp back of Timpson's Creek. The overseer said he was shamming, said there weren't no snake, I didn't see no snake, keep on workin boy, or you'll feel the lick. And Cyrus' daddy had worked on, so they said, till he collapsed in that ditch muttering as to how he couldn't see and he couldn't draw breath. The others dragged him up out of the water and carried him back to his shack. He bloated, blackened, and after seven days he died, stinking of bodily poisons. Cyrus was maybe four then, and still he remembered the smell of his daddy, dying from the inside out.

Steal away, he whispered to himself, half-singing the

words, gouts of white mist spilling from his lips, Steal away, steal away to Jesus.

They'll catch you, fool.

No, they won't.

He knew the odds. Three times in his life, and he was now thirty-three years old, he reckoned, he had seen runners caught by the slave-catchers. He had seen them dragged back beaten, cut about, mutilated, mauled by dogs, exhausted beyond exhaustion, eyes bulging with fear, stammering pointless excuses and futile apologies to Mas Tyler, praying like fools, like he was some gentle Jesus as he stood there stern as Moses, soiling themselves, more desperate than they had ever been before they ran, and by then the human part of them, the realization of which they had hoped to run towards, and which was indeed the whole point of their running, was still farther off, receding fast and then irrevocably gone. Once as a boy, twice as a grown man Cyrus had seen this, and just last year he, along with all the other hands, including even the fine ones from the Big House (because they too needed to be reminded what they were and to what they could be so easily reduced) had been jolted from their sleep one night by yells and bangings on the walls, summoned to the yard to watch as Mister Johnson whipped Williams the stable boy for running.

It had been a stifling night, hot and without a breath of wind. Cyrus' nostrils had filled with the dense smell of oil as it burned in the three lamps positioned roundabout the whipping horse triangularly, their placement conceived to make a show and throw light on every detail and let no part of it be concealed. And the show was the whip, and Cyrus smelt the iron smell of Williams' blood as it ran from his splitting latticed back down over his bare buttocks and thighs, mixing with the salt bite of urine as it spattered down and blackened the dirt between his twisted calloused feet; and the crack of the whip and Williams' screaming was rammed into Cyrus' ears like stakes driven into the hard ground, one blow at a time, as the eager skeeters cloud-clustered round the gouting welts, and the noises Williams made turned from something human into something animal.

And Cyrus had stood it as they all stood it, looking across it at an angle, as it were, so as not to fully see what was occurring as Mister Johnson complained of how his arm was tiring him, and Cleve Olsen stepped forward with a flushed face and sapphire eyes glinting from drink and took over from him, and whipped the life from Williams. And Cyrus saw how a beating can kill a person without bursting the heart or lungs or brain or bowels; how the repetition of brutality can in and of itself destroy. And a part of him died when Williams died, a part of them all left when what was inside Williams left with a sound like a sigh that was in fact a wrench, something that seemed like acquiescence but was a rape, and that was what Mister Johnson intended, no doubt. But energy being neither creatable nor destroyable, and balance being compelled by some force deeper than humanity, or nature even, a defiance was born at that self-same moment, in Cyrus, in all of them, a defiance magnified by finding themselves that night compelled by the overseers into a singular black mass, one thing, but human, and with a will. And Mister Johnson had detected that magnification and had cut his lesson short, hacking Williams free and leaving him lying there in the yard, issuing only the crude instruction, Get rid of it, of Williams' body, and that not to anyone in particular, but to the mass of them all at once, and then they knew his fear, although they did not act on it, knowing too that fear makes men act worse, worser even than they had already acted that night.

He seed too much, Bella said once the white men had gone, as she washed the blood from her son's wrecked and still-warm body. Ridin out with Mas Tyler like he did. She wrung the cloth out on the ground, then pushed it back into the bucket. Goin to town. It spoiled him.

Hush, Bella, Samuel said. He at peace now. He's with the Lord, praise Jesus.

Praise Him, Bella echoed emptily, her eyes downcast, intent on her task as the body passed to that curious coldness that is somehow, in defiance of natural law, colder than what surrounds it, as if the departing spirit takes with it more than the final breath and leaves some dark and icy thing that cries out for restitution in this world of flesh and earth.

And Cyrus had looked on Williams' torn body, face-down in the dirt, this sagging thing that was once a person and now was not, this white triumph, and thought, Naw, he ain't at peace. Ain't no peace in this world for a nigger slave. Nor in the next world either, I reckons. Sides, when you dead, you dead. But to Samuel he said, Amen, brother, amen.

And now Cyrus was running as Williams had run, under the relentless, dazzling moon, and with no better hope, just a compelling need. No chance but a small chance. But they would not bring him back, that much he had determined on: if they brought him to bay out in the brake with their dogs and rifles they would have to finish him there, for he had with him not only a knapsack of supplies but also Nate's whittling-knife, and he would fight to the end. His death would not become a lesson or a show: drag the remains back, they could do that, but no black man or woman or child would hear him scream, hear him beg.

Jus see the ol sack an thas it, he thought. Spirit be somewhere else.

Don't know where, though.

But it seemed like something that mattered; as if the exact manner of Williams' death might have tethered his spirit to the place of his dying in a particular and perpetual bondage; as if dying out there, beyond the bounds of what he had been born to, might mean that even in the defeat of death, somehow Cyrus would be free.

Not free like Samuel says though. Not climbin up to no white man's heaven, thas fo sho. Somethin else, maybe. Befo that, befo Jesus. Some place where the spirit can wander any way it takes a mind to, like it was befo the Word was made Flesh and the Flesh got chained and the Flesh got whipped.

He was nearing the boundary-fence now. No lights were visible in the land beyond it, but somewhere in the formless darkness ahead a dog began to bark. Cyrus pulled up sharply at that, his heart ramming itself upwards in lurching beats so violent his rising gorge choked him. How far off was it? And at what angle to the angle of his motion? Did they already know he was gone? Did the patrollers know?

Can't know, he told himself. Not yet. Night like this, bodies keep theyselves indoors, an crackers like they comforts same as the rest of us. Dog just smelt some haint, not me. An don't matter how clear the air is, wind's blowin my way, not his. I can go on.

Yet a weariness swept over him then so complete he thought he would fall where he stood, even pass out entirely; as if he was at an end not a beginning.

Gots to get goin, he told himself with an effort. Gots to get gone.

Though all was black about him he would have known his way blind, the many thousand times he had walked this and every other path on Tyler. He started forward again with a rising sense of urgency, hurrying towards the fence that marked the limits of all his certain knowledge of the world. Within its confines he was steeped in the wisdom of the soil and the seasons and the slow-passing years, and his mind was rich in the dense concentration of minutiae that circumscription brings; but he knew nothing of what lay beyond, for he had never so much as entered the opaque wall of woods that limned the estate, never mind passed through it into whatever waited on the other side.

Yet as to what might lie out there, Cyrus did have some notion; did have a map of sorts. It was a map that existed only inside his head, it was true, a map made up of rumors and images, dreams and tales and taller tales; sketches of strange things he supposed to be this way or that but would never know for sure until he saw them, if indeed he ever did see them, his only certainty being: the further he got, the wronger would his every notion be, as is inevitably the way with speculative knowledge.

But still, it was something.

Looking up at the sky, he sought out the one thing that was constant above all else: the North Star. It was this the relentless clarity of the frozen night had given him: the certainty of a course to take, a point of reference fixed as a silver nail tapped into the black tar-barrel of the sky; it was this that had decided him to run.

It was Abednego the junior butler who got Cyrus started on thinking of escape in a way that was real: putting a map in his head where before there had been nothing but a throbbing gray block, turning what were only dreams towards something that as he said maybe might could happen. Abednego, who worked up at the Big House, in which Cyrus had never been, nor ever would expect to be; and which, though it loomed large in his mind as it did in the minds of all the hands, he rarely even ever saw, the cabins and the fields in which he and the others toiled being largely screened from the white folks' view by a double line of pine and cypress and, below their fanning branches, densely-planted bougainvillea, for the fine white folks did not, it seemed, wish to see that which sustained them. But that excessive delicacy, that compulsive shielding of their sensibilities, created, entirely against its intention, a shielding for the field-hands too, allowing them the possibility of both unseen action, however often Mister Johnson and Mister Olsen and the other overseers rode by, and its corollary: private thought; interiority.

Abednego waited table in the Big House, serving food and drink to the Tylers and their guests. Anyone with eyes could see there was white in him, on account of his toffee skin if not his features, which were African enough, but Abednego thought himself no better than the others on account of that, not like some in the Big House; nor because of the fine linen shirts and soft leather boots he was given to wear, or the grease he used to slick back his naps till they lay straight as an Injun's. And when he had a little time to himself he would come down to the field-hands' cabins and visit there like family. He was maybe twenty-four years old.

Ain't my clothes anyhow, he said one evening, to Cyrus and Bella and anyone else who cared to listen, standing in the yard before the cabin. Zeke sat on the step and stroked the strings of his banjo, half-strumming some melody that had one afternoon come drifting over from a party held on the wide and unseen lawn beyond the hedge of bougainvillea, to which he had taken a fancy; Bella was preparing a meal.

Mas Tyler, Miss Tyler, they change their mind bout how they want me to look, that's up to them, not me, Abednego said. I gots to do what they tell me. Wear what they tell me. Like a doll. Like a mannykin. Ain't got no choice in the matter. These clothes ain't mine any more'n yours are your'n. Silver collar still a collar, same as if it was made of iron, an you know it gon chafe the same.

Don't talk that way, Bed, Bella said, stripping the skin from a sweet potato with blunt, deft strokes of a peeling knife. Not out loud.

Don't tell me what I can and can't say, woman. Abednego stuck the butt of a cigar he had produced from his top left vest pocket into his mouth and moved it to one side. Left by one of Mas Tyler's gentlemen guests from town, he said through clenched teeth. From Havanny, they do say. An island in the seas.

I ain't tellin you, Bella said as Bed entered the cabin, in search of the candle that burned on the unpainted sill. When did I ever tell you? I'm just sayin is all. She glanced up at him as he leaned into the flame and sucked fire and life into the cigar-butt. Don't let Samuel hear you.

I ain't afraid of Samuel, Abednego said, smiling at Bella with his teeth but not his eyes as she quartered the sweet potato and dropped it in the pot, his derby cocked at a jaunty angle, and Cyrus had been drawn to his boldness and lack of fear.

And Bed had kissed Cyrus once, when the spring growth was high and thrusting wild, behind the winter store of fire-wood; pushed him back against the close-stacked height of pine-logs and kissed him on the mouth. The logs were budding resin and the sticky, aromatic fluid dotted and stained Cyrus' shirt where his back was pressed against the split and oozing bark. The firewood stack rose eight feet high beneath an open-sided shelter, shielding the two of them from the view of any passer-by.

It was a sudden kiss, a kiss without preamble, and Cyrus had not reacted to it one way or the other, had in a sense not understood it, but as Bed's lips pressed firm against his own a warmth had opened in Cyrus' chest and down below, and his heart had hammered so hard that he had had to catch his breath. Yet taken by surprise as he was, more surprised perhaps than he had been by any event in his life up to that point, in that instant Cyrus had neither rejected the kiss nor welcomed it; and faced with Cyrus' lack of clear response, either for or against, Abednego had stepped back and looked at him with naked, uncertain eyes. Then, without speaking a word, he had turned and hurried away, the fear on him clear, as Cyrus was to understand soon enough afterwards, that he had been mistaken; that his need, his desire for Cyrus had generated in him not a perception, as all who desire hope and believe, but a misperception, a betrayal that could be disastrous.

What it mean, Cyrus asked Bed the next Sunday, after morning service was done. The two of them were standing a little apart from the others, but not so much so as to draw the attention of Mister Olsen, who attended the slave service each and every Sunday, not out of piety, nor even to remark on the piety of the Tyler Negroes and thereby magnify his own quality of spirit, but to serve as a perpetual reminder that just as the Good Lord sees all and knows all, so does the overseer. Leaning against the trunk of a cypress and grinning like a fox as they bowed their heads to the Almighty, hips at a louche angle, he was both predatory and intrinsically blasphemous.

What what mean, Abednego asked.

What we did, Cyrus said.

Dint mean nothin but what it was, Abednego said, tipping his hat to Bella as she passed on the arm of another woman, smiling briefly at her, eliciting a tight smile in return. A kiss.

Sho, but –

You liked it?

Sho, but –

You like to do it again?

Sho, but –

Sho, but what?

Sho, but when we gon do it again, Cyrus asked. An where?

At that Abednego's full lips split into a smile that he as soon reined in, a smile quite different from the one he gave to Bella, deeper and brighter both. Soon as we can, I reckons, he said.

Then, sensing without so much as glancing in his direction that Mister Olsen's eyes had stopped on him, Bednego added in a louder voice and a shriller register calculated to be clearly heard, I best be hurryin back up to the Big House now less Mas Tyler be needin me. Praise Jesus, he added in the general direction of the others, who were by now themselves dispersing and returning to their Sunday duties. Amen, brother, some among them responded as he went, and Cyrus watched him.

That was a season of snatched moments for Cyrus and Abednego, scattered like playing cards through months of heavy toil. For the field-hands each day began before sun-up with the lighting of the pine-knots they had prepared the night before, the teams making their way to the cotton-fields in darkness so as to be ready to begin laboring at first light, and continuing in their toil with but a single break for sustenance until the sun had arced and sunk below the other side of the sky and night had fallen once again; whereupon, following the completion of their other duties – chopping wood, grinding cornmeal, feeding the oxen, mules and swine – they were permitted an evening meal and a scanty few hours' sleep. February Cyrus and the other hands spent their days in gangs dragging and forcing the plow through the old growth of the year before, turning the dead, fibrous vegetable matter under with brute strength, preparing the soil for the planting of the new crop. It was wrenching, muscle-tearing work, for they had to force the bladed prow of the plow to hold straight and steady as at a snail's pace it broke up the heavy, half-frozen silt and dessicated, tenacious vegetation; and they whipped and beat their mules as they themselves were whipped and beaten, to urge them on to get the job done.

Then came the weeks of seeding, when the women joined the men in the fields the whole day long; then weeding and tending the shoots as they emerged, slaves and overseers and owners alike tense through fear of frost, for a failed crop would mean hardship for all, and the hands knew full well that it would be they who would bear the brunt of any constriction or shortage; so there was for that brief period a true sense of commonality between all, through fear. But that year they got clear past March without a frost, and the shoots grew calm and orderly into young plants, and the hands tended them loveless- ly but as if with love as spring passed into summer, sunk on their knees at first, later bending their aching backs below the blistering sun as they labored without shade and, it felt like, end, slaves both to the unyielding demands of the burgeoning, blossoming, boll-heavy plants and the rotating seasons that promulgated their development; toiling beneath the glinting, squinting eyes of Mister Johnson and the other overseers, who sat high on their horses complaining of the parching heat as those do who maybe might could choose to move out of it. And the bolls began to dry out and split as the long dusty hours and weeks and months of the picking season loomed.

Across the hottest of those days, when he could, Abednego would bring Cyrus sweet things from the kitchen of the Big House, coming jauntily down the dusty track bearing bread and ham and slices of fruit cake in a small knapsack slung over his shoulder, once even a half-bottle of wine all the way from France, he said, which was it seemed a land of vines; and he and Cyrus would share their feast on the edge of the field at that time when the sun was at its height and Mister Johnson, wanting to escape the blistering heat for a time himself, would let the hands take a short break in the shade of the dusty scrub oaks scattered along the fields' edges. And Cyrus and Abednego would find some spot where they were out of the overseer's line of sight so as to be intimately together for a time, a task that came easier as the cotton grew past waist-height. The other hands in Cyrus' gang would laugh and make remarks when they saw Abednego making his way towards where they were resting, but not cruelly, and they would watch for Mister Johnson on his roan and whistle bird-chirrup warnings if need be; and if he could Abednego would bring them small things too, but they accepted that he came for Cyrus.

Abednego's visits to the cotton fields ended one day in July, when the overseer came upon him sudden as he was jogging up to the edge of the field Cyrus and the others were working, thirty-nine of them, strung out in a long line. The sun burned overhead, the land was parched, the air was thick with dust, and they could do nothing but watch the encounter in stolen glimpses through eyes stinging with sweat, for Mister Johnson had not yet signaled that they could cease their laboring.

No more, my Lord, Solomon sang out.

You, boy, Mister Johnson said.

Cyrus twisted his head and saw the overseer was speaking to Abednego, and fear flushed through him like poison in the blood. No more, my Lord, he and the other hands responded, and they too were watching.

Me, suh? Abednego said, at once dulling his eyes.

(Lord, I'll never turn back no mo)

You. Bednigger. What you doin down here?

Jesus the man I am lookin for, Solomon sang, raising his voice up so Mister Johnson glanced round, giving Abednego a moment to gather himself.

That sure is a fine mare, Mas Johnson, Abednego said, grinning up at the overseer, squinting in the dazzle, his handsome face slick with sweat.

Can you tell me where He's gone, Solomon sang.

What's in that knapsack, boy, Mister Johnson demanded.

You means this knapsack, Mas Johnson?

Don't take me for a fool, nigger.

(Go down, go down to the flower yard)

Miz Tyler tol me to bring you a little somethin fo refreshment, Mas Johnson, Abednego said, not breaking his grin.

(Perhaps you may find Him there)

So give it to me then, Mister Johnson said. And next time don't be so slow about it.

Yassuh, Mas Johnson, suh.

And Abednego had handed the overseer the knapsack, and Mister Johnson had taken from it a bottle of cider, a leg of chicken wrapped in a linen napkin with a monogram 'T' embroidered in one corner, and biscuits, and had thrown the knapsack back in Abednego's face.

Now get gone, nigger, he said. Less you want to come down here in a permanent capacity.

Yes, Mas Johnson, suh, Abednego said. I mean, nawsuh, Mas Johnson, suh. And he had hurried off in the direction of the Big House, stumbling as he went like an oversized child, or a natural idiot, and Cyrus had to watch the overseer on his roan eating the food and drinking the drink that had been intended for him, and choke down rage.

Abednego had never risked coming down to the fields again, for he knew Mister Olsen felt for him and all the house slaves a deep and abiding and utter hatred, envying as he did their proximity to the master and his wife and daughter, envying the freedom of their hands to touch those finer things that he himself would never touch; and therefore Cleve Olsen sought always for reasons to punish the house servants, to tear from them that privilege that was closed to him for all the whiteness of his skin, for all the blackness of theirs, by reason of his station, by reason of his lack – strange troubling phrase – of breeding. And Abednego's lie had implied that Cleve Olsen was in Miz Tyler's eye when he was not, when the fact of it was

Cleve Olsen had been described by Miz Tyler in Bed's hearing as Barely better'n a nigger, the words spat out between drawn pale lips and over bluish teeth. So Abednego needed to be absent from the fields lest his returning presence remind Mister Olsen of Miz Tyler's thoughtful gift and the implied sentiment behind it, for Mister Olsen would surely seek to test the truth of that asseveration, and would as surely be rebuffed. And what would follow then would be the inevitable conversion of his humiliation into Abednego's agony, for he would without question slash his shame into Bed's skin with whip or tawse, and in that way transpose and exorcize his degradation by proxy.

But Mister Olsen never spoke to Miz Tyler it seemed, and for Cyrus and Abednego there was a sweetness to that summer, for there were many moments they managed to steal together. Cyrus taught Abednego how to tickle the languid catfish in the creek, catch them with his bare hands and toss them up onto the bank. How to gut them and cook them on an open fire. How to snare a rabbit and prepare it. For Abednego had been kept from such things, at least in part, Cyrus reckoned, to keep him from running; deprived of those skills that let a man survive in the wild places without any resources save his own hands and wits, just as he, Cyrus, had been kept from reading and writing and wider knowledge of the world, and chained to the few things he knew for certain, to deter him from running. And Abednego told Cyrus of counties, and states, and that there was a government over all, and towns and cities, and roads and railroads connecting them, along which latter great steam-engines rushed with pounding pistons, drawing a dozen mule-trains' worth of carriages filled with people and goods; and most astounding and strangest of all, that there were places not in Africa but in this country in which they had been born, in which they labored and lived their span beneath the lash, where a black man might be free.

Places where folks can just be together, equal, black and white, Abednego said in a low voice as they lazed in the kindly green shade of the great cypress by the fishing hole one Sunday after worship, lying back against its rough and angled, fissured trunk, leaning into each other as if sharing a hammock, and Cyrus' arm was round Abednego's shoulders. Bed glanced

17

about him as he spoke, as if he feared being overheard, even here, away from everyone, or so it seemed to Cyrus. They don't have no slavery up there you know, he said. Up north.

Where the star points, said Cyrus. Abednego had showed him once: by the bowl of the drinking gourd.

Abednego nodded. They even gots what they calls a movement. His voice sank still lower. Calls itself Abolition.

Naw, Cyrus said. He was unable to conceive clearly what a movement might be, out there in that world of which he had neither experience nor certain knowledge, but considered it must involve travelling from someplace to someplace else hoped for and better. Fo real? he added doubtfully.

Yes, my heart, Abednego answered. A movement to bolish slavery. Put a end to it. Course I ain't never seen none o them places, he admitted. His eyes hazed as he thought of them though, as if they were mud stirred up at the bottom of the clear pool of his mind.

So how you know they real, then? Cyrus asked, shifting his shoulderblade against the nubbled bark to ease the weight of Bed's head on his chest. Sounds like pipe dreams to me.

Owin to Mas Tyler an Miz Tyler, an the folks from town when they comes a-visitin, goes on an on about em, Abednego said. An they gets mad an they sounds afraid. That's how comes I know it's true. Ain't no-one afraid of what ain't real. It's why we ain't spose to talk about it. Bout freedom.

And Abednego had kissed Cyrus, and this time Cyrus, intoxicated by his talk, by his presence, by the heat of him, by the muscular fullness of his lips, had kissed him back, and a bright new joy had arisen in him as Abednego's strong arms slid around him and drew him close, and a breeze shivered the cypress leaves above their heads and set them dancing. And Cyrus had lain with women, and Abednego had lain with women, but this was something different. It was something right that yet like many right things could not be spoken and had to be concealed; both of them knew as much without a word being said, almost without a thought being thought. And if the others knew, and they surely intuited some change in the flow of energies between the two men, they knew only that the count of joy in the world had been increased and that was good, and were careful not to inquire further: they let it lie, all save

Samuel who preached on Sundays, who was the only one to raise what might be the case between two grown men so much in each others' company.

So you friends then, he said, some months along in Cyrus' and Abednego's knowing of each other.

It was the quieter part of the picking season and dusk was drawing in. They had toted their sacks, heaving and distended like prolapsed innards, to the gin-house, where the contents had been weighed and trodden down for storage. Cyrus and the others had finished their evening meal and were resting their aching joints and muscles a little before putting out the lamp, quietly enjoying the extension of that brief time before the oblivion of a sleep that was but the bitter prelude to a harsh awakening to yet another day of unrewarding and unrewarded toil.

Sho, Cyrus replied. He like a brother to me.

The others were listening without watching, some lying back on their blankets, arms folded behind their heads, staring at the ceiling; Nate sat in the open doorway, looking out at the night, his back to them, smoking his pipe.

Brother, you callin it?

What the Bible callin it, Cyrus said. Like to ol King David and his friend Jonathon.

Samuel grunted. He opened the door of the unlit stove and tipped the contents of his pipe onto the cold ashes within. Just like, he said.

They all sat quiet for a time. Then Samuel asked, You thinkin bout jumpin the broom?

What you mean? Suspicion put an edge on Cyrus' voice.

Time you settled, I reckons.

Yeah?

Bella's been giving you the sign, brother.

Zat so?

She ain't too old yet and you ain't neither. Settle befo the Good Lord. Go forth an multiply.

Fo what? So they can – Cyrus cut himself off. The others stirred.

Fo the Bible tells us so, my brother, Samuel said.

Well, I don't want Bella, Cyrus said.

She knows how to make a home.

Don't want a home, preacher.

Or children?

She won't want to raise no mo, I reckons, Cyrus said. Not after Williams, nor with what happened with them others neither. And he and Samuel locked eyes then, and it was Samuel who looked away first.

They's others, though, Samuel said, plowing on for all he couldn't match Cyrus' gaze. Melia. Daisy.

Cyrus grunted.

Women, they more rooted to a place than a man is, Samuel continued. Somethin in their bodies, I do believe. They can sweeten the sour.

Like yo Sarah?

Like my Sarah, Samuel said. Fifteen years we been together, or close on. Marriage is a blessing, Cyrus.

Don't want no woman, Cyrus said.

Cause you got a friend?

Cause I got me a friend.

Nate stood up then, knocked his pipe on the frame and closed the door, and Cyrus put out the lamp.

Samuel never again raised the subject of Cyrus marrying, and Cyrus and Bed continued to snatch what moments they could away from prying eyes, flirting in their deeper minds with dreams of an elopement of sorts, while always remaining aware that their brief absences from their duties might be at any moment misconstrued as contemplated or, infinitely worse, actually attempted flight; a double danger, then, wherein each alibi was more deserving of punishment than the supposed crime from which it provided an exoneration. But still they risked it, so strong was their compulsion – so strong was what they shied from calling by its rightful name: love.

Several times they swam naked in the cool clear water of the creek, and afterwards their lambent skins prickled in the warm air as it called to the warmth within them and was answered. They lay together naked in the tall grass on the bank, shaded by the fanning trees, and though the cotton grew high and burst free, demanding picking, Cyrus' hands, hands that had never been used for anything other than thickening, callousing toil, that had never been much more than the instruments of Mas Tyler's will, those hands learned new

lessons that season, becoming something simply and profoundly human as they touched Abednego's body and Bed exhaled
softly and a shudder ran through him and his nipples hardened
as when a breeze caresses the skin.

And Cyrus thought of Bella, and he thought of Sarah and
Samuel, and the burdens of women, and the pain and awful-
ness of loving a woman who, even in the married state, was not
permitted to decline the attentions of any white man of any
standing whatsoever or no standing whatsoever at any time,
and who could be, and would be, and had been so used. Not a
one of them had not been broken in by Mister Johnson or
Mister Olsen or Mas Tyler himself; no black man on the Tyler
estate, nor any other estate as far as Cyrus knew, could penetrate his woman without the burning, heavy and unbearable
knowledge that a white man had been there first, deep in her
deepest places, planting his seed in her, whether there was
issue or none. It was an ugly weight, a screen of silence pulled
down forever between slave husband and slave wife, those very
words themselves a parody, being as how vows made by
chattels, by things, were of no matter to their owners. And
though they could share no marriage bed, Cyrus and Abednego,
in their secret love and their secret places, were free at least of
that.

Then the rains came. For days and nights the skies opened
without pause. At first the hands were compelled by Mister
Johnson to labor on in the relentless downpour, in the febrile,
chilling humidity, attempting to salvage what they could of the
erupting cotton-fibers before they were wholly ruined through
saturation and the consequent inevitable rot; but on the third
day, declining to stand another twelve hours' soaking of himself
and his fellow overseers, Mister Johnson ordered the picking to
be abandoned, and sent the hands back to their cabins to rest
up and dry out.

The rain continued falling, and as the yard before the cabins became a steadily-deepening lake it insinuated itself into
the chimney-flues and hissed in stoves and fireplaces, making
the charring logs pop and smoulder. It drove rats and mocca-
sins from their hiding-places and sent them swimming this way
and that, the cold-blooded preying upon the warm, and talk

turned to the river bursting its banks and flooding the fields if the rain did not stop soon, for the richness of the plantation's soil was on account of its being on alluvial land, and therefore low-lying; and the river, they knew, was rising remorselessly.

Like the Great Flood come again, Samuel said.

Amen to that, said Lil Joe. He was placing damp kindling in the stove one small piece at a time, hoping the heat of the glowing embers would dry the wood out enough to catch and not make a smother. And they all shivered as the rain beat down on the shingled roof, and their joints ached.

Least the rain's beatin down the skeeters, Nate said, staring out of the door they had left partway open in order to allow for some circulation of the air in the sulfurous humidity of what was, despite the seeming interminability of the downpour, high summer.

Even if it does stop soon, the river still gon bust out, I reckons, Solomon said. He was sitting hunched up on a stool with a blanket pulled close around him, his eyes bright with fever and his brow shiny with sweat, but they made him keep bundled up.

How comes, asked Lil Joe, hooking the door of the stove closed.

Solomon cleared his throat. Owin to the weight of water what's built up upriver, he said. They ain't enough room for it to come down orderly.

We in God's hands now, said Samuel.

Amen to that, Lil Joe said.

Crop ruined anyhow, Cyrus said. Can't plant again, not after May.

Fo better or worser, Nate said.

Fo better or worser, Cyrus agreed. He rubbed an aching shoulder and thought of Abednego's strong right hand gripping the back of his neck, the ball of Bed's thumb moving around, finding and deftly pressing on bundled nerves, freeing them up. But Abednego was up in the Big House with no excuse to leave it. Fine and dry up in the Big House, Cyrus thought, and for a moment he almost hated Bed.

You reckons any o the crop be saved, Lil Joe asked.

If the rain stop soon? Half, maybe, Cyrus said. Solomon nodded, cleared his throat again.

Maybe mo, if the frost come late like it can do, Nate said.

Like say November time.

Plants keep givin, we keep toilin, Lil Joe said.

Till frost kills em, Cyrus said.

Then we gets to rest.

The longer they last, the mo we picks, Samuel said. Toil or no toil, that's somethin.

And Cyrus recalled a Bible verse Abednego had told him once, something about the lilies of the field: For they toil not, nor do they spin.

You know what lilies look like, he asked.

What you talkin bout, said Nate.

Nothin, Cyrus said. Just thinkin is all.

Flowers, ain't they, said Samuel. Mostly fo funerals, I hears. I guess they would look fine.

Frost kill em too? Cyrus asked.

Samuel shrugged. I would suppose so.

Hard to think on frost right now, Lil Joe said. His boyish face was greasy, and his half-unbuttoned shirt blotted black with sweat where the curves and angles of his body touched it.

Could do with a lil frost on me, Solomon said breathlessly, and he coughed again, and his cough now had a seed-pod rattle to it that disquieted the rest of them and stopped their talk. A little while later Samuel put out the lamp and they all attempted to get some sleep.

Cyrus lay in the dark staring up at the ceiling, listening to the rain clatter on the shingles and Solomon breathe. Don't stop, he thought. Keep goin. You strong, Solomon, stronger than all of us, I reckons; stronger than me fo sho, and I'm strong.

He was distracted by the whine of a mosquito. He waited until it settled on his forearm then crushed it into a bloody smear; then lay back again. The rain fell as if it would continue until the end of time. Cyrus realised he could no longer hear Solomon breathing. He turned over and looked across to where the other man lay huddled, a black outline, and Cyrus held his breath and the blood thudded in his ears as he strained to detect some movement in that outline. There was none. Solomon, he said hoarsely, Solomon?

Solomon stirred under the blanket and snored softly. Cyrus exhaled. Here yet a while, he thought. The rain clattered on.

*

None of them slept well that night, and all woke aching. The following two days and nights passed in the same torpid, dispiriting way.

On the morning of the sixth day, shortly after dawn, the rain continuing relentless, the overseers, thigh-booted and clad in oilskins, came banging on the cabin walls shouting as to how the river was going to burst its banks if nothing was done, and they needed all hands to sandbag it at its weakest points.

The clouds so wholly occluded the sky that sunrise or no sunrise it remained near night-dark, so Cyrus lit the lamp with a spill from the stove-embers; then he, Nate, Samuel, Joe and Lil Joe forced their weary limbs into the still-damp shirts and pants they had hung on lines around the room the night before, lighting the stove despite the boiling heat in a vain attempt to get their garments at least partway dry while they slept, and pushed their sore, bruised feet into still-dank, split and mud-clogged boots and shoes.

Solomon, however, was too sick to stand, and Nate was deputed to tell Mister Olsen so. Through a curtain of falling rain Cyrus watched Mister Olsen curse Nate then strike him about the head with the butt of his whip, raising a welt on Nate's temple for having the temerity to tell a white man a fact he did not wish to hear. Nate stood there impassive, uncomplaining, taking the abuse until somehow he was transmuted by the energy of the assault from victim or object into some manifestation of endurance, and seeing that transmutation Mister Olsen restrained himself, a queer look in his light eyes. Then he stomped into the cabin to see if Solomon was shirking, reinflating the bladder of his rage with every heavy-booted step.

God-damn idle niggers, he said as he pulled the blanket off Solomon, ready to kick and otherwise belabor him, but Solomon was shiny with sweat, wild-eyed and shivering, and the hoarseness of his breathing was near-unnatural in its intensity and curiously projected, so Mister Olsen threw the blanket back in his face. God-damn it, he said. Like you done it on purpose, on account of there's work needs doin. God-damn it. He turned. The rest of you, I need you in the big barn.

Yassuh, Samuel said, bobbing his head. Right away, Mas

Olsen, sir.

A piece of old grain-sack covering his head against the still heavily-falling rain, Cyrus hurried with the others over to the big barn behind the stable-block and smithy, sloshing thickly through the pooled water as he made his way diagonally across the yard in split-soled boots held together by wound and knotted twine.

The barn was raised on brick supports to deter rats, and, being also situated on somewhat higher ground, had a plank floor that was still dry, to the relief of all, men and women alike, though for most of the men the respite from being soaked through would be brief. In short order the women were put to sewing sacking, and they and the youngsters and the old men were charged with filling the resultant sacks with sand and dirt that was to be barrowed in by the field-hands from a great heap round the back of the stables, left over from the digging out of the barn's foundations two years back. The mouths of the filled and stone-heavy sacks would then be stitched shut by the women.

One third part of the male hands were to be employed shoveling, barrowing dirt and slinging the filled sacks onto the backs of three open wagons, while the rest were led down to the river by Mister Johnson to unload the sacks when they arrived there and, under the overseers' directions, pile them at the weakest points along the bank. Mas Tyler's grooms and stable-boys were to drive the laden wagons down to the water, unlade them, then return post-haste for fresh loads in as near to a continuous relay as could be managed.

Cyrus was set to shifting dirt, his arms and shoulders soon enough commencing to burn from the weight of the barrow he was wheeling, exposure to the heavy and persistent rain rapidly lowering his spirits – lowering all their spirits – while at the same time inducing a hysterical sense of urgency. His only respite on each fast circuit was a brief half-minute standing in the downpour by the mound, heaving for breath, his cramped hands tingling as, backs bent, Joe and Lil Joe spaded in the sodden dirt, rapidly refilling the barrow until it was once more heaped and heavy and hard to manage. Cyrus had then to take hold of its handles, lift its back end, haul it cumbersomely round on its wooden wheel, brace up and set off at a stumbling run back to the barn, and there raise and empty it.

Thunder rumbled overhead and lightning lanced down repeatedly into a belt of woodland on the estate's eastern border, presaging, unbelievably enough, an intensification of the deluge, and creating a sense of panic even among the overseers that resulted in their laying about them with their whips to no useful end but the expulsion of their own intensifying emotions.

Still the work got done: first one heavily-piled wagon rolled out, then some ten minutes later a second, their axles groaning, the pairs of horses pulling them straining vascularly in their harnesses, for necessity compelled the wagons' overlading. Cyrus and his team were dragging and swinging the sodden, sand-filled sacks up onto the third wagon, Cyrus leading the call-and-response, when one of the overseers who had accompanied the second wagon on its way, returned breathless on foot and hurried up to Mister Olsen and spoke to him in urgent tones. Mister Olsen cursed and told Cyrus' team to leave off what they were doing, take up some planks and follow him.

Wagons are boggin down, he said. Ground's like swamp out there.

Cyrus, Nate, Samuel, Joe and Lil Joe picked up several of the lengths of timber that had been set aside to season in a lean-to by the smithy, hefted them to their shoulders, and followed Mister Olsen down the riverward path, he on his mare, them on foot, and each step they took was made heavier and more difficult by the wagon-churned, sucking mud, and the weight of the wood they carried drove their feet down deeper.

Twenty minutes later they reached the mired second wagon, and as the lightning flashed, before their eyes it slid obliquely into a flooded drainage ditch that ran alongside the track. The back axle twisted like a cat's spine and the left rear wheel sank into the mud and water to more than half its height, and as Robinson the groom belabored the struggling, wild-eyed horses, like bowels opening the wagon began to disgorge its weighty load of sacks. The horses reared and screamed and attempted to pull forward, but they could not drag it up out of the ditch however hard the groom flogged them, and the greater part of the sacks went slithering and tumbling into the water like millstones. At this abrupt lessening of weight the wagon momentarily lifted free of the ditch, but the edge of the bank gave way and it once more slid back, pulling the snorting, heaving team with it, and tilted swayingly, and now the left front wheel was also sunk in the water.

Boy, stop that, Mister Olsen yelled at Robinson, who was wielding the whip frenziedly, his other hand tight about the reins, his thighs tense, both feet braced against the buckboard as he was all but flung from his seat. Don't mark them horses. Them horses is valuable, you hear me?

We best get these planks placed, Cyrus said to Nate and Joe in a low tone. There an there, he indicated. If they don't break under the weight, we can roll it up on the slant without the axle bustin.

Whip them horses again I'll put some stripes on you, Mister Olsen roared. God-damn it. You, boy – he turned on Cyrus. You got them planks down yet?

Just doin it now, Mas Olsen, suh, Cyrus said, as he and Nate slipped down into the ditch. Thigh-deep in water they wedged the ends of the lengths of wood beneath the iron-hooped wheels of the wagon, angling them obliquely so as to form a paired ramp by means of which the vehicle might be impelled forward and up out of the ditch.

Well, put your backs into it then, Mister Olsen said.

At that moment a bolt of lightning struck a nearby pine, the sap within, raised instantaneously to boiling point, expanding wildly and bursting it to pieces. Mister Olsen's mare screamed and reared and he was flung from it and landed in the mud by the wagon hard and at a clumsy angle. Cyrus, Robinson and the other hands watched, for a moment entirely still save for their chests rising, falling, rising, falling as the rain came down straight and the sweet, aromatic scent of heated pine-resin filled their flaring nostrils, and the wood inside the split trunk showed pale and pithy.

Mas Olsen, suh, said Samuel, the tone of his voice rehearsedly solicitous though he made no move toward the fallen white man, who lay there immobile, unresponsive. Mas Olsen, suh?

You reckon he dead, asked Lil Joe.

No-one answered. Then Mister Olsen kicked and jerked and rolled over, coughing and cursing. As one, the hands rushed forward, so as to be seen helping him to his feet. He shoved them away angrily.

God-damn niggers, he said. Then, seemingly dazed, he staggered in a tight circle like a hound before it lies down, holding a hand out in front of his face as he did so, as if blind. Where's my horse, he asked.

I gots her, suh, said Robinson, who had jumped down from the wagon and caught the reins of the eye-rolling mare, and was quieting her by stroking her neck: There now, sweetheart. There now –

Gimme those, said Mister Olsen, yanking the reins roughly from Robinson's hand. Gripping the pommel he stepped into the stirrup, and with a grunt swung himself up into the saddle, his face contorting with pain as he did so, suggesting he was attempting to mask an injury to the arm he had fallen on that was more serious than it seemed, so as to not appear weak in front of the hands. One side of his head was plastered with mud, hair sticking up wildly.

You alright, Mas Olsen, suh, asked Robinson, his eyes blank in the way a slave's eyes are always blank when showing solicitous concern for his master's well-being.

Mind your business, boy, Mister Olsen snapped. Pass me up my hat.

Robinson did so. Thunder rumbled overhead again, and Mister Olsen was for a moment distracted by preventing his horse from rearing, so as not to be flung from the saddle a second time within the space of two minutes. When he had done so he said to Robinson, Get back in your seat. The rest of you get back of the wagon and put your shoulders to it. Robinson, on my word whip up them horses –

A moment later Cyrus, Nate and the others were back in the ditch, throwing all their weight against the back and left side of the wagon as Robinson once more belabored the bucking, struggling horses, and the men's feet like the buttresses of some subsiding cathedral were driven deeper and deeper into the mud beneath the water until at last, with painful slowness, the horses began to drag the wagon up from the ditch. With an audible sucking sound the wheels pulled free and it began to creak its way up the planks, which bowed ominously beneath its weight but remained in place. Then came another crash of thunder. One of the horses in the team reared in panic and, kicking, half-slithered into the ditch. Before it could right itself the wagon slid sideways off the planks, and the left rear wheel rolled back onto Nate's foot and crushed it, crippling him instantly.

Keep pushing, yelled Mister Olsen as Nate collapsed screaming into the water, whipping Cyrus and the other hands around the heads and shoulders as he saw them threatening to throw their efforts aside in order to go to Nate's assistance. Keep pushing, you God-damn no-good lazy niggers –

And with a yell from the gut and a final wrenching effort they forced the wagon back up onto the track, its weight settling level at last, its frame and wheels undamaged, though it had shed more than two thirds of its load into the flooded ditch in which they stood, now waist-deep. Their task done, heaving and panting and drenched, the hands turned to Nate, lifting him by his extended arms like an agonized Christ. He was moaning and shuddering, and his foot was burst open as the pine-tree had burst open when the lightning struck it, blood gouting freely into the muddy brown water.

Leave him, Mister Olsen ordered. Can't do nothin for him now. Leave him be and get them sacks back on there – and his whip struck Cyrus across the shoulders for not turning quickly enough from where he had set Nate down on the sodden ground beyond the ditch. I said load them sacks, God-damn it. Won't do him no good if the banks burst.

Later they carried Nate back to the cabin and cleaned and bound up his foot. There was talk of sending for a doctor but no doctor came, and he burned up with a fever even worse than the one that had laid Solomon low, and within a week he was gone, and so Cyrus came by his knife.

The river continued to rise, and Cyrus and the other hands, house-slaves and all, none exempted, even the elderly and infirm, were sent down to sandbag the banks at their lowest points. The rain beat down on them with stinging force, and they worked in teams with only the briefest intervals to catch their breaths, and there was no shelter. Once every piece of sacking that could be stitched had been turned into a sandbag, however misshapen or odd-sized, and toted the half-mile from the big barn to the river, the women who had been sewing, and any children past toddling age, were sent down to sandbag with the rest. And so it went on, hour after hour: the battle to raise the banks to a greater height than the one to which the river was, it seemed, ineluctably rising.

At one point, as the afternoon was wearing on toward dusk – not that there was even the suggestion of an opalescent disc perceivable through the obscuring bruise of cloud by which to gauge the hour, just a further general draining out of color – Cyrus found himself laboring alongside Abednego. Bed was stripped to the waist, and his torso was lean and strong, and his sinews serrated as he hefted each sack into place, and the two men toiled side by side a while, building a near-vertical wall against the rising of the waters. Round Bed's skull was a piece of oilskin, the torn brim from an overseers' discarded hat that he had knotted like a headscarf to protect his greased hair from the rain, and the sight of it made Cyrus smile.

Gots to tend to what matters, Bed said, and his bare shoulder bumped Cyrus', and the contact sent a thrill of pleasure coursing through Cyrus' body, bone-weary though he was.

Still the river rose. The sense of urgency was such that even Mister Johnson and the other white men climbed down from their horses to toil beside the hands in common purpose. And Mas Tyler rode out to supervise, sitting erect in the saddle of his great white charger on a nearby rise of land, in his oilskins like some great black shiny beetle, its pallid mouthparts, his stubbled jaw, grinding, his eyes shadowed by the brim of his hat as he looked up and down the river's length and radiated dissatisfaction. A colonel he had been, and he shouted orders, but that availed him nothing now.

And the river rushed by, gray and swollen and spiny with branches and even whole fallen trees, possessed of some strange animal quality of eagerness and the foreknowledge of the triumph of the elemental. And the thunder rumbled overhead as if up there great boulders churned and rolled.

For that brief span of hours no white man's whip was raised save to urge on the horses and mules that brought down comestibles, for all minds and bodies were bent to a common task: to protect their land, their crops, their homes from the coming of the waters; and beneath the deepening and Apocalyptic gloom the sons and daughters of Ham labored until they reached a level of exhaustion that even they – slaves born of slaves born of those long-ago Africans who had survived the obscene holds of the white men's ships and the deep and vast Atlantic swell – had not conceived was possible. And the rain, relentless, lashing, chilled them to the marrow; nature's whip, or so it seemed to them that lightless day, that lightless night.

We outta sacks, Cyrus said: already they were moving them from place to place, wherever the need seemed greatest, the breach most imminent.

Samuel was toiling nearby. We be needin a ark soon, he said.

Amen to that, brother, Abednego said.

Around midnight that sixth night the rain finally fell off, and their spirits lifted, and they felt there was hope. Every sandbag was in place, and they ate, and then there was nothing more to do but pray, and so they prayed, even Mas Tyler bowing his head as Samuel spoke humble words of supplication and beseechment to the Almighty. But the river burst its banks the next morning regardless, and the whole of the cotton crop was carried away with barely a young plant salvageable; also the vegetable gardens behind the cabins that the slaves cultivated in their brief periods of free time, and upon which in large part they depended for variety in their sustenance. Chicken coops and bundled firewood and haystacks were swept away, supplies of meal and maize and feed were spoiled, and the foundations of cabins and outbuildings damaged and undermined. No lives were lost save later Nate's, for all managed to remove themselves to areas of higher ground as the levees gave out, but there was nothing to be done but watch the lead-heavy, gray-brown water pour on and on through the points of rupture, overwhelming everything in its path. Eventually the waters broke around the base of the rise on which the Big House stood, submerging Miss Tyler's croquet lawn until only the tips of the tops of the curves of the hoops were showing; but it rose no higher: the Big House was spared.

Three days it took the waters to recede. Then followed weeks of dispiriting toil in mud so heavy and cloying that each step taken required a spine-damaging wrench; a failed attempt at a second planting, and a building sense of foreboding as talk of financial ruin filtered down from the Big House, and they all knew what that might mean.

Abednego was sold.

At first Cyrus refused to believe it, and day after day at work's end he waited by the track that led up to the Big House. But Bed never showed: he was gone and it was done and Cyrus knew they would never meet again in this life. A chasm opened in his heart, and it was then that he reckoned he knew how Bella felt when Mister Johnson took her twin baby girls to sell.

She done went crazy fo a time.

And so did Cyrus: he answered back to Mister Olsen over some trifle and was whipped before the others as Bella had, in her wild grief, been whipped. There were other times across the years he had been punished in that way, of course, as had all the hands at one time or another, even the most delicate of the girls, such were the overseers' caprices and sudden, lust-bloated or liquor-sodden furies, and they, the suffering hands, bore those punishments of necessity, for what else could they do? – drawing such fortitude as they were able from being observed by those who understood; who did not merely watch, but more profoundly witnessed. Yet this time was different: this time the pain inflicted on his body, which was at once both a manifestation and a symbol of his powerlessness, seemed a piece with the pain in his soul, wherein each cut of the whip into his bared back, each bite of that sick length of braided leather seemed intended specifically to destroy the pleasure he had but newly found in the skin's receptivity to fond and loving contact, to subtle sensuality; burning it out, cauterizing its possibility and supplanting it with agon: a repossession of his spirit through his flesh. And on that day there came into his mind the sense that all delusion had been stripped from him in order to reveal the bleak, crystalline and essential truth: that they would wreck you; that they would delight in wrecking you in every way save the one that made you useful to them; that they knew what they were doing, and that to them it was good.

White folks don't let you keep nothin, he thought, nor even stake no claim to it.

Stay behind.

Stay behind like Nate with his bust-open foot.

Stay behind like my snake-bit pappy.

Stay behind like Moses' folk in Egypt land, waitin on God's good time.

Stay behind an toil.

Stay behind an die.

And so he closed the shutter on the lantern of his mind, withdrew and became sullen, waiting on his chance and the burgeoning of his need.

Chapter Two

Fall passed and winter drew on. Bella gave Cyrus a coat she had made from scraps, coming up to where he was sitting on the cabin porch one evening and without greeting or even looking at him placing it around his shoulders, her hands pressing softly on his upper arms as she did so. He felt the heat of her then, but there was nothing in him that could respond to her, and so he failed to raise even a nod of acknowledgement of her gift, of her attempt to stake a claim in him as she had attempted to stake a claim before, after his whipping. That time he had driven her off, repudiating her in a burst of pain and anger that was, somehow and undeservedly, a rebuke of her for nothing more nor less than being a woman.

Let Lil Joe do it, he had snapped, pushing her away with a grunt and a curse, throwing the rag she proferred to the young man who hung back big-eyed in the doorway, holding up an oil-lamp, behind him the black block of absolute night. Joe caught the rag in his free hand and came forward, slipping past Bella hesitantly and sideways on, glancing at her fixed, impassive face as with bared teeth Cyrus lowered himself slowly onto the heaped, belly-prickling straw, his stripped back tightening with crust and vibrating with pain.

Don't want no woman's fussin, Cyrus said thickly, turning his head to face the wall.

Bella set the bucket of water she had brought down on the plank floor with a clunk and left, and Cyrus had closed his eyes tight against tears and exhaled through clenched teeth as Lil Joe washed his wounds as gently as any woman could and thereby brought him some relief, though he wasn't Abednego either.

Lonely, Bella said, removing her hands from his hunched shoulders and straightening up, and Cyrus did not know whether she meant herself, or him, or black folks in general; or even human beings taken all together, knowing as they did that when life was done the grave would divide them from all earthly love, and that there was no certainty as to what lay beyond, for all the Bible spoke of milk and honey and many mansions.

He glanced up at her then, giving her face and form a brief consideration that she affected not to notice. She was wearing a faded lavender dress that fitted close about the bust and was embroidered with small blue and yellow flowers, and round her shoulders was an old blanket cut into a shawl that she had hemmed with lavender thread. Though she wasn't near as dark as him she had the African coil in her hair, however violently she brushed it back and ribboned it into a bun; and her nose, though not as wide and flat as his, was wide. Sometimes she worked in the kitchen of the Big House, but never was she permitted to be seen in the white folks' rooms.

Not with them features, Bed had told Cyrus once; not while Miz Tyler has a say.

For, much as she hated the lighter ones too, knowing as she did the inevitable source of that lightness, and calculating as she surely must have done the odds of which exact white man it might be did what where and with or to whom, polluting and diluting both, and excluding from that reckoning neither her own father nor her gone-away brother; like some steamboat card-player placing bets in her mind as to whose blood ran where, and weighing up the concomitant corruption of the spirit, Miss Mary Anna Tyler placed blame with her own, Bed said. But she hated the darkness more, out of some fundamental place and passion deep within her, and wished never to see even the fact of it. And so Bella was excluded as surely as any field-hand, as surely as Cyrus himself, from the fine rooms of the Big House.

She shifted from one foot to the other, letting the shawl slip to show, in defiance of the chill air, the smooth line of her neck. Cyrus turned back to the nothingness into which he had been staring before she came: the confusion of undergrowth that had erupted so violently from the alluvial mess the burst river had strewn across the land, and which was now fading into gray oblivion under a drained autumnal sky.

A sister an no more, he thought. She ain't got what I need. She ain't Abednego.

It was only after several months of their being together, by which time they had learned the use of their mouths on each other, learned the taste, the rising juiciness and intensifying rigidity, the need to stop sucking at the exact moment of salty explosion to avoid giving pain, that Cyrus had allowed Abednego inside him. At first it hurt so sharply that Cyrus wondered why he had felt such a sudden and consuming need for it to be attempted, for it had been an action without precedent, and one that his body had somehow and of its own volition suggested to his mind with such an overwhelming forcefulness that he had been compelled to give it voice, to manifest it both in words, in a pleading request that burst from him as an urgent, blood-heavy demand, and in the reflexive positioning of the limbs of his body so as to open itself to Bed. And Bed had understood Cyrus' need and had responded, easing his way in with the grease Mas Tyler's groom used on the horses' flanks to guard against the chafing of the saddle, for that afternoon the two of them were in the stable, lying together close and warm and naked on heaped straw, in the stall furthest from the door.

All the horses but one were out being exercised. It was this mundane fact that had assured Bed and Cyrus there would be small likelihood of interruption, and thereby permitted this new and deeper exploration of each other as desiring and desired subjects. The horse that remained behind, a piebald mare with a torn tendon, was tethered in the stall next to the one in which they lay hidden from sight. Somehow her tongue-warm breath filled the close, dim single-story building, mingling with the sweet scent of fermenting hay and horse-dung and the stolen pomade in Bed's hair, and she moved restlessly in her stall as their passion built and the hay beneath them compacted, split and liberated dust-motes that rose up and floated golden in the slanting sunbeams of the afternoon, and their gasps grew louder.

To begin with, though, Cyrus had wanted to beg Bed to leave off pushing up inside him, arching his straw-prickled back and struggling to keep his backside in place on Bed's lap, throwing his arms up above his head and his strong thighs wide, and keeping his open, extended legs as straight out as the toil-tightened tendons would permit, his brow furrowing and popping sweat, but once again his body took control of his mouth, this time locking his jaw and stopping his tongue from uttering protestations, and so Bed had continued, his hips moving regular, rhythmical, and each movement pushed him deeper into Cyrus, and after a time the pain had thinned and widened and pleasure had risen up through it, and alongside that a relief so ecstatic Cyrus had finally shouted aloud, exultant at this strange new openness, and Bed had clamped his hand over Cyrus' mouth and for a moment they had frozen, fearful they had been overheard. But no-one came, and their fear subsided and the heat rose up in them again, and Cyrus felt Bed's rigidity pulse inside him and nodded and Bed once more began to move against and within him until Cyrus rose to his conclusion. And then taking up the saddle-grease Cyrus had done the same to Abednego, using what he had learned from his own experience to ease Abednego's discomfort and bring him the quicker to that holy place of pleasure and release.

Perhaps five more times they had managed such a meeting, and on each occasion Cyrus opened more easily; and as his broad chest heaved and his erection jutted like the prow of some voyaging bark, in parallel to Bed's erection jutting deep inside him, he marveled at this transformation in the functions of his body, at its capacity to become the locus of a pleasure so intense it was beyond controlling; and the deployment of those most private muscles, the ring and the staff, to bring that pleasure to them both; and the unexpected accommodation of the male body's design in relation to that mostly-disavowed possibility, the giving by one man of sensual satisfaction to another, seemed a new thing to him then; and he was set free by the hot, carved curve and weight of Abednego's frame as Bed rode him hard, and at times he sat astride Bed, all muscles flexing, compressing and moving in unity as he, Cyrus, did the work, enjoying the exertion of a control that was also the giving of delight.

This was both a fresh claim on his body and a reclamation, and was made the sweeter by its secrecy, though afterwards Cyrus' thighs trembled when he stood, and for ease he moved as though he had been riding a mule, and those were things visible to others, though not, he hoped, correctly interpretable. He clenched his softened sphincter to keep Bed's seed inside him until he felt the need to open his bowels for the usual reason, by which point the loss became not loss but a simple, indeed a necessary bodily expulsion. And at night Cyrus would lie beneath his blanket imagining Bed behind him and inside him, and would feel both an agony of longing that sent tremors coursing the length of his body, and the sweet consolation that he had learned what gave him primal release, and that this released Bed too, for the taking of pleasure had also to be a giving or the satisfaction achieved would be a selfish, impoverished thing.

But it wasn't that that Bella could not give to Cyrus, though of course she could not, a man being made as he is and a woman as she is, and expectations of what should occur between them being what they are; rather it was the profounder business of spirit.

Still, the air was cold and Cyrus took the coat she had placed about him and pushed his arms into its sleeves. And that day, needing comfort, he did not chase Bella away. In his action and non-action she perceived encouragement and so without invitation she sat, near, but not so near as to incite him to drive her off, and looked out at the same gloomy gray tangle into which he was staring as the dusk deepened.

What you see, she asked eventually.

Dead stuff, he said.

It ain't dead, she said. Just sleepin. Come spring –

What?

It'll start over.

Cyrus nodded. Women and seasons, he thought. Over and over. That's how they is an they endure it. Maybe even grow on it. But mens got to go forward an onward. Can't jus go round an round makin somethin into somethin else.

He thought of his mother, who he had never known, who left neither keepsake nor image, her face to him only what he guessed was not his father's in his own. He thought of Abednego. Inside he felt heavy as lead.

You know where they went to, he asked.

Who?

Them ones got sold.

You mean Bednego, Bella said, and he could tell she was pushing down resentment.

All of em, he said, hating himself even as the words left his mouth; hating Bella for fooling him with her attention into revealing part of what lay within him, because what could she know that he did not already know?

Daisy and Louisa, Bella said. Davidson and Ruth.

Yeah, said Cyrus. An the rest.

The servants in the Big House, unlike the field-hands, had been purchased more for ornament than productive toil, so it was from their ranks that the greater number had been culled as a consequence of the failed harvest and the resultant need for economies on the estate. But Abednego was the only one Cyrus had cared for, the only one who had moved willingly between the house and the fields.

He gone, Lil Joe had said, putting his hand on Cyrus' shoulder one afternoon as if he understood, and for all Cyrus knew perhaps he did. Cyrus had been standing staring up the trail again, a small hatchet in his hand, hating with a senseless passion the rampant masses of bottlebrush, phlox and wild garlic that threatened to overwhelm the way along which Abednego used to come, their fecundity promiscuous and even perverse, fed by the silt from the flood, incontinent life born from destruction rapidly obscuring what had been with meaningless new growth, a vegetable surging and ebbing; endless and repetitive as the ocean tides that were slaved, so Bed had told him, to the rotation of the cold, unfeeling moon. And he had hacked at the mass in a frenzy, wasting strength and energy as no slave should, as no man should, until the moment Lil Joe placed his hand gently on his shoulder and said, He gone, Cyrus. And Cyrus had wept then, and only Lil Joe had seen, and he never told.

Where you think they sold em onto?

Other places, Bella said, a hint in her voice that she might know more than she was letting on; as if Cyrus might tease it from her with the right formula of words, or by the right actions. She rubbed her arms as if to ward off the cold, moving a small nudge closer to him as she did so, seemingly by chance and not intention.

Worse places, you reckons?

Bella shrugged. Better or worser, she said. He partway light. That'll help, most likely.

Cyrus grunted. Maybe, he said. You reckon they was sold all together?

Bella didn't answer. From a breast pocket Cyrus took out his pipe and Nate's whittling-knife and began to scrape out the bowl.

I don't know, she said.

Do anyone know, you reckon, he asked, turning away from her and knocking the bowl on the porch-frame.

I gots work to do, she said abruptly, and she got up and left him. He didn't watch her go, having no reason to: he could never care for this woman in that way, and to pretend otherwise would only punish her more. He sat where he was until his bones were heavy with cold and the moon was coming up. Bednego, he thought, staring at the bright white horn-tip as it broke the splintered black spine of the tree-tops. Where you at now, Bednego?

Bigger'n it looks.

That was what Bed had told him, as they stood side by side at the edge of the slave gardens, leaning in like any courting couple and gazing up at the cornyellow globe of a harvest moon, a lifetime ago it seemed to Cyrus now, Bed's straw hat tilted way back on his slicked, kinked scalp, the wheel of its brim a solar echo of the lunar disc above.

Like a ship on a horizon, Bed said, but bigger still.

Cyrus grunted. The widest water he had ever seen was the river, and it had no horizon, just a farther bank, plain to see. Somewhere, somehow he had heard that the world was a globe, as was the moon, though he had no notion of how this could be so.

They say there's deserts up there, and mountains, Bed said. And Cyrus had looked up and wondered what kept the pale sphere in its place, just that piece bigger or smaller across the seasons, nearer or further away, he supposed, and sliced thinner or thicker as it rose and fell night after night, and why that should be so.

How you know bout deserts an mountains, he asked.

Top flo o the Big House they gots a room, a attic, Bed said. They took off a part of the roof an put in glass.

Like a window?

Uh-huh, but fo lookin up. Skylight, they calls it. An old Mas Tyler senior, he put a telescope up there.

41

A what now?

Tubes of brass, one slid inside the other, and at bottom curving discs of glass that bring what's far away to the eye an make it look closer. Bout so big, Bed said, gesturing with his hands maybe a yard apart.

What fo?

To know stuff.

Stuff bout what?

Bout how things are.

What things?

Bed shrugged. I ast him once, You see God that way, Mas Tyler? You see God up there? He laughed and ast, did I want to take a peek.

An did you?

I set down my tray and looked. I saw the moon and I could see what looked like dried-up lakes and plains and mountains up there, all tiny and far-off, like on a map. Ol Mas Tyler called one of em a name and said it was old-time talk, and it meant Sea of Tears.

Sea of Tears, Cyrus said. Someone sure was sad when they named it.

It's just a name, Bednego said. Sides, they all dried up now. And he had turned to Cyrus and smiled, and they had kissed, and Cyrus had pushed his tongue into Bed's mouth and Bed had gasped.

Now he was gone and Cyrus was alone; more alone by far than if he had never known what true companionship could be.

He had reached the edge of the estate now. A low fence barred his way, ribboning off in both directions, vanishing into the featureless dark, its whitewashed pickets glowing ghostly in the moonlight, its line undulant and seeming to float above the rise and fall of pitchy, unseen land beneath it. Beyond the fence was a wide, rutted roadway, the region's main thoroughfare. To the east, to Cyrus' right, it ran past the Oglesby estate, with which Tyler shared a border in the swampland out past Timpson's Creek, the exact delineation of which was the subject of much litigious disputation between the parties concerned. Beyond Oglesby, and facing it on the generally-uncultivated hillside north of the road, there was, in a bowl of poor but workable land just outside the alluvial plain's largesse, a patchwork of smallholdings known as De Bray's Bend. It was from De Bray's Bend that the majority of the overseers were drawn, and accordingly it was ill thought of by the slaves of the surrounding estates.

To his left, to the west, the road ran in a die-straight line past Tyler's other neighbor, Bell, thereafter curving away northwards, hugging the bases of Colt Rise and Squaw Hill before bridging the wild Illitabi River on its way to Tannerville by way of the hamlet of Tanner's Cross. Illitabi was an old Indian name, Cyrus knew, for this was once upon a time Choctaw land, and Cyrus had been told, by whom he could not now remember, that the name of the river meant Dead Killers, but whether that name was given for the vanquished or the vanquishers he did not know.

That was all Cyrus' certain knowledge of roads. But whatever route he chose he would take no road, nor pass through any town, until he was many miles from where he now stood. The word telegraph flew into his mind then, but he did not know why, nor could he remember what it meant; just that it did not reassure him.

To the south all three contiguous estates, Tyler, Oglesby and Bell, were bounded by the Nooseneck River. Directly ahead and due north, beyond an intervening blackness of woods, he could make out the shapes of hills the contours of which he knew blue and lavender by day, his eyes graphing the line where the clotting of the stars was cut off as if by blocks of solid nothing – nearest to, the rise known as Stricken Pine, that further up became Coleman's Hill, named by and after the first white man, Colonel Thomas Amity Coleman, to set his eyes upon it one hundred-fifty years before. To the east the hillside fell steeply down and clove in two to form the bowl of De Bray's Bend. Beyond that it sank to the alluvial plain, then rose up again in a slow sweep on its way to a tilted plateau, at the far and subsided edge of which De Bray's Town was situated.

Cyrus had long since determined he would above all keep his distance from De Bray's Bend; and of De Bray's Town all he knew was that it was large, the principle town of Welt County, that it too was on the Nooseneck River, and that they held auctions there.

Ahead and to his left was Colt Rise, and a good way beyond it Squaw Hill, and between them, Bed had told him, the Illitabi ran wide and fast through a deep gorge named Black Bear Gully that was near-impossible to ford at any point north of the bridge at Tanner's Cross. For which reason Cyrus would not go that way either; instead he would do as he believed he was destined to: follow his star, and head due north through the steepest, wildest and least populated country: he would go by Stricken Pine and Coleman's Hill.

With a final glance behind him he clambered up onto the fence. For one brief moment he straddled it. Then he was over.

The tussocky ground immediately beyond the boundary fence felt no different under his feet: the transition he had made was metaphysical, ontological. Until now every step he had taken had been just a step, something that might cause certain questions to be asked, that might earn certain punishments, but only within the limits of what was prescribed and pro-scribed: prowling about at night. Each step he took from here on out, however, was a crime, and not a small one, but the largest and most outrageous crime that Cyrus could perpetrate: stealing himself.

His heart was hammering. Still he could go back; he could undo what he had done, creep back to the cabin.

Where you been, Solomon would ask.

Never you mind, Cyrus would answer.

No, but where?

Nowhere, Cyrus would say. Just lookin at the moonlight.

Damn crazy fool, one of the others would say. And: Close the door. It cold enough in here already.

Or more kindly: Lay yoself down. Rest them weary bones an let us rest ours. It gon be cock-crow soon enough.

And Cyrus would remove his hat and the coat Bella had given him and hang them on the spike by the door and lie down and think as he thought every night, Bednego gone. And his days and nights would wear on in that way, and his loss continue unrelenting until he was ended.

Naw, he thought, tugging on the leather strap that ran across his chest, shifting his knapsack round so it sat square between his shoulderblades. I'm goin on.

44

And with that he stepped onto the road, and there was a strangeness to his movements now, as if something was tilting him onwards like a wheel on an incline, and he felt within himself a churning chaos of sensations. Most of all he wanted to run, but he knew that at that moment what mattered most was not simple speed but mental clarity; that to survive this he must not rush; he must be attentive to every tiny sign and sound about him.

Slow an steady, he thought.

Yet as he stood there in the middle of the broad, bleached road, gathering his thoughts in the bright moonlight, it seemed to him he must be garish as a bonfire and brazen as a brass band, so clearly was he lit, so black was his shadow; so loud did his heart pound and his breath rasp. Ahead the pines stood waiting. He crossed the road, and a minute later entered the welcoming darkness beneath them. Glancing up at the sky before the needle-furred branches wholly obscured it, he noted the position of the North Star and set his course towards it, moving fast and smooth, face set, hips and shoulders aligned, a tight spring in his stride, all purpose and intent now, and at first there was little undergrowth to impede his progress, and the spongy undulations of fallen needles beneath his feet made only the smallest of soft, crisp sounds in the windless night.

It was profoundly strange to him to be passing into new territory, and he found himself nervy as a rabbit or a fox. He was all present and no future now, a mass of bundled nerve endings co-extensive with everything around him, and each step he took remade him as something new and unfamiliar, and that alteration, that evolution was not unwelcome. Ahead of him the land rose up, as yet unsubordinated by human will or hand, and in that resistance Cyrus found a strange relief, hostile though it might well prove to him; for it mirrored what lay deepest within him and, like a looking-glass, for it was without will, yet not, for it was also somehow sentient, returned something to him of himself: it gave him both resolve and somehow, and more obscurely, a sense that all of this was his, though until this night he had never had set foot in it; and that he belonged to it, in an interpenetration, as it were, of spirits.

Beyond that initial belt of trees, and before commencing the rise up Stricken Pine, the land ran briefly down a spell, and it was a declination increasingly obstructed by the tangled debris of the summer's growth of jasmine, woodbine and phlox. Cyrus stepped more carefully now, concerned to avoid the making of any more noise than could be helped as he pushed his way through the brittle sprawl of dead growth; and also avoid as best he could the leaving of too visible a trail for his pursuers. At the bottom of the incline a small, frozen-over creek ran directly across his path. He made a rush, jumped it, and scrambled up the bank on the farther side. From then on the land began to rise in a linear fashion, and that gave Cyrus heart, for he had lived his life wholly on the flat, and to be ascending, it seemed to him, was a good and even a wondrous thing. The trees, in the main pines, grew closer together, and his way soon became obstructed by not only old growth but fallen branches and even whole dead trees, over which he was obliged to clamber. At one point he passed through a grove of bare-branched sugarberry trees whose slender, silvered trunks, dotted with dark warty patches, added to the dazzle of fragmented ink and quicksilver as the harshly-moonlit wood closed in about him, becoming, as he moved within it, queer and kaleidoscopic. The ghosts of the Choctaw were said to haunt these woods, and though he had no fear of them, for he feared only the living and not the dead, still Cyrus had no wish to meet one.

The thought of spirits made him reach inside his coat, and push his already cold-stiffened fingers through the opening of his shirt to touch the leather pouch he wore around his neck. Old Africa had given it to him. She had been the oldest slave on the estate, milky-eyed and wandering in her mind, so old that she was, it seemed, without sex: breasts withered flat, head all but hairless, dried body stringy with sinew like a man's. In her dirty, dilapidated and unlit cabin she would sit crouched on a pile of rags, the shaking of her body continuous, and weave baskets and panniers and summer hats from straw with fingers that were buckled like tree-roots but still somehow strong and capable. That was her work, and she sang low and tuneless while she did it. To the overseers she was worth less than an old dog, and excited in them less compassion. Her fellow slaves brought her food and cared for her when she would surely otherwise have died, yet that too was done not from compassion, or not wholly so, but owing to their belief that she had power, that there were things she knew, things she could do that maybe might extend beyond the passing of this life, and that was her other work, hoodoo work to help or harm, and so they sought her good opinion. Samuel the preacher hated her, for he divined correctly that she was not only his rival in shaping the souls of the black folks on the plantation but deeper and more abysmally, that she was somehow his own self as it would have been – should have been – in the world that came before, the world of haints and drums and ancestors in robes and crowns who carried spears and hunted lions under wide, forgotten skies, a world that now was shrunken down, diminished to the Word of God and trapped in pages fine as wasp-paper between black leather and heavy, gold-stamped covers. And Cyrus brought Old Africa a wad of tobacco, and she tore off a corner of the wad and packed it in a pouched cheek in her toothless mouth and said, Three days.

What's in it, he asked her three days later, two days before he ran, when she handed the packet up to him from where she squatted on the floor.

Why, she asked in return. You know the right herbs from the wrong? The right bones from the wrong?

You dint ask what I wanted it fo, he said.

I knowed what you wanted it fo.

Zat so, he said, an edge to his voice.

Wing-bones, she said. Fo travelin. Thas what's in there. An other stuff you don't need to know about.

Travelin, he said.

She nodded.

You won't tell nobody, he said.

Who listens to Old Africa, she said. She travelin already. And with that she went back to the wide-brimmed hat she was working on for Miz Tyler's niece.

That night Old Africa died. The next morning Cyrus was one of the hands deputed by Mister Olsen to dig her grave. And be quick about it, he said, there's real work needs doin. The pouch hung round Cyrus' neck as he drove the spade-head hard into the frozen earth.

Bella and one of the other women from her cabin, Melia, laid Old Africa on the blanket next to the cot where they found her dead, folded it round her and stitched it closed with twine, beginning at the feet and finally reaching her face, then closing that off too, signifying that yes, she was gone from this place. Cyrus and Lil Joe carried the wrapped body from the shack to the burying-place beyond the sheds. It was curiously heavy, as if dense with something hidden.

We could use the barrow, Lil Joe said on feeling the weight of her.

Naw, said Cyrus. That ain't respectful.

It's a burden, Lil Joe said.

We gots to bear burdens, Cyrus said. Come on.

So they had carried her the half-mile to the burial plot between them, and laid her in the grave they had dug for her, and spaded in the dirt till it was filled. And come evening they and the other hands gathered there, and Samuel, barely concealing his exultation at the victory the passing of the years had finally bequeathed him, spoke of her as their sister in Christ. He gave her name as Mary and said as how she would be in Abraham's bosom now, and at peace, and so she departed disrespected and denied, or so it seemed to Cyrus.

Touching the pouch now Cyrus sensed in it not heat, or no heat greater than that which his body had imparted to it, but an indefinable radiant energy that comforted him a little, though he knew Bed had not believed in the power of such things, in charms and hoodoo chants; nor in prayers on Sunday neither. Bed had lived in unbelief, had called himself a clear-sighted heathen and free.

Free.

Where you at now, Bed? Where they send you?

After Bed was sold Cyrus had made such small enquiries as he could concerning his possible whereabouts, but to no avail; no information was forthcoming from the Big House.

Not to Oglesby, he considered. They was flooded bad as us, or nearly so: they'd be sellin, not buyin. Nor would Abednego have been sold to Bell: though they had been spared their neighbors' catastrophes they too had lost a good part of their harvest to the rains, a quarter, maybe more, and so would hardly be looking to take on more house-slaves, however affordably the severity of the seller's economic calamity meant they were priced. In any case, had Bed been sold to Bell or

Oglesby Cyrus would have heard, for there was regular traffic between the three estates in the form of the hiring out of skilled hands, and, consequently, some sharing of news.

South of the Nooseneck River were the Sharp and Harrington estates. The ferry, just upriver of where Timpson's Creek joined the Nooseneck, was well-used, and the constant comings and goings along the ferry road made Harrington a near neighbor; and Bella had once told Cyrus as if he could possibly care that Mas Harrington's son was intending to propose to Miz Tyler, or so the wagging tongues in the kitchen said. The Harrington estate had entirely escaped flooding, but Bed was not there either: Cyrus would have heard. The Sharp estate, however, though contiguous with Harrington, was farther east, and there was no river crossing closer to it than the ferry, which to Cyrus gave it a quality of remoteness, for all its fields would have adjoined the Tyler fields but for the river between them.

I would of heard though, he thought. You was there, you'd've sent me word some way. Naw, you was sent to De Bray's Town, all of you was, to be sold on.

The rise grew steeper, pitching him at times near on all fours. Through a brief break in the branches he saw above him, jutting out from the hillside off to his left, a great black rock, and considered that if he climbed it he might gain a view of his surroundings beyond the already-confounding maziness of the moonstruck wood, and confirm his bearings by the stars. Pushing through a dense thicket of dry bushes he worked his way over to the outcrop and clambered round and up onto it. It was rough with lichen and thrust upward and forward like a balcony, though one of course without rail or barrier, and he approached its forward edge with caution and, crouching down, looked out across the alluvial plain where his entire life up to that point had been spent, and the estate whose bounds contained his every certain piece of knowledge.

Cyrus had never seen his world from such a vantage-point, and looking down on it, more distant from him than he had ever envisioned or conceived, he thought of Abednego, gazing up at the desert oceans of the moon in ol Mas Tyler's attic-room, and of toy farms made for children, carved and still.

Almost it seemed he was looking backwards in time, for all he saw was now behind him. Yet perhaps others who ran had looked back from this very rock and felt that selfsame certainty, others who were brought back as Cyrus had determined he would not be; who had gone on to die as they had lived, toiling in the Tyler fields, but still he felt the conviction that for him it would not be so.

From this height and at this remove all appeared peaceful, orderly and prosperous, as if governed by natural harmony. Cyrus shifted his gaze and looked down on the road he had recently crossed where it showed palely beyond, and in parallel to, the black line of the pine-trees now far below him. It was, so far as he could see, empty of traffic, though to the east a small ridge of dense woodland cut off his view where it turned in the direction of De Bray's Bend. To the west, in the direction of Tanner's Cross, his eye was caught by the steeple of the white folks' church, thrust up like a knife-blade. Generations of Colemans, Tylers, Oglesbys, Bells, Sharps and Harringtons lay buried in the churchyard there, he knew, and there was a marble cross taller than a man put up by the gate, a memorial to the white men who fell against the Choctaw in the Battle of Coleman's Hill, and to those who fell later, in the war against the British, their names incised in the pale, veined stone, one above the other, each incision painted in with gold. They too were in Abraham's bosom, Cyrus supposed, along with Old Africa, who Samuel had called Mary, and Williams the stable-boy, and the ways he could not conceive of such a thing were legion.

Like a spread blanket the Tyler estate stretched all the way to the distantly-glinting Nooseneck, and everything but the river's surface was fixed as whittled bone. To one side of the drive that ran up to the Big House, beyond a small area of pastureland for the grazing of cattle, was the large, neatly-planted kitchen garden that served it. On the other side of the drive, past some orchards, were the overseers' houses, all at that hour in blessed darkness; and at the drive's end, on a rise of land that obscured from Cyrus' view the outbuildings and slave-quarters clustered behind it, the Big House stood. It was strange to him to see the shape and extent of it in that way, obliquely and from above, as if distance and angle somehow revealed what close-to was hidden: its finite quality. Just a house. In several of the rooms on the upper stories lamps were lit even at that late hour. Perhaps, Cyrus thought, ol Mas Tyler was looking at the moon.

The notion of someone looking out from those windows, even though they surely could not see him at such a distance and in the dark, returned Cyrus to himself: it was time to quit wondering and move on; in fact past time. It struck him then that his freedom was conspired against by all manner of forces unseen as well as seen: above all, those buried, perhaps beyond excavation, within himself; and that he was his own delay. In a sudden fury he shifted the weight of his knapsack onto one shoulder, turned away from the view, and made his way back along the rock. A moment later he had put the estate behind him and the outcrop vanished among the crowding trees.

He moved quickly, less fearful now he was away from the road of making noise as he pushed through the dead masses of honeysuckle that proliferated there. The hillside grew steeper and the woodland denser, and all became a struggle. Above Stricken Pine, Cyrus knew, came Coleman's Bluff, and above that was Coleman's Hill, though he did not know, nor did it matter, what were the precise divisions between them.

Up and on, he thought. Over the bones of Injun braves. Almost it seemed a song to him: up and on and over.

We sung in the white folks' church. They made us sing, took our throats and souls for they betterment, for they elevation an entertainment. Wade in the water, we sung. Was that advice? The white folks suffered Samuel to preach, and smiled tightly as he spoke beneath the peaked, reverberant roof not of Judgment Day and endings, as was his habit, nor of the Children of Israel's sojourn in Egypt Land, but of obedience to the Lord, who in His wisdom ordered all things; of forebearance now in hopes of reward, certain reward he said, beyond that line in the dirt where life and certainty came to an end.

Beyond Coleman's Hill was wild country that ran on untamed for many miles, or so Cyrus had heard, and that was in large part why he had chosen this route: not only because the North Star hung above it like a lamp born by a kindly guide, but also because, being the least cultivated and least routinely penetrated by man, wild beasts or none, it was his most hopeful way forward. Yet just a little way further along he came upon a narrow trail running on a slant that, judging from the slashing-back of brush along its length, was regularly, and had been recently, traversed by men moving with a purpose.

Cyrus stood there for a moment, uncertain. Even to step onto the trail made him uneasy, for always near the front of his mind was the fear of pursuit by dogs. Thoughts came to him then of night-hunts for possums and coons, memories of the distant blasts of white men's shotguns violating the night as he lay awake in the cabin staring up at the ceiling, willing dawn not to come; memories of the short, excited barks of hounds as they darted after a rabbit or some other small nocturnal animal.

But I hid my beddin, he thought. They ain't got nothin to get my scent from cept straw, an straw is straw.

He had bundled his blanket, tied it with string and thrown it up on the winter wood-pile, out of sight of all. Everything else he called his own he wore or carried with him. And surely, he considered, the fact of it was his scent ran down every path on the estate, pervading its ways with all the years of him, the decades of him, and thereby resisted, surely, easy or clear transection by the surgical noses of the hounds.

To his left the trail slanted up into the deeper woods; to his right it ran downhill, in the direction of De Bray's Bend.

Go on like I was or go up left, he thought. Trail's faster'n thickets and breaks, but it gon be faster for the catchers too, once they gets on my tail. An they will. An I don't know where it's headed. Still, though. Speed now.

After a long moment's hesitation Cyrus took the trail, heading crosswise up Stricken Pine faster and easier now there was no undergrowth to slow him. The brief relief served to remind him that he was in the world of men not ghosts or memories, and so he directed his mind toward the wholly practical, as it might well be he was not the only night-time user of this track that ran between where and where else he did not know; and so his movements, though swifter, were warier too.

A little way on, the leafless branches began to tangle so thickly above his head that it seemed to Cyrus he had entered a tunnel of twisted roots, and he slowed abruptly, for he was now compelled to grope his way forward in near total darkness. To his right he could hear the sound of running water, and he became aware that he must be traversing some sort of narrow ridge split off from the general rise of the hill, for rather than above, the sound was below him. He came to a halt, uncertain as to how best to proceed.

Evidently he had reached the ridge's peak, for at that point the vaguely-descried path ahead fell away steeply into total obscurity. Fearing that were he to continue to follow it, it might curve round and lead him back down to the road, and thus defeat his purpose almost before he had begun, he at once struck away from it at right angles, in the direction of the running water and his original line of ascent. This too involved a sharp initial descent, and, he soon discovered, offered the additional hazard of unseeable twigs and small branches jabbing at his eyes and poking into his mouth. Spitting bark and dirt and muttering muffled curses he slithered down into what proved to be a fair-sized gully, along the bottom of which ran a large stream he guessed was most likely the upper course of Timpson's Creek. Lower down it turned lazy and split into slow channels that meandered through the swampy ground east of Tyler. In this season those often froze over, and one time in a course out there Cyrus had found a catfish caught as if within a brick of glass. Up here, however, the stream was too fast-moving to freeze, and in the rays of moonlight cast through the gaps in the branches above he could see its supple centre, black and unreflective, while at its margins the water broke on smooth pebbles in oscillating silver parings that, at the shore's edge but only at its edge, Cyrus could see were accumulating rigid and still.

It was too wide to jump and yet he knew he must get across it somehow, and without delay; and also he was eager to put moving water between himself and his pursuers, in order to throw off the noses of the hounds; so he sat on a moss-covered boulder at the creek's edge and quickly unlaced his boots and worked them off his feet. The icy stones burned his bare soles as he stood to let down his pants. He stepped out of them, the skin on his exposed legs bristling in the cold air, his genitals shriveling. Keeping his hat pushed down firmly on his head, he unbuttoned and took off his coat, and wrapped boots, pants and knapsack up in it, using the coat's sleeves to knot the bundle. With shudders running from his crotch to his collarbone he rolled his shirt up to just below his rib cage, knotted it in front of him, picked up the bundled coat and, holding it against his chest like a swaddled infant, stepped into the creek.

The water was of an aching coldness that at once penetrated to the bone as if there was no intercession of flesh, and he did not know how deep it would get. The unseen stones in the creek-bed were greasy beneath his rapidly-numbing feet and the current was strong enough to make it hard for him to keep his balance. He knew if he stumbled and fell, if his clothes got soaked, he would most likely die, or at the least be reduced so quickly to a state of near paralysis that the matter of his capture would be a foregone and scarcely-delayed conclusion. He waded on, sinking down steeply with each step he took, and in three steps the water was up to his knees; three more and it was halfway up his thighs. Something bumped him from behind and he started, struggling to keep his balance as he glanced round, fearing even though it was winter-time the presence of some wakeful alligator or swamp-adder, but it was just a tree-branch carried down on the current. He took a breath and steadied himself as it rotated round him, and watched as it spiraled away downstream, glinting faintly in the flume. Once it was gone from sight he continued on, sinking deeper with every awkward step. Eventually his testicles slipped below the water's surface, and a pain knifed up through him at that sudden violation, but still he kept on. His bladder constricted unpleasantly as he sank in past his waist and he would have voided urine had his penis not now shrunk to a point of near-vaginal retraction into his body cavity, and he was not yet halfway across. His lower body felt abstracted from him, and burdensomely heavy. At the mid-point, or so he judged it in the obscuring dark, the water touched the bottom of his ribs, and his gut began to spasm as the heat was evacuated from it with the suddenness of a fall, and he feared what would happen should the water reach the level of his heart, and he sank still further and the water threatened to lift him, tilt him, float him and bear him downstream helpless as driftwood.

But the mid-point was, as he had prayed, the deepest point too, and he began, step by ponderous step, to emerge from the icy water of the creek, rising up as he moved forward, each hesitant placing of his splay-toed feet somehow a sainted act of mercy bestowed upon him. On the far side of the creek he threw the bundle he had by then been carrying high over his head down on the frost-stiffened leaf-mold and collapsed on top of it, shuddering and gaping like a catfish thrown up on the bank, and he was for a time wholly unable to move.

I'm all clean now, he thought obscurely, and he thought of newborns and the baptized.

Trembling violently, and swallowing raw and painful breaths that tore at his lung-linings, he unbundled his coat and tipped boots and pants and pack out onto the ground. Before dressing, with rapid strokes of his coat he brushed down his wet belly, buttocks, groin, thighs, calves and feet, drying them as best he could while taking care not to soak the material through to the inner side at any point. The rough movements sped his blood a little. He rolled down his shirt, struggled into his pants, tucked the shirt in, knotted the rope that served as a belt, and pushed his numb feet back into his boots. He thrust his arms down the coat's sleeves, pulled it closed around him, turned up the collar and sat there on the ground, hugging himself and rocking until the shuddering passed from him and dissipated into the surrounding air. Time passed and the water flowed smoothly by, and it seemed to him he sat there for hours and seconds both at once, an eternity and a moment. Everything had changed somehow; and something, some doubt, some lingering claim made by the land behind, left him.

He got to his feet, slung his pack across his shoulders, and made his way up into the dense woodland that covered the hillside on that side of the stream: Coleman's Bluff, he judged it to be. It was steeper than it had looked from the other side, and soon he was pulling himself up on branches that functioned when his frozen fingers found them as floating ladders in the dark, and it was indeed almost wholly dark down there, for the moon was commencing its declination and the hillside, being back-lit, was all in silhouette.

Night's more'n half-gone, he thought, and he forced himself to move more quickly, for he knew that these few hours of darkness were his block of grace; that once the sun rose they would know for sure that he was gone and the pursuit would begin.

For now he was in some absolute and epistemological sense

free.

He toiled on and, after an hour of steady going, the rise began to plane off and he found he could once more walk upright, though the undergrowth grew no less dense, tangles of dead briar now joining the desiccated fingers of phlox and woodbine clutching at his ankles and making his movements stumble-some. He was feeling almost warm now, and his thighs ached from the unaccustomed use, climbing not being a task to which his muscles were habituated, for all the long years he had, with thews bulging and calves straining, forced the plow through the mud of the Tyler fields. He came to no other stream and crossed no other track, and an unfamiliar sense of solitude began to settle on him. He thought of Lil Joe and Zeke, Samuel and Solomon and the others back in the cabin, sharing dreams as he believed.

Never see em no mo.

A desolation sank into the depths of him then, like dew sinks into dried-out earth. It did not, however, slow his stride nor deter him from his purpose, for he had long understood that a dash for freedom would compel the sacrifice of everything he knew, including people. Still it came on him now, and with an intensity he had not foreseen, as a deep betrayal on his part; as if he had shouted in the faces of his fellow hands, Nothin none of you gived me was ever worth a damn.

Not you though, Bed, he thought. What we had between us, that was somethin else.

His feet told him he had finally reached the crown of the hill. In his mind's eye he had pictured this moment as occurring on some speculative elevation or promontory from which he would see as in a revelation lands born new to his eyes spread out all ways before him, but it was not so: the darkness of the night and the density of the tree-trunks around him combined with the lack of a vantage point to constrict that new horizon for which he had waited so long to not much more than the size of a barrel-hoop.

Moon's near gone, he thought, glancing up at the black sky above, and the realization of its all-too-rapid submersion caused fear to surge through him for the first time since he had forded the creek. Gots maybe two hours fore they miss me. Fore dawn breaks.

He hurried on, determined to keep going as far as possible in a straight line until exhaustion overtook him and he could go no further. The ground began to slope downhill at a gentle gradient: Coleman's Hill, it seemed, had only one steep side, the side he had just now ascended. The close-crowding hackberry and hickory trees through which he had been passing gave way to larger, taller and more widely-spaced sycamores and cottonwoods. The undergrowth thinned too, easing his progress.

All too soon predawn light commenced to underpin the dark dome of the sky. Panic flooded through him when he became aware of this, and he broke into a shambling run. Distantly, somewhere off to his right, he heard a cock crow, and as a clammy sweat broke out in his armpits he wished he had a better grasp of the geography of the area he was now traversing, for the sound surely connoted human habitation. With the trees being less dense and the land sloping away from him he could see further ahead now, but all he saw was woodland: sycamore that some way off yielded to spruce and cypress.

Cypress. That'd be swampland, he thought, slowing to catch his breath and attempt to get his bearings. To his left, above the treeline, rose a wooded mass he took to be Coleman's Ridge, on the far side of which the impassable Illitabi River flowed through the deep ravine of Black Bear Gully. The ridge itself ran off into the distance without break or let. To his right he could make out nothing beyond the trees, but he recalled that the road that passed the Tyler estate on its way to De Bray's Town bent north-east, and that De Bray's Town was situated at the confluence of the Nooseneck and another river, Goose River, Bed had said it was called – and so De Bray's Town would, Cyrus reckoned, be almost directly due east of where he was now standing, maybe twenty miles away.

All this confirmed him in his simple plan to head as directly north as possible until forcible obstruction compelled a detour. Beneath a sky that was brightening relentless fast he could just barely make out, as it faded into the paling blue, the last glint of the North Star. He adjusted his course accordingly: this would be his last moment of certain orientation until night came again.

And thas only if they ain't no cloud, he thought.

To his right the first glints of sunrise broke through the blackly backlit branches in a golden dazzle, latticing his way with spikily elongated and harshly-angled tree-shadows. Just short of a run he went on, jumping several small, frozen streams in quick succession, and at the edge of a cane-brake he came upon a congeries of rabbits. Startled, they scampered off, vanishing into the dense dead brush, flashing their white tails as they went this way and that, and leaving small black marks on the frosted ground that led Cyrus to realize that he too was leaving a tell-tale trail of ink-prints through the sparkle behind him.

Time anyone gets here they be gone though, he thought. Sun's bright enough to blur em out by then, I reckons.

I hopes.

It was unquestionably morning now. High above his head a hawk hovered in the brightening blue and he found its solitary presence disquieting, an ill omen or symbol of betrayal, for all it was likely just scoping for rabbits, perhaps the very rabbits he had just disturbed. For a moment he contemplated setting a snare, to try and get himself some meat, but reckoning he had supplies enough for the next three days or so, he kept moving.

Everything now was open wide, the horizon, the sky; and the air was piercing cold and utterly still. Colors were both sharpened and heightened in that light, and to his eyes seemed altogether new and unexpected: wonderful save for the circumstance in which he was seeing them; and each brown and silver trunk and branch and stem sparkled with white sugar.

Like Bella brung once from the kitchen, he thought, remembering the sweet granularity of it on his tongue and between his teeth, and how later they had ached.

Whichever way he looked there were no tracks or fences visible, no beasts or buildings, nor any sign human beings had ever been here; just the great salted haunches and rusted iron bones of the land, absolutely, unyieldingly itself. He twisted the cork from his water-flask and swallowed its contents, determining to refill it at the next stream he came to that wasn't frozen solid, wiped his mouth, then pulled down his pants at the front and urinated steamingly over the dead growth at his feet.

They gon be up now, he thought. Lil Joe, Solomon an the

rest. An the white folks soon enough. Who gon tell Mas Olsen I gone.

Samuel, I reckons.

The scene rose in his mind like a dead thing bloating and rising up in a well. He thrust it back down. Their pain being also and always his own made the mere visioning of it, combined with his certain knowledge of the chastisement they would inevitably endure as the consequence of his flight, a source of anguish to him, as did its corollary: that they, though understanding at the most profound level the necessity that compelled it, would hate him for running. Then. He shook his head and hurried on, shoulders hunched as though their eyes were on him, weighted and wounded by a guilt that was at that moment barely supportable.

Gots to be free though, he muttered, glancing about him as if he feared they might in some obscure way be spectrally present among the surrounding trees, suspended at some raised point among the tangled branches like clinging mist, their recriminatory faces gazing down upon him as though the bodies that supported them had been strung up, one way or another.

Gots to get free. If I can. He moved faster.

An hour later he heard, faint and far-off, the barking of dogs.

Chapter Three

Cyrus came to a halt and listened. He felt no great fear at that moment, knowing as he did how clear air brings far-off sounds closer than they truly are. Rather it was as if the intermittent barking of the still-distant hounds signified to him nothing more nor worse than his reaching the true beginning of his journey, a journey to which the night's travails had been no more than an arduous prelude; his journey and his trial. It was to be, he knew, a trial by ordeal, predetermined in this world where he was, randomly as it seemed to him then, and whether there was a God or no, and without any reason beyond the servicing of those interests of white men that were primarily venal and secondarily venereal, a possession to be reclaimed, a beast to be hunted down and run to quarry: a nigger. For all under the sky was as it was meant to be, or so he was told the Bible proclaimed, which was to say all was as it was, the consequence, if not the meaning, much the same, regardless of whatever was the truth of it.

Cyrus wiped his mouth with the back of his hand and rummaged in his pack, bringing out a greasy bundle of bacon rinds he had stowed there before setting out. Mas Tyler, most likely to build up their strength for the labors in the season ahead, had arranged the evening before last for the stiff, salted slivers to be distributed among the hands. It was a rare treat, for meat of even the basest sort was largely kept from them, and most had eaten their portions at once. Unlike the others, and for no clear reason he could have given at the time, Cyrus had taken care to save his portion: a prefiguration, as it transpired, of his decision to run. He ate a third part of the rinds now, standing, turning his head this way and that, listening with the acuity of a hunted thing, his jaw flexing as he chewed and shreds of gristle caught in the gaps between his teeth.

The hounds fell silent. Their barking had come from behind him, of that much he was certain, but how far behind? From the presumed habitation to the east, the existence of which he had inferred from the crowing of the cock some time earlier, no further sounds came; nor was anything to be heard in the land ahead of him, and that made his choice simple. Briskly parcelling up the remaining rinds and shoving them back into his knapsack he took a swallow of water, stoppered his flask and hurried on.

They be castin about on the other side of the hill fo a couple hours yet, I reckons, he thought as he strode along, his hands thrust deep in the pockets of his coat for warmth. They can't know what way I went, not fo sho. I could of headed north, east or west, thas three ways; even south if I made me a raft or stole me a boat. And I could of.

The fingertips of his right hand found the deer-horn handle of Nate's knife. The weight of the blade tilted its sharp end down into the lower forward corner of the pocket and lifted the haft towards his palm, as if the knife were preparing itself for imminent and proper use.

I hid my blanket. Ain't nothin fo them hounds to get they noses into, just the general funk from where we all lays down to sleep, and what'll that get em? Nothin.

They got horses to speed em.

How many gon come after me?

Cyrus knew word of his flight would quickly reach the residents of De Bray's Bend. An they's nothin them po whites like more'n a nigger hunt, an a chance at gettin paid fo catchin an fetchin me back.

They ain't gon catch me.

He had twelve hours' start on them, however many they were, dogs or no, horses or no, and though he did not know the land he was at least his own fixed point, and so could not be mistaken as to the location of his own self in relation to itself; whereas those who pursued him would be compelled to cast about this way and that, uncertain in their progress towards him, a shifting dot in the landscape; and at times, he hoped, they would follow false trails and be compelled to double back, thus gaining him further advantage.

They won't give up, though. That he knew from the return of other runaways days, sometimes weeks, on one occasion months later. They gon keep on after me. So I gots to keep on too. Till I drop. Or I'm away.

The barking started up again, then stopped. It sounded neither closer nor further off. Had they found his trail? It might be they were not after him at all; maybe someone was out hunting rabbits or possums on this fine, bright morning.

Naw, he thought. It's me. They onto me now. In his mind he saw the dogs bounding up the steep side of Coleman's Bluff in great eager leaps.

Cyrus picked up his pace at the thought of that, not running, for he recognized the need to husband his reserves of energy for the innumerable miles that lay ahead, but stepping fast. The land continued its gentle downward slope, the trees growing wider apart, and the underbrush gave way to scrubby grassland. The sun continued its silent ascent, and from its rays came warmth enough to take the frosting from the trees and blades of grass, and quiet the black of his footfalls.

He had been passing through that country for close on two hours, the dogs barking intermittently behind him, when he saw, some way off to his left, a thin blue line of smoke, rising up straight from beyond a gray-brown mass of furze.

Determining to keep his distance from any human contact, Cyrus skirted the area, cursing the unseen woodsman under his breath as he did so, for the smoke rose to a considerable height, and it was certain his pursuers would suppose Cyrus to have lit the fire himself, and so would be drawn the more directly to the vicinity he was now by chance traversing. Yet provided he was able to cover sufficient ground before they did so, that too might prove a useful distraction, causing a delay in fruitless talk, and allow him to maintain some of his advantage.

He kept on for another hour or so, and all the while fear rose in him, for the barking grew slowly and steadily louder, and now and again he caught distant shouts that, though he could not make out the words, had an intent that was directive. He pushed himself harder, only one notch off a run now, and began to sweat heavily for all the persisting coldness of the air, and his mouth cottoned. His boots, his pack, his coat, even his hat became burdensome to him, turned as they were by circumstance from items of comfort and protection to things of clogging cloth and leather that frustratingly and perversely obstructed the free-flowing vascular, muscular and ventricular mechanisms of his body.

In Africky they goes bout naked, they says. And he saw the sense in it for all the bite in the air. Without breaking his stride he unlooped the woolen scarf from round his neck and shoved it in his left-hand coat pocket.

The trees started to close in again, the widely-spaced sycamores and cedars giving way to an increasing density of cypress and swamp-oak. Their branches began to meet over Cyrus' head, reducing the now steeply-angled rays of a sun well past noon to a honeycomb of shafts increasingly unable to penetrate the steadily-deepening gloom that gathered beneath them. The ground, having for a time run level as though some bottom had been reached, grew first damp then boggy underfoot, forcing Cyrus oftener and oftener to slow and pick his way, or risk plunging through some great pane of ice that overlay what swallowing depth of sucking swamp beneath its glazed fragility only chance or fate would determine.

Slow them crackers up too, he thought, glancing breathlessly behind him. Thas somethin. There can't be paths they know, not through this.

The sound of his pursuers, which had formerly been so clear, was now muffled by the mass of intervening trees, but there was no question they were catching up to him. How they get onto me so fast, he wondered, and his thoughts turned to betrayal, and the faces of Samuel and Bella slid into the shotgun breech of his mind, vivid as the flash of the wings of a pheasant flushed from the brake. Then he thought, If them crackers goin twice as fast as me fo the best part of the day, they'd catch up to me bout now, simple as that.

Wearily he looked about him. The swamp spread out wide and dreary and seemingly without end, for in every direction as far as he could see dispiriting gray-green tunnels ran off into dusky obscurity. In pool after widening, deepening pool great cypresses, silent, fissure-barked, thrust down extruded, buttressing roots into the murky water. Between the pools ice-fringed mud-banks broke the surface like turtle-backs, bare and comfortless.

At least no skeeters, he thought as he searched with his eyes for a way through; and he thought about alligators, and whether what he had heard about reptiles turning drowsy in the cold was true, and how drowsy drowsy was if it came to it and there you were, nose-to-nose in the mud with such a creature. Cyrus had never seen a live gator, but one time when he was working some ground on the edge of the estate a cart on the road to Tanner's Cross had bumped past with three dead ones piled up in back of it, and he had left off what he was doing to stare in fascination. Their bodies were rough as bear-corn on top and dark as dirt, and their undersides pale as something drowned, and segmented like worm-rings. Their small splayed limbs pointed up and down like something on some heathen cross, and their eyes were yellow with slit pupils that made him wonder what it would be like to see with such an eye, and even in death their snouts grinned. Like it was all a joke and they was in on it, he thought; and their tails had protruded heavy and log-like over the back end of the cart, for from nostril to tail-tip the creatures were near on nine feet in length, and their teeth were uneven. And then Cyrus had felt the lick across his shoulders from one of the overseers for his idling and had looked to his hoe.

His hand went to the knife in his pocket, though he could hardly believe its blade could penetrate a hide of such scaly toughness.

Still, now.

Looking about him he saw no mark nor presence in the swamp of any life beyond the insensately vegetable, which was itself in stasis in that season; not even the small incisions of bird-feet in the mud. An ancient language sometimes those had struck him as. The barking of the hounds and the shouts of men were drawing nearer now. He peered back into the gloom through which he had passed but saw no sign of his pursuers.

Time yet, he thought. Ain't failed yet.

He took his hat from his head and wiped his sweat-greasy brow with his sleeve, then jammed it back in place. I could lay me down a false trail with the rinds, he thought. Put em off a while that way. But since he had not yet found a true path through the swamp the idea of setting a false one could not be given shape. How far this mess go on anyway, he wondered, as for all he could see the swamp might spread out hundreds of miles north, east and west; and for all he knew that was the reason no slave had ever made it up north from Tyler, Oglesby or Bell; was how come they was always brought back.

White folks'd tell us that right off, though. Stop us even tryin. Kill hope.

Just as worrying as its unknown extensiveness, he did not see how he could continue crossing the swamp once the sun had set, and already it was tilting hard westwards and commencing to flare copper through the slices of sky that showed between the gray-brown, blackening tree-trunks. The barks of the hounds and the calls accompanying them were very close now. They seemed spread over a distance, as if his discouragingly numerous pursuers were advancing in line, so as to preclude his doubling back and evading them in that way. Reflexively he touched through the rough fabric of his shirt the cloth packet hanging on his breast, but it was cold and without energy, and a sense of abandonment pierced his heart. Jus bones and feathers an mumbled words an nothin else, he thought, cursing Old Africa in her grave and cursing himself for believing in her foolishness. Jus me now. He glanced westward, into the last of the declining sun's striated, epileptic dazzle, and thought at least the failing of the light would make the marks he was leaving behind him in the receptive and tell-tale mud that much harder for his human pursuers to make out.

They won't see much of nothin soon. Less they light lamps. An if they lights lamps or knots I'll see em a long ways off an dodge em easy. But they's the dogs: they noses. An they can see in the dark better'n a man.

In what seemed to him his one chance to put off the dogs or be seized on within a matter of minutes, and heedless of the discomfort to his feet and the damage to his boots, Cyrus waded out into one of the widening lakes. Its nearmost shore, which was all he could make out in the now-onrushing dusk, was no more than limned with rime, for it was too large a body of water to freeze over, never mind through, the simple volume constituting a form of insulation from the surrounding iciness. Perhaps too, as Cyrus had heard tell, the mud that was most likely fermenting rottenness beneath its surface gave out heat gaseously, thereby in some obscurer fashion preventing its freezing, though the water that flooded his boots nonetheless felt first painfully, then numbingly cold around his feet and lower legs. He hoped the lake would not get too deep, for he could swim but briefly and splashingly; and that through its broad and featureless extensiveness it would serve his purpose and throw off the hounds.

Ain't no current to carry my scent off, though, he thought as he sloshed through the ice-water and the thicker layer of unseen, cloying mud below. No wind neither. But they noses can only reach so far: if I go out a ways I can beat em yet. Out a ways an outta sight. They won't wanna go nigger huntin in no swamp by night, not an wreck they boots.

The water came up to his knees but mercifully no higher.

On Cyrus toiled, penetrating ever deeper into the intensifying gloom, and for a time it seemed to him his pursuers were falling back. The challenge of maintaining a line where each man could at all times see his fellow to both right and left was hindering their progress, maybe, the more so as the trees grew denser and night fell; and while Cyrus went forward in a straight line, water or no water, he did not doubt that those following him would be reluctant to wade through swamp-water pools of uncertain depth only a spot above freezing, and would therefore take time to seek out paths among them, regardless of how much it slowed their advance.

After maybe an hour of sloshing along, during which time he had seen no-one and the sun had disappeared altogether below the horizon, Cyrus found himself approaching the trunks of two towering cypresses that stood apart from the rest, and loomed up in the dimness like sentinels. Stricken by disease or old age they had like lovers fallen against each other and, root-jutting at the base and tangle-crowned at the head, made what seemed to Cyrus a vast asymmetrical doorway that gave onto some hallow of primordial origination, beyond which all was absolutely still.

This is somethin, he thought as he passed beneath the arch they made.

Exhaustion overwhelmed him then. His thighs burning and his chest heaving, he dragged his clogged and sodden feet up onto a wide and featureless mud-bank that emerged reluctantly from the gloom a hundred yards or so beyond the archway. Ahead was the endless, hopeless swamp. Cyrus' gut was tight with hunger and fear and the tendons of his heels ached from wrenching his booted feet repeatedly out of the thick subaqueous mud, his dry tongue clove to his parched, gluey upper palate, and he was breathing hard.

No water fit to drink.

Just as he was staggering up onto the mud-bank, barely able to keep his weary self upright, excited barking broke out hard by him to his right. Turning as fast as he could on the glutinous mud he saw a large brindled hunting-dog burst from the cover of the trees some twenty yards away and come racing towards him. Sinews striated its taut limbs as it pelted along the firm ridge of the mud-bank, its red tongue lolling, its panting breath smoking in the chill air, blackly-freckled foam-flecked pink lips drawn back from pointed teeth in slavering jaws, amber eyes pupil-pin-pricked with savage eagerness.

Before Cyrus could do more than throw up an arm to protect himself it was on him, its jaws clamping vice-tight round the forearm he had raised to shield his face and throat, its weight and slab-like, muscular impact throwing him backwards onto the mud, for it was heavy as a man, and without fat. Bracing itself up in a lean instant so as to straddle him with all four legs, its backside high it wrenched his arm snarlingly this way and that, shredding the mercifully-thick felt of the coat-sleeve and ripping into the shirt beneath while Cyrus frantically attempted to slam his knee up into its concave belly or kick at its dangling testicles, trying at the same time to wrench and damage its thickly-muscled neck as its locked jaws jerked his right arm one way then the other, threatening to dislocate his shoulder, poking at its yellow eyes as best he could with the fingers of his free left hand, his knife all too unreachable in his right coat-pocket. Ropes of drool broke from the dog's mouth and spattered like ejaculate onto Cyrus' grimacing upturned face. Somewhere close by there were shouts.

With a squirming thrust born of pure desperation Cyrus flung the beast onto its side and then, after a frenzy of scrabbling in the stiff and stinking mud, during the entirety of which it never ceased to keep its jaws clamped tight around his forearm, he somehow managed to clamber on top of the muscularly-twisting thing and jerk it round until he had it pinioned on its back, and now he was lying flat with the full weight of his body on top of it. Its spine flicked supply one way and then the other as its back paws kicked and scrabbled at his groin.

Jumping his hips forward so he was straddling the chest of the writhing, slavering animal, riding it as if it were a log, keeping his arm jammed in its mouth and keeping it pinned firmly on its back, he pushed it with punts of his bent knees down the bank, inching it head-first into the water he had but recently emerged from. Its body pulsed hotly against his groin. Its ears and eyes were underwater now. With all his weight and all his strength he arched forward and pushed down, his forearm still trapped in its mouth, his free hand underneath its jaw, forcing the head first back and then eventually altogether under the freezing water. The dog gurgled and kicked and scrabbled frantically, catching him in the gut and balls with its back legs and clawing blindly at his face with its forepaws, cutting his cheek and gashing one eyelid, but he did not flinch and he did not release it. At one point it almost got itself free and he was forced to push it and himself deeper into the mud and ice-water, soaking his knees and chest as he pressed himself down on it until with a sudden, violent convulsion all motion ceased.

Dragging ragged breaths into his aching lungs Cyrus wrestled his bloodied forearm free of the dead beast's jaws and struggled to his feet, leaving the carcass as impacted in the mud as a fossil in slate, stumbling about dizzily, wiping blood from his face and right eye, trying to ready himself for action, for surely his pursuers were on him now. He raked the zone with eyes only half-focused but focused enough, as it transpired, to reveal a pair of figures standing watching him no more than ten yards away along the curve of the bank: Mister Johnson, broad-brimmed leather hat low on his head, eyes obscured by shadow, unshaven jaw thrust out, a long coat on, a bullwhip coiled in his right hand; and, holding back with a leash a second, now loudly-snarling hound, a terrified-looking Lil Joe, hatless for once and with no coat on, just a shirt lacking half its buttons, hunched and shivering, and Cyrus guessed he had been compelled to join the chase at dawn, with no time to prepare any proper defence against a long day and now night out in the bitter air; and surely too he was afraid at what he might witness here. They carried neither lantern nor pine-knot, either for purposes of stealth, or from the presumption that the pursuit would be concluded by nightfall. Lil Joe kept his hand tight on the leash, leaning back so as to counterbalance the eager, straining kinesis of the hound, though his body-weight barely exceeded its own, all the time staring at Cyrus with wide, stark eyes.

Well, let im go, you dumb nigger.

Yassuh, Lil Joe said, but he did not let the dog go, paralysed by something within him it seemed, a need to resist, perhaps, or simple dread, or complex shame, and Mister Johnson struck him a sudden blow on the side of his head, the blunt, heavy brass base of the bullwhip's haft raising an instant knot on his temple.

What you waitin for? God damn it boy, let im go.

Fearing another blow Lil Joe released the second hound, and it too came bounding for Cyrus across the mud, its leather leash skittering behind it like something alive. But this time Cyrus was ready: he had Nate's knife gripped tight in his right hand, and though the other hound had torn the skin of his right forearm its teeth had not damaged the web of muscles, tendons and sinews beneath; had not impaired the functioning of it. And, too, for it was the twin almost of its mate, Cyrus knew what to expect of the creature; how it would most likely attack him. Rather than being caught off-balance and falling backwards as he had before, he now crouched down and, as it leapt upon him, threw himself against it so its weight would not send him tumbling onto his back, almost leaping himself, this time bracing his left forearm against its chest to keep its slavering jaws from his face, and in the long moment their conjoined momentum held them there he stabbed it repeatedly in the side of its muscular, vascular neck, forcing the blade into the firm flesh all the way to the handle over and over, and the steaming blood spurted and spattered onto the cold mud below, and the hound collapsed to the ground and lay there whimpering and twitching, expiring one bellows-push at a time, and Cyrus turned to Mister Johnson and Lil Joe, bloody blade thirsty in his hand.

Moving through other parts of the swamp, beating brush and hallooing, he could hear the rest of his pursuers. Not on me yet, he thought breathlessly. Gots me a chance yet.

Here, Mister Johnson called over his shoulder, keeping his eyes on the wild and bloodied figure now squaring off before him. Cyrus took a step forward and Mister Johnson called again, louder this time: Over here, God damn it.

Seeing his fear and aloneness, Cyrus now advanced upon him fast along the mud-bank, clear in his mind as to what his need necessitated: the taking of a man's life; certain too of his power to achieve that end, until from the pocket of his pea-coat the overseer drew forth a revolver, dully-oiled and long-barreled, and, with a single, practised movement of his thumb pulled back the cocking-piece and from his waist aimed at Cyrus' gut. Cyrus froze. He and the white man were now no more than three yards apart, a tableau as it were, an exemplar from which each figure drew opposing moral lessons, the only movement the rise and fall of their chests; and Lil Joe watched motionless, and he too was a part of this.

I could kill you now, boy, Mister Johnson said.

And Lil Joe could have told Cyrus the gun in the white man's hand was named a Walker Colt; that it was six-chambered and loaded with what were called picket bullets; and that this knowledge had come to him because, out of some inexplicable and capricious fondness for him which Mister Johnson had lately contrived, a fondness Lil Joe knew contained within it a justification for his own future chastisement or even possible murder as a nigger who had come into possession of dangerous knowledge, Mister Johnson had compelled him that very morning to load chamber after chamber with those self-same picket bullets until all six chambers were filled and the Colt snapped closed and the chambers spun.

Then you gon have to kill me, Cyrus said. Cause I ain't goin back.

God damn you, what you mean, you ain't goin back, Mister Johnson said. You'll come back an I'll split your God damn hide for you.

Nawsuh, Cyrus said, and he began to move sideways, for it was in his mind to circle Mister Johnson and in that way attempt to gain, in the scant moments remaining to him before the arrival of the others with their weapons and ropes and chains, some small advantage of incline or sureness of footing on the mud-bank.

Yes, sir, Mister Johnson said, his eyes on Cyrus' as Cyrus

circled him, you shall. To Lil Joe, who was now standing
diagonally behind him, he gave the order, Holler, boy. We gon
need help bringin this buck down.

But Lil Joe did not holler: rather he set his jaw and flared
his nostrils, in cool decision it seemed to Cyrus; and when a
moment later Mister Johnson threw Lil Joe a glance, as he
could not restrain himself from doing, Cyrus, seizing the tiny
chance the youth's silence had afforded him, and with all the
strength remaining to him, threw himself forward in a wrenching lunge. It was, as it transpired, a fatal misjudgment on
Cyrus' part, for as if he and Cyrus were components of some
interlocking mechanism wherein one movement of necessity
compelled the next and with near simultaneity, Mister Johnson
raised his gun, and the instant the barrel was aligned with
Cyrus' throat, and at a distance of less than two feet, discharged
it.

The sudden explosion of sound impacted the air both flatly
and ringingly as it was flung among the cypress-trunks and
bounced off the water and the mud. An instant later it was torn
through by the serrated blade of a second sound that, though
less physically damaging to the ears, assaulted the mind and
soul more violently than that initial black powder blast, for it
surely came from the throat of a human being, yet one reduced
by agony to the level of a beast.

Two men were standing, one was prone. The stink of burnt
sulfur filled the standing men's nostrils, and a haze of blue
smoke hung suspended above their heads like gauzy tenting, an
ectoplasmic mass rising as it were from a séance where the
contact had been broken, as if it were returning to some upper
air of spirit. And through that still moment moaning pain
thrust itself like a spike.

Mister Johnson lay on his back between Cyrus and Lil Joe,
his body twitching, his face shredded by the explosion of the
revolver, the sockets of his skull splashes of red where his eyes
had been, shards of blown black metal embedded in the seared
flesh surrounding them, his right hand a scarlet ruin like a
torn-up chicken-carcass encircling claw-like and redundantly
the splintered grip of the devastated weapon. Cyrus ran a hand
quickly over his own face, for he could feel speckles of hot
metal itching and burning there, and the powder-flash had set

flaring, phosphorescent spots floating before his eyes, but he could see, and bar the cuts he had received from the paws of the hound he had drowned, was unbloodied and otherwise unharmed. Something exultant coursed through him then, and he felt more alive at that moment than he had ever felt before, save for that first time Bed had slid inside him.

Help me, Mister Johnson gasped, turning his sightless head this way and that, his long, pale hair flopping in the mud like a knotting of dead snakes or rotten reeds.

Sho, I'll help you, Cyrus said, and he kicked Mister Johnson in the side, just below the ribs, compelling a groan from him. You need mo help, Mas Johnson, he asked, his eyes lighting on the bullwhip lying looped on the ground nearby, the brass butt of its handle winking at him invitingly.

An I could now, an it'd be so easy. See how that white skin cuts up. See what's underneath, if it's the same as ours. So they catch me an kill me, it might be worth it, even so.

But Lil Joe, as aware of what was rising up in Cyrus' mind as if he were Cyrus and Cyrus were himself, caught Cyrus' arm and mouthed the word, Go. Then, as if fearing the punishment the blood-soaked figure on the mud would later seek to exact for his failure of service, Lil Joe said to Mister Tyler, Don't you worry none, massa. I'll go get help – adding in a hoarse whisper to Cyrus, Don't you worry, brother. When they comes I'll send em the wrong way.

And Cyrus looked at Lil Joe then and loved him. He pocketed the knife he had been holding all the while and extended his hand, reddened by the blood of the hound and full as it seemed to him then of the power of living, veins pumped and proud as mountain ridges on the moon yet sensate and animate. Come with me, he said, and at that moment it seemed to him an easy thing to ask.

Can't, Lil Joe said.

Come with me, Cyrus repeated, the longing for a companion on the road rising up in him strong.

I can't, Cyrus, Lil Joe said. Not just like that. An even if I could, not just like this, neither. He gestured to the mostly-buttonless shirt that was all that covered his upper half, and which he could not stop from gaping open to expose his chest to the bitter air any more than he could still the increasingly violent tremors the cold was forcing up through his slight frame. Get gone, Cyrus, he muttered. Fore they gets here. I gots to call em soon or it'll go bad for me.

Cyrus nodded and backed away a few paces as if to keep his offer open, then turned and fled into the deepening night. And he never saw Lil Joe pick up the bullwhip and beat Mister Johnson in the face with the same brass haft that had lately raised the welt on his own forehead, calling out with each impact of weighted metal on seared flesh, Here, he's here; nor did Cyrus ever know that by the time it came to load Mister Johnson's revolver Lil Joe had learned they were going on a nigger-hunt and had therefore, with forethought and intention, loaded the bullets into their chambers back to front, which error was possible in a weapon of that type, and was to lead to its subsequent obsolescence, aiming to produce a misfire, in fact causing the entire six chambers to explode in one when the hammer hit, and shatter the gun to pieces.

Cyrus ran.

Chapter Four

Cyrus ran, following the curve of the mud-bank deeper into the swamp, heedless of any direction taken beyond the most general, the immediate need of his heart being to put a distance between himself and the grim red scene behind him.

Lil Joe, he thought. You should of come with me.

Within five chains the mud-bank gave out and he was back in the water, once again wading through what seemed an unending nightmare succession of sludge-bottomed, bitingly-cold pools, stumbling up and over the serried, inhospitable and interminable mud-banks that broke surface rib-like between them; blundering blindly, painfully, over and over, into the black and rotting branches of dead trees that thrust up from the water like spears of buried Choctaw braves; stumbling repeatedly over roots that, whether on land or submerged, caught at his feet like hostile stirrups. It felt to Cyrus the swamp was somehow sentient, an animate entity, and, whether living or otherwise, whether obscurely corporeally manifested in every trunk and branch and root, or else discarnate, ghostly and somehow exerting a spirit-pressure upon his will, was seeking to impede his flight; the landscape as it were a beast he could neither whip nor drive on, though it compelled him to bestride it. Did it resent all presence of, all penetration by men, whatever their color, whatever their need? Hanging mosses trailed across his face like veils or spider-webs or clutching haints.

At times he tripped, went skittering forward on all-fours like the animal they had his whole life endeavored to make him believe he was, then forced himself to once more, as it were, evolve upright; then fell again, rose again, plunging on without a backward glance into the dense and reeking darkness; keeping moving forward until finally the giddiness arising from oxygen deprivation in the canal-systems of his brain, and the arrhythmic lurching of his heart, compelled him to come to a stop as absolutely as if he were a tethered dog that, forgetting it was tied, had given chase and reached the full and inelastic extension of its leash.

Exhausted and dizzy he lent, just for a moment as he at first intended, against a broken, rotting cypress-trunk jutting up obliquely from a low mud rise that but barely broke the surface of the water. The moment distended: Cyrus' whole body came to a standstill, every muscle bar his hammering heart starved to a carbon-poisoned paralysis by a suffocating loss of breath. He dragged the painful air into his lungs with gasping swallows so violent they snapped out and bruised their lobes against the encircling cage of bone, and a tearing came in his gut, and a heaving of the viscera that was near to vomiting. He bent over, sinking to his knees, but nothing came. For a time he could not straighten up, and he knelt there immobile as the praying angel carved of stone that knelt atop Coleman's tomb. A shiny black miasma drifted before his eyes. He closed them, but the miasma persisted.

He breathed.

He breathed: just that and for a time nothing more; experiencing in the stillness and now blessed silence of the night the rise and fall of his chest as if it were in miniature the passing of the seasons, and his body the replenishing land.

Strange, he considered, how simply breathing could set things right, and he thought of God breathing life into Adam, and the lancing pain in his stitched side made him think also of how God made Eve from Adam's rib. Yet how could man come before woman when he came from woman? It seemed to Cyrus then without sense, for all it was in The Good Book. The minutes passed, unmeasured save by his subjectivity, such was the formlessness of the darkness that had closed in around him. The worst of the pain and nausea passed from him; the inky glitter rose up diagonally before his eyes and slipped away like some floating creature seeking a new environment. His heart slowed. Now he could stand upright, though still there was pain in his side. He wiped stinging sweat from his eyes and looked back the way he had come, fearful he would see the firefly movements of lanterns or torches. But there was nothing; nor was there any sound.

Must of put the fear in em, he thought: a hound choked an drowned, another stabbed over an over. An Mas Johnson by em with his face blowed off, maybe dead too: that'd scare em mighty bad, don't matter what happened was his doin, not mine. An now it's night, an they can't follow my trail without lights, an they know if they use em I'll see em a good way off an get gone easy. So I gots me some time to rest up.

Cyrus hawked and spat then looked about him, but could make little of his surroundings, for the darkness in the swamp was now unrelenting heavy and opaque. He looked up and found that either clouds or swamp-vapors had stealthily gathered overhead and now wholly obscured the sky, leaving him with neither the moon to light his way nor the stars by which to orient himself; and in his panicked, zig-zagging flight he had lost all sense of which way he was headed.

Long as I ain't goin backwards, he thought. He felt reasonably sure that he was not, but whether that was due to the amassing of subliminal details he could not name yet correctly perceived or the delusion of wishful thinking, he did not know. He had his knapsack with him still, and he swung it round and rummaged in it for the packet of rinds. He ate the rest of them hungrily, then shoved the wrapping-cloth back into the pack.

Don't leave nothin to draw no hound.

Abruptly self-conscious at the memory of the dogs he had killed, even though in the dark he could not see the blood on them, he squatted and washed his hands in the icy water, then scooped up a few mouthfuls from where he reckoned he had not troubled the mud. The coldness of the water made his teeth ache, but food and drink revived his spirits. With that revival, however, came a resurgence of a sensitivity not only physical but also mental, and the horrors of the last few hours returned to him then with a saturation of feeling that came close to overwhelming him.

Mas Johnson, you was a unkind man, he thought. A cruel man, and you would of treated me worser'n a dog if I'da gived you the chance. An if I'da had to, I do believe I would of kilt you. But still I pity you the loss of yo eyes.

And back on the Tyler estate, though Cyrus was never to know it, Samuel preached regular from that day on, on how if thine right eye offend thee, you should pluck it out, and on an eye for an eye; and he spoke of how bright sapphires may become muddy rubies but God's good grace is a diamond and precious above all, and his preachings were heard by his colored congregation, and understood.

Bednego, Cyrus thought, longing for a hand to reach out to him, Abednego's hand, flesh and blood and warm and full of life, but there was nothing, only the cold and tenantless swamp. Such was the night's opacity Cyrus was now compelled to feel about him for clues as to even his most immediate surroundings, deducing by touch that he was standing in the middle of a small ring of spars and tree-trunks on a slight rise of mud, a crown as it were, atop the swamp's emergent skull, and all was dead. A fallen log lay at its centre like a bench, as if placed there for a traveler's ease. Lowering himself onto it, Cyrus found he could lean back against one of the all-but-invisible upright trunks behind him, and in that way rest supported, rather than being obliged to crouch on the cold, bare mud. His thighs ached. His legs below mid-thigh and his feet were soaked from his traversing of the pools, and the bottom of his coat was sopping, stretched and heavy. Though the rest of him was damp only with sweat, as it cooled it added to the pervasive chill that ate into him as he sat there.

When it's et all the way through I reckons that's me done, he thought. So I can't stop here for long, don't matter how tired I is. Gots to get somewhere fore I freeze up for good. Fore I'm stuck like that catfish I found froze in the creek. Gots to find me some shelter better'n this nowhere place. Wish I could build me a fire, but I can't risk it.

Even had Cyrus not feared that any fire he lit might be seen by his pursuers, the saturation of the air about him would, he judged, have precluded his finding any twigs or sticks dried out enough to catch; even the hanging moss was dank.

Still it was a relief just to sit, however cold he was, however cold he would become; a mercy to be for a brief spell beyond pursuit; and he determined to use that time to gather his thoughts. Lacking a wider geography he had no solid sense of how to move forward from this place, and the fear built in him that when he left it he would, in the absence of starlight to guide his way, and while imagining himself to be going in a straight line, through the bias in the land inadvertantly curve round, and so find himself stumbling into the presence of one or more of those behind him who had not abandoned the chase that night.

He placed his hands palm-down on the log, braced his arms and pushed up his shoulders, thereby relieving the ache in them a little. Feeling crisp and yielding moss compress beneath his palms, a thought came to him as to the differentiation of rates of growth in vegetable matter; of the many different types of plants and their particular natures; and whether there might be a plant whose favouring or avoidance of sunlight could suggest to him the sun's arc, and therefore the points of the compass. Yet even had he known of such a plant, and he did not, the darkness was too absolute for the putting into action of any such plan. Bending over with a grunt, he wrestled his flooded boots off his numbed feet and tipped the water from them, as near futile an act as could be conceived in the pervasive damp, and with the swamp extending in pools and lakes every way about him.

Everythin I tried done gone wrong, he thought wearily.

He could of course go back: flounder through the mud and water and offer himself up to his captors, take his whipping and whatever other punishment Mas Tyler chose to visit on him – branding, perhaps, or the splitting of his ears or hacking off of his nose, for Mas Tyler would be indifferent to his appearance; survive, probably, being as how he was a hard worker and therefore represented a considerable dollar value to his owner; and Mas Tyler would not, after all, profit by his death, neither by his permanent incapacitation, and so would most likely pull back somewhat on the chastisement.

An scar me up too much an he can't even sell me on, Cyrus thought. They'd look me over in the pen an say, well, that there's a trouble-maker, we ain't buyin no trouble-maker. Still, though, he mad enough, he'd do it. Kill me. Or if he away, the overseers'd lay it on me hard, on account of one of their own got hurt, whether I done it or not; lay it on me till I'm dead.

Truth to tell, this here's like a place o the dead. Everythin here dead cept me. An I'm gettin so I ain't so sure bout me.

He peered out into the darkness. Nothing but the vaguest shapes were apparent to him, black on black, distinguishable only because edged with what seemed like an oil-ring burst by a soap-bubble: spatiality itself, perhaps. He sensed no presences, human, animal or spirit, within that blackness. A curious calm came upon him then, as though he were at that moment beyond everything, in a place where nothing mattered or could matter because all was done that was there to be done. How you feel when you dead, he thought. But I ain't, Bednego, I ain't. At the thought of Bed's name a pain knifed through him that was a different sort of cold; a bitter loss.

Bednego, I –

He knuckled sudden tears from his eyes. The longing to be held by another man, by this man, reared up overpowering strong in him; that utter vulnerability he could not, would not disavow. Gots to find you, he thought. If I can. Don't know how, but I gots to try. Can't bear it otherwise. You an me, Bed, we one. We men but we got the ownin of each other's hearts. Even if we never thought to say no vow nor jump no broom.

The revelation came to him then, sudden as sparks up a chimney, that this was the true reason for his flight: to bring him to this dismal and forsaken place where nothing lived, where there was no dwelling and no shelter; where, despite all, his mind could be free; or free enough at least to reach the certain conclusion that north for him was, as perhaps it always had been, less a place on a map he had never seen than a symbol, and that his North Star shone in Abednego's eyes.

Spirits brung me here, he thought. As if they got a plan. An the firin piece blowed up just when I was done for, cornered. Maybe they did that too.

The idea of unseen, benign guidance gave Cyrus heart, and the sense that the swamp was set against him left him then, the ring of thrusting spars surrounding where he sat seeming now less a crown on a dead king's head than a stockade ringed round with spears fixed against a charge. He stood and stamped his ice-block feet and rubbed his numb and burning hands together, not with any hope of warming them, but to stir up a little the blood that had sunk down in him like dead leaves in a still pool while he sat torpid and stiffening as does a toad in winter. The gristle in his neck crackled as he rolled his head, and he recalled Bed's hands on his shoulders, his strong thumbs forcing out the knots. Cyrus closed his eyes and sighed.

Hope Lil Joe don't get a whippin, he thought. They guesses he misguided em, it might go bad fo him. But how they guess it, cept they never caught up to me. That ain't proof. Not that a white man needs proof fore layin on the paddle: they don't get what they want, somethin in they head blows like a overcooked still.

He reckoned, however, that the combined effects of the garish severity of Mister Johnson's injuries and the corpses of the dogs would distract the other slave-catchers from Lil Joe's giving of muddle-headed directions – if, that was, the pursuit was even continued past that point, as maybe it was not. Crazy nigger, he imagined them saying, none eager to lead the chase into the fallen night: wild.

Cyrus placed his hands on his hips, pushed his pelvis forward and stretched out his aching spine, then sat back down to await the dawn. Hard-eyed and chilled to the quick, he was sure sleep would never reach him. Yet somehow it did, for he started awake some hours later, confused as to where he was, almost falling from the log on which he had been awkwardly reclining, waking from a dream that felt like no dream but more a dispiriting continuation of his ordeal in the waking world, for in it he was toiling through bitter cold, muddy water in pitch darkness. In the dream he had trodden on something large and leathery and living he could not see, and with a gurgling exhalation it had flicked up like a monstrous lily-pad, fore and aft, and he had somehow gained the impression it was thick-tailed at one end, blunt-snouted at the other, yellow-eyed and grinning eager.

What the –

Cyrus struggled up from the log with a cry, throwing his hands in front of his face, only gradually becoming aware that there was no gator, and he was standing on firm mud not knee-deep in water; and then he remembered where he was. His wrists and ankles ached shootingly and his spine, like a tree-bough distorted by the compelling of its growth through or around some unyielding obstacle, had seized up as he lay there in the damp and dark, leaving him buckled like an old man whose body had been wrecked by the pitiless passing of the years, and by toil. Using a spar for a support, carefully he straightened up. Something in his lower back had gotten wrenched, a different kind of damage to that produced by laboring bent over in the fields, but no less painful or incapacitating. His feet felt dead, yet within that abstraction was a throbbing like a tooth-ache, deep in the bone; deep in the marrow, in the nerves; and in the depth of its penetration, dangerous. His fingertips were numb and his neck had locked.

Hooking his arm around the spar and using it as a brace he leant out over one of the pools and, the weight of his body suspended above it, reached down and scooped up a mouthful of water, then another. With a grunt he swung himself back onto land, then, after straightening up again, dug in his pack for the heel of a loaf he had stowed there along with the packet of rinds. He tore off a piece and ate it, chewing slowly, for his jaw ached and his swollen tongue felt bruised, and looked about him. A predawn gray had begun to underscore the edges of the sky, and though the opacity of the clouds above precluded the breaking through of any actual ray of sunlight, because his eyes had grown accustomed to the gloom Cyrus realised he was now able to see a good way in every direction.

He seemed to be in the blighted heart of the swamp. Many of the trees, which were mostly cypresses, though here and there on the banks stood swamp oaks, with patches of scrub beneath them, were dead; and spars, branches and whole fallen trees lay mute in the still pools surrounding him. The mud rise on which Cyrus stood was not circular, as he had taken it to be in the dark, but tear-shaped. Its pointed end extended out into a narrow natural causeway that ran just barely above the waterline a hundred yards or so before striking a larger and higher bank that crossed it on the slant and offered, at least briefly, dry passage in two opposite directions.

Rightways look much the same as where I is now, Cyrus considered: swamp an cypress. But through them trees to the left they's a mass of somethin might be rhododendrons, the kind of plant neighbors a swamp but won't grow in it. So left is better. Don't know if I'm gon come out the swamp sideways, frontways or backways, but I gots to come out, an fore they catches up to me again. An if thas back the way I come in they can't watch the whole of it, not all at once, so they'd still be a chance for me to get away, an they surely won't expect me to come straight back at em. An they ain't got no clue where I is now, or not much of one, so.

He shouldered his pack, left the circle of spars, and made his way along the bank. Reaching the junction he turned left, and the choice felt good. The simple act of walking began to return his body to life and lift his spirits, for the pain in his bones and joints and muscles was no longer that of inertia, and the coldness of his flesh was less that of a corpse in waiting than something for a living body to defy. He moved less awkwardly now, felt looser.

The bank ran straight for a hundred yards or so, then forked. Cyrus took the right-hand fork, for it seemed to head most directly toward the sort of dense underbrush that grows only on solid ground, and too in that direction there seemed a greater ratio of oaks to cypresses. A short way on, however, the bank dipped below the waterline; but it rose up again five feet beyond, and with the gathering of his reviving energies he was able to jump it and continue on his way without giving his boots another soaking. The earth-bank ran on level after that, some five feet above the water's surface, curving round on itself somewhat as it went, but not so much as to lead him back into the swamp; therefore he kept on with it, and as he went, soft gray light slowly filled the air.

Colors returned to the world, muted at first, but growing richer and more differentiated as the sky lightened, and the swamp opened up before him in tunnels and vistas of ochres and umbers, pearls and flint-grays, soft ambers and cadmiums cut through with flashes of emerald. The pools, once considerable in size, Cyrus saw were now increasingly broken up by a network of emergent tracks and banks that commenced to lattice their surfaces, and here and there were water-panes small and shallow enough to have frozen over. Rhododendron bushes, their leaves glossy green even in that season, massed in ever-deepening profusion beneath the great, bare-branched oaks that rose up before Cyrus in a wall that signified the swamp's end.

I been through somethin, he thought, moving forward hopefully. He slipped a hand inside his shirt and touched the cloth packet that hung there on its loop of twine. Despite his fingers being too numb for their tips to tell him whether it held any energy or warmth, still it reassured him. Can't let a setback take your faith, he thought. Nawsuh. A short while later he had left the pools altogether behind him and was back on firm ground, much of it densely covered with layers of crisply-frosted leaf-mold that yielded only slightly beneath his boots.

Due to the sodden state of the leather and the soaking of his feet the night before, Cyrus at first gained little relief from being on dry ground beyond the fact of its making stepping easier; a small mercy so soon acclimated to as to be near at once forgotten, as is the case with the removal of any such impediment or source of suffering.

The ground rose gently then leveled off, and the rhododendron bushes, which for a time had become so dense as to cause Cyrus to have to push and struggle through them, leaving behind him a trail of tiny, snapped, bright yellow-green and sap-revealing twigs any huntsman could follow without difficulty, rapidly thinned out, being no more than a belt, as it transpired, and his way became easier, though he was both tired and hungry, and had no sense at all of where he was.

Didn't see none o these kinda bushes where I went in, he thought. Thas somethin.

He looked up at the sky, which spread out gray and uniform beyond the bare, immobile tree-tops, trying to determine on which side of the opal bowl the sun was going to rise, but the opacity of the cloud-cover defeated him. The air was bitter cold and absolutely still, as it had been the day before, and he wondered at that; at how there had been no wind to bring the clouds in in the first place yet here they were. But then he considered how they looked in their soft furrows to be clouds of the upper air, and who could know what different breezes drove their paths up there when all was still below?

He recalled one summer's eve in the cornfield by the burying place, he and Bed lying side by side among the stooks, sharing a cigar-butt and, as sunset came on, taking turns to blow baby cloud-puffs at the greater clouds above, their bellies underlit in flaring gold and scarlet, some nearer, some further off, some moving fast, others still as paintings, or so Bed said, and the phrase struck Cyrus though he had never seen a painting, only applied whitewash to a wall or creosote to a fence. Feeling shy in his ignorance, as he sometimes did with Bed, he had not asked him what a painting was. They had been warm then, side by side on the crumbly, radiating soil, as he could not imagine being warm here, alone, in this other place and season.

He continued on through the oak-wood. Frost sparkled on

the dry brown loops and twists of winter underbrush, and on the moss that draped the branches of the trees in gray-green festoons, like wreath-memories of Christmas gaiety. He came to a small creek, knelt, broke the ice at its edge, filled his water-bottle, and drank. Though painful to his teeth and tongue and throat, the creek-water tasted almost sweet after the stagnant swamp-water he had been forced to consume the night before, and swallowing it down relieved a pain that had been gnawing in his stomach since he awoke that morning, perhaps a sort of poisoning arising from his forced consumption of the decay-contaminated fluid. After drinking his fill he wiped his mouth, immersed the flask in the creek until all the air had left it, corked it and returned it to his pocket.

He went on then, but in no great hurry, for he knew neither where he was, nor in what direction he was headed, north, south, east or west; nor did he have any information concerning the land beyond the wood he was at that moment traversing. In any case all had changed, for he was now searching not for the north and the dream of freedom it offered but for Abednego and another kind of freedom, that liberation that consists in following in its wildest extremity the dictates of the human heart. What he needed now, he saw, was knowledge; knowledge of every sort as to the workings of the world, and most particularly knowledge as to where Abednego had been taken on being sold; but before that, and he had no notion of how he might attain any of it, Cyrus needed food and warmth and shelter.

A short way on, as abruptly as if a wall had been reached, the wood came to an end. Hanging back among the concealing trees and shielded by the underbrush, Cyrus looked out at what lay beyond: an expanse of farmland, low, flat and open save for here and there several small copses of trees, and, some way off and clustered together, groups of gray and white farm-buildings. This being the quiet season the bulk of the fields had been plowed under, though in some clover, small-leafed and low-lying, had been seeded, to replenish the soil for the next year's planting; in others winter crops showed: collard greens and turnips, their leaves gleaming a muted viridian in the drab predawn light, grown, Cyrus supposed, to fatten hogs, or feed hands; in the fields alongside these alfalfa, lettuce and sprouts grew in orderly lines.

Some way off, like ripped black paper in a vortex, crows flapped and rose and drew back down to worry at something in a furrow in one of the fallow fields, cawing raucously under the leaden, immobile sky.

The fields ran on to Cyrus' right and left as far as the eye could see, and he realized this was not, as he had at first assumed, a single vast estate, but one of a series of contiguous smaller holdings. Here and there along the fences edging the nearest fields pickets were slumped or fallen and not set back upright; and the underbrush that spread forward eagerly from the wall of the wood had not been cut back that year, nor, Cyrus estimated, the year before. There was hardship here, he concluded: poverty arriving on the coat-tails of prosperity as it had on Tyler, coming, maybe, with the root-rotting rains, though these farms, these estates, were nothing in scale to Tyler or Oglesby or Harrington or Bell.

Cotton ain't they crop then, Cyrus thought. It'd be rice, maybe. Or tobacco.

By chance he had emerged from the wood at the boundary between two properties, for there a fence taller and more sturdy than the others strode away across the fields; and roughly equidistant from each other, though still some considerable way off, were set, he now saw, two near-identical sets of outbuildings, and beyond, but close to each, stood larger structures, likely the main houses of the respective estates and, under their watchful eyes, he did not doubt, the slave-cabins. A short way beyond those was what Cyrus took to be a road, though it was at that hour empty of traffic. It was somewhat raised above the level of the surrounding fields, a dyke as it were, running straight and unbroken to left and right, and marked along its way by skinny pines spaced evenly five chains or so apart, the trees left over, he supposed, from the clearing of the land, or planted after so as to assist any soul who lost their way to find the road again. Beyond it the land evidently continued low-lying, for Cyrus could see nothing of it in the predawn pallor, excepting at a great distance what appeared to be more woodland – a gray-brown smudged line – and past that the pale lilac of what were maybe hills: he was, then, still on the alluvial plain of which Tyler was a part.

The crows rose and fell back again. In the entirety of the landscape there was no other sign of movement: no bird, beast or man; no gush or trickle of stream or river or twisting, squeaking weather-vane. Both main houses were in darkness, and no smoke rose from either set of chimneys, for at that hour no-one was out of bed, or if they were they had not yet lit the fires.

Anytime soon, Cyrus thought. They'll be pullin back curtains, openin shutters. Be at windows, lookin out. If I wants to get me some supplies, or at least scope the place out, I best do it now. I can always go back in the woods if it look too chancy to stick around.

Since its outbuildings were a hundred yards or so nearer the wood's border than those of its neighbor, and just two fields away from where he stood, he chose the lefthand farm. The closest of its outbuildings was a large, windowless barn, and he saw that if he made his way along the wood's edge a little he could place the barn, a two-story building, between himself and the main house, and thereby afford himself a covert line of approach to it.

Gathering his courage he broke from the cover of the trees and, keeping low and glancing this way and that, loped along the edge of the first of the two fields, keeping to where his tracks would be least visible. Then, cutting away from the fence, he headed diagonally across the second, moving fast and directly toward his goal. Thrills of fear ran through his chest at finding himself for the first time since he had commenced his flight on open ground, and the crows rose and fell, rose and fell, ineluctable as waves on sea-shores he had never seen; as seasons. The plow-turned furrows of the fallow field, alternately frozen stiff and suckingly yielding, made the going cumbersome and yet, though it felt an uneasy long time exposed beneath the sky, soon enough Cyrus reached the back of the barn. Its whitewash was faded but otherwise it was in good repair, deteriorated boards having been replaced with new since the worst privations of the previous season. Beyond it other buildings were arranged in such a way as to create a yard or square among them. As there was no way of entering the barn from the back, Cyrus made his nervy way round to the front, keeping shoulder-brushingly close to the walls as he went, pausing at each corner and peeking round. Still no-one was about.

The wide barn-door was closed, but fastened only by a latch. Cyrus lifted it and quickly passed inside, carefully pulling the door to behind him. The latch clicked. He looked about him. Pallid light filtered in weakly through the gaps between the boards of the barn's walls, revealing on either side rows of stalls, in one of which was tethered a milch cow; and her breath, and the particular fermenting scent of stored hay, sweetened the cold, dim air. Constrained in her enclosure and aware of his unfamiliar presence, she moved uneasily, lifted her tail and urinated spatteringly and copiously, sending a channel of rank, steaming fluid coursing across the dirt floor.

In the center of the barn a ladder ran up to the hayloft, which took up the entire upper story and offered itself immediately to Cyrus as a possible place of concealment and rest. Before climbing up there, however, he first took a bucket and stool from where they stood ready by the door and slipped into the occupied stall. The cow, her udder swollen morning-heavy and waiting, tossed her head restlessly at his intrusion but made no effort to impede him, only watching him sideways-on as Cyrus set the stool down by the barreled curve of her belly, level with her yellow-tan hindquarters.

There now, he murmured, stroking her flank with firm, rough movements. I'm just gon take some pressure off you here.

He positioned the bucket and sat, his knees clicking as if he had aged a year for each of the thirty-some hours since his escape. The heifer's stiff, rubbery teats were no warmer than his fingers as he took hold of them and commenced to pull, but the milk that hit the bottom of the pail in noisy spurts steamed. Once he had gotten maybe two pints from her he quit what he was doing, left the stall, drank the milk down, replaced the bucket and stool, and climbed up into the hay-loft, his gut gurgling fiercely from the sudden intake of fatty fluid.

Up in the transverse the straw was heaped in pitched mounds that came near ceiling-high. These had been forked together but not unduly compressed, and so Cyrus was able to worm his way through them until he reached the barn's front end, into the wall of which three ventilation holes, echoing the triangularity of the building's upper frame, had been incised so as to prevent the stored hay's inevitable fermentation from reaching a point of combustion through providing some circulation of the air. Cyrus found he could lie stretched out in the hay-mound and through one of the ventilation holes observe the yard below with no chance of being observed himself. The straw both insulated him from the cold and gave off a muted, self-generated heat of its own, and for the first time since his flight Cyrus began to feel something near warm. Nearby a cock crowed, then crowed again. Nothing happened. Cyrus sat up and unlaced his boots, wriggling then wrenching them off his feet, and afterwards packed them tight with straw to speed their drying. With another handful of straw he rubbed his frozen, aching toes, their undersurfaces crinkled and near to splitting from the repeated soakings they had undergone, and as the blood began to circulate his spirits lifted.

Hearing the sound of a door opening and closing, he turned back to the ventilation-holes. Out of his sight-line something wooden was slid up, then another something, then a third – pop-holes as it transpired, for the sounds were followed by squawks, and then fowls came pecking and scratching their way into the yard, a rooster and nine hens. Cyrus knew them to be Dorkings, for the rooster had a black body and tail, and a cloak of white feathers as it were thrown about his shoulders, and the hens were silver-backed and rust-bellied; and at once he thought, I could have me one of them, wring its neck, draw its guts an it'd last, and still no human being appeared.

He heard the door open and close again: the somebody who had let the fowls out going back inside, he reckoned, and that decided him. Leaving his straw-packed boots up in the loft he squirmed backwards through the hay and clambered barefoot down the ladder, shedding whistles and gold dust as he went. Carefully he lifted the latch, cracked the door and looked out, saw no-one, and a moment later he was in the yard. The birds carried on about their business, searching for grains and seeds. He moved towards them at first on a slant of intention, as it were, so as to neither alert nor alarm them. Then, bending and sinking with a dancer's grace, he placed his hand on the back of one silver-gray hen and pressed her smoothly down, his thumb and finger splaying and then slipping easy round her neck, and the hen was calm as he picked her up and with a simple but relentless turn wrung her neck, the bones inside breaking with a crisp click, and she kicked and clawed and voided down one side of his coat, and the others, their wing-feathers clipped, jumped and squawked but did not move away, so ingrained was their habit of territory. Cyrus shoved the dead hen headfirst into his knapsack and hurried back to the barn, concerned the noise of the others would alert whoever had opened their pop-holes.

Don't know when I gets to cook it though, he thought as he snuggled back down in the warm, enclosing hay, for he could not imagine risking a fire out in the woods, or not for many long miles yet, and even then only with the impossible certainty of there being no human habitation anywhere nearby. I needs me some ready victuals, he thought. Somethin fixed.

A young black woman in a short-sleeved gray blouse and wearing a white apron over a long gray skirt, came into the yard then, her face at that angle concealed from him by a white cap, and she was carrying a blue enamel basin from which she scooped handfuls of grain to toss to the fowls. They gathered round her eagerly, pecking at her skirts, the recent demise of one of their number as utterly forgotten as if it had never occurred; yet Cyrus could tell from the inclination and then turning of her head this way and that that the young woman had realised one of her charges was missing. She dumped out the rest of the grain from the basin and moved off quickly in the direction the birds had come from, then a moment later returned, looking about her to see if the hen had wandered, her movements nervous as the birds', and Cyrus feared his theft would earn her a beating or worse.

The girl cast about, studying the ground, and Cyrus' chest tightened as she stooped and picked up a whistle of straw that must surely have fallen from his coat or hat when he crossed the yard, and he moved back sharply as she looked up at the ventilation-holes, not expecting to see anything in particular, he supposed, so much as obeying that reflex that makes a person seek out the eyes even of a building; yet he feared she might have seen his movement as she stood there twisting that piece of straw between her slender fingers. Should of kept still, he thought. Fool. A moment later he heard the latch clack and the barn-door creak open though he did not hear her step inside, yet why would she not? It banged shut, then juddered open again, creaking on the hinge. In, out? He held his breath, fearing to move again as she would surely hear the furtive shifting of the hay and know there was someone up there.

She goes back in the house I can run, he thought. Catch up my shoes an be gone fore she can fetch someone. Yet the thought of returning to the woods, the swamp, appalled him.

I knows you in there.

Her voice was hoarse and whispery, light with a tremulousness beneath it. She don't know, he thought.

They's hay-stalks an dust goin up the ladder. I knows you in here. You took that hen.

She talkin low, he thought. She ain't tryin to raise no-one. Okay, then.

Taking hold of his boots, he worked his way backwards through the hay and over to the open trapdoor where the ladder came though, and looked down. She was standing by the door; had come no further into the space than that, a silhouette in the pale oblong iris of the slowly widening doorway. Wary then; aware of her vulnerability.

Come down, she said, and he obeyed her, descending frontways, one step at a time so as not to alarm her, bare feet, calves, then thighs, hips in shapeless gray pants, hands loose, empty; torso enveloped in the gray felt coat Bella had given him, and halfway down the ladder he squatted and let the rails of blanched light strike his face and reveal his features to her while her face was hidden from him still, for the rising dawn was behind her, and so he could not read her response.

You runnin, she asked.

He nodded.

No-one's been here lookin, she said. Not yet.

Thas good, he said.

She studied him, he presumed, out of the blackness of her silhouette, and he studied her. His nose itched from the straw. He brought a hand up slow and rubbed it.

You gots blood on yo hand, she said, and a hollowness ran through the centre of her voice like the vibration in a reed.

They put dogs on me, he said. One caught up on me.

An you killed it?

Uh-huh.

She moved a step closer, and now the light fell upon her face as it had fallen on his, revealing youthful features, wide, tired around the eyes, her nutmeg skin carved from the purple-blue shadows by the oncoming light, a girl made too soon into a woman, one way or another.

How old is you, he asked.

She shrugged, folding her arms so as to frame her breasts, unselfconsciously as it seemed, and perhaps unmeaningly. Fifteen, she said. Maybe. He grunted, looking away from her then as does any man or woman who fears to look into a mirror knowing what he or she will find reflected there. I'll say a fox must of got that hen, she said.

They gon believe you?

She shrugged. Give me some feathers, she said. Rip em out in clumps.

He nodded, went into his bag, tore several handfuls from the dead bird and held them out to her, a soft mass turned out porcupine-like with quills and blood at its expanding end. The girl did not move forward: Cyrus was compelled to go down and cross to where she stood. Gently he placed the feathers in the hand she now held out to him. The blood marked her palm.

What's yo name, he asked.

Esther.

An this place?

Hart. When you run?

Night befo yesterday.

Don't go by the road.

I wasn't plannin to.

They's patrols, she said. More'n there used to be.

She glanced round at the barn door half open behind her and Cyrus thought, You plannin to run too. Maybe not yet, but soon.

Where the road go, he asked.

North is Cooper, she said. It's a town but it ain't big. South-east you got De Bray's Town. Thas bigger. Asides the road there's the canal, runnin mostly longside it. South you got the delta an, her voice trailed off. You goin north?

I was. Now I gots to try an find my friend.

You lose him?

He sold.

You know where to?

I knows they took him to De Bray's Town to sell on.

That ain't much.

I know.

Esther looked at him levelly. You can rest up here today.

It safe?

Safe as anywhere, I reckons. Mas Hart's off in town, on business or so he says. Not that much business gets done round here, he here or not. We strugglin.

Cyrus grunted.

I'll gather up these droppings, Esther said, gesturing to the bits of straw he had let fall on his earlier descent. They glowed golden, bright in the general light of a dawn that was now extending like a lime-wash across the yard. Go on back up, she said.

He nodded, and retreated.

Chapter Five

After his ordeal in the swamp, to rest in the dry was sweet, though Cyrus could feel his muscles once more seize up and his joints commence to lock as he lay there among the straw. His scalp, sweaty along the stained and buckled leather band that gave shape to his hat, itched him. He removed the hat and scratched the stubble field growing there, and thought of Abednego lathering his scalp: the licking coolness of the frothed fox-brush on his skin, the undertone of warmth from the water steaming in the dish nearby into which it had first been dipped; the tickling of suds slithering down his neck inside his shirt; Bed's fingertips firm on his skull as he wielded the cut-throat he had abstracted from Mas Tyler's dressing-room, and the others in the cabin looked on, drawn in by what was on so many levels a transgression.

Keep still now, Bed said, and Cyrus was both braced up and wholly relaxed, and the sensual scrapings of the blade on his scalp sent ecstasy coursing through him, and he exhaled and suppressed a delirious shudder as Bed wiped the white, black-coil-and-speckle-filled ladings of foam flat on the thigh of his pants, smiling and with a cigar-butt in the corner of his mouth.

You cut me an I be mad wit you, Cyrus said, taking care not to shift, his eyelids heavy as if sleep was coming on him fast.

I won't cut you.

In the yellow light cast by the oil-lamp hanging high on its hook Lil Joe and Zeke and Nate and Solomon watched, in one way puzzled, in another understanding, as Bed shaved Cyrus' head with small deft movements that he interspersed with flourishings in which the blade caught the light. And he was true to his word, for not once did he nick Cyrus' scalp, leaving it instead gleaming flawless and oily smooth; and when Cyrus rose to step out into the yard, to bend from the waist and tip the water over his head and rinse away the ghost-rinds of the lather, they saw and did not see the jutting in his pants, and in that instability of vision, as it were, and unknowingly, they conspired against Samuel and his preachings, reaching somehow both forwards and backwards, to a time before books they none of them could recall, even in dreams, and a time unimaginable, after The Book was done and gone, when a new world was built upon the ruination of the old.

What's it made of, asked Lil Joe, for all of that was unsayable, even had they had the words, which they of course did not – directing his eyes towards the razor's ornamented handle.

Ivory, said Bed. Ivory an silver filigree.

What's ivory?

It comes from a big gray animal call a elephant. Its teeth grow an grow like a monster hog till they longer than a man is tall. Or so they says.

Where they live, asked Solomon, curious despite himself, for he was aware as they were all aware that the more a man knew, the more he knew of what he was deprived.

Africa, Bed said. An the Indias.

Solomon nodded. He had been brought to Tyler along the coast by boat when he was a boy; had had the ocean beneath him. You couldn't see no end to it, he told Cyrus once, when Cyrus asked him what it was like, and his eyes went far away.

Lil Joe hooked the stove door open and lit a spill for his pipe. That Mas Tyler's razor, he asked, drawing on the bone stem and brightening the bowl.

Bed nodded. An I best take it back befo it's missed.

Ain't he gon notice it blunted?

I'll rub it on the strap fore I puts it back, Bed said. Clean it an keen it.

You shave him? Cyrus asked, suddenly jealous at the thought he was sharing this newly-discovered intimacy with another, with that particular other above all, though perhaps an overseer would have been worse, and regardless of whether the sharing was compelled or otherwise; and in that way having his intimacy with Abednego defiled by association, or at the least diluted.

Naw, I don't. Bed smiled but it wasn't the warm smile of before, more a baring of what he on occasion called his ivories. He don't trust no nigger to put a blade on his neck. He shaves his ownself.

Huh.

Bed folded the cut-throat and slipped it into the left breast-pocket of his fancily-embroidered vest. Samuel came in then and gave him a look. Bednego, he said.

Preacher, Bed said.

I was thinkin bout prayin some, Samuel said.

Amen to that, brother, Bed said, and he left the moment and Samuel hanging as he took a spill to the stove as Lil Joe had done, raised it to the cigar-butt between his lips and sucked, and the others looked on as the gray stub commenced to glow like stained glass in a sunbeam, his chest swelling his linen blouse as he puffed; and Lil Joe hooked the stove-door closed for him and watched him close, and perhaps Cyrus was not the only one in love with him that night.

And Bed left them to their worship, duty his excuse, trailing behind him an aromatic scent that was more as it were melodic than the harsh smell of the overseers' cheroots, and of a certainty more costly: even a field-hand's nostrils could tell that.

Cyrus ran his hand over his clean, smooth scalp and felt both purified and full of the heat of the flesh as Samuel led them in worship, and that evening the preacher's prayers were fulminations both against a heathen past full of bodies without shame, and against a future in which all certainties might be thrown down, for he sensed, as did they all, in the tightening of white knuckles round the handle of the whip, in the tightening faces and throats of white folks overheard speaking of what they plainly feared was coming, and soon: an Apocalypse in which faith itself might be consumed entirely, and Judgment Day miscarry, and saint and sinner alike fall into the abyss as the devil took all. Yet as they said their amens that night each man thought perhaps, and Cyrus thought for sure, would not that risk be worth the taking, to overthrow what was. For what was, it seemed to him, was not supportable, and Cyrus had never heard a prayer answered yet, save on those occasions when what was delivered by the Almighty was what chance might have in any case supplied.

Bed had taken pleasure that evening in giving his lover the outrageous best, in public, and at some risk to himself, for a slave found with an object of both value and danger upon his person risked extreme chastisement, even permanent mutilation, and a house slave with split ears or a hacked-off nose, being no longer pleasing to the eyes of the white folks, would be expelled from that privileged zone, that approximation of Heaven on Earth away from the dirt and stink of the field-hands' cabins, the sweaty, spirit- and body-wrecking toil of the fields. Yet Bed did it, in that and other actions evincing a power of spirit, a heart that was rare, for most in the Big House would not risk their advantage, and who could blame them for that?

Better to rule in Hell than serve in Heaven.

Bed said that was from a book, and ol Mas Tyler would repeat it with relish at table, to the annoyance, or so it seemed to Bed, of his son and spinster daughter, smiling as he did so, showing false teeth that fit ill in his mouth. The teeth, set in a brass-hinged wooden frame and padded with leather, were white and flawless, and had been extracted with pliers from the gums of slaves in order to enable his feeding of himself; to permit his smiling. Better to rule in Hell, he said, and ain't that what we do, amen. And Cyrus pictured his gelid eye roving the room, and the servants looking down harder than was their custom, fearing he would compel a response from them, for any response, any response at all would lead to retaliatory punishment by the scions after the old man had been helped drunk and grinning to bed.

Don't want to serve or rule, Cyrus said as he and Bed stole one last kiss in the blue night outside the cabin.

Now it was Cyrus taking a risk, the largest risk he could take, though perhaps it was in his turning aside for another that his courage mostly consisted. Not that he would have called it courage, for in the calculating part of his mind he considered danger hemmed him in on all sides equally, and therefore whichever direction he struck out in was as hazardous as any other. The duty of the heart, he might have called it; a duty he had not been able to see clearly until he had commenced to run; until he was past the Tyler plantation's bounds and, however briefly, free, which state bringing, once a haze of confusion and even guilt had dispersed, a clarity that was fearful and profound.

I am a shootin star, he thought.

His stomach grumbled and he felt an overpowering need to open his bowels. Awkwardly he squirmed his way round and diagonally across to a back corner of the hay-loft, pushed down his pants and in a squat emptied himself, wiping his backside after with handfuls of straw. Though the smell of what pumped out of him both turned his stomach and worried him as constituting an odor that would in time become detectable to others, the simple bodily relief was nonetheless strengthening. He packed straw tight round what he had voided and worked his way back to the ventilation holes at front of the loft to resume his vigil on the yard.

Finding himself dry-mouthed, he unstoppered his flask and swallowed the last of his water. He wondered if he might ask Esther to refill it from the well they likely had thereabouts, but doubted the wisdom of leaving his hiding-place now others would be up. Too, he could feel building in him a general reluctance to leave, for any reason whatsoever, the shelter of the barn. This and other feelings – fear, dread, longing and desire – now rushed in on him, and Cyrus found them hard to disentangle, for they were occurring in a context wholly unfamiliar to him: as a running man free in the free world. But he understood this: that fear of the lash for disobeying a command, or speaking back to an overseer, or for simply happening to be within reach, was of a different order from fear of the lash for running, however identical the agony of the leather splitting his back would be; an order of sensation if not higher, for what would that mean, then somehow further out. Beyond.

Beyond the farm was the road, raised, lined by pines; past that, the as-yet-unseen canal. Road and canal, running north, or south-east to DeBray's Town. And that latter was to be his way, resisting the call of the star in order to follow the needle in his magnetic heart. Yet how could he find where Abednego had gone to? His eyes moved restlessly as his brain stacked up what he knew, what he might do.

Several times Bed had talked to him of running; of those who ran. Mostly they's the ones can pass, he said, fo Mexican or Spanish. Quadroons or octoroons.

Bed was lighter than Cyrus, but still brownskinned, and, handsome as he was, his features declared his heritage on his mother's side, whatever mix his father might have been: the sculpted fullness of his lips, the wideness of his nose and its low bridge; the height of his cheekbones, and the kink in his greased and glinting hair, blazoned it. And there was within him a pride that Cyrus knew would scorn to pass, even had it been a possibility, as it was not; though Bed would, Cyrus supposed (as who would not) privilege, if it came to it, survival over pride. He thought of ears nailed to a plank then sliced off with a knife, of red holes rimmed with gristle. But it was too late now.

Most of those who ran, Bed said, had skills that led to their being hired out. In that way they became accustomed to a certain breadth and freedom of movement, and learnt more of geography than was usual for the slaved. Being known to the white folks of the district, they could commence their escape under cover of performing tasks assigned by their masters, and in possession of passes to ease that commencement – all of which Cyrus knew, of course; but Abednego had laid out the possession of those advantages with a clarity that sharpened his thinking.

An I gots me none of em, Cyrus thought now. No pass; no hope of passin.

But the blood that had dried in the creases in his palms itched him, reminding him: I'm the runaway choked a hound in the swamp an stabbed another till it dead. I blowed off half a white man's head, maybe even kilt him. I'm already a tale. An they's power in that.

He thought of Zeke, strumming his banjo as he sat in the cabin doorway after the day's work was done, his rough, sweet voice catching words that descended from the sky, celestial, or rose up from the earth, chthonic. So Zeke would tell his story. But how would it end? His hand went to the knife in his pocket. He could defend himself; could cut his own throat if it came to it (his vow). And in the meantime gut the hen he had taken. He might have drawn it where he had emptied his bowels, but had not thought to do so. Well, it would keep a few days yet.

Esther and an older, heavy-set woman, also in white cap and apron, came into view then, bearing a basket of cut branches between them, walnut from the particularity of the twist, and tipped it out in the middle of the yard. The older woman took the basket back in, leaving Esther to pull the branches into a well-ventilated, conical construction, which task she carried out briskly, thereafter setting some kindling, which she produced from a pocket in her apron, in the midst of it. The older woman returned balancing a piece of glowing charcoal on a scuttle and tipped it onto the pale yellow kindling, which caught at once. Esther took the scuttle back inside while the older woman stood watching the fire build, puffing on a corncob pipe as she did so; the younger girl returning a minute later, carrying somewhat awkwardly two stools, a hoe and a pail of cornmeal dough with a roll of red-and-white check cloth laid across its rim. She set down the stools and the older woman sat first and then gestured to the younger that she might join her, which she did. The older woman was very dark-skinned, flawlessly so, and handsome, and her bust and hips were broad. Esther twisted the hoe idly in her hands, looking down at the glinting, freshly-scoured blade while they waited for the heat to build. Neither looked toward the barn.

She tol bout me, Cyrus wondered, though nothing in either woman's bearing suggested so.

One of the hens made its way over to where they sat, its eye on the meal in the pail. The older woman brushed it away with a reflex movement of her plump hand, and it was strange to Cyrus to see actions so familiar performed by strangers: a lesson in how the world was; how things were everywhere at once different and the same.

Fire's hot enough, she said after a little time had passed, during which Cyrus had heard doors open and close around the place, and had begun to feel uneasy at the general rousing of the household.

Yes, Miz Peartree, Esther said, and she tore a ball from the meal-dough in the pail and pinched it out flat and round on the hoe-blade, which she then set as far into the fire as she could without having the flames lick round it and scorch the cooking cake.

Bracing herself with a hand on Esther's narrow shoulder, with a grunt Miz Peartree stood and returned to the house. Esther spread the check cloth out on her vacated stool and stacked the hoe-cakes on it as each one was cooked through. The smell of the baking drifted up and set Cyrus' mouth watering. As she was alone, Esther now shot occasional glances at the upper story of the barn. Somewhere a dog barked. Cyrus' chest tightened, but it seemed only the sound of release or recognition, not pursuit.

Time passed slowly. As Esther was nearing the bottom of the dough-pail another girl, of the same age as her or therabouts, Cyrus reckoned, but skinnier and light-complected, and with floured hands, came hurrying out. You heard, Esther, she said in a rush.

Heard what, Ditie?

Runaway, the other said, looking about her dramatically, clearly enjoying the chance to share the news. From Tyler, she went on. Night befo last. They say he kilt a white man with his bare hands.

Cyrus knew Esther must be exerting considerable willpower so as not to look towards the barn, towards the ventilation holes and the dark face pressed up behind them, its features screwed up in listening. Probably went downriver, she said as if indifferently, turning another toasted cake onto the pile. That'd be easiest, I suppose. Get on a log, get carried along like driftwood.

Naw, Ditie said, wiping her hands on her apron, oblivious to the wistful tone in Esther's voice as she spoke of floating away on the current, he come this way. Mas Hart's man tol Emory an Emory tol Miz Peartree an she tol me. He come all the way over Coleman's Hill an got in the swamp, likely got all the way through, an they ain't caught him yet. A killer! Best keep yo eyes open, Esther.

An you best get back to the kitchen fore the shortenin gets stiff.

Girl, you ain't scared of nothin, Ditie said admiringly.

I'm scared of plenty.

Want I should take the cakes in?

I'll bring em when I'm done.

Ditie? Ditie! Miz Peartree called. Girl, where you at?

Comin, Miz Peartree, Ditie shouted. She gave Esther another big-eyed look, then hurried back to the house. Esther's eyes followed her as she went and Cyrus heard the clatter of a screen-door, following which Esther looked up at the barn once more. Cyrus could not read her expression, but she stood and, setting the hoe aside, took two cakes from the heap and moved quickly in his direction, and he heard the clunk of the latch and the creak of the door, and squirmed his way over to the trap.

Leaving his boots, barefooted he descended to find her once more waiting, her chest tense, holding the hoe-cakes in front of her stomach, midway between a cradling and a supplication.

It true, she asked as he came to her, gentling his features as best he could, not drawing so close as to be a threat, but near enough that they could talk without body in the voice.

Yeah, he said. Different from how that gal said, but yeah.

She likes to swell a tale, Esther said. Like a toad. When Cyrus didn't reply she added, I brought you these, and offered him the cakes.

Thank you, he said, taking them from her with both hands, his mouth springing wet with hunger. And then he paused, awkward for no reason he could figure over eating in front of her.

What you waitin for, she asked. They done.

He watched her watching him as he nibbled the edge of the topmost cake. I eat fast as I want to, I'll choke, he said. Can you fill my bottle?

Sure.

He dug it from his knapsack and passed it to her. Don't let no-one see you, though.

I ain't stupid, she said.

Naw, he said. You ain't..

Take me with you, she said in a sudden uprush, and it struck him that maybe she was pregnant, or feared to be, two contrasting horrors.

Can't, he said.

Why?

He shrugged.

I'm strong. I got my wits.

My north ain't your north.

Her hands hung by her sides and she gestured twitchingly, powerlessly, and he knew all that was warring inside her then, all those things unanswerable, of which perhaps the most central was this: amidst madness what course is sane; and from that: what survives when what has survived is debased so far beneath its nature it forgets that nature?

She reached out and touched his upper arm. Strong, she said, and she forced a smile in the face and fact of his unresponsiveness, which she did not understand: not that he did not want her, which she understood easily enough, as all are not desired by all, but that it came from something she only dimly sensed that was deeper, or if not deeper then off at an oblique; and if as a rejection it was cruel then it was cruel in a way wholly different from anything of which she had knowledge, a novel species of indifference, and indifference, by its nature, cannot be stirred or fired up, and in that way remains remorselessly itself.

She turned her head then as if she had heard a sound, though he knew she had not; rather had needed a reason not to look at him while allowing him to look at her, and her profile was fine, and her chest rose and fell, delicate and vital, but to look at her that way only made him recall another event, one that had occurred a decade before, and had seeded in him a profound confusion, and had shadowed and closed his mind, his spirit, still further against the things of this world until the coming of Abednego; that had caused a withdrawal of shoot and root back into the wood-hard seed of him, a recoil as it were from a soil that was without those mineral nutrients his nature could draw upon, though he had not understood that then, for until that day his flesh had been used for laboring only, and not to fruit or pollinate – quadroon, octoroon, mulatto, the product of white men's pleasure and discharge, being one thing, and stock for breeding another, and arranged accordingly.

Cyrus had been just shy of twenty-two, and he, Solomon and Nate, along with two other hands, Volt and Shadrach, both a couple of years Cyrus' and Solomon's seniors, had been shackled together and loaded into a caged cart one sweaty Sunday morning close to the end of picking season, and the humectants air was dense with blood-stealing skeeters. Joseph and Lil Joe were absent, being at that time boys whose parts below a rude inspection by Mas Johnson's hand had determined were not yet full enough to function as required; and Samuel and Zeke were not yet purchased.

What day it was he recalled clear because it was the one part-given them for worship and, once their other allotted tasks about the place were done, the tending of their own plots, by which industry they supplemented the bare adequacy doled out by the overseers; and the cart was drawn by a bullock, its testicles swinging pendulum-heavy between its narrow haunches, and they were collared and chained and padlocked inside the cage on the cart's back. They passed the orchard, the branches at that season burdened with fruit and languid with foraging bees, and the overseers' cabins, and on the porch of one of the cabins stood a thin white woman in a long, straight dress of orange gingham with wavy orange hair and pale eyes, unbonneted, watching them. Cyrus recalled wondering what she knew of what her husband did, and with whom, and under what duress, presuming that was she was a wife and not some spinster sister, (though such a person, he reflected later, could also be a desiring one, perhaps the more so in the routine frustration of her desires); and what that knowing made her, through her condoning of it, tacit or otherwise, and regardless of her lack of choice in the matter, for she was in some way free to leave and therefore culpable, or so it seemed to him both then and later.

Leaving the estate the cart turned left, towards Bell, passing a half-hour or so later the white uprightness of the church at Tanner's Cross, at that hour of the morning sun-struck and glaring blindingly, and outside were buggies and their drivers, and from within came singing in which there was no admixture of blackness. And the drivers watched the caged Tyler hands pass as they waited on the worshippers inside, and, guessing the reason for their transportation, none risked a hail and some looked away.

How much had he and his fellows known or guessed of it beforehand?

Cyrus struggled to recall that now, standing before Esther in a state of mingled rage and grief. To be chained and collared had been ominous, and the swelter of the day unpleasant and unclean. That morning, before the worship from which they were to be excluded, they, the young men of the cabin, had been made to strip naked in the yard in front of everyone, male and female alike, and the two overseers, Gooderson and Molt, had thrown over them buckets of water the women brought from the trough at their command. Then Mister Johnson had inspected Lil Joe and Joseph, spitting tobacco juice on the ground and laughing as with burning faces the two boys, summarily dismissed, leaving their clothing, ran naked into the cabin, not looking back, the bright rabbit-tail soles of their feet red-gray with mud, and probably they were crying. To do with our private parts, then: that they had known for sure as they pulled on their pants and shirts and Mister Gooderson and Mister Molt (both dead since from drinking and no tears there) came forward with the collars. And the others watched from the sides of their downcast eyes as the white men fastened the collars round the necks of Cyrus and Solomon and Nate and Shadrach and Volt, a padlock at back of each, and ran the chain through a hoop set in front of every collar for that purpose, and led them to the caged cart. In this they could sit only if their heads were bowed, as if by symbolic intent, though perhaps it was merely to use the least amount of iron in its construction, the symbol but a by-product of thrift that was surely pleasing to its commissioner.

And so the cart, heavily-laden, creaked on at below a walking pace, the iron-hooped wooden wheels turning slow on the rutted road, Gooderson and Molt up front on the buckboard, the one fat, the other scrawny, passing between them a bottle of something they half-concealed as they passed the church, either on account of liquor being ungodly in and of itself, or through some sense that to be witnessed consuming it by slaves they did not have the whipping of would be a degradation of skins that were, despite the reticulated redness burnt into their surfaces by outside supervision, beneath that, white.

Cyrus and his fellows were not permitted to speak to each other while in the cart; nor had they had a moment to share speculations concerning their situation when, gathered together in the yard and, in front of the others in their Sunday best, they had been ordered to commit the sin, as they knew it to be from the casting out from Paradise of Adam and Eve, of nakedness. Yet this was not a theological or spiritual matter: they knew that also. And they knew of stock, and breeding and crossbreeding, of multiplication of stock and white men's profit thereby; of foaling and calving and babies black brown and yellow torn from their mothers teat for sale the instant the milk was done and the breasts were emptied flat; of the impossibility of comforting mothers for whom they could do nothing, who they could protect from nothing, and of the madness thus induced in those mothers and in themselves: that tearing of the heart beyond repair as a woman's private places are sometimes torn in birthing and never heal but thereafter pain and leak, defeating function and denying even the smallest possibility of future pleasure. But until that day they had not, or so it seemed to Cyrus in their shoulder-touching wordlessness, heads bowed like statues of saints, sweating in a caged cart, conceived their part in the production of that tearing: that it would be in no way chosen, or not by them, but on both sides forced. Until that Sunday he had understood their pain to be that of passive failure: to fail to feel loss as deeply as a woman, since it was from within women's bodies that babies came, the man's contribution being only his own release; and then to fail to protect either the bodies or the hearts of those women thus overwhelmed by feelings both tender and violent. Now they would understand a pain, a horror that was the worse for its impurity, its sticky, blood-engorged collusion.

The church-bell began to toll. Cyrus looked back at the grooms as they commenced to smarten themselves before the white folks emerged through the pointed double-doors. A strange illusion it seemed to him then: a world where all was clean and orderly – smoothly brown-skinned men in tailored uniforms of good material and cut; horses glossy-flanked and smartly docked, ribbons gay in their manes, brasses gleaming; the accordion bonnets on the brooms all levered up, waiting to screen their soon-to-be-ascending passengers from the rays of a sun that would otherwise steal from them their marble whiteness. And on one side lay fields neat as a tiled floor and tidily fenced off, the cotton rising, or further on and down the rice, as if orderliness was their natural inclination; and on the other, under a cloudless blue sky that seemed eternal, lay the wild country, fecund, untamed and yet inert, obligingly awaiting conquest.

There was a time befo, he thought: just the land an the red men. Deer an buffalo an bears an such all over.

But there was no power in his mind to summon the Then to defy the ineluctable Now. And Bell, when they reached it an hour later, was in its setting out, which was, after all, no more than a reflection of its function, a mirror of what they had come from, implying to Cyrus the possibility of an infinity of multi-plications, and nothing beyond those multiplications to which a person might escape, which impression was, he saw now, intended.

He did not wish to remember all this, looking at Esther's profile, but he did.

The humidity intensified as the cart turned in and they were born slowly between cotton fields in which, by chance or design, no hands were at that hour toiling, coming after a short but endless-seeming while to a congeries of roughly-built, whitewashed clapboard outbuildings. A group of white men, several of whom were overseers, judging by their whips, and various others were waiting on their arrival in the blue shade of a barn, among them an older man, perhaps Mister Bell himself, for there was in the bearing of the rest a deference toward him.

The Habsburgs, the older man was saying, his manner instructive, his gray eyes appraising Cyrus and the other black men as the cart drew up before him and stopped not in the shade but in the blaze. Now, they married in until their women-folk brought forth nothing but idiots and defectives, and that is why their empire fell, holy or otherwise.

Roman, one of the other men said, nodding.

Heathen, said another.

Blood gets stale, the old man said. Played out, like a field. I believe in the scientific method. These your best, he asked as Molt and Gooderson stepped down from the cart.

I believe so, sir, Molt replied. He belched, and the older man's lips pruned in distaste.

Mister Tyler reckons so, Gooderson added quicky, an he's a judge.

The older man came forward then, to the very edge of the shade. He wore a bright blue velvet frock-coat buttoned high and tight despite the heat, and the frilled shirt within pushed out of the top of it like the breast of a fighting-cock. His boots were of a soft, pale leather and he was droopingly moustachi-oed and thin and did not sweat. A judge of men, he said drily. Not bucks.

Gooderson and Molt looked at each other. They got they equipment, Molt said. An there's always chance in breedin anyhow. Throwbacks.

I do not believe in chance any more than any other true Christian, the old man said, looking first Solomon, then Volt, up and down. They stared ahead, emptied out already. All is as He ordered it.

Amen, Gooderson said. His face was red and he was sweating heavily from the beating of the sun and the drink he had consumed. Neither he nor Molt had been invited, nor granted permission, to step from the sun's glare into the privileged Bell shade, though unlike Cyrus, Solomon, Nate, Volt and Shadrach, the Tyler overseers had at least the protection of their hats. So where we takin em, Gooderson asked, when it became apparent no such invitation would be extended.

In there, one of the other white men said, pointing to a rectangular, single-story shed the doors of which stood open, waiting.

Gooderson went round to the back of the cart and unlocked the cage with a key from a bunch at his belt. Without conscious thought Cyrus and the others took note of which key it was. Though dread was heavy in them, and growing heavier by the second, it was a relief to get down from the cart and stand up straight, even though still burdened by the weight of the chain and the collars, the latter abrading the skin, in particular over the clavicle, at which delicate point neither muscle nor fat was thickly present enough to keep the nerves from being ground against the bone by the unyielding weight of iron, and this was sharply painful to endure, even for as comparatively short a time as the journey from Tyler to Bell.

Chinkingly chained together they were led into the shed, Volt in front, then Shadrach, Solomon, Cyrus, and lastly Nate. There were no windows, but the sunlight penetrated gaps in the planking walls, and their eyes adjusted swiftly to the cross-cut, gray-yellow gloom within. Along the walls on both sides were stalls in which a parsimonious amount of straw had been strewn on the compacted dirt, and from which livestock was, it seemed, absent, though the smell of recent animal voidings was thick in the air; and at the far end stood a trough of water and a feed-bin. At a tug of the chain by Molt they were led to the trough and permitted to drink either by lapping like dogs or scooping with their hands, no cups or ladles being provided. Mindful of Bible tales, as if this were some test of fitness, all scooped with their hands, and warily. The water had a taint to it.

After, they were made to stand in line in the middle of the shed as Mister Bell, or his head man as it might be, looked them over and made marks with a tiny, silver-shod pencil whose tip he licked to darken the lead, in a small, leather-bound book kept it seemed for that purpose, for a glance showed Cyrus there was a pattern to its pages, and that the new marks made seemed an extension of that pattern. Otherwise he, like the others, stared ahead, mind blank, and the white men murmured to each other behind their backs, and there was laughter that had about it something that made Cyrus' skin crawl worse than the sweat and tickling skeeters had done.

Unchain em, the older man said, snapping the little book shut and sliding the pencil down inside its spine.

Yes sir, Molt said, and he unlocked and unhooked the hasp of a large padlock, one of a pair which had been closed on a doubling-over of links at either end of the chain, by which simple expedient preventing its removal; and he and Gooderson fed it through the loops on the collars, disconnecting Cyrus and his fellows from each other. The collars too? Molt asked.

That ain't necessary for the purpose, the older man said. Leave em on. Get their clothes off.

You heard, Gooderson said, and, with eyes downcast in a shame that was different from, but no less intense than the shame they had felt before the cabins, Cyrus and the others obeyed, fumbling shirts up over their heads in slow silence; even more slowly unbuttoning their pants and letting them fall, their private parts shriveling under the white men's gaze as their humanity shriveled like tender shoots beneath a burning, relentless sun.

The old man walked back and forth behind them as they stepped out of their pooled pants. They all been whipped some, he observed.

They surely have, Gooderson said, his tone halfway between a brag and an apology.

Bucks with no spirit ain't no good for breedin, one of the Bell white men said.

The old man nodded. Weak stock.

Too much spirit ain't good though, said another. You breedin in trouble.

Broken spirit is best, the old man said. He was standing directly behind Cyrus now and Cyrus could smell the liquorice sweet on his breath.

We break em, Molt said quickly, and Gooderson nodded. Break em good, he echoed.

There was a silence then, a pause it seemed, during which an appraisal was made that was evidently of the quality of the overseers rather than the hands, for in the corner of his eye Cyrus saw Molt's face redden.

Well, I'll be leaving you gentlemen to your entertainment, the old man said.

Get in there, a harsh voice said behind Cyrus, and before he could think to move he and the others were manhandled naked into separate pens. All you niggers face the wall, the voice said. Keep facin the wall. And Cyrus did so, and he supposed the others did so too, for he heard no crack of whip or smack of leather or paddle, and there was no cursing by the white men.

Bring em in, the voice said, and now it had a smile in it that was nothing but unpleasant to the ear, and Cyrus had not known until that moment how sweat and heat and stifling closeness could be as bleak as a bare field in midwinter, not until a body was thrust against his back, and at the sudden prickling contact with another's bare skin he turned and saw before him a girl with a scared face, and hair divided in pigtails tied with white cotton strips, and behind her, beyond the stall's entrance, the white men standing about idle, watching what was occurring in the various pens with expressions on their faces he could not read then and would never truly fathom, nor cared to try, for to understand would be a possible connection: a fearful, even dangerous thing.

He allowed the girl to press herself against him, for it shielded the fronts of both their bodies from the flint glint of the vulpine watching eyes. He tried to ask her name, but his tongue clove to the roof of his mouth.

I'm Dinah, she said anyway, and she smelt a little sweet, of cinnamon, from the kitchen he supposed, and that made him ashamed that he himself did not smell pleasant, though no doubt her sweetness was a source of shame to her: an enforced preparation intended to disguise what was bitter beyond bearing. She was dark and small and pretty.

I'm Cyrus, he managed to say. From off of Tyler.

I know, she said.

Was that Mas Bell?

Who?

The ol man with the book.

Mas Bell at church with his wife an children. That was Mister Gray. He got notions.

Behind her a voice said, Get to it, though whether the order was directed at himself and Dinah, or at one of the other pairings Cyrus could not tell, for his vision was in some way sheared off, his eyes and head locked at some angle preventing his looking past her, or at the least preventing his focusing on anything beyond her.

And he knew then what he would have to do in order to reach the day's end; what he had never done in his life, though Volt and Shadrach and Solomon surely had, but not this way, not without the choosing and the eagerness of the girl they came to, and not before white men for their sport and thus wholly robbed of joy. This act that he had never in his twenty-some years had any urge towards, not understanding it, nor understanding the reality of it in the desiring parts of others; preferring the company of his hand and – once that was done without thought or image in his head, just the calling of hot palm to aching rigidity – the sexless company of his fellows. The act that loomed before him now in this beast's pen was false as burnt cork on the face of a white minstrel in a coon show, a grinning mockery: that which he was not.

Get to it.

One of the white men came up behind Dinah and shoved her into Cyrus hard, sending him staggering back a step through transmission of rude male force and, it seemed, anger. He held onto her to stop her slipping to her knees on the straw and dung beneath their bare feet and there were tears wet and warm on her cheek where it pressed against his chest, skin soft as air almost, and tears started in his own eyes as he kept close in to her to avoid seeing the expression on her face, the wound; to escape that unbearable interpenetration of irises gaping in spirit shadow. Get down, the voice ordered. It's only shit. Later Cyrus sensed there had been bets made, and Volt confirmed it with a wordless nod: money lain against who would be done with rutting first by his build and bearing, and the curve of her breasts and hips and mouth and what else neither Cyrus nor Volt nor the others could guess, save that it maybe might be what Mister Gray considered 'scientific'.

And amidst filth and thus compelled they lay down woodenly together, he on top, shielding her as best he could, which was in truth not at all, his weight pressing her down into that selfsame filth; and a boot cold and smooth against his bare backside obliged him to move his hips against Dinah's to the accompaniment of laughter from beyond the stalls and, he supposed, though his ears could not receive them save as beast-noises, urgings. And to his disgust and her disgust their being pressed together, having been brought here for this purpose and no other, and it therefore consuming all their minds, led to his arousal, an unclean heat gathering down there that extended his private organ until it was blood-filled enough to enter her sucking muscularity, which itself gained in shameful wetness as he inched inside her, easing his passage and making the performance possible. As he moved his hips against hers in that way, smothered gasps and moans from the other stalls came to his ears, disconcertingly magnifying the event, disgusting yet also shamefully provocative, for the animal self knows nothing of morality, only its own mechanically arousable nature; and that was the one and only time Cyrus knew a woman, in that animal pen, in that shed, on that Sunday.

Afterwards neither he nor Dinah could look at each other, an evasion he supposed the others shared, though they never spoke of it, such was their mortification; and after all what would be the benefit?

He was fourth of the five to be pulled from the stalls to dress wordlessly and with nerveless fingers in front of the cheerful white men, the girls left behind in sweaty opened silence on the straw and droppings, Dinah's juices drying but still sticky on his flaccid member, revealing her arousal, suggesting his, and therefore collusion with the white men's orders, as in the fifth stall Solomon struggled away gruntingly and one of the white men said, Big buck shy of wenches. Goddamn – and handed to another silver coins from a leather purse. Glancing at the fronts of their tight breeches Cyrus saw it was as if candles of differing sizes had been wedged in at various angles. The close air was sharp with the smells of sex: sweat, seed and juice, and Cyrus wanted powerfully to run, and at that moment something in his head departed and did not return, as sparks do not return to the fire but rush upwards and expire.

Eventually Solomon emerged blank-eyed and they looked away from him, avoiding his half-rigidity; and from the stall he left came sobbing. He dressed without a word or a backward glance, and joined the others in line as the white men threw into the stalls, one after another, shifts disbursed from a bundle brought in by a scared-looking black girl wearing a prettily-puffed, sky-blue apron, a little girl of maybe nine who looked down at all times, and moved awkwardly as though about to wet herself. She left fast without seeking leave, which caused some laughter among the white men, one of whom said, She don't need no crystal ball. And Cyrus prayed they would be taken away before the women emerged from the stalls, be spared that, but no: there they were kept until the women had dressed and left, at least doing so behind their backs, and so they did not have to face their violation.

By the time the men were chained and led out into the yard the women had returned to their duties elsewhere, and so neither sex had to meet the eyes of the other in the exposing glare of the afternoon sun. But they all felt dead inside as they stepped up, tremulous as old men, into the caged cart, and bowed their heads even as they would have done had the frame of iron bars not compelled it; and Molt and Gooderson were silent, and later Cyrus supposed there was a possibility they felt a little shame at what they were a part of. Or perhaps they had no more than lost a wager on an ill-chosen pairing of buck and wench and felt shame, if indeed they felt shame, only at their own poor judgement and resultant impecunity.

That day, a day so many hands had endured and would endure until the wearing out, it seemed to Cyrus, of the world itself, he had long pushed from his mind. Now, in the curve of this girl's collarbone, he was brought back to it.

Tell me bout De Bray's Town, he said.

She looked at him. He broke off a piece of the second hoe-cake and held it out to her, a gesture of connection, of civility, though it felt perverse to offer back to someone what was their own. But then he knew, and she knew, that it was not her own: that she, her hands and skills, the dough, the pail, the hoe were chattels all. She shook her head. Don't eat what I cook, she said.

You been there?

I come from there, she said. Well, through. I was young, though. Don't member much.

Uh-huh. An it big, you said?

Growin all the time, they say. On account of it's on two rivers, an the canal.

Volt and Shadrach had been hired out to dig that canal; had died hired out a year later, and were buried unmarked somewhere along its banks. Shadrach had been wed to Bella, for what that was worth, which was precious little, it being unrecorded in writing or marked by the exchanging of rings, and nothing any white person need take account of, though among his fellow slaves it was an assertion of human feelings acknowledged and respected; and too it was a claim upon fleshly pleasure: an assertion of the will to power made by a man over a woman, and such assertions, while not admirable, Cyrus knew were human too. Shadrach had fathered Williams, who last year had been whipped to death for running; and Bella made for Cyrus the coat he was wearing now. Confronted by these interconnections he felt both burdened and emboldened, for they ran out this way and that like rhizomes, ready to spring up in unexpected places, and break through the crust of his ignorance with small iris-blades of knowledge. And town felt like knowledge, or its possibility.

You hear news from there, he asked.

Some, she said. She watched him as he finished eating the second cake. That good?

Uh-huh.

You best go back up. I'll fill this. She held up his flask.

Thank you.

It'll be a while. I got chores.

He nodded. Pushing the flask down the front pocket of her apron, she turned and left the barn, pulling the door to behind her, closing the latch with care so it did not click. He climbed back up to the loft and, taking his boots with him, returned to his watching-place. Once there he tugged out the straw he had pushed into them earlier, it being, as he had intended, damp from the moisture it had drawn from the sodden leather. The interiors smelt brackish, so he left them empty and set them to air by the ventilation holes alongside his hat, and watched idly as Esther briskly cooked the last of the hoe-cakes, folded the cloth up round them and went inside, leaving, and then returning for, the now-empty pail, the hoe and the stools.

Blue smoke rose in a thin column from the brightly-crackling fire and the fowls pecked at the ground, and he wondered how long it was wise to remain here. If Esther could find time later on to come and talk with him, and give him useful information, then that would make his lack of progress during daylight hours worthwhile. In any case, to try and move on beneath the sun's exposing eye would surely be a perilous, perhaps even fatal mistake. Yet would not the slave-catchers endeavor to search just such outbuildings as the one in which he now lay concealed? And would not the owners of those buildings, however great their habitual pleasure in cheating one another on every deal made or attempted, and however minded they might be to stand on the rights of property, collude in such a search, it after all being in all their interests that no black fugitive successfully flee his or her captivity? The reward for his taking would surely be large, the more so since the events in the swamp that had branded him a Bad Nigger.

How many estates and holdings were there in this part of the country, he wondered; and he felt a longing for the raw simplicity of the wild and empty places, where the greatest test was of endurance. But he had turned his back on that, at least for now.

Town.

What did he know? What had Bed told him? All was built on toil and trade, he knew that. Slaves, then. Cotton, rice, tobacco and in a small way fruit of various sorts; mulberry leaves for the spinning of silk by way of feeding particular worms. Canals cut between rivers to permit the easy freighting back and forth of what was traded regardless of weight. Punts and rafts, boats and, though he had never seen them, ships. On roads like veins were carts, carriages and wagons drawn by mules and horses, sometimes bullocks. Coaches bringing mail – letters, packages – from all over, with teams of horses waiting fresh at inns along the way, to keep the mail moving in relay and with a minimum of delay.

Out beyond were also, so Bed had told him, great piston-engines, furnaces on iron wheels that rolled along iron rails nailed to planks to keep them in line, that pulled more wagons than a man could count, and faster by far than even a team of whipped-up horses, for many hundreds of miles; and somewhere the iron was dug from the ground, he supposed, and he didn't doubt by slaves. And he knew of De Bray's Town and thereabouts the curious fact that the enslaved outnumbered by a considerable margin the free; the black outnumbered the white: hence the intensity of the fear the white people felt that was so often palpable in the air surrounding them, like the tension before a thunderstorm.

Okay, then.

It was little enough, and gave Cyrus no sense of how he might move forward on this new course he had set himself. He had no pass, and could not read: how then could he make enquiries about the selling of the Tyler Negroes and, in any case, of whom? He supposed himself not particularly memorable in appearance, but perhaps he would be remembered well enough to have a portrait drawn of him by one or other of the overseers, or by some skilled hand under their combined direction, for he had on occasion seen sketches of runaways on handbills, as well as the perhaps more fanciful illustrations of those being offered for sale, no doubt exaggerating whatever the seller believed would make them most desirable to a purchaser; and, if that was so, if he was caught in a picture, he would be unable to, as he might have hoped, disappear among the crowds he had heard tell filled a town – a multitude of strangers together, in the main unknown to each other, and so unable instantly to determine who belonged to whom, and who did not belong at all.

Though scars from whippings were of course commonplace to the point of universality, the particular pattern on his back was, inevitably, unique: a signature of sorts that he supposed the one who inflicted it might possibly remember, and mark down in a drawing, and could thus, should Cyrus be captured, betray him. But his back would not be on general view: that was something.

Drawing or none, there was little he could do to change his appearance: his height and build and complexion were what they were, his face was, as was his habit, smoothly shaved, his hair was cropped short; and he foresaw no opportunity to change his clothes.

Night be my best friend still, he thought, and that decided him to try and snatch a few hours' sleep, though his feet remained distractingly cold. He took a minute to rub a little life back into them. They were at least now dry. He stretched out on his side, pushing them into the straw where it was denser and so a little warmer in its fermentation. Through the peep-holes he now saw only a pair of gable-ended rooftops, and where they met a chimney, the smoke from which was of a piece with the scalloped, pearl-gray sky behind it. He imagined Bed pressed up behind him, Bed's arms around his waist, and hugged himself and closed his eyes.

Chapter Six

H e woke with a start from jumbled dreams of pursuit.
Beyond the airholes the dusk was drawing in, and the
chill air was stirring, signifying that a change in the
weather was on its way.

Someone was moving about below. Esther? Ditie, deciding
on her own initiative to make a search? Cyrus sat up slowly so
as to avoid making noise in the heaped and shifting hay,
reached for his boots, pushed his feet into them, knotted the
laces, and with the same silent care set his hat on his head. His
joints ached, his hands and feet were cold, and his blood had
sunk down like mud in water. Yet a body running towards
freedom feels its hard use in a different way from one toiling
unremitted for the profit of others; and too there was a zest in
unfamiliarity, even in unfamiliar suffering, and so the pain was
supportable; proof, even, of life, of possibilities.

Still as a set-aside pitchfork he waited in the straw and listened, but no-one climbed the steps to the loft. Could it be
Esther, waiting for him to come to her as he had both times
before? Stealthily he wormed his way through the hay until,
after what seemed the longest time, he was once more at the
trapdoor's edge and peering down into the dimness below.

Two figures came into his field of view, a man and a woman, both dark-skinned, she in apron and cap, leading; he in a
short coat, tight about the waist and with brass buttons set in
polished pairs across its front, white breeches and black, knee-
high boots, being led. They had with them neither lamp nor
candle, and to a speculative eye they might be lovers in search
of some discreet, if chilly, place of assignation. But when they
reached the foot of the steps they looked up, and the woman
was Esther, and she carried a milking-pail by way of a justification for being there. Her eyes met Cyrus', she nodded, and he
came down to meet her and the man with her.

This Emory, she said quietly. One o the grooms. We used to
have four, now we got just two. Emory, this Cyrus, from off of
Tyler.

Emory gripped Cyrus' hand in his, and his broad, smooth face was hard, and his dark eyes were probing. He was tall, strongly-built, and younger than Cyrus by some years; or perhaps, and judging from his dress, chance had spared him the aging toil of the fields. His short hair was greased back as Abednego's had been.

Esther led them to a stall a few along from where the cow was tethered by the door, in the shadows of which they would not be seen by anyone who came only as far as the barn's entrance.

So you runnin, Emory said.

I'm aimin fo De Bray's Town.

You knows people there, or along the way?

Cyrus shook his head.

There's patrols, Emory said. More'n there used to be.

Esther tol me.

We had visitors in the ante meridian, Emory went on. She tell you that too, I dare say.

Cyrus glanced at Esther. Was they from Tyler?

Naw, but they knew you was.

How many?

Fo on horseback, two on a wagon. The ones on the wagon stayed up on the road; the others come up to the main house. They had rifles an pistols.

But they went away?

They went. But they be back soon, I guess.

Why?

On account of Mas Hart bein due back now or rounda-bouts.

Less he get so drunk over card-playin he stops where he is, Esther said. He got rooms in town, she added, by way of explanation.

Emory went on, They needs his permission to search an he's particular on that point, an the daughter told em so. Kept em out on the verandah while they was here. They dint like it. When they was leavin they told Green – he one of the overseers – they done searched the other holdings hereabouts already an with no trouble. Green would of let em search here too, fo a cut of any money they got if you was caught, an was all for overridin Miz Hart, on account of she fraid to leave the house when her daddy away so what she gon do, but they said no to that an left. Green a drunk too.

An vicious ill-tempered, Esther said, glancing over at the barn door which, left unlatched, had swung partway open in the breeze. The skin on her neck prickled.

Seems I best move off directly, Cyrus said. There many whitefolks bout the place?

Mas Hart's brother an wife, Esther said, an they got two sons comin up on fifteen, sixteen eager to prove they men. As she said this she moved a shade closer to both Cyrus and Emory, and they to her. Mas Hart's own son an daughter, they in they twenties, but ain't neither married. Four overseers, three wives mean as cottonmouths an a parcel o younguns, none over ten years old.

An blackfolks?

In the house, nine. An forty hands.

There flamed up in Cyrus' mind then thoughts of insurrection: forty-nine – fifty if he included himself – against thirteen or fourteen, and the most competent and therefore dangerous of the latter drunks, and unsuspecting. Acting in concert, could he and the others not speedily dispatch them all with what was readily to hand – hoes and rakes, forks and spades, hammers, saws and hatchets; and, from the big house kitchen cleavers, carving-, gutting- and filleting-knives? Wait for the return of the errant master, drag him from his fly and finish him fast? That done, wait for the patrollers, invite them in on the pretext of having information to share concerning the runaway, dull their wits with amiable hospitality, and then take hatchets to them? They surely could. But what then, within that charmed zone of butchery, all connection with the wider world thus abruptly amputated? Could they make a pretence that nothing had changed? It would be a façade impossible to maintain for more than the shortest time, he could see that; and then obliterating violence would descend on the transgressors, and tortures be inflicted worser even than could be imagined by those like himself – like each and every one of them – who knew what torture was. And would all, in such a situation, act in concert? Would not some betray, seeking advantage from what was to their eyes – and likely also in reality – vainglorious, futile; or, more excusably, from simple fear of torment?

Inevitably so. Hadn't Esther said of the state of the estate when he first asked her, We strugglin?

We strugglin.

Still and all, here she was, and she had brought with her someone of sense, it seemed, in Emory, whose interest in her Cyrus perceived at once in the bright lamps of his eyes, as, simultaneously, he perceived by her bearing in the young groom's presence Esther's lack of reciprocity – a lack already implied by her preparedness to run without consulting this man so well-placed to assist her in such a venture. So Emory was there to on some level prove himself to her, and that would place a limit on how far he would transgress the bounds of self-preservation. To be here now, illicitly, gaining nothing for himself but her esteem, was risk enough for him, perhaps.

Any o the others know I'm here, Cyrus asked.

Esther shook her head. An we can't be out here long or we be missed. Emory knows more'n I do, so I ast his help.

Cyrus nodded as Emory produced a piece of creased brown packing-paper from an inner pocket and smoothed it out against the side of the stall. On it were charcoal marks. Can you read a map, he asked.

Can't read, Cyrus said.

But you can reckon?

Reckon?

Like proportionin a thing put down on paper.

A thumb mean a foot or a yard? Sho, I can do that.

Then look here, Emory said. Esther, we needs to risk a candle.

Esther nodded and produced a candle-stump from her pocket, which she handed him, and a tinder-box.

Couldn't of chanced a lamp or lit candle crossin the yard, Emory said to Cyrus as Esther moved to the back of the stall.

Breeze would of took off a candle-flame anyhow, she said, striking the firesteel on the flint, sending sparks into the tin box where she had set it on a ledge.

The repeated sound of steel on flint, though small, seemed to Cyrus as drawing to the ear as a woodpecker's beak on a hollow tree-trunk, and as revealing of purpose as a robin dropping with hungry persistence snail-shells on a rock. Quickly enough, however, the sparks caught the charcloth within the box. Esther blew on it till it glowed, then laid the sulfur-tipped head of one of the accompanying match-spills against it. The spill flared into brief life; just time enough to light the candle-stump Emory held up as she turned with the flame cupped in her hands. That done she extinguished the spill with a flick of her wrist and put it back in the tinderbox, which she closed to smother the charcloth within, and returned to her pocket as Emory carefully set the candle on the ground. Thus illuminated all three looked about them, but the yellow light seemed contained within the stall, cut off by its chest-high sides from the view of anyone who might appear in the doorway.

They squatted down as Emory placed the unfolded brown paper on the ground next to the candle. Stains from whatever it had wrapped made irregular dark shapes that seemed like, but Cyrus knew were not, symbols of places and phenomena. He knelt and studied the paper intently as Emory pointed out the lines he had drawn and their meanings.

This the canal. This the road. They runs side by side all the way to De Bray's Town. I reckons it twenty-five miles, maybe. They's three estates past Hart, all bout the same size an set in a line, an they's the same number facin em on the far side of the canal. Ain't no fords on a canal, but each estate got a couple ferry-points an rafts, an a dock fo sendin off loads by barge. Mills, gin houses an such is mostly in the flood fields between the road an the canal. Road's on top of a kinda dyke, raised up, with ditches on either side.

How long them other estates run on fo?

Bout three miles, I reckons. Thas where you in mos danger if you takes the road.

On account o the traffic between em?

Emory nodded. Even by night. An that's on top of patrols. Else you could go back the way you came an skirt round, but that'd put you in the swamp again. With no moon to go by you'd get lost soon enough, an not to yo advantage: you'd likely be doublin the distance an treblin the exertion.

The road runs straight an level, Esther said. Keep yo eyes open an you can duck down them side-ditches if someone comes along.

Ten miles on, you in the woods, Emory continued. They

somewhat swampy, thas how come they ain't been cleared yet, but they'll give you cover. Does the patrollers know the direction you takin?

Naw, they'll guess I'm headin north. How long them woods run on fo?

I'd say ten miles maybe. Past the woods is a crossroads with a inn, a stable, a couple houses an a sto. Thas where the road from Tyler comes in. Then it's open fo a spell, then mo estates, runnin into town on a slow decline.

Tell me bout town, Cyrus said.

Emory shifted on his haunches, and though he was crouching he straightened his back and pushed out his chest. The brass buttons on his coat glinted in the candle-light, and Cyrus saw his black eyes deepen and become remote both at once, and they too caught the light and glinted. His thus-heightened physical presence and simultaneous psychological withdrawal made Esther become attentive to him as she had not been before. For if he had, as it seemed, declined to offer her the potentially lethal dice-throw of a dash to freedom, his connection to wider possibilities was not something to discount; and perhaps only Cyrus' sudden appearance had caused Esther briefly to forget that fact.

They's people by the thousand, Emory said, livin, tradin or just passin through. They's a harbor, an all the trade is set round that; warehouses, offices an such. Thas where the rivers meet, Nooseneck an Goose, an the canal deadends there on account of a row of hills. They lookin fo subscribers to finance diggin through, but don't none o them white folks want to pay. The river runs on down to the delta, an a way past that, the sea. At the far end o the hills, they's a bluff overlooks the town, an on top of it a big pressin mill. They gots great wooden screws in there, turned by mules, to press the bales down tighter an smaller than a ordinary press. That way they can fit mo in the holds o the ships an make mo money off of each trip. They slides em down a long chute from the mill to the dock. On the side of the bluff is a whole heap of big, fancy houses with pillars in front. The rich white folks, merchants they called, or I heard speculators, an they kin, they likes to be up in the fresh air, lookin down on they wealth growin in the dirt below.

Cyrus nodded, finding he could in some measure envision

such a vista. An down below, he asked.

Houses fo them what ain't so rich, some of em called row cause they share walls, an stores for all manner of items. Fancy clothes an boots an millinery: what they calls fashion.

Fashion?

Things what ain't got a use.

Like brass buttons on a coat that don't close it, Esther said, teasing Emory a little, moving closer to him. He gave her a look, and went on: They's inns an hotels – places a traveler stops when he tired out an gets a bed an victuals an stablin fo the horses. Confectionaries fo the sellin of liquor. Cat-houses. The buildings is crowded in down there, some wood, some brick, an near the docks the streets shrink till they so narrow they only gets sunshine at noon. By the docks is warehouses fo goods an produce, an between the hotels an inns an cat-houses, an next to the courthouse an a big white church, they's the auction house.

Cyrus' irises tightened. Thas where I gots to get to, he said.

Thas where you likely end up anyhow, Emory said, and his eyes met Cyrus', and were at once a mirror and an interpenetration, and full of feeling; and Cyrus glanced down.

Thas it, he asked.

Thas it.

Emory held the corner of the paper in the candle-flame, and it caught and they watched as it flared and was consumed. We best leave you now, he said, reaching for and pinching out the wick. Passing Esther the candle-stub, he stood up, then helped her stand too.

Cyrus rose with her, and looked over at the partways-open barn-door. Through the gap, outside the night was black. Esther pressed something wrapped in cloth into his hands. A slice of pie, she said. Oh – and she pulled out and passed him his flask, the weight of it telling him she had filled it. He had no words with which to thank her, or Emory, and understanding, they expected none.

What it wrap in, he asked, as he slipped the package into his knapsack.

Nothin they could figure comes from here, Esther said, at once catching his meaning and his concern for her safety. And then Esther and Emory were gone, closing the door carefully behind them. Cyrus listened out for the sound of the screen-door to the kitchen as it creaked open and then, perhaps more loudly than need be, banged closed, waited a minute more, crossed to the barn door, opened it, and slipped out into the yard.

Dark though it was, he had at once the sense of being exposed. The air, which in the yard was only stirring, became, as he reached the corner of the barn and looked out over the fields, a cold wind cutting across his face. Cloud-cover had wholly robbed the night of star- or moonlight, and he could make out little of the land before him.

A shrill iron crying high above told him a weather-vane was turning. Across from the yard a fence ran away into the night; by the fourth picket it was wholly swallowed by the dark. As he recalled from his view of the configuration of the fields earlier that day, all those to the east were rectangular and set out in parallel to the straight line of the road; and so he determined to follow the fence and, guided as much by touch as sight, at the field's eventual end to turn left, follow the right angle he presumed to be similarly fenced along, and in that way reach the unseen road without difficulty or risk of encountering anyone along the way.

Glancing about him, he made his way to the first picket and passed it. Goin an gone, he thought. Alongside the fence the earth had been trodden into what passed for a path, and it indeed ran straight, as he had remembered. He went at a steady pace, brushing the pickets as he passed them with his fingertips, and encountered no obstacles. Perhaps a half hour had gone by when he reached the field's end and found as he had hoped that the fence turned there and ran towards the road. He followed it for what seemed a long time, though in the darkness time and distance were hard to figure. The wind, stiffer now, blew straight into his face and made him squint, and it was in that way, through watering eyes, that he became aware of a prismatic yellow dot, a light somewhere up ahead.

Although it seemed directly in his path, Cyrus did not slow, for though it was surely on the road, it was also some considerable way off: a wagon or carriage with a lamp or lamps upfront; and as such was a confirmation of the correctness of his direction – Mas Hart, perhaps, being driven home dead drunk.

In any case, by the time Cyrus traversed the rest of the field and reached where the light was now, it would have long since passed on towards its intended destination, and why should either driver or passenger trouble to look back?

And then he thought of the patrollers: they would be looking all ways, no doubt, back and forth and to either side, with eyes like boring beetles. But without moon- or starlight how far could even those eyes penetrate the ebony of the night? No more than five yards, likely, and so the dark was, as it seemed to him it should be, once again his friend. He matched as best he could his rate of progress to the procession of the floating lamp, it growing neither larger nor smaller as he went on. Perhaps a mule- or cattle-cart, then.

Eventually, after clambering over a boundary-fence, he reached a large and steep-sided drainage ditch. Gathering himself he leapt, and by throwing himself flat on the muddy, sharply-cut far incline, managed to avoid falling back or slithering down into an unknown depth of black water below. He scrabbled his way up onto a flat area where small stones were spilled about: the edging of the road; and stood up. The stones made a crunching sound underfoot that was distinctive, and so disquieting. A step further and he was on the road itself. Composed of impacted stones and dirt, it ran away pale and straight and level to left and right; nothing was nearby save a tall and skinny pine-tree, and the wind blew more harshly here, as if across flat emptiness.

Still as a signpost Cyrus stood in the middle of the road and listened.

Chapter Seven

The wind, streaming across the road, the unseen canal, and the flat and equally unseen expanse of fields on either side of it, stirred the pine-boughs above Cyrus' head sighingly. No lights were visible in any direction: even the carriage had passed from sight – turned a corner, passed behind a wall or hedge, descended a dip in the road. Though its absence was a relief, a sense of aloneness fell on Cyrus then. He took a swig of water from his flask. There was nothing to do but go on.

The road, being well-laid, made for easy walking, but the wind pervaded his clothing and chilled his torso. It carried sounds away across the glacial plain, giving rise to the possibility that any horse on the road, whether behind or ahead, might get closer up on him than he could wish before he heard its hooves or the jingle of its harness. A slow cart didn't worry him, but riders on horseback did – though he supposed that on such a lightless night, even on so straight and generally unobstructed a road, they would be obliged to carry lanterns, and would thereby, if approaching from ahead, alert him to their presence a sufficient way off for him to conceal himself by slipping down the side of one of the ditches. Perhaps for that reason the patrollers wouldn't be out tonight, and for sure dogs would have nothing to trace him by. But they knows I'm out here someplace. An they knows I kilt a white man, or weren't that what Ditie said: killed?

Steady now.

Pulling his hat down tight he leant into the angle of the wind. The presence of the pines, regular markers in the formless dark, reassured him he was making progress; and to be free for a while of the need to make any decision was a relief. Get to the woods, get through the woods, was all he needed to hold onto for now. All here was of the physical realm – the chill, persistent wind, the pale road long and hard and level beneath his booted feet, the pine-boughs creaking above – yet it was as if he was walking in a dream.

Mas Johnson dead, he thought. Um-hum.

Mister Johnson, who had whipped Cyrus for insolence in the midst of his heartbreak after Bed was sold; who had had him stripped to the waist and compelled Solomon to hitch him to the tall post in the stable-yard that was set there for that purpose and no other; who had left him with beltless, unstrung pants sagging and threatening to drop and add further humiliation to his ordeal. Solomon's eyes had been lowered in shame, their mirrors hidden beneath twitching lids as he pulled Cyrus' arms above his head, stretching out muscle and ligament with a terrible gentleness before tethering Cyrus' bound wrists to the iron ring at the post's apex, tugging the knots tight with an exhalation of breath that was indeed a loss of spirit, an expiration; after which, and following an unbearable, vibrating moment of cat-gut fiddle-wire anticipation, Mister Johnson had laid on the lash with grunts like those of a copulating beast; and Cyrus grunted too, at first, then on the fifth cut yelled out, which release it seemed further excited the overseer's arm.

Teach you to sass, he said, laying the whip on harder. That'll teach you, God damn it. I'll bare your strings.

Something died within Cyrus that day, as something dies in any person from whom all control, all independence of action, is ripped away; the more so when such an extinction of self is the intention of the system in service of which, or so it seemed to him then, the entire world turned, an outside barely conceivable. And yet through Bed that outside world had become conceivable to Cyrus; and even in the midst of the extremity of agony and debasement he was enduring he drew a little heart from that, a resilience beyond the knowledge that cuts healed, that flesh knit back together, that even bones resedimented themselves, albeit oftentimes misshapenly. And he came to understand that just as the hearing of a blind man sharpens, the eyes being extinguished, or the wit of a homely woman grows bright, so a compensation of function could develop within the brain or spirit to take the place of what was lacking or destroyed; and thus it was that he and his fellows could endure the whippings, the beatings, the bridling, the branding, even the amputations, and still remain, in defiance, surely, of what was intended, and through the operations of the spirit that remained vital, if muted, within them, human.

Still it was a terrible hard thing to bear. And such compensations could, should they become too numerous, and too little of the original being remain for them to draw upon, become deformed and even malignant. This too he had seen: mental monsters. Salve, he thought. Salvation.

Then: If he dead, I'm glad he dead.

He thought of Lil Joe then, and missed him; and Joseph and Zeke and Solomon; and Nate, though he was dead and so not to be returned to while life was in him. But he missed Abednego more, and so he looked ahead into the night, into the future. He began to hum as he walked, not loud, but in its vibrating through the roof of his soft palate up into the bones of his skull loud enough, and with enough of a tune to carry his spirit forward.

After he had been going two hours or so by his reckoning, he noticed some way off to his right lights that suggested to him in their lack of movement a building. It was likely located beyond a belt of trees, his angle to which had slowly shifted as he trudged along until its lit façade now stood revealed to him; and indeed a little way on he came to a wide driveway running off towards the source of the lights over a low, ditch-straddling stone bridge, and at the far end of this driveway, beyond an intercession of opaque black nothing, he now saw a mansion, its mass and proportions established by a framing grid of lamplight that bled through closed shutters on two substantial stories. This grid flanked symmetrically a pilastered portico tall as the tallest barn on Tyler, beneath which broad steps led up to a great front door. Flaring torches were set in flammifers on either side of this door, which stood, it seemed by intent open, and the wind, which set the flames fluttering like rags on a scarecrow, conveyed faintly to Cyrus' ears fiddle music and, fainter still, sounds of merriment within.

They'll be carriages on the road then, he thought.

Would the passengers in those carriages be wary, he wondered, knowing a desperate and indeed murderous black runaway might be in the vicinity of this fine house, lurking in the darkness? Or in their soap-bubble-bright lives of lace and velvet would they fancy themselves immune to such a danger, floating somehow above it? Did they imagine they could set lamps on all sides of their lives and thereby, through some trick of arrangement of the facts, perpetually expel the shadows?

Not enough lamp-oil in the world fo that. He touched Nate's knife in its pocket, kept on humming. Well, then.

He went on, leaving the fine house and its music behind him, and as he walked he took from his knapsack and ate Esther's slice of pie – peach, it turned out. The pastry was crisp and sweet, the fruit vivid. A bone-hard fragment of peach-pit had got in there, and he rolled it round his mouth a while, then spat it out onto the road. The scrap of material she had wrapped the slice in he bundled after wiping his mouth and hands on it and flung in the direction of the ditch. Bella came into his mind as he did this. She won't understand how comes I run, he thought, though he also thought perhaps she might, for it was only once Abednego was sold that she had formed the habit of seeking out his company: for sure she had seen that much of it. Of him and Bed. He felt a little guilty then at his cruelty towards her, though his predominant sense of himself in relation to her was as a fire into which she insisted on putting her fingers, despite knowing or at the least guessing its intrinsic nature and qualities, and what blame can flames carry and what tears would they cry for the burns and weeping blisters they inflict?

If Bed was walkin with me now, he thought, and the image of Abednego at his side made him stand straighter and push out his chest, wind or no wind. We both be upright as pines an as strong. Hand in hand. Together.

Through the interruption of another belt of trees the house was cut off from his view, and the dreamlike quality of the landscape returned. He passed another well-laid side-road, this time running away to his left, and presumed it led to the estate's mill, barns, drying-houses for tobacco and suchlike, and the jetty by means of which commerce was enabled and the mansion he had passed sustained, the road on which he walked now as much a dividing line in the wealthy white folks' minds as that between Earth and Heaven, or Earth and Hell, though which was which was, in God's seeming absence, perhaps no more than a point of view.

Briefly he considered a detour, wondering if he might conceal himself on board a barge and head to town that way, floating on the water effortless as a willow leaf. Having no friend or ally to aid him, however, and lacking knowledge of how big such barges were, how high they might be piled with bales and barrels, and how far what was stowed on them might be covered by tarpaulins beneath which a man might conveniently conceal himself, he abandoned the notion and continued on.

Thus far, bar what he took to be Mas Hart's carriage returning home, he had seen no-one on the road. How many estates had he passed in the dark? Surely the brightly-lit mansion had been too far beyond Hart to be the first, but was it the second or the third? At this late hour all buildings not hosting some extravagant social event would likely be in darkness, their inhabitants in bed; and any window still lit that happened to face away from the road he would not have seen. He had passed a good many smaller paths as he walked, extending to both left and right over flat, wood-plank bridges set above the drainage-ditches that were, it seemed, a feature of the area: only the lit-up house had had a stone bridge and a continuous roadway.

On some impulse – owing perhaps to the intervention of a warning haint, or else through some animal sense that penetrated his mind below its conscious level – he looked back then, and saw a light behind him on the road, and seeing it, heard, though still some considerable way off, the clatter of hooves. One horse, he thought, goin at a trot.

Finding himself by a path that ran off to his left, he at once stepped off the road, turned about, and on hands and knees scrambled feet-first backwards down the incline of the ditch beside the wooden bridge that spanned it. From there he wedged his backside into the V of one of the bridge-struts and, by peering round and up, was able to see, while remaining concealed, whatever passed by when it drew sufficiently near, though in the meantime he had no wider view of the road. And so he sat there above the icy ditchwater, his legs dangling, in rising discomfort, for the square-sawed cross-strut soon cut off the circulation to the backs of his thighs; and he waited for what seemed a wearisome length of time.

Just as he was beginning to conjecture that the carriage had made its way down one of the earlier turnings and so he

might safely move on, by some carrying or suppressing trick of
the wind the clatter of hooves and jingle of harness rose up
clear, and a moment later a corona of lamplight filled one
corner of his field of vision. Then the conveyance came briefly
into view. It was a compact but fancy open carriage of lacquered black and gold, seating four, with a Negro groom, in
livery and muffled up with a scarf against the cold, perched up
front between two lamps that swayed wildly on account both of
the cross-wind and the bouncing of the springs, for it was
moving fast, and he cracked the whip. Four white folks, two
sets of men and women, sat facing each other behind the
groom, who stared earnestly ahead, and through the zoetrope
made by the rotating spokes of the great whirring carriage-
wheels Cyrus saw the bonneted women bundled in capes of
turquoise and crocus yellow, and the men in great wool coats
buttoned high and top hats, all of them stiff-faced and pale and
upright.

They fraid of me, he thought. They wasn't when they was in
there dancin in the light, but they is now.

The carriage passed. He waited a while, then swung out
awkwardly from his hiding-place and climbed back up the
bank, keeping crouched until he judged it sufficiently far off for
those looking backwards to be unable to see him in the swallowing dark.

In this way he went on, being obliged three more times to slide
partway down one or other of the roadside ditches in order to
conceal himself from passing conveyances. The requirement to
press himself flat against the angled mud meant he could see
them only some time after they had gone by, when he raised his
head back up above the level of the road's surface. Digging the
toes of his boots in and sprawling out on the slant was more
tiring than sheltering under the bridge had been, but was not
difficult, and each time he did so he judged his positioning
more economically. Twice as he watched the receding backs of
one-horse buggies, those without grooms that were driven by
one of the pair of passengers within, he noted the tail-boards
for luggage at their rears, and considered how he might
scramble up from where he was, sprint after them and stealthily climb aboard. The second time this thought occurred to him,

the image was so vivid it was as if from where he hunkered down Cyrus could already see himself drawing away, clinging there like a frog, flat against the varnished wood and curving leather.

They'd know, though. My weight'd make it sink some an give me away.

And he was not, or at the least not yet, for all the fury forever within him, and for all the tales he did not doubt were already being told across the county, a killer of men, never mind women, as might likely be the case in such a buggy, passenger wife accompanying chauffeur husband.

During the long hours of night-walking his senses had become as used to darkness as a man's can be, and in a short while he became aware of vague low shapes beyond the ditches that by the sound of the stirring in the wind were surely bushes. Then came trees and more trees, the wood thickening, he could tell, though he could not see it, by the increasingly voluminous rushing noise above, and the simultaneous stilling of the air below, where the massing trunks obstructed and diffused the wind. The road ran on near-straight but the ditches became increasingly choked with old growth of hackberry and woodbine.

How long Emory say the wood go on fo? Ten miles an a maybe.

Cyrus was tired now.

Something up ahead – a small scuffing sound, a movement of shadow within shadow – made him start. Chest tensing he froze and peered into the blackness, attempting to force through exertion of will some further penetrant dilation of his irises. He sensed as much as saw another movement by that something, a movement that seemed to him wary without being furtive, which was in a small way a reassurance, and then he made it out: a doe, watching him with eyes that were wholly black. She was perhaps twelve feet away from him. One ear twitched. After a long moment she turned her head, stepped off the path, sprung over the ditch to his right and, with a flash of white hindquarters, was gone.

Cyrus determined to keep on until the first streaks of dawn revealed his surroundings to him more plainly. He could then, he hoped, seek shelter among the trees, maybe even find one he could climb up into and thusly remove himself from the eyeline of any passer-by; rest up some and reckon his best way forward, perhaps for a second time travel, as seemed to him surely the safer choice, under cover of night, especially if the clouds cleared. His stomach made a liquid sound and he thought of the chicken in his knapsack, and how even deep in the woods it would still be too dangerous to make a fire to cook it over. He thought of eating it raw if need be, and the point at which that would not repel; and he thought of thieving should the possibility arise.

An ain't I owed? Work I done.

Ain't we all owed.

He paused to urinate into one of the ditches and continued on, though his ankles, knees and even his hips were aching now, and with each step he took the never-fully-dried leather of his boots dug cruelly into the backs of his heels, making him drag his feet in order to obtain a slight relief. The stones embedded in the road, while small enough to create a visual impression of evenness, were too sharp for him to go barefoot, even had the cold not made the prospect offputting. And so he went slowly on, until the edges of the sky grew pale enough for him to differentiate them from the dark horizon of the forest about him, though with the dawn no color came, only a variegation of grayness; and the roof of cloud was disclosed as crowding to the mind and spirit as the vault of some low stone tomb; and the forest changed before his eyes from a depthless black tarpaulin backdrop to a receding pillared hall of trunks and branches, beneath which was spread a fretwork of skeletal and lightly-frosted underbrush.

Cyrus looked to his left, seeking the canal, but its route had at that point diverged from the road sufficiently for it to be out of view, beyond a strip, as he supposed, of woodland. How wide the strip was he did not know, though the presence of low-lying mist suggested the comparative nearness of a water-course. Considering it prudent to locate it, and perhaps get a wider view of the country about him, he jumped the ditch and made his way into the trees. Concealed by the ground-mist the soil was boggy, but, owing to scads of fallen leaves, tolerably firm on its surface; and so long as he stepped briskly, it did not unduly pull on his boots.

After passing through a belt of oaks just a few chains wide he found himself abruptly at the canal's edge. Looking out, on the far side of the canal, which was sixty feet or so in width, he saw a pallid, orderly landscape of fields that were in the main at that season fallow. The mist lay milky across earth and water, and each was as motionless as the other; and the air at that hour was still. Somewhere nearby a lone duck quacked. In its singularity it seemed to Cyrus like a signal. He stepped back under the cover of the trees and listened intently but no more quacks came, and then from that same direction he heard a brief clatter of wings.

Beyond the fields opposite, which ran on a long way, he could make out what seemed to be faint gray forest. Here and there were groups of farm-buildings, and these too appeared gray, with no lights evident within or without, and, as yet, no smoke rising from any chimney. Even had he been able to cross the canal – and looking in both directions there was no sign of any ferry or landing-point on either side – none of this was encouraging.

At his feet a narrow track much marked by the hooves of, he guessed, dray horses, ran along the canal's edge. Judging it to be more generally exposed to view than the road he had left, rather than taking it Cyrus turned back. Traversing the wood slantwise, so as to be making progress rather than returning to the road at the point he had left it, after a short while he adjusted his course so he was moving parallel to it while keeping it just in view. His stomach was growling now. Should of run when there was fruit on the trees, he muttered to himself. Though it was his habit to talk little, he was unused to being alone; and finding himself deprived of either the endorsement or refutation of his unvocalised thoughts by the utterances of his fellow hands, he felt now the need to speak those thoughts aloud, so as to make them – and thusly himself – real.

Like we was one.

He began to look for a tree of good size, with branches of a lowness, scale and configuration up which he might climb without too great an effort and, at not too great a risk of falling, rest among; perhaps even doze a little.

Pine's no good, nor willow. Cypress a maybe. Oaks is best.

After a while he came upon what he sought: a great old moss-bedecked oak, its sprawling lower boughs sagging near the ground as if exhausted by their own weight. He clambered up onto one of the boughs without difficulty and made his way higher, discovering some way above a forking of the trunk into three substantial tines, among which he could sit in tolerable comfort, and against one of which he could lean back with a fair measure of safety. From this elevated viewpoint, which was some twenty feet above the ground, he could see, through a haze of twigs that would, he felt confident, conceal him from any returning gaze, whatever passed on the road; and all he wore was in any case drably brown or gray, and so in this season positively concealing, and his brown skin was, he did not doubt, ashy as the dead moss patching the tree's trunk and depending from its branches. Though he could wish for sunlight to warm him, and the clouds' departure, he was thankful the wind had fallen off. He bent round a small, twiggy branch to act as a sprung, spiky pillow for his back, reclined on it and looked up at the lightening but resolutely gray sky.

I'm like a bird up here, he thought. But birds went places, far places, and then came back, year after year, and, though it had not been his choice, this drab wood was the farthest he had ever been. And birds had feathers and hollow bones, and though high up and as it were perched, he felt heavy and earthbound.

In the massed twigs in front of him sat suspended an abandoned nest, in which he saw, when he bent forward to examine it, amongst feathers and moultings, two split-open eggshells, each the size of a thumbnail, and pale blue. The splits were in the form of craters, suggesting a pecking-in and not a breaking out: predation; a sharp beak or incisor tooth, and the sight of this small calamity struck him powerfully then, though had he found such eggs whole he would have eaten them without compunction.

He thought of his mother, or rather his not-knowing of her; the nothing that had been said of her; the lack of even a wooden marker in the burying-place just past the sheds where they had laid her down alongside the other worn-out sacks of brown skin and white bones, disposed of with a shrug once they were used up. His mother. But she had not mothered him; had only birthed him, and in that had died and offered him no more, and the nothing he knew of her meant he felt no guilt at being the cause of her bleeding out, or no guilt that could, as it would have been able to, perhaps, were it directed towards a known person, feed on him and grow. Her name, they said, had been Sarah, but that name, having been bestowed upon her by her owner, and likely without care or consideration as to aptness or signification, told nothing of her truth beyond that she was, indeed, owned.

'Mother' was at least a statement of some degree of fact about her, though he had never known her breast, the other women who had milk at that time suckling him with what little they could spare. Had his father begged that of them? Had he had to beg? Had they begrudged him? He supposed it to be the case. Yet if so, less, surely, than they begrudged the whey-pale Tyler babies, to whose pouting, sucking mouths they could not, under pain of the lash or the bridle, refuse the intimacy of their nipples, even at the expense of their own newborn. A reverse, he dimly apprehended, of the venom of snakes, from the fangs of which it was said a milky fluid could be drawn, but was in the main injected and not extracted, though were these white babies not in a like manner venomous? He thought of his father, who he had barely known, and barely remembered save for the manner of his dying, in bloated poisoned agony; and he thought of Bed, and another source of milky nourishment with a taste and tang like nothing else, and his crotch tingled at that.

It was curious, he considered, what tied the heart and what did not. Suckling him had not, he felt, bound those women who did so to him, nor he to them. Neither, he suspected, did it, for how could it, bind them to the white cuckoo-babies who latched so readily onto their brown breasts; or if it did, it did so only for that short length of time when they were wholly vulnerable, without will, and made up of nothing but inborn impulse; for when they were grown they became something else entirely, something soon enough revealed to contain glands generative of a venom that, once developed, could prove lethal to those human beings possessed of a darker skin who were obliged to be in proximity to it, including even those who had nourished these same children when, for reasons of excessively-cultivated delicacy or biological insufficiency, their pale mothers had declined to do so.

When Cyrus was a boy there was another colored boy named Billy who, being pleasing to the eye and bright in manner, was permitted to play with Mas Tyler's young son whenever he was outdoors, and was his companion in roaming and exploring the estate. Cyrus did not witness this joyful intercourse, being as he was never near the Big House but intended always for fieldwork; but he and Billy were of an age, and Billy would often tell him of the games he played with the young master, and the toys they shared in easy comradeship, one time showing him by way of proof, and reproof at Cyrus' scoffing, a gaily-painted tin spinning-top he had been permitted to borrow for the afternoon. Was Cyrus envious? He did not now recall, and the ending of the tale made it hard to think so, though the brightness of the top, the widely-grinning coon and clown motifs on its metal surface, and the cunning of the spinning pump within he recalled even now as a delight.

One day – Cyrus thought it had been about six months along in this great friendship, though he did not much trust his childish reckoning on that point; but more than a season, for sure – Billy came staggering into the yard in front of the field-hands' cabins, holding his belly and crying. Sensing something in the tone of his cries beyond a child's small upset, Cyrus and some of the women hurried over from their grinding of corn-meal to comfort him. He and Mas Tyler's son had had a fight, he said, wincing and gasping as he hunched over between sobs, over nothing much, as is the way with young boys – perhaps, though Cyrus allowed it might be his fancy, the spinning-top – and in consequence Billy had knocked the young master down, and was sitting astride his chest in the dust of the yard behind the Big House, when Mas Tyler, who had seen the fight from his study window, stormed out purple-faced in his great coat and heavy boots and fetched Billy a kick in the side with all the strength and viciousness his rage could muster. This kick, as it transpired, had burst something inside Billy, and blood came from him later when he urinated, and he could not open his bowels, and he swelled unnaturally in the belly and died in screaming agony and great confusion of spirit and weeping a week later, a month short, his mother Etta reckoned, of his eighth birthday. The master attended but once, looked vexed, and went away, sending the next day a man said to be a doctor, who probed Billy's swollen belly, each touch expelling a scream and tears from Billy, and pronounced that nothing could be done, that in his estimation the muck of the split stomach had spilled out amongst the boy's viscera and set them rotting. The young master never showed his face, and the hands were scolded and felt the lash around their ears and shoulders for tardiness in coming to the fields, and for idleness when they were there, the loudness of Billy's trials having shattered their sleep for many nights and thus slowed them in their toil; and his mother was sold away soon after, so as to spare the young master the sad reminder of his former playmate.

Cyrus' father had died two years before Billy. Cyrus seemed to remember sitting on his knee one time, though perhaps it was many times condensed into a single memory, his father's arms strong and close and warm about him, a particular smell of sweat and an enfolding solidity; a safety, but one that he had sensed, even at the age of three or four, and as no child should, was somehow incomplete; or so it seemed to him now, though perhaps the memory was in its entirety a fabrication. It had come to him when he was first in Abednego's arms, and whether that made the likelihood of its being true the lesser or the greater he did not know. He had no real memory of his father's face.

They says I look like him.

It was in its lack and secondhandness an echo of some greater amputation of the past, of all forebears and lineage, a symbol of the dividing ocean he had never seen, the waters of which were like tears salt, and so poison and madness to drink, though creatures dwelt and thrived therein.

The blown blue eggshells looked up at him like the reproachful eyes of some small spirit of the woods, so he lay back and, once more staring up at the sky, tried to let his thoughts fall away. Though his perch lacked comfort it proved to be tolerably secure. He loosened his boots, and after a short while managed to drift off into a shallow doze, albeit one that was striated by jolts of anxiety that shook him into twitching wakefulness. These, however, in the manner of storm-clouds on a high air-current, slowly passed off; and despite the grumbling emptiness of his stomach, his sleep deepened, and if he dreamed, his dreams were without narrative form.

He awoke abruptly he did not know how much later, with something sharp in his nostrils: drifted tobacco-smoke, he realised, though the animal part of his mind had told him he was in danger before the considering part assessed what exactly the odor was, and therefore what it signified. Attempting not to breathe aloud for fear of being heard by the smoker of the tobacco, who must surely be nearby, very slowly Cyrus sat up. He felt the twigs stir poppingly at his back and stilled himself; then, once he sensed they had settled into the natural pattern of their expansion and would make no further noise, he bent forward and looked down. Peering through the branches at the ground below, a mosaic of brown and yellow leaves and black mud, sharp-etched now the mist was gone, he saw two white men, one urinating against the trunk of the tree and groaning painedly as he did so, the other turned away from him, puffing on a cigar. Their faces were from that angle concealed by the brims of their hats, two leather discs as it were floating above the stained glass of the fallen leaves, but the skins of their hands were visible, albeit in the case of the man not emptying his bladder only in the gaps between his coat-sleeves and the beginnings of the yellow calfskin gloves he wore.

Cyrus looked over toward the road and saw, tethered to a sturdy branch that grew out horizontally like a hitching-rail, two horses. Both were glossy and trim, one a chestnut mare, the other a large white stallion that, as he watched it, tossed its head and rolled its eyes, straining at the constraining rein and setting its bridle jingling. It was surely, Cyrus realised with alarm, the charger ridden by Mas Tyler himself, impossible a coincidence though it seemed that he should be in this exact place, at this exact moment; an instance, surely, of prayers answered or prayers denied; or of the futility of prayer in a creation that was in fact a chaos and nothing more. The mare had no distinguishing marks, and so Cyrus could not tell by looking at her whether the man accompanying Mas Tyler was known to him or not. Don't look up, he thought, fearing as he did so that the intensity of the thought might in some occult and perverse way remotely induce exactly the action that was feared.

The other man, who was not dressed so well as Mas Tyler, but well enough that Cyrus guessed him somewhat above the rank of overseer or patroller, while continuing to micturate, drew a flask from his coat-pocket. He uncorked it one-handed, took a swallow, and offered it to Mas Tyler, who took it, wiped the lip with his sleeve, and likewise drank. The flask was evidently nearly full, for neither man tipped his head back far enough as he swallowed to see Cyrus splayed owl-still among the branches above; and now he thanked the clouds for continuing so resolutely to obstruct the sun, or else his shadow would have been thrown most distinctly upon the ground directly at their feet, making his detection certain. Both men wore polished black riding-boots and had pistols holstered at their hips, and the man who wasn't Mas Tyler had draped like a chain of office round his neck a heavy tawse.

Go, Cyrus willed, though he knew he was most in danger of discovery should they start to leave and then for whatever reason – and he supposed them no less in possession of the subtle senses than himself – look back as they neared their tethered mounts, and see him perched up there. He wondered if he could endeavor as they went to slip like a squirrel down the side of the great oak's trunk that faced away from them, and in that way remain unseen even if they did look back. Or might it be better to this instant jump from his place of concealment, aiming to land boots-first on one of their heads at least, heavy as a tub of nails, in hopes of felling one man instantly, perhaps cracking open his skull; at the least concussing him; and snatching up his pistol before the other, thus surprised, might think to draw his weapon.

As likely break my own leg as his head, he thought, fallin twenty feet. An if I does, then what? No hope at all. An I ain't never fired no pistol neither. I seen it done, but I ain't done it. He glanced over at the horses again. Had he not earlier discovered that here the wood was not at all wide, if the two men had decided to go in deeper he might have considered attempting to steal one, though in his life he had ridden only mules, so as to flee the area as fast as possible.

But if Mas Tyler out on the road, they's patrollers all over fo sho. First one I comes to I'm done: even if I took me the plain brown mare they'd know. An I tries an gallops I'd likely end up in a ditch or bust my neck or both.

God damn clap, the white man who wasn't Mas Tyler said, buttoning his fly. It stings like God damn hellfire when I piss.

Don't be bringing that to any of my stock, Mas Tyler said.

Since when was your wenches too good for it, the other said. You ain't runnin no school for colored deportment nor no nunnery neither; I know you put em to breedin soon as they bleed.

Offspring gets tainted, Mas Tyler said.

You spoil your niggers, Tyler.

The produce comes out idiots and incapacitated, Mas Tyler said, and most times it shows before they can be sold off, and the owner is lumbered. As labor they're next to worthless but they live on, consuming profit to no good nor Godly purpose.

So tie em in a sack and drown em.

I am a Christian, Mister Penbury.

Well, so am I, Mister Tyler, and I say the Lord give us dominion over all living things.

On that we agree, Mister Penbury, but even so I am too sentimental to drown a cretin infant.

You'll see a grown buck whipped to death, though.

Because he is deserving of it.

That remark seemed to draw them to some purpose, for their manner of speech changed then, becoming less playful, and Cyrus, who had never in all his days heard but a few words from Mas Tyler's mouth, and those in the main pieties delivered sermonically, listened in fascination, realizing as he did so that some form of practice had been worked persistently upon him, upon all who were enslaved – and moreover, he in some way intuited, upon all who are poor and powerless, regardless of skin – its intent being to conflate aristocracy of wealth with aristocracy of sensibility, the ability to afford to purchase a fine thing with the ability to appreciate its refinement, and at all times align fiscal with moral elevation. And Cyrus thought of Samuel, preaching on the Good Lord and His ordering of all things as He thought best, and he cursed him.

This nigger of yours killed a man, Penbury said. I won't say he was a good man, but he was a white man, and the news is spreading like a plague.

I'd bridle every God damn one of em if it were practical,

Tyler said.

It ain't just nigger tongues that wag.

Tyler made a noise in his throat.

Patrols been to Hart, Greenfield and Packenham, Penbury said. Turned em over an found nothin. He ain't had time to get further out than that. He's either back in the swamp or cut over this way.

Maybe he crossed the canal, Tyler said dourly, and spat on the ground.

Can he swim?

I don't believe so. But fools leave boats tethered places. I've had messages sent round the holdings opposite to keep their eyes open. And let em know any nigger caught helping a runaway'll get a whipping and a brand on the hand or worse.

You'd know him if you see him?

He'd know me.

You reckon he'll head for town?

I doubt it. He's never been off the estate, and town requires a kind of brains and manners a field-hand has no knowledge of. I consider he'll skulk in the woods and starve. He ain't smart, running in this season, and he took nothing with him by way of supplies or money that I can find out about.

He'll give himself up, maybe.

Not now he's a killer.

By this time they were moving away from the tree and heading back to their horses, and the charger was placid now. Their heads remained cut off from Cyrus' view by the discs of the brims of their hats, which deprivation of features imparted to him a magnified sense of the strangeness of the moment, and put him in mind of masks from long ago. Old Africa had several times spoken to him of masks as if masks were people, but when he asked, could not say what she meant by it.

And then what, said Penbury. Once he's caught?

A harsh example, said Tyler. A whipping, naturally, and a bloody one, then I'll have his ears split and his nose and lips cut off. God damn it I'll do it myself, and in front of every nigger in the place too, and I'll feed what I cut off to the dogs and they'll watch me do it. I'll show them not to make a mockery of me. But I won't let him die. I'll get my money's worth from him year on year and they'll see me do it.

But he kilt a white man, Tyler. You can't ignore that. He should hang for that.

I'll see Charlie Johnson buried decent; put something towards a marble headstone for his wife's sake. But I won't let these God damn ungrateful niggers bankrupt me, Penbury. I'll get a good return on my investment.

You still plannin on runnin for Congress?

God damn you, Penbury, you son of a bitch. Hand me your flask.

The two men passed out of Cyrus' hearing, and with all speed and all the care he could manage, gripping firm with his knees, he slithered down the trunk of the great oak on the side turned away from the road, his actions eased by its leaning in his favor. At the tree's foot he waited, out of the line of their sight should they glance back, and listened, still barely daring to breathe. Chancing a peep round the trunk, he saw the pair of them swing up onto their horses and set off, in no particular hurry it seemed, in the direction of De Bray's Town.

Only once they had passed from his sight could Cyrus allow himself to fully exhale. Almost it seemed the two white men had been inside his head, and he found himself curiously dizzy now they were gone. He turned away, arched his back against the trunk of the tree, and with difficulty fought an urge to shout aloud, for he needed to in some way release the vast tensity swollen within him. Instead he gulped in the chill, damp air like a gaping catfish until his expanded lungs pushed out his cramped and confining rib-cage and he felt once again in full possession of both his body and his mind. Reaching inside his shirt he found Old Africa's charm, its presence a reassurance, though if her magic was effective, why had it done her so little good in her own life?

Cause sometimes we can only do fo others, he thought, not fo ourselves. So he knew mothers often felt, and sometimes fathers too. And lovers?

Am I doin this for me, or fo Bed?

Fo sho I'd take a whipping fo you, an worse.

So what I'm gon do now?

Amidst uncertainty there was this: the one place they were certain he was not, was where he was; and where he meant to go was where they were convinced he lacked the wits to go. He had, then, and for the first time since being brought to bay in the swamp, a small advantage.

Chapter Eight

Remaining where he was being of no benefit to him, Cyrus determined to move on at once, and continue parallel to the road for as long as the saturated ground remained traversable. He guessed from the uniform radiance, muted though it was, of the gray sky above him, that the hour was around noon. As he walked, and having rested up his pace was for a time brisk, he had to jump a number of small streams, one of which was clear enough for him to fill his bottle in. He drank deep, drained the bottle, and filled it again. Light with hunger but well-hydrated, he went on.

Three times in the hours that followed he heard horses on the road, and twice carriages, and each time he crouched down in the underbrush until they passed. One was a group of four white men on ill-groomed horses, the ribs of which were visible through their pale, matted coats. The men wore gray felt greatcoats hemmed with leather, and seamed, mud-spattered leather boots. Their jaws were unshaven and their hats pulled down so low on their heads that the brims met their eyebrows, and they were, he did not doubt, a patrol, perhaps the same one that had gone to Hart the day before. They were headed that way again, it seemed, and he felt uneasy for Esther and Emory, hoping that Ditie had learned nothing that she could either inadvertently, or for reasons of malice or misguided loyalty or profit to herself, betray.

Lil Joe and Solomon, Joseph and Zeke and Samuel came into his mind then. Least Mas Tyler dint say nothin bout them, he thought; how they must of knowed I was goin an likely helped some.

At one point an ox-cart passed him, bearing a load of timber in the direction of town and going only a little faster than he did on foot among the trees. A man with a long whip sat up front, bundled up in a long scarf and hunched over the reins. From his features he might have been some shade of mulatto, or maybe Spanish or some such. There were plantations on islands way out in the sea, Bed had told him, whose names were given in the Spanish tongue. Cyrus supposed there were plantations most everywhere, and slaves, and masters. He did not risk approaching the driver.

He thought then of the north, which had been driven from his mind by his change of direction and purpose, and tried to picture himself and Abednego headed there, drawn by and lit by starlight, and though the image was nothing real, still it gave him comfort, and even a little hope. The north itself he could not picture in any way that was not entirely fanciful, though he knew for all his dreams of it that it was as real a place as where he trudged now; as possessed of bitter cold and stifling heat, storms and skeeters, moonshine and sunshine, human beings and their virtues, frailties and immoralities.

No plantations there, was all he knew for certain.

Dusk was coming on, and the driver of the ox-cart, which had by now drawn some way ahead of him, lit a lamp, and Cyrus tracked its friendly glow as the trees about him faded into the deepening dusk. Freed from fear of losing the road so long as he kept the lamp in view, the coming dark troubled him less than it would otherwise have done; and soon he became aware that not only was the ground growing firmer underfoot, but that the trunks and branches interposed between him and the lamp's light were thinning out: the wood was coming to an end.

What Emory say? Beyond the wood a crossroads an a inn.

But in the fast-descending dusk all he could make out before him was a dim vista of low-lying scrubland, flat, empty and uncultivated, with here and there black clumps of trees. No buildings were visible, only the floating lamp of the ox-cart, now a good way ahead on the long curve of the road. To his left, marked by intermittent pines, the canal ran on in a near straight line, an unrolled strip of dully-polished pewter mirroring the failing light above. There was at that hour no movement of craft upon it, though Cyrus supposed it much used in daytime.

Seeing no light other than that of the cart, he decided to risk returning to the road, planning to proceed as he had the night before, ducking down in ditches when the need arose. He very much feared being pursued by dogs, but doubted such a hunt would be attempted when the night was lightless, not without some concrete knowledge on the part of those hunting that their quarry was in the vicinity. By the time he reached the road he could see almost nothing about him, just the single lamp up ahead, small and far off.

After several more hours trudging, during which time his heels began to pain him severely, being already blistered, and the blisters having burst and been torn open, and the raw skin beneath them further abraded by the leather interiors of his boots, he had lost sight of the cart, and found himself once more among trees, in the main pines, and wholly in darkness. He had up to this point passed no dwellings he could see, and since there had been no forks in the road, nor side-paths or tracks of any sort, he kept on. It proved no more than a narrow belt, and on reaching the farther side of it he saw, a hundred yards on, lights and a cluster of buildings: he had reached the crossroads.

The largest building, which he took to be the tavern, was wide-fronted, two-storied, peak-roofed, and shingled in white cedar; it appeared in good repair, and lamplight spilled from its front-facing windows and splayed out across the crossroads-yard. On either side of it were single-story sheds of various sizes, all of which were in darkness, and in the main free-standing and without windows. One of these Cyrus guessed to be the stable, as it directly adjoined the tavern and ran width-wise, facing forwards. Opposite this was a building, also two-story, in front of which was a wide porch and a hitching-rail. Cyrus took this to be the store Emory had mentioned. It, and the house behind it, were in darkness. In the centre of the crossroads, at which four ways met, stood a square, brick-walled well with spindle and hanging bucket, and by it a wooden trough; and the roads, framed at their interstices by clumps of cedars, ran off into the invisible night. From within the tavern came a shout, a burst of raucous laughter, the clatter of things set down – though these friendly-seeming sounds struck nothing but chords of fear in Cyrus, being but the revelation of the presence of his enemies taking their ease when he could not, where he could not.

At that moment he heard horses on the road behind him, coming at a canter; without pause he jumped the ditch to his left and hunkered down among the dry and spiny hackberry bushes that were massed there. Shortly thereafter the four patrollers he had seen earlier sped past, their captain lighting the way with a blazing pine-knot held aloft. This he threw down in the yard as they pulled up in front of the tavern. It lay there spurting flame as the oozing resin flared, and their pale horses steamed in the lamplight from being run hard, and Cyrus wondered if they had heard news, of himself or some other benighted runaway.

Baines, the lead man called. Baines! Send your boy! We got horses need stablin.

A heavyset white man in a green apron appeared at the tavern door, his head backlit by a lamp hung on the wall behind so it seemed faceless, a black blank framed by spun white hair fragile as dandelion seeds. Yes sir, Mister Adams, sir. I'll call my boy. Vernon, he shouted over his shoulder. Tend to these gentlemen and be quick about it.

A smooth-skinned and very dark black boy of maybe fifteen hurried forward in response to the landlord's call, and was obliged to awkwardly squeeze past him in order to come out into the yard; and he was dressed smartly, in a full-sleeve white shirt and gray pants, though barefoot. Yassuh, Mistuh Baines, he said, as Mister Adams swung down from his horse. Right away, suh.

Nigger-huntin's thirsty work, one of the other white men said as he dismounted.

It surely is, Mister Rees, Mister Adams agreed.

I don't reckon he's in these parts at all, said the third, handing his reins to the waiting Vernon, who took them from him without quite looking at him. He'll of cut back through the swamp. You wouldn't run, would you boy, he said to Vernon.

Nawsuh. I gots me a good master.

There's a coin in it if you rub them horses down an get em good an dry.

Yassuh.

And a floggin if you let em catch cold, Mister Adams added.

I'll get em dry, suh, Vernon said. I'll shine em like a wine-glass. But already the white men were not listening, were swaggering over to the tavern-door, and Cyrus watched them go in, and the door close, and Vernon led the horses to the stable, two sets of reins in each hand, and they went along easily, as if they were familiar with him, or perhaps it was his gentleness in handling them.

Straw an oats, Cyrus thought, wondering if there might be other foodstuffs stored in the stable, or if he might get into one of the neighboring sheds without making a disturbance and perhaps find apples bedded in straw or stored sweet potatoes or even onions he could take. Better to starve and be free: but that was a hard thing, and with little nobility in the suffering of it. Would it be wiser to attempt to explore the sheds now, when there was noise from the tavern to act as cover but all were awake, or later, when there was silence, but most were asleep? The boy, of course, might be expected to sleep in the stable to prevent theft of the horses.

As he was weighing these things up, Cyrus became aware of lamps on the road that ran away to his right, which led, from what Emory had told him, first to the hamlet of De Bray's Bend and then on back to Tyler; and within a short time two smartly-lacquered covered Broughams, each pulled by a pair of gaily-plumed horses and driven by a liveried black groom, had rolled into the crossroads yard and come to a halt before the tavern door. Tasselled blinds pulled down in the glazed windows wholly concealed their passengers from view. A door swung open and from the first Brougham a top-hatted and clean-shaven young white man in a green velvet frock-coat stepped down, and he carried a silver-shod cane. He vanished into the tavern, returning a short while later to have some words first with his fellow passengers, and then, by means of stepping up to the side-window, with those in the other carriage; and an agreement evidently having been reached, both sets of passengers debouched into the yard. In all, their party was six men and six women, the latter in silks and satins – fabrics Cyrus knew from scraps Bed had smuggled out from the Big House and encouraged him to rub between his thumb and forefinger – and fur-trimmed capes and extravagant hats, in one of which Cyrus espied, he was sure, a stuffed and glass-eyed mocking-bird; and all of them were smooth-faced as china dolls, and red-lipped and young.

The landlord appeared once more in the doorway, compelling another household servant, dressed much the same as Vernon but several years his senior, to squeeze by him in order to hurry out and take down the bags and trunks from the backs of the carriages, which he did without help from the grooms, who did not deign to descend from their seats, preferring to remain where they were: for there are degrees of station even in Hell; and these must constantly be asserted as, if neglected, they will burn to ashes just the same, and as agonizingly, as the rest.

Mister Bell, welcome, sir, to you and your party, the land-lord said, and it seemed as though he might extend a hand to shake, but then thought better of his presumption, instead stepping back and sucking in his gut as best as he was able, in order to let the foremost young man pass him by without obstruction, followed by the ladies and then the other gentle-men. Your private sitting-room has been made ready upstairs, Mister Baines continued. Your drivers may go round the rear and be fed in the kitchen.

My drivers are fed well enough at home, the young man replied, to which statement the two black men in their livery reacted as stones react to the rain, which is to say, not at all; for when all is known, what need is there of response to it? Only once the tavern door had closed did their braided shoulders sink slightly. A little time passed; then, their master not having returned for some small chastising trifle or other, they clam-bered down from their seats. Leaving the blinkered horses standing idle in their shafts, the taller of the two unhooked one of the still-lit carriage-lamps, and, holding it high, the pair sauntered towards the stable.

Vernon, the taller one called quietly, boy, you in there?

You feelin prayerful, called the other.

We brung the devil's bible, the taller man said with a grin in his voice; and producing from a pocket a deck of cards, he and his comrade went inside, illuminating briefly the stalls and the backsides of their equine occupants. A tail rose on reflex, and droppings fell steaming from a sphincter.

A notion came to Cyrus then, one requiring a form of cour-age different from that which he had had need of before, and he determined to act on it at once. He took off his knapsack, his hat and his coat, and, leaving them piled by a tree-stump for easy location and retrieval later, crossed quickly to the trough by the well, pulling his shirt up over his head as he went. The air was so cold on his bare and prickling skin it was like a vice gripping his chest and needles piercing his nipples, but he set the shirt aside on the well's edge and without delay plunged his head and arms and the whole of his unclad torso into the icy black water filling the trough. The blood shrank to his core in a violent contraction, as when a haint gets a hold of a person, and, thus submerged, he yelled bubblingly into the water, compelling it to absorb the sound, and forced himself to stay there a long, excruciating minute before straightening up, chest heaving like a flogged horse's, flicking droplets every way.

Gots to get clean an not stink of no swamp.

He rubbed his fingers roughly under his armpits, splashed more water up there, then, after dunking his hands in the trough to clean them off, ran them over his head, brushing twigs and straw and mud and bark-bits from his scalp. Looking about him he saw, next to the trough, a piece of sacking lying on the ground and, shudders now running the length of his bare upper half, he picked it up, wetted it, bent down and rubbed it over his boots fast, in that way getting the worst and rankest of the mud off them, then rinsed it out in the trough and sponged the cuffs of his pants. That done, he picked up his shirt and flicked it out repeatedly to make it seem a degree less sweat-worn and slept in; then put it back on, tucking it into the waist of his pants with more care than was usual for him. The trough-water on his skin blotted the coarse cotton where it clung, wetting it, but any sort of covering was a help against the bite of the air, and his shuddering grew less.

I ain't no Bednego, he thought regretfully. But it was the best he could do to make himself presentable, and, before fear overwhelmed him, or discovery defeated him in advance, he crossed the yard, skirted the stable and made his way round to the back of the tavern. To the rear it was less well-kept than in front, and extended in a jumble of interconnected single-story sheds and shacks, likely added without much planning as the need arose.

Up three steps a screen-door led into the main building, and Cyrus climbed the steps and knocked on the frame of the door as though he had business doing so.

A heavy-set, flat-faced and dark-complected black woman in red kerchief and white apron appeared beyond the mesh, blocking the back doorway as the white inn-keeper had the front, and looked at him with a hostile expression.

I'm Mas Bell's man, Cyrus said.

The woman said nothing, and he wondered how he appeared to her; whether Mister Bell in his fancy clothes would keep a servant as unkempt as he; whether this woman would know enough to make such a judgement, and therefore question his claim. Or would she simply assume what was often the case: that, like many of the most finely-clad masters or mistresses, Mas Bell took a puritan pleasure in depriving those he owned of all but the meanest coverings? Still she said nothing; gave no ground.

Mas Bailey said if I come round you'd fix me some victuals.

Grudgingly she unhooked the screen-door to admit him. Don't know bout fixin, she said. We might have some leavins you can have.

I'm obliged, Cyrus said. I'm Billy.

Come through, she said, leading the way up a short passage to the tavern kitchen. We jus done servin the guests. You can sit by the stove.

The stove was large and gleamingly black-leaded, and set into a wide brick fireplace up the chimney-breast of which its pipes ran, though despite both pipes and flue the air was eye-stingingly smoky from the frying and roasting that had been done earlier. A young, light-brown girl with big eyes was scrubbing a table with soda crystals and vigor, a pinkness to the corona of the suds suggesting raw meat had been dressed there; another was bent over a sink washing dishes; a third was drying and stacking them. An elderly woman with polished chestnut skin and no teeth sat in a settle to one side of the stove smoking a pipe, and three black men sat on benches at a table without a cloth, eating from wooden bowls with spoons and breaking off bits of cornbread from a pile on a china plate.

Ladies, Cyrus said, his stomach shrinking and pinging from the kitchen smells. Gentlemen.

This Billy, the large woman, who was plainly the head cook, said. He from Bell.

They looked him over without comment, their expressions neither friendly nor otherwise; then went back to what they were doing. Noise from the saloon and the other public rooms was audible from a passage past a door that stood ajar. Not presuming to join the men of the household at the table, Cyrus took a seat on a low stool on the other side of the stove from the old woman. She watched him intently. Her hair was wiry white, and brushed back firmly in a bun. You et, she asked.

No, ma'am, he replied, turning to the orange slots in the stove and blessing the warmth it radiated, and understanding exactly why, as he had heard, men in olden times worshipped the sun, and warmth, and spring, and other things basic and profound.

Etta, the old woman said, and the young girl drying dishes straightaway broke off from her task and took a bowl from the stack and came and filled it with a ladle from a kettle on the stove and handed it and a tin spoon to Cyrus.

Thank you kindly, Miss Etta, he said, and she smiled shyly at the courtesy, and she was pretty, and he was pleased to be smiled at, for the first time, it seemed to him, since Abednego was sold.

Take care on account of it's hot, she said, returning to her task.

He nodded, and the steam wafting up from the bowl filled his swelling nostrils with the aroma of corn and millet and somewhere traces of pork, or pork-fat at least, and the stew was spicy with black pepper and bay. Setting the bowl on his lap he took a careful spoonful and it tasted better to him than anything had tasted in a long time. Don't eat like no starvin man, he warned himself, though he reached out quick enough when one of the men at the table turned and offered him the plate of cornbread.

Bell decent, the man asked as Cyrus took a bite.

A full mouth his excuse, Cyrus shrugged a wordless assent. He young, he said eventually.

The man nodded and went back to his supper. He and the others were dressed as the boy, Vernon, had been, in what was evidently the uniform of the house, and were likewise barefoot. Cyrus wondered if he might without occasioning comment remove his boots and set them to dry before the stove, though, thus exposed, the state of his feet might tell against his account of himself. A fourth man came in through the back door then, accompanied by a gust of chill air, and to his unease Cyrus saw it was the one who had been unloading the Bell party's luggage from the carriages out front, having for some reason gone round the outside of the tavern rather than through it. He took a bowl from the pile of dried crocks by the sink, served himself from the kettle, and went to join the others at the table, the only free space facing in Cyrus' direction. His eyes were gray and he was somewhat redboned.

Patrollers in tonight, he said as he swung a leg over the bench. Who this?

Bell's man, the man who had offered Cyrus the cornbread said.

The baggage man looked at Cyrus for a long moment, saying nothing, then nodded and began to eat.

The door leading to the public rooms was yanked open sharply and Mister Bailey thrust his head through, bringing with him the odor of tobacco and beer-slops. His fat face was ruddy and his nose a textured mass of burst veins, but his eyes, though reddened, were bright and sharp as flints.

Eunice, he said. Cyrus lent back on his stool, so as to be as far out of the inn-keeper's line of sight as possible without drawing attention to himself.

Yes, Mas Bailey?

Fetch two bottles of rum and three of champagne. The priciest we got.

Yes, Mas Bailey.

Have Etta take em up on the special salver.

Yes, Mas Bailey.

Eunice was the woman who had admitted Cyrus. He now saw she had a bunch of keys hooped at her hip, and she bustled over to a padlocked store-room, unlocked and opened the door, briefly revealing a windowless space stacked floor to ceiling with racks of glinting bottles.

Make sure to mark what you take in the book.

Yes, Mas Bailey.

The landlord withdrew as if retracted on a spring, and the door slammed shut, cutting off the sounds of carousing from the saloon that had formed a backbeat to his instructions. Eunice bent over, selected and brought out bottles. Etta put down her drying cloth and her eyes blanked over and Cyrus saw the task was not to her liking, and he was struck by the smooth line of her neck and the delicacy of her clavicle, which showed above the line of her dress with the sweep and swoop of a swallow's extended wing.

I'll take it, the man who had first questioned Cyrus said, getting up from the bench as Eunice set the bottles on a silver tray that had also, it seemed, been kept locked away for just such a use as now required it. It was ornately-molded, with serpent motifs for handles. The man was young, solidly-built and well-made, and brown to Etta's brown, kin maybe, or otherwise close in loving spirit.

Mas Bailey said Etta, Tory, Eunice said, turning away to bring down from a high shelf elegantly-stemmed glasses, and carefully setting them next to the bottles on the tray.

I'll take it, Miss Eunice, Tory repeated in a level tone.

Mas Bell wants Etta.

Tory's eyes met Eunice's, and his chest and her breast rose in unison, and a vein in his smooth neck pulsed visibly and squirmed like a viper beneath a brown satin cloth; and Etta looked down at the plank floor like a little girl awaiting chastisement. All at once and in a smothered rage Tory turned and left the kitchen fast, strode down the outer passage, and banged out through the screen door into the night. No-one else reacted. Eunice placed a silver bowl of sugar, silver tongs and a jug of water on the tray, and Etta picked it up, and slow as some dead thing and not through care to keep it level, she went off down the passageway in the direction of the stairs that led to the private rooms above.

Young, one of the other men said, in echo of what Cyrus had said of Mister Bell, and the air was heavy and not with smoke or burnt fat. The man who had first passed Cyrus the plate offered him more cornbread, and Cyrus took it.

You heard the news, brother, the gray-eyed baggage man asked, after time sufficient to carry out her errand had gone by and Etta had not returned.

What news, Cyrus asked.

Someone run. From off of Tyler. Kilt a overseer an lit out.

I heard somethin, Cyrus said, reckoning that since Bell neighbored Tyler he would have known about it. Likely he went north. Followed his star.

God speed him, said one of the others, an older, stooped

and very dark-skinned man with a shaven head and sleepy eyes, looking over at the door through which Etta's defender had gone out.

Amen to that, said a third, and Cyrus nodded, and though his situation was precarious, and the longer he remained among them the greater was the chance that he would be exposed by the appearance of Vernon or either or both of the Bell grooms, the warmth and food and company gave him so much heart he could not up and leave. He chanced bending over and working off his boots so he could warm his bare feet by the stove, and no-one paid this any mind, and so he sat quiet, listening to their talk.

Patrols out in force, the last man to speak said, an they gon likely be that way fo weeks.

Means I can't chance goin to see my Amy, the man with sleepy eyes said.

Maybe when Mas Bailey sends you to go fetch that lumber off of Ansen.

Maybe.

He gots to give you a pass an I reckons you can make up some time.

Even if you gots a pass, they stop you, you get a whippin.

Worth it to see my gal.

I won't risk no whippin, not for no gal, nawsuh.

Nor her getting caught an cut up neither. Thas worser.

Amen to that, brother. Pass me the cornbread.

Ain't no better to be had in this county.

It was disorientating to Cyrus to be sitting in this room, accepted by these strangers, at least to some degree, and find himself in proximity to what had all his life been entirely withheld from him – china, patterned and edged in gold; silverware; glassware; gleaming copper pans; substances for cleaning things so deeply and so thoroughly it was as if they were turned back to new; materials in colors someone had chosen them to be; a window with glass panes in its frame; pepper and salt and all manner of spices from faraway lands lined up orderly in jars. He felt closer to Abednego then, for this, surely, was what life in the Big House must be: a constant nearness to things that both elevated and mocked and lowered those in their seductive ambit; that could seed confusion, as was no doubt intended, in the minds of those so exposed. We strugglin, Esther had said, we, though she had not been confused, as nor had Abednego been, or he never would have come down from the Big House to the Tyler field-hands' cabins, as others had not, and did not.

And had he not, and had Cyrus never seen him, would he, Cyrus, ever have understood or even known the deepest parts of himself? Would he have – why should he have? – come to understand that even the act of seeing is not a simple thing; that it is a matter not of the merely mechanical function of the eye but of the interpreting mind that receives its images, that creates meaning from the optical information, that is by its nature or design symbolic and hierarchical and not merely an unthinking and receptive mirror? There were things to which, when he noticed them now, he assigned a significance he would not have done before Abednego; things he would not have considered to hold any particular meaning, though certainly they had always pleased him: the width of a man's back and shoulders in relation to his beveled waist; the upsweep of the twin grooved muscles that flanked the back of his neck as he bent to a task; the rise of his chest and the connected swell of his arms; the cording in his forearms and the strength in his hands; the curve and angle of his jaw; the twin blocks of his buttocks and the bulk and mystery in the front of his pants: all that was male was, he had come to realize, a source of pleasure to him. Had he not known Abednego he would have assumed, for why would he not, that the other field-hands, the other men, saw these things as he saw them; and that while they also saw the physicality of women and its particularity they, without disparagement, felt it less deeply, as he did, regardless of how vigorously they spoke of it, of women and desire. And in that, he came to learn, he stood apart from them, but, with Abednego, not alone.

The talk around the table had died down to disconnected remarks and the old woman was puffing wordlessly on her pipe and watching him. He flexed his toes and wondered, though it was six months ago, if he could ask these people about the selling of the Tyler hands; if they might know anything of use to him.

Had me a friend, he said, and was surprised to hear the

sound of his own voice. The men fell silent and looked round at him. Eunice did not: she stood bent over a ledger open on the table the youngest girl had been scrubbing, her brow furrowed in concentration, making careful marks with a pencil; the girl herself had gone out to empty a bucket of scrubwater.

Over on Tyler, Cyrus said. In the Big House there. Got sold.

Owin to the flood?

Yeah. I was wonderin if any o you might of heard where them Tyler hands got sold to.

You reckons maybe he the one runnin, asked the baggage man.

He said sold off Tyler, the old woman corrected him. Not runnin from there.

He sold, Cyrus agreed. If he run, I don't know from where.

Mos likely they was sold in town, said the sleepy-eyed man.

Sometimes they gets sold other ways, Cyrus said, recalling somewhat the story Abednego had told him of being bought by Mister Tyler not in town by auction, but afterwards, along the way, having first been purchased by someone else – for some reason of financial advantage to one or other of the parties involved, Bed had supposed; or owing to some practice that was fraudulent or otherwise dishonest, and therefore to be perpetrated out of the sight of others.

Sometimes they gets sold here, Eunice said, looking up from the ledger, and the others nodded. He got a name, yo friend?

Abednego.

Came out the fiery furnace livin, the old woman said, puffing on her pipe. Shadrach, Meshach an Abednego.

Amen, the baggage man and the sleepy-eyed man said together.

Abednego, Eunice said. Never heard it outside of the Good Book. Never come here that I know of. You know how many was sold?

Twenty-five, thirty, maybe, Cyrus said.

In one lot?

I spose. They was took off all together.

Tyler won't let this one get away, the old woman said. Too valuable, even though he kilt a man.

Used to be a person might strike a bargain, the baggage

man said. Buy yoself free. Not no mo.

Buy your own self, one of the others nodded.

An who ain't been cheated that way, said the old woman, and her bright eyes went to Eunice, who was once more bent over her accounting book. Accused of stealin what they scrimped an saved an sweat fo; an if they ain't, an if the money ain't took from em in a so-call loan to they master or mistress, when the day comes, the buyin price doubles.

Eunice closed the book and put it in a drawer, then came and cleared the bowls from the table. She met no-one's eyes, and Cyrus could guess easily enough that this was her story, though for all he knew it was the tale of everyone in the room. He wondered briefly if she had children; if they had lived; if the old woman was kin to her. Steal away, he thought.

Keep the faith, Eunice, the baggage man said, touching her arm as she gathered the bowls.

Don't I always, Eunice said.

A loud burst of laughter came through from the public rooms. We bes fetch up a couple o barrels fore they called for, the sleepy-eyed man said.

He and the third man got up from the table and went in, leaving Cyrus with Eunice, the old woman by the stove, and the man who had unloaded the carriages, who was once more looking him over intently while Eunice busied herself in putting the crockery away. His face was freckled, and his short hair was brushed back and greased glossy, and he nodded as if he had reached a decision.

Tilson, he said, extending a hand.

Billy, Cyrus said, aware as he shook it that his own was that of a laboring man. Off of Bell.

Uh-huh. You said. Billy Bell. You come with Carl an Cole?

Sho.

Mm-hm.

Cyrus shifted on the low stool and added, They playin cards with Vernon in the stable.

An you ain't?

I don't never touch the devil's bible.

You ain't a gamblin man?

Cyrus shrugged. Livin's enough of a gamble fo me, I reckons, he said, and that was true enough.

Amen to that, brother, Tilson said. An a marked deck too.

Cyrus did not take his meaning. So my friend was likely sold in town, he said.

Tilson nodded. An likely further south.

Why?

Cause that's the way the river runs.

Thas so.

Warmth or no, company or no, Cyrus knew he should get up and leave, and on the instant, but did not; and wanted to ask how far it was to town, but did not, for as the companion of Carl and Cole he would be supposed to know such things. But he thought of time rushing past like a river in flood, like the wind in the pines, and of what was of value being born away and not returning; and what he was attempting seemed no less impossible to him then than it had been when Emory showed him his map by candle-light in the barn, yet no less necessary.

Gots to get gone.

It struck him then that Mas Tyler was likely still in the area; and that rather than staying in De Bray's Town, some miles from his hunting-ground, he might have taken rooms in this very inn, being as it was set so conveniently at the meeting of the roads; and that though he himself would be unlikely to appear in the kitchen, some accompanying servant might at any moment do so, and that servant might recognize Cyrus and betray him, inadvertently or otherwise. To remain here, therefore, could not but increase his danger, and made him a danger to those around him. Reluctantly he bent over and prised the mouths of his boots open.

Here, said the old woman. For yo heels; and from her apron-pocket she produced a ribbon of raw calico a thumb's length wide and a yard and a piece long, and offered it to him.

Thank you, ma'am, he said, taking it from her.

Cut it in half, she said.

He had left his knife in his coat, out in the night. Ain't got nothing sharp on me, he said, feeling as he did so that it was perhaps unwise to confess his lack of any weapon but his fists. Owing to some shift in the upper air the wind rushed in the chimney then, making him look round, and the stove clanked as if being riddled by hands unseen and the close air in the room stirred.

Change comin, the old woman said. Through the stove-vents Cyrus saw the embers within glow more intensely, then subside.

Tilson reached across the table and offered Cyrus a clasp-knife with a deer-horn handle. Cyrus took it, doubled the length of calico over and sliced it in two, closed and returned the knife to Tilson, then bound up his bloody, blistered heels, pulling the calico tight, but not so tight he trapped the blood down there; afterwards carefully knotting the ends around his shins. That done, he worked his feet slowly back into his boots, making sure not to ruck up the bandaging, and carrying out various small adjustments for comfort as he did so, then laced them up firmly. His heels ached in a dull, bruised way, but the padding spared him the slicing pain he had been obliged to endure before.

I best check on Carl an Cole, he said. Tilson nodded.

Reluctantly Cyrus got to his feet. His thighs and calves were tight from sitting. You can take em these, Eunice said, lifting down two corked stone pint-jars from a cupboard shelf and passing them to him. Apple cider.

He took them from her with only a little guilt, not knowing whether she guessed the truth of his situation, or if she did how much; nor how much Tilson guessed, or the old lady sat by the stove, her eyes defocused now; just glad to know he would have a warming drink to help him through the night.

I'll go now, he said, cradling the clinking jars in one arm, somehow still unable to break the moment, and the wind moaned in the chimney discouragingly.

At that, the door to the public rooms was pulled open and once more Mister Bailey thrust his face in, a gust of shouting at his back. Tilson, he said, Mister Tyler got two horses need stablin.

Yassuh. Tilson got up smartly. Right away, suh.

As he came forward with the required show of eagerness Tilson interposed himself between Mister Bailey and Cyrus, it seemed to Cyrus intentionally acting as a screen. But the landlord looked past his servant at this unfamiliar Negro male standing in the middle of his kitchen, grimy-shirted, his pants stained round the cuffs; booted, sure, but his boots were battered; in his arms two jars of cider.

Who you, boy?

He takin somethin to warm Mas Bell's grooms, Eunice said quickly. He from Bell.

With flesh-pouched arrowhead eyes the landlord skewered Cyrus like raw meat, and, as before, while up in the tree, Cyrus had the sense that this white man, despite his being unknown to him, was somehow inside his head, even in some incomprehensible way inside his soul; and that, being an agent of the power that lay behind the construction of the systems of the world, he knew all Cyrus' truths and all his lies, and that, therefore, nothing was concealable from him any more than it was concealable from God.

Cyrus' hackles rose as if lightning was striking the ground beside him, and he found himself unable to even attempt to stammer out a few collusive words that might legitimize his presence in that room, or at least partway excuse it. But just as the extension of the moment became unbearable to him, and the kitchen-knives and the stove-poker called to his hand and to the white man's gut and skull, someone from behind the landlord shouted for more beer, and the flint eyes receded like a twisted focus into gray-blue dullness, and Mister Bailey grunted and withdrew, Tilson following hard on his heels.

You best go now, said Eunice.

Cyrus nodded, and left.

It was with a sense of dislocation that he abandoned the warm, friendly and treacherous kitchen and found himself once more out in the bitter air and disorientating dark. The wind was rising, and as he made his way round the back of the tavern, passing a row of sheds, it and the cold reminded him he must retrieve his coat and hat directly, otherwise he would all too soon be drained down to his previous level of chilled depletion, and then sink lower still. With his heels bound he was at least now able to walk in a fairly normal fashion, and he had a full stomach, and was dry.

On reflex he tried the door of each shed he passed. Only one had no padlock on it and opened to him. He took a moment to lean in and feel about inside, but found it empty save for a low, broken plywood box spilling dry, granular soil. This he explored by touch, retrieving two sweet potatoes that were wizened but firm enough to his fingertips to be worth the salvaging. He went on, skirting the back of the stable, from which, though there were no sounds of card-playing within, glints of lamplight escaped through gaps between the boards; and quickly made his way over to the pine-stump where earlier he had left his coat and hat and scarf and knapsack. His memory did not play him false, even in the dark: there they lay, bundled and orderly, though after the warmth of the kitchen his coat, when he pulled it back on, felt discouragingly clammy and heavy and pulling on the shoulders. He slipped the cider-bottles and sweet potatoes into his pack. The knife waited in his pocket like a friend, like a small warding spirit. He placed his hat on his head and gave the brim a tug so it was set right.

As he reknotted the scarf around his neck Cyrus took a final look at the crossroads yard, and watched Tilson lead a restless white charger and a placid chestnut mare to the stable. The sight was, despite its being proof of the proximity of his enemies, reassuring to him. I know where they is fo sho. They don't know where I is. Fo sho.

Still, though, there was no doubting that the arrival of Mister Tyler might cause a spark to be struck in the tinder of the landlord's mind, and cause a connection to be made between the unfamiliar and only partly accounted-for servant lately in his kitchen and Mister Tyler's surely much talked of runaway buck. And too there would be the matter of the reward money that was surely offered for his capture, and the presence of a financial incentive would likely fire up the landlord's wits sooner rather than later.

Cyrus left the cover of the trees and passed a second time behind the tavern. The darkness back there was near impenetrable. Despite it he moved fast, fearing further delay might prove lethal; and was proceeding almost at a lope when to his alarm he blundered into someone else, a presence invisible, still and silent as a fence-post, standing there, waiting, as it might be, for him, or for another. Cyrus barely suppressed a shout as he pulled back from this unseen person, every muscle in his body at once tautening to such a tensile extremity that he was drawn up on tiptoe.

Who that, the other said, alarmed.

Cyrus thought he recognized the voice as that of Etta's Tory; it was at least not the voice of a white man, and he chanced on answering in a hoarse whisper, It Billy from Bell.

Tory, invisible in the dark, said nothing. The wind gusted. Tory, Cyrus said. Tory, you there? He reached out a tentative hand but the black air before him was empty: the other had left him.

Gots other business, I guess.

Cyrus took a breath to steady his nerves and went on, more carefully now, but encountered no-one else. At the far corner of the inn he hung back and listened for horses. Hearing nothing but the stirring of the wind he left the shelter of the building and crossed the narrow western road, jumping small ditches on either side of it to do so, and passed through a clump of cedars to the wider and better-appointed road that led south-west to De Bray's Town, and was therefore, though he could see nothing of it whatsoever, his way forward.

Something made him look up then: high above he sensed the wind in the upper air was commencing to tear at the clouds that had for two days and two nights entirely quilted the sky.

Chapter Nine

Cyrus was now in grave doubt as to how best to proceed. This surely was the road that led to De Bray's Town, but what lay in between, and how far off was his destination? Many miles and more, and the cypress boughs creaked about him, a melancholy and wearisome sound. He thought now of the vastness of the world and how little a way he had so far come, and how he was for all his exertions still in the midst of his enemies. Dared he chance the road again? No other way seemed possible in the blind night. From what little he could make out, the ditches flanking it were well-maintained and free of brush, but much shallower here than they had been on the road from Hart, as though the crossroads marked, as perhaps it did, a change in the mineral composition of the land beneath his feet, and consequently an altered potential for cultivation and therefore drainage.

Well, then.

He jumped one of the ditches. As before, the road was smooth and level beneath his feet, and in that way at least, the easy and natural choice, and so he began to walk. Though the wind blew strong and tiring in his face, he sensed the land about him was less wide open than before, as if he had passed beyond the valley's end, and as he went on the road began to rise, or so his thighs soon enough told him, though the gradient was slight. For a time he found the warming of his muscles an encouragement; and to be once more alone, and freed from the need to guard his words and guess the minds and motives of strangers, was a relief.

Time and space began to fall away, for on this road there were no paths running off on either side, no pines or posts to stand as markers; and progress, beyond a mounting weariness in the bones and a growing heaviness in the feet, seemed an illusion. Now and again he became aware of unseen presences flitting overhead, bats or owls, to which the darkness was nothing; was in fact their preferred element. These presences did not trouble him, bats and owls and the prey they sought being wholly of the natural world, and thus reassuring in the formless emptiness of the unknown night: here, then, there must be burrows and therefore earth to dig them in, seeds and grains to eat and therefore cultivation; and tree-branches on which to perch, and from which to watch and listen with penetrant ears and scotopic eyes. And should they prove to be not beasts but spirits, that too reassured Cyrus, for it reminded him that there were hidden powers other and older than what was set down in the Bible; and beings unchained by the Word, as a man also might become unchained, in spirit and in body, if he could but see clearly in the dark.

Bednego, I will seek you out. Believe. And his faith in his love and his mission was strong in him then, and of a depth and wonder beyond the memorized, memorialized quotations and unanswered prayers and blind and cyclical amens of Eunice and Tilson in the tavern kitchen as they were betrayed, over and over, as if God was blind and deaf, or dead.

But what if you is dead, Abednego?

It was perhaps the contemplation of spirits that put the thought in his head, and the seeming nature of the unseen landscape about him; for would not the lands of the dead be similar to what was around him now, without warmth, and sunk in gloom and obscurity? And here too time was confused, as it surely would be once life was done and all progress, even the simple, unwilled organic procession from umbilical infant vulnerability to maturity to senescent decay, concluded. He felt a rod of bitter, burning cold rise up from somewhere deep below, and it slid up through his asshole into his guts, and rose through the middle of his chest, and at once a vision came to him of Abednego, naked and wild-eyed, white bones painted on his brown body, a skull painted on his face, dancing before a blazing bonfire, and whether he was living or dead Cyrus could not say.

An if he dead, what then? I hopes he ain't, but hope can't undo what's done already, no more than prayin can.

If I knowed it I would go north.

But he did not know. A desolation settled on his heart, accompanied by a growing sense that he was not only making no progress but worse, was somehow moving backwards, as in a dream; getting less than nowhere as doubts heavy as ankle-chains multiplied around him in the dark, eager to reduce him to shuffling servitude. Taking out one of the stone bottles, he uncorked it and swigged. The cider was autumn sweet, with a slight effervescence that settled behind his back teeth, and it warmed his gullet as he swallowed it down. He took a second swig, pushed the cork back in tight, returned the bottle to his knapsack, and went on.

Time passed, or didn't pass, as he trudged; and then, finally, the wind in the upper skies tore the clouds apart, layer upon linty layer, until the stars showed in the illimitable beyond, and the black striated strips of shredding cloud were for a short while backlit and coronaed by moonlight; and then the moon itself showed, large and riding high, and cast its light upon the land, and for the first time since he left the tavern Cyrus was able to see all that was around him.

To his surprise it was an orderly and well-cultivated landscape that met his eyes monochrome in the moonlight. Neatly-fenced rectangular fields spread out like quilting on both sides of the road, which ran on level in a long, pale thigh-bone curve. The furrowed fallow fields were sharp-etched black and silver where the plow had scarified the soil alternately crosswise and lengthwise, and looked as though they had been combed or carded by some giant hand or mechanism. Others had been seeded with clover, to rest and restore the soil, and these appeared as darker patches, the leaves, for some reason of biochemistry or optics, absorbing, rather than reflecting, the moonlight.

The drainage ditches, he now saw, had petered out, and at irregular intervals on both sides of the road ahead dirt paths led off to clusters of farm-buildings, all in darkness at that late hour. To his left the canal, now further off, was a spilled mercury strip, and here and there among the fields were dotted clumps of trees, orchards maybe, or copses of oak or cypress that had been suffered to grow up for timber on land not required for raising crops; or pines for the manufacture of turpentine. Though it was hard to tell boundaries, these seemed to Cyrus to be in the main smaller holdings than Hart and its neighbors, and were without question smaller than Tyler, Bell and Oglesby; and he reckoned they might, rather than cotton or rice or indigo, supply the town with staples. If that was so, it might be nearer than he had come to believe as he plodded through the endless night. For all the questions it begged as to what he would do when he arrived there, the probability of proximity to his destination was encouraging.

The landscape itself was not, however: its regularity had within it something mocking and treacherous, for in the event of pursuit he would have two choices only: to keep to the road, which in its naked linearity would speed towards him pursuers by definition already gaining on him; or take to the mud-clogged, rutted fields, across which he would be compelled to struggle laboriously, and dividing them was fence upon fence, over each one of which he would have to clamber as best he could.

And now came the sound he had been dreading since he left the inn: dogs barking. It was the particular sharp cry of hounds on a scent and eager to share the news, but were they ahead of him or behind? All at once the lines of the fields and furrows seemed to him to run not, as they surely did, at right angles to each other, or in parallel, but like spokes in some wheel of psychic convergence, and whether he kept going or stood still he was at its centre. He came to a halt, turning his head first one way then the other, trying to figure whether the wind was making what was far off seem close by or, which was without doubt the greater danger, deceiving the hearer that what was in reality near to was safely remote.

He became aware as he stood there on that pallid, empty stretch of road that the temperature was falling fast, the removal of the clouds above permitting an uprush of what until that moment he had not realised was an insulating mildness, and his breath gouted thick white fog, and his heart beat in his prickling chest, and the blood rushed in his ears as loud as the kitchen chimney's updraft, obscuring other sounds.

They behind, he decided.

The wind was strong in his face, and so bearing all sounds backwards. Therefore what was behind was closer than it seemed, and he did not doubt pursuing him, though surely there were other trails than his spider-webbing this land. Or did perhaps the longing for freedom have its own particular stink and spoor that a hound could be trained to follow, some pineal secretion that in its radiant intensity overwhelmed all others, and that the wind was now carrying back to the eager nostrils of the dogs? He could believe it.

He ran, booted and heavy-coated, and with his pack awkwardly shoved round onto his back, its strap, harness-tight, constraining his chest and shoulders. It was a lumbering run, and his heels soon began to pain him sharply again, but he kept on. All he could hope for was to come to some stream or river that, if he could ford it, might carry his scent away; some confusion of buildings containing the scents of many like himself amongst which he might lie concealed; even a manure-pile, the stink of which might overwhelm his own; but the road continued straight and with no turnings-off to right or left, for he was, it seemed, on both sides equidistant between two holdings. He gripped the handle of Nate's knife, unlikely though it was that he would have the chance to use it, for the patrollers, doubtless knowing his reputation, would be wary as well as savage in their taking of him. Reputation, he thought, and somehow that was something in the midst of the terror that threatened to wholly overwhelm and blind his mind. His breath was coming hard now, and his heart pounded as if his chest were an anvil and the dogs' barks the hammer, and he did not look back.

He ran until burning, bursting lungs and a heaving gut compelled him to slow to a stumbling stagger, then stop and bend over. The barking was, so far as he could tell above the pounding in his ears, neither nearer nor farther off. His legs were heavy as lead, burdensome weights rather than mechanisms of locomotion: no longer his; a prefiguration of defeat and dismemberment. Cotton-mouthed he looked back along the ivory inlay of the road. Flaming pine-knots danced there as his pursuers rushed towards him, surely less than a half mile distant now, and any small remaining hope he might have had that they had other moonlit business was torn from him with a cry. Again he ran, straight, for he could think of nothing else, keeping to the road, for there was no cover in the bright silver fields, and with the dogs on his tail he knew he would be caught and brought down in the mud before he reached the first fence.

Cut my own throat, he thought. He had slaughtered hogs and knew how it was done. Rob em of that much. Show em I own my ownself. Not get took back. I swore.

Now concealment was impossible he was heedless of the noise his clomping boots made on the impacted clay beneath his feet, concerned only with continuing to move forward while he still could. But his gut began to heave uncontrollably again, and his gorge rose as if some animal composed entirely of terror was seeking to be born from the womb of his stomach through the tearing vagina of his mouth; and though the base functions of the body cannot be transcended more than briefly by the will, still he ran on, plungingly, blood energies surging galvanically within him, forcing him onwards, and it was as if he would burst to pieces.

The road continued to rise, its gradient accelerating, though he did not perceive this in the chaos of his anguish until he reached its crest and saw what lay beyond: a plain of fields and more fields, but also just a little way ahead a fork in the road, a greater branch to the right, a lesser to the left, and along the lesser road a covered stage-coach was speeding, lamps swinging, drawn by four black horses and coming straight towards him. Rapidly it drew near, and Cyrus saw the top-hatted driver on the pillion was a white man, and at that sight he came to a halt in the middle of the road, defeated: nowhere to run, and all he had was his knife, the instrument of his self-extinction if he had the courage.

Won't get took back.

Bednego I'm sorry.

I ain't afraid to die.

I ain't afraid.

His feet, it seemed, were already chained and weighted to the ground, and for a terrible moment Cyrus thought he would be run down by the rapidly-approaching carriage, reduced by blindly trampling iron-shod hooves and heavy spinning iron-rimmed wheels to shattered bone and split, silver-bloodied, tormented and expiring flesh. But the driver, at the last moment seeing him standing in the middle of the road, as unwilling or unable to yield the way as a stone pillar or a tumbled boulder, pulled back on the reins, and turned the coach so sharply that its wheels on the far side for a brief instant left the ground and put it in danger of wholly tipping over, which, had it done so, would, in the continuance of its momentum, have seen Cyrus crushed beneath it. The wheels, however, slammed back down and the coach came to a halt just yards from where he stood and where the road divided, its compartment pitching toward him and then sinking back, settling on its springs. The driver had by chance or purpose maneuvered it so it was sideways on, as if he might go on in either direction, towards or away from town as pleased his mood, and the door faced Cyrus as if it was waiting for him to climb aboard; and the horses whinnied and stamped, champed their bits and tossed their heads.

Cyrus saw it was a mail-coach – such coaches came to Tyler regularly, bringing the white folks letters, newspapers and small packages – and it was seemingly without passengers within, for none appeared at the window to berate the driver for his abrupt and indeed hazardous halt; and it was lacquered black, and the wheel-spokes were painted a red that even by moonlight was detectible as such. On the roof piled sacks were tightly tethered, and on the folded-down through-brace to the rear several large trunks were stacked. Around these were draped a pair of leather flaps part-closed against the weather and the dust of the road, and the trunks were tethered by a rope.

The driver wore a long, heavy, black wool coat, his low but wide-brimmed top hat shadowed his eyes, and his jaw was the jaw of a young man, and clean-shaven. In one gloved hand he held a whip doubled over like the feeler of a crawfish. The other held tight the reins of the steaming, restless horses; and Cyrus looked up at him like something wild, and from a position of hunched-over elevation with the moon ancient above his head the white man looked down on Cyrus.

You runnin, he asked.

Cyrus said nothing; to deny it seemed futile, to admit it a mistake, and in any case he could barely breathe. The barking of the hounds behind him, which had ebbed and surged as he ran, now exploded with renewed nearness and excitement, and made him turn and look back. Though his view of them was cut off by the rise, without doubt they and their masters were about to breast the hill.

You runnin, the driver asked again. Tell me.

There was an urgency in his voice, as if, in order to reach some decision, he required from Cyrus a confession, and Cyrus, wholly lost now, nodded dumbly. For a fleeting second he imagined some sort of competition occurring between this white man and the others over who should claim his capture and thus the reward; some possibility of a situation that might work out to his advantage, though how he could not conceive. Certainly he could run no further, and this white man was one man, not a posse, and had no dogs.

Quickly the man climbed down from his seat, and his movements were agile. Cyrus kept a grip on the knife concealed in his pocket. The hairs on his forearms and the back of his neck prickled, and curiously he felt all at once as if he were a kitten whose mother's jaws were closing round its nape to pick it up. Stab an run, he thought as the white man, now ignoring him, went round to the back of the coach. Jump up front, whip up them horses, Cyrus thought, though he had never before driven any sort of coach, only mule and bullock-carts. How hard could it be? The man pushed the leather flaps aside and untied with rapid, jerking movements the ropes that held the stacked tin trunks in place.

Cyrus glanced to right and left: nothing but the fields running on and on, and where the road split a scattering of trees and more fields beyond them, and all was exposed under the bright moon. How thick was the man's coat, he wondered. Not thicker, surely, than the blade of his knife was long. The barking dogs were inside his head now, and his mind was blazing and flaring like the pine-knots, and his thoughts scattered as though the brain that housed them was already hacked to pieces and dragged. The white man flung the ropes aside and they lay on the silver ground like dead albino snakes as he yanked the lid of the topmost trunk open with a clank.

He turned to Cyrus and still his eyes were hidden in shadow. Well, get in, he said, in a voice that was thick with something. What it might be Cyrus could not tell, though by the gesture of frustration the white man made when Cyrus did not straightaway obey him it was evident he thought it obvious that this would be his offer; that of course these would be his words, and he did not even look at Cyrus but past him at the rise of road; and abruptly aware that this young white man it seemed feared his pursuers too, or at least feared an interruption to his current activity, Cyrus hurriedly stumbled forward and clambered up into the waiting trunk.

Lie on your side, the white man said, and Cyrus did so, drawing his knees up towards his chest as does an unborn child when it has grown large in the womb. The man reached in past him and tugged from under him a length of heavily-embroidered material, a curtain maybe, that had about it a scent of age and costliness, and pulled it over Cyrus like a caul. The man closed the lid and with a blow of his gloved fist tamped it down. Cyrus feared he would be smothered, but could do nothing save listen as the white man busied himself retying the ropes, and the barking of the hounds drew nearer, and with it men's voices shouting. A moment later there was a tilting in the springs and the coach jerked forward as with a cry the driver whipped up the horses, and the coach turned and the barking and shouting fell away as it quickly gained speed.

Constrained uncomfortably within the trunk, Cyrus was joltingly aware of every irregularity in a road that had seemed smooth when walked and even run upon; and though he was amazed to find himself accelerating away from his pursuers in so wholly unexpected a fashion, still he did not trust the white man who had confined him in this low-roofed metal box. With some difficulty he managed to twist round so his torso lay flat and chest-down, and from that position, though his hips and thighs remained sideways on, he was able to brace his back against the lid, and, with both hands palm-down beneath his breast, push up with his arms and arch his spine against it. The lid didn't move, and he wondered if some catch held it closed, but when he pushed up a second time it shifted a little, and a third effort on his part freed it entirely.

Propping himself up on one elbow, Cyrus raised the lid just enough to peep out, and through the gap in the leather curtains saw the road roll away with the rapidity of a rushing river, and he was moving faster than he had ever moved in his life. Yet before he could feel any relief his pursuers came into view. They were on horseback, the flaming knots they bore to light their way revealing them as leering devils and striping the flanks of their wild-eyed horses red and orange; and they were rapidly catching up to the coach, which now, ominously, began to slow.

Glancing to left and right Cyrus saw only a continuation of

the plowed fields that had kept him trammeled to the road before, and he calculated that there was, therefore, no advantage to him in attempting a hasty disembarkation and flight cross-country: for though his pursuers had in their enthusiasm outrun their dogs, under the revealing, relentless moonlight their eagerly-scoping eyes would surely spot any fleeing figure, and he could not outrun their rifles.

They'd wing me, bring me down in the mud an wait on the dogs. Keep theyselves clean.

They were hailing loud now, and the driver drew the mail-coach to a halt, to wait, it seemed, for them to catch him up. Cyrus watched as long as he dared, long enough to count that they were five in number, and indeed had rifles slung across their shoulders, before letting the lid fall back down, and his mouth was dry and his heart was pounding. His hand brushed a leather strap, one end of which was affixed by screws to the inside of the lid, and he wrapped it tight around his fist, determining that if it came to it he would attempt to hold the lid down, in hopes that any searcher would assume the trunk was locked and therefore quit his search and pass on.

Long as the dogs don't come sniffin.

Seeing the coach had halted, the patrollers ceased their shouts, and it was only by the approaching thud of hooves that Cyrus knew they had drawn level with it. Gentlemen, a voice said that he took to be that of the coachman. What brings you out at so late an hour and so hot-blooded?

You seen a nigger?

When?

Just now.

I have seen no-one.

We was on him till the fork. Then the hounds lost the scent. You pass anyone?

I have not; and I would have surely done so had he come this way. Perhaps he cut across the fields?

He done that, we'da seen him. Where you come from?

My last deposition of the night, at Mister Willett's farm yonder.

An you didn't see no nigger, neither on this road nor that?

I did not.

I consider that surprising.

Mister Willett's land is somewhat neglected and grown up, the coachman said, and so might offer cover to a fugitive.

I allow that's so, the other said, grudgingly.

And I confess I was deep in thoughts of my supper and my bed.

Maybe we oughtta go warn old man Willett, another of the patrollers said, Cyrus presumed to the others in his party; then, more loudly: This nigger's dangerous. Kilt a overseer over in the swamp by Hart. A white overseer.

Troubling, the coachman said. Has he distinguishing features or marks?

He's a field nigger, built strong, six foot or thereabouts. Bout thirty years of age. Dark-skinned. Back cut up some. Pretty much of a shaved head, no beard or moustache.

I will keep my eyes peeled, the coach-driver said. I'm obliged to you gentlemen for the warning and the information. My name is Rose, James Rose.

I'm Penbury. This is Olsen.

A pleasure to make your acquaintance, gentlemen, albeit in upsetting circumstances.

There's money just for news of him, Penbury said. An two hundred dollars for a capture.

A tidy sum, sir. May I inquire as to who is posting the reward?

Tyler. It was one of the Tyler overseers got kilt.

My second cousin – Cyrus recognized the voice as Olsen's. May his soul receive its just rewards.

The coachman's encomium seemed a conclusion of sorts, and the men fell silent. This was followed by some muttered talk that Cyrus could not make out, and the sound of hooves stirring erratically, as when horses are being urged to turn about. Then the thud of horses cantering off the way they had come, and the diminishing jingle of harnesses. Cyrus let out a breath he had not realized he had been holding since the first patroller spoke.

The mail-coach sat there immobile. Cyrus did not dare peek out from the trunk, however, for there was the possibility that one of the patrollers might, for reasons unknown, have silently remained behind. Several minutes dribbled by, during which nothing happened. Cyrus wondered if, in light of the information he had just received that the Negro absconder he was assisting was a killer, and of white men, the coachman would come round and interrogate him, but then there came the crack of a whip and the coach was once more set in motion.

Pushing the lid up a little for air, Cyrus turned back onto his side and tried to rest, though hunched up as he was he could feel his tendons tighten, and his muscles lock as if with rigor mortis; and thus confined, and in pain, he lay as one buried alive. There were now no thoughts in his head, such small reserves of willpower as remained to him being wholly deployed in maintaining a responsive readiness to face what-ever random event might occur, but despite these tensions of mind and body the sway of the springs, the gently hissing turn of the wheels on the crushed stone road, and the sprightly clitter of the horses' hooves were, in their regularity and everydayness, quieting to his racing heart; a seduction of sorts. Goin the right way. At least that.

Once again he found he could not easily measure the passing of time, his cramped discomfort soon enough making what was surely short seem interminably long. His irregular peekings-out through the gap between the leather curtains told him it was still night, and its being darker now than it had been before told him the moon had set. Despite being wrapped in the curtain, owing to his immobility he began to feel extremely cold, and he longed to open his bowels.

A thought took hold of his mind then, that by its nature soon enough birthed others: They offer in a reward. He a driver an that ain't much. They told him I was from Tyler. What if he takin me back there?

Whether or not this was so, and whatever the man's true motivations might be, it came to Cyrus that it might be best to get out of the trunk while he could, and slip off into whatever cover might fortuitously offer itself; and that it would be best to make the attempt while darkness was still a shield, however exposed and exposing the landscape might prove to be when laid bare by the yellow eye of the predating morning sun.

But there ain't no road to Tyler. Not less we goes back to the crossroads. Emory said, an he knowed the lay of the land. An we ain't turned. Even layin in this box I'da knowed if we turned, an Lord knows I ain't slept none: we been goin nothin but straight. So it look like this white man takin me where I wants to go. He don't know it; he don't know nothin cept I was runnin an they's a price on me.

And then this thought came to Cyrus: He know I know bout the price an what I got waitin for me if I gets took back. He know I could slip out this trunk real easy an go, an he don't reckon I will. He dint lock me in, an he could of, twice.

He a friend?

It seemed unlikely, if not outright impossible, that this could be the case, and even were it somehow so, some friends were surely too dangerous for a black man to have – though Cyrus did not forget how, back on Tyler, there had been those who came close to saying the same of his friendship with Abednego; and he had chanced that, and with an eager heart, and had had less than no cause to regret it; had, indeed, been transformed by it. What, then, might this sudden and unexpected friendship, if it was a friendship, mean?

He recalled a time when Bed had told him of Bolitionists, white folks who were, it seemed, so passionate against slavery they felt compelled to act upon that passion, coming south in secret from the Free States to help those bent beneath its yoke, though how and in what manner Cyrus did not know, and Abednego had not said. Bolitionists, Bed said, were reviled by the white folks of the South, both those of quality and those of none, and were considered lower than niggers and thieves, worse even than rapists and murderers; and were loathed and feared in equal measure as most unnatural betrayers of their skin. They went abroad in the land and, like Satan, it was said, tempted innocent and ignorant Negroes to defy biblical injunctions and run from their lawful masters. Above all, they desired to overturn the divinely-ordered nature of things and were, therefore, Abednego said Mas Tyler and other white folks of standing declared whenever the distasteful topic was raised, not only a danger to orderly and gracious Southern living but also both blasphemous and unnatural; in short, insane.

Was this white man, then, insane? Cyrus had witnessed insanity among his fellow slaves a number of times across the years, though never in his experience was it turned outward into action, as might be the case here. Rather it was the collapsing inward, like a rotten squash, of a ruptured mind and spirit: it was eyes that could no longer bring themselves to meet the eyes of others but only look down at the unresponsive ground; a voice that was reduced from its proper function of communication to indecipherable mutterings meaning less than the lowings of beasts, less even than the creaking of boughs in the breeze; a spinning wheel that had no longer any yarn to draw but could not stop whirring round, accelerating uncontrolledly towards a flying apart of the mental mechanism, combined with a lassitude of body so profound the threat and application of the whip, the paddle and even the brand could not dispel it. All these things Cyrus had seen, in the young as well as the overwhelmed elderly, male and female alike. But perhaps white madness was different.

Yet did he not know white madness already, and profoundly? Was it not true that he and all of them, slaved and free, existed in a world wholly created by it; were in fact procreated by it, forcibly birthed by it from pairings equally forced? He perceived at the margins of his understanding that the very words with which he struggled to formulate his thoughts were themselves a product of that same insane system; themselves a sort of chaining of the mind, for the words allow the thoughts. And if that was true, as it surely was, what escape was possible for him, for any of them? A person could not escape the organization of his brain anymore than he could escape the earth beneath his feet or the sky over his head, not and live. Perhaps the knowledge, deeply felt, that that was the case was the beginning of a form of liberation, a progression or return to sanity and profound selfhood. He lived under white madness, then. But his concern at that moment was the danger posed to him by one, singular white man. Could a white man be insane against slavery?

Be foolish to trust. Worse'n foolish .

Gots me my knife, if it come to it.

Gots to be vigilant.

Cramp lanced through him.

Gots to stay strong.

Movement was awkward within the trunk, and not helped by his being tangled in the length of material that was doing so little to warm him, but he managed to wrangle his knapsack round so he could tug one of the cider bottles from it and take a series of clumsy, sideways-on swallows, though to drink reminded him that he now needed to open his bladder as well as his bowels.

As he pressed the cork back into the mouth of the now near-empty bottle the coach began to tip about: it had, it seemed, turned off the more even main road onto a lane the ruts of which were beyond the compensatory capacity of the carriage-springs. Propping himself up on one elbow and lifting the lid he watched a narrow avenue of star-silvered pines receding at an unhurried pace into the general darkness of the night. Was this the driver's destination, he wondered, or had he some other delivery or collection to make along the way? He had spoken to the patrollers of home and bed, yet Cyrus supposed the coach would stop anywhere it had a business to; and the driver's words might in any case have been a lie.

Cyrus yawned: he had not slept, except brokenly in the tree, for more than thirty-six hours, and was aware that his joints were now so wholly seized up that he would be little able to defend himself should the need arise; and that, chilled to the bone as he was, he would be unable to run more than a few yards without collapsing. Like a iron machine thas done sat an rusted to a solid lump, he thought, and he thought of mainte- nance, of oiling and greasing, and there came a stirring in his crotch at that, that almost as soon as it began became confused with the need to relieve himself. Strange, he thought, how the parts of the body could be wholly one thing and then wholly another. He was too tired to consider why this might be so, or what, if anything, it might mean for the organs of excretion to be also those of intimate pleasure, though he knew the coinci- dence to be a source of unease for many. Pollution, Samuel would say, though Cyrus had never understood his meaning, nor cared to ask.

In order to distract himself from the worsening discomfort of his confinement Cyrus tried to imagine Bed behind him, Bed's arms warm and strong around his waist, Bed's breath warm on the back of his neck, and to draw from that sense- memory a little sustenance.

He ain't dead, he thought. He was dead, I'd know. Fo sho I'd know.

He clung to his conviction like a raft, like oars, for it was the whole of his purpose, and beyond it he would not allow his mind to be swept, because to face the possibility of a survival that entailed crippling whippings, bridling, the cutting of the ankle-cords, amputations of nose, ears or genitals – degradations that were for Cyrus all too easy to envision, requiring, after all, no imagination on his part beyond the transposition of such punishments as he had witnessed from one writhing face and body to another – to Abednego, was to pour lye into an open wound: unbearable; and to what purpose?

I'd love him still, is all.

A fence began to run alongside the lane to his left, the pickets close together and orderly. Somewhere up ahead a cock crowed, and crowed again: the night was nearly done. The coach slowed and made a leisurely turn, passing through a five-bar gate that had been left open. A short way on it came to a stop. The springs shifted slightly as the driver climbed down. Cyrus did not hear him walk away; nor did he come round to the back of the coach to check if Cyrus was still there.

Cyrus waited a minute then pushed the lid of the trunk all the way up. With a barely-suppressed grunt of relief he struggled onto his knees and lent forward, pushing his head and shoulders through the leather curtains to look about him, though he had barely time to catch a glimpse of to one side pines and to the other a small orchard and the corner of a farmhouse, before a voice nearby made him withdraw so quickly the leather flaps caught his ears painfully and almost took off his hat.

Round the back with it, Thomas. It was the white man.

Yassuh.

Stack it with the others.

Yassuh.

Lamplight spilt past the side of the coach, and Cyrus barely had time to hunker down and drop the lid on himself before the flaps were pulled aside. To his alarm he became aware that a further trunk was being piled on top of the one in which he was concealed, and it was heavy, for its weight pushed the lid of his trunk down tight. His mind at once ran to suffocation, and he cursed himself for not having taken the chance to run before. The sound of the ropes being pulled tight over the piled trunks was like two deft strokes of a saw. There followed some quiet talk he could not make out, then the slight dip of the driver retaking his seat; and a moment later and without further words, or even the audible flick of the whip, the coach once more jerked gently into motion. It made a circle in front of the farmhouse before, Cyrus supposed, returning to the main road along the lane by which it had come.

Though sufficient air penetrated the key-hole of the trunk to prevent his imminent suffocation, he now felt nothing but uncomfortable, and as if he were encoffined – not that any slave, never mind one who dared to steal himself away, would warrant more than a winding-sheet, a length of cotton that if he was fortunate, and for all it could conceivably matter to him, being dead, was clean; a box, even of plain pine, being reserved for those more elevated in the living world than himself.

Spose it keeps the dogs an critters from yo bones. That's somethin, maybe.

Or nothin.

He thought of the Judgment Day of the bible, and the resurrection of bodies, of bones that were long scattered coming back together and at their joints engristling, of flesh somehow restored, poured over re-knit bones like candle-wax, he supposed, and bagged in new skin, the dressing of a carcass in reverse, and the idea seemed grotesque to him, and the intent plain foolishness, for he knew that those who did harm faced no judgment in this life, in this world that God had, after all, ordered as pleased His whims, so why would they in the hereafter? Yet there were also, he knew, other worlds that were not so ordered by that Word that suppressed all other words, for in his dreams he had seen them and, rightly or wrongly, called them Africa. In his Sunday sermons Samuel said Africa was benighted – a dark continent he called it, because the Word had not been brought there, but to Cyrus it seemed it was the Word that brought the darkness.

He squirmed about in the trunk to try and get more comfortable, though the endeavor was futile. Was this, he wondered, how a baby felt as it expanded in the womb, the sense of constriction increasing alarmingly as its mother's belly reached the limits of the skin's elasticity, aching to be born not in any knowing way, but simply to escape the intensifying agony of a potentially lethal confinement? He supposed it so. Birth was mechanical, animal, almost vegetable in its mindlessness, and did not involve, indeed supervened, the will: the cord fed the uncrying baby and could not refuse to yield the nourishment; breasts swelled and leaked for the baby that was dead. Was rebirth, the rebirth as a free man that he craved, the same as birth, an organic rather than a transcendental matter? He had been born; he had, since fleeing Tyler, passed through water, and that had been a sort of rebirth, or so it had seemed to him then; a first stage in his transition from slaved to free, sealed perhaps by the blood sacrifice of the hound in the swamp. Now he had need of a second rebirth, a basic and visceral one, for his bodily discomfort had become so acute that tears squeezed from his eyes, and he fought the urge to moan and groan aloud, to manifest if not a release of the body a release at least of the breath, of the voice.

Make pain into a thing that might be any other thing, he thought, somethin that don't matter to you one way or the other, like the color of a thing: fool the mind an you be free of it.

Leastways fo a short while.

His bladder was now an aching stone block inside his guts but he took a few more sips of cider anyway, just to wet his mouth.

Though the keyhole was too small to afford him any view, he became aware that through it pale light was now entering. Morning had arrived, but he felt nothing: by now all he wanted was to be free of his confinement. After a while he began to hear noises about him, and by way of distraction he bent his mind to figuring what they were. The snort and whinny of horses, for sure; the turning wheels and creaking axles of carts or wagons or carriages; men and women, black and white, calling, traders maybe; clatterings, clinkings, thuddings; a white man cursing someone; barrels being rolled; dogs barking joyously and not in pursuit.

Town, he thought: I'm here; and at that, despite his discomfort, he felt a sudden excitement. The coach seemed to be going more and more slowly, impeded, he supposed, by the people and vehicles around it. His mind returned to the idea of being among strangers, men and women not only unknown to himself but to each other, and the possibilities that lack of knowledge might afford a running man without distinguishing marks.

Gots me other problems first, though.

The coach came to a halt and the driver got down, and by the shifting of the springs Cyrus reckoned the bags were being unloaded from the roof: some sort of destination had been reached, then. The coach rose a little on its springs as the trunk above his was lifted off, and at that he felt a lessening of the pressure on his spirit, and simultaneously a rising anxiety as to what would happen next.

Bring that one in, said a voice that might have belonged to the driver, and evidently hands laid hold of the trunk Cyrus was inside, for a moment later, and accompanied by audible grunts of exertion, it was lifted up, at first tilting sideways, then leveling off, likely owing to being placed on men's shoulders, and Cyrus had the curious sensation he was floating. This was brief, for soon enough the trunk was tipped on its end, and he slipped down inside it head-first, and had to try and slide his hands round to brace himself up a little and take some of the pressure of the weight of his body off the compressing verte-brae of his neck without alerting those carrying the trunk that something sentient was within it. Feet clonked hollowly on wood and he was bumped about as the trunk was manhandled up a flight of stairs. Then it was level again, presumably being carried down a passage. A door opened, and the trunk was set down with a jarring heaviness that told him its owner was likely not in the room. The feet went out and the door closed.

Unable to bear another instant's confinement Cyrus twist-ed round and braced his shoulder-blades against the lid, forcing it up with two determined archings of his back. Keeping hold of it so it couldn't swing fully open, strike the floor behind him and make a noise, he struggled up onto his knees.

Nervy as a rabbit emerging from its burrow and scenting foxes he looked round and found he was alone in a smallish, white-walled, plank-floored room with an unlit fireplace and a single, glazed and curtained window. The room's furnishings comprised two narrow beds, on which were gray blankets, and under which were chamber-pots; a wardrobe with one door slumped on its hinge; and a chest-of-drawers upon which stood a china wash-bowl and an enamel pitcher. In one corner a curving rail had been bent round and attached to each wall high up, from which a length of curtain hung, to be drawn round so as to create a private space should, as he supposed might be the case, strangers be obliged to share: certainly this was not a private home, for it had nothing personal about it, and Cyrus took himself to be in another inn of some sort.

With an effort he struggled to his feet, letting the length of material in which he had been wound fall from him. Simply to straighten up was a relief so intense he almost cried, and could not prevent a creaking groan like a moan of ecstasy escaping his throat. Like every field-hand he had born much pain in his life, but there were, as he was coming to learn, many different varieties of pain, and habituation to one did regrettably little to ready the sufferer to endure another. Using the raised lid as a prop he stepped out of the trunk, breathing heavily as he did so. If this was a rebirth it was an agonizing one, requiring that he endure the burning restoration of circulation to his extremities, and the spasming realignment of ligaments around the nerve-strung stack of his spine. He extended his arms scarecrow-crucifixion-wide, stretched out his shoulders and tilted his head back, and groaned again, for it felt heavy as a stone that had replaced a sunflower atop its stalk. Feet came clomping along the passage beyond the closed door then but he found himself wholly unable to move, never mind attempt to conceal himself. Instead he just stood there, staring at the door as if watching something inevitable as a weight falling. But the feet passed on without pausing, and some other door further along the passage opened, then closed.

Cyrus drew a ragged breath. I could of closed the curtain an hid behind it, he scolded himself. I could go under one of the beds. If I can stand to hunch up again I could go in the wardrobe. I could stand up right next to the door an be behind it when it open – the placing of the hinges told him it opened inward – an not get seed if a person stands there an don't come in. Whatever I does I gots to keep way from the window, on account of someone might look up an see me where I don't got no business to be.

On impulse he crossed to the door and tried the handle, and though he probably would not have risked opening it, he found he was locked in. This was both a worry and a relief, for though it plainly proved he was the prisoner of his rescuer, it also ensured there would be no accidental incursions from other inhabitants of the inn.

Though disposal of the results seemed an impossibility, he had now as a matter of pressing urgency to empty his bowels and bladder: the discomfort was at such a peak that he was becoming unable to think properly about anything else, and he had, it appeared, an unlikely private moment in which safely to do so. He took a chamber-pot from under one of the beds and retreated to the curtained part of the room, turned into the corner and emptied his bladder, the urine flowing with an interminability that was disconcerting, painful cramps tugging at his insides as the membraneous bag collapsed within him and grudgingly shrank back to its usual proportions. Then, pulling the curtain partway across so that, while to some extent sheltered from view, he could still survey the room, he pushed his pants down, squatted over the chamber-pot and opened his bowels, keeping as low down and close to his heels as he could, so that what fell from him wouldn't splash the urine already foaming there. He pushed, in order to expel whatever might be left inside, and then he was done. The chamber-pot had had a white linen napkin placed on top of it. He wiped his backside with it, stood, pulled his pants back up, knotted the string that served him for a belt, then placed the napkin soiled side down over what he had voided, so as to somewhat contain the stench in the small room, which, the window being closed, was ventilated only by the fireplace.

Thus emptied out, and no longer as hobbled by his waste as a pregnant woman is by the child within her as it nears full term, Cyrus felt better able on every front to face what was to come. He crossed to the chest-of-drawers. There was water in the jug that sat there, for washing he reckoned, but he took a deep swallow from it nonetheless, barely noticing its flat, dusty staleness.

More footsteps came along the passage, and this time they stopped at his door. A key slid into the lock, and turned.

Cyrus' hand went to his knife. His heels pulsed.

Chapter Ten

Noiselessly Cyrus closed the lid of the trunk so it would appear undisturbed, and with two quick steps positioned himself so he would be concealed behind the door when it swung open. He did not draw his knife, just gripped its handle inside his coat pocket.

Don't let em know what you got. Not till you needs to.

The door opened inwards and the white man James Rose entered, and his eyes, as Cyrus had anticipated, went to the trunk, and he likely assumed Cyrus was still inside. Before he had a chance to so much as think to close the door behind him, Cyrus slammed it shut. The white man turned in surprise and alarm, stumbling back as Cyrus advanced upon him, holding up the room-key as though it were evidence of his good intentions; or perhaps, like a heathen, he believed it to be in some measure talismanic. His eyes were bright as a bolt of blue silk Cyrus had seen being delivered to the Big House one August morning while he toiled in the orchard pulling peaches; and as the black apertures of James Rose's pupils snapped open, giving sudden birth to fear, and swallowing the surrounding cobalt coronae of the irises, Cyrus felt charged up as by the tensity before a storm, that is, electrostatically, for he had never before had occasion to see a white man's fear, still less to know that he had by his actions induced it, and at that moment his world changed. The knife drew itself from his pocket, as much a part of him as a talon is a part or extension of the prehensile foretoe of a bird of prey. The white man was hatless and young, side-burned though otherwise clean-shaven, pale-skinned, and his hair was straight and oiled and shinily brushed back, the purity of its blackness a suggestion of Indian blood in him, perhaps; and Cyrus shoved him, and the force of Cyrus' palm on his chest split the shiny mass in black blades like the flight-feathers of a crow, and these fell forward over the his flushing face, and seeing the knife in Cyrus' hand he breathed in sharp but said no word.

And so they stood facing each other, chests rising as much

in unison as if they were conjoined parts of a single bellows, and the moment and their locked eyes the forge; and from the small window sunlight cut across the room and lay gridded yellow at their booted feet, and the dust-motes drifted up sparkling from where they had been pounded from the floorboards.

Best I lock the door, the white man said eventually, his blue eyes on Cyrus' brown ones. Sky an the river, Cyrus thought, the one reflected in the other. Still the white man did not move. To forestall the incursion of the household staff, he added. His voice was level and its tone was even, though as a tone is even on a fiddle-string, that is owing to its being at full stretch. Cyrus nodded and stepped back, and the white man moved to the door, inserted the key in the lock, and turned it.

Leave it in there, Cyrus said, and the young man did so, and again it was a revelation to Cyrus that he could give an order to a white man and have it obeyed, and he saw in the quick movements of the pale hand as it were a secret exposed, though he had surely always known that white men and white women were no less physical beings than black men and black women; no less susceptible to sickness, to cuts and bruises and broken bones, to death in childbirth and in infancy, to the organic failings of encroaching age; that they were not, that was, in any way exalted beings. He had known this and yet somehow simultaneously he had not, owing perhaps to the different valuations assigned a black life and a white one, truth being, after all, a function of power, and all things being relational.

Put up the knife, friend, the white man said. My name is Rose. James Rose. Like the flower.

Why you tell me Get in the trunk, Cyrus asked, keeping his eyes on James Rose's and not putting up his blade.

Seeing a fellow human being in distress it seemed my Christian duty to do so.

Uh-huh.

I have no weapon, friend.

James Rose held his coat open and the jacket beneath was gray and pearl-buttoned and tailored to fit close about the body, and if he had concealed somewhere within it something that could do Cyrus harm, it was at the least not readily accessible. Seeing this, and knowing himself to be heavier and stronger than the white man, and knowing the white man knew it too, Cyrus considered it might signal weakness on his part to continue to have his knife drawn, and so he returned it to its pocket. Just as he did so, a knock came at the door. Cyrus' hand went to his pocket again but James Rose shook his head sharply. Go behind the curtain, he said.

Cyrus had little choice but to obey him, the guest, after all, being known by the staff of the hotel to be in his room and the key in the lock. He crossed to the dressing-corner and drew the curtain round, leaving a gap through which he could, unobserved, see all that was occurring in the rest of the room. Holding his breath he watched James Rose open the door. Standing there was a housemaid holding a laden tray, young, pretty, and with skin the color of a nutmeg. Her eyes were downcast and her hair was put up in a white cap, and she wore a clean white apron. James Rose stood aside and she entered quickly and with hunched shoulders, and set the tray down on the chest-of-drawers next to the water-pitcher and bowl. Her nose wrinkled at something: Cyrus' waste, he realised, the odor from which was now pervading the small room, and the chamber-pot was at his feet.

James Rose noticed the girl's response and at once crossed to the curtain, reached round and drew from behind it the stinking china pot with the soiled cloth laid across its mouth, forestalling the girl from doing so herself, as was surely her duty, and thereby inadvertently discovering Cyrus. James Rose handed the pot to the maid, who, giving him a look both blank and strange, took it from him, turned and left. She was forced to cradle it briefly in one arm in order to close the door behind her.

As James Rose turned the key on her Cyrus let out a breath. He hoped the white man's violation of proper conduct in performing a part of a slave's disagreeable duty for her would not excite in her mind undue speculation as to why he should have done so. Yet why should she bother to waste thought upon it? No doubt her predominant feeling on exiting the room was one of relief that no carnal imposition had been made upon her. It was a melancholy and scraping thing for Cyrus to see close to, what he had known only at a distance:

what black girls endured from white men; and it fired anger in him on behalf of them all, as the look on Ella's face had done, when she was ordered from the kitchen of the crossroads tavern with the snake-handled silver salver.

James Rose went over to the window and hooked it open. Cold air and street-sounds came in, and despite the sunshine its small panes were on the outside rimed with frost. Cyrus emerged from behind the curtain and his eyes went to the tray, on which sat a pewter jug filled to the brim with foaming drink of some sort, half a loaf of bread, butter in a dish, a knife and fork, bone-handled, and a china plate on which were buck-wheat cakes, scrambled eggs, bacon and grits. His mouth began to water and his stomach grumbled.

Seat yourself, the white man gestured.

Cyrus lowered himself awkwardly onto one of the narrow beds. It felt taboo to do so while a white man stood, yet equally it was taboo to refuse a white man's command, however unusual the circumstances, and however ambivalent the issue of who, here in this locked room, had the power to command. The bed was at once softer and firmer than the husk mattress on which he had been accustomed to sleep, though after several nights in the open, heaped husks would have felt like luxury. He watched James Rose divide the meal in two, transferring one half to the tin plate on which the loaf had been sitting. This latter he tore into two roughly-equal pieces, one of which he handed to Cyrus along with the now-loaded tin plate, then, handle-first, the knife; and taking up the other plate and the fork, James Rose sat on the other bed, directly opposite Cyrus.

In watchful silence the two men ate. James Rose drank half the contents of the foaming jug and passed it to Cyrus, who turned the rim about, then raised it to his own lips and took a swallow. It tasted sour and was somewhat effervescent, but since the white man had drunk it before him with no sign of distaste, he finished it, guessing it to be beer, as it had a warmth similar in nature to cider. He mopped up the last traces of fat and gravy with the bread, hurrying to do so before the white man concluded his own meal; and before James Rose could stand and possibly ask for his plate, Cyrus got to his feet and took the white man's plate from him and went and set it on the tray, stacking it under his own. Then, there being nothing else to do, he sat back down.

You enjoyed that, James Rose asked.

Yassuh. He would have said the same had he been compelled to eat hog excrement.

They serve a good breakfast here, James Rose said. Well above the average.

Cyrus said nothing.

Why did you run?

Cyrus wrinkled his brow and looked away and looked down, wondering what answer James Rose wanted to hear, for that, not the truth, was what mattered here; and the world being as it was, the help this white man had offered him, since he was white and Cyrus black, had not earned him an honest answer in return. Yet with no knowledge of James Rose's motivations, how could Cyrus tailor his replies to reflect what the white man expected to hear? And so he shrugged and gave no answer.

They made out you killed a man, James Rose said.

Cyrus stirred uneasily, feeling the power in the room pitch and shift beneath him. Nawsuh, he said. I did not kill him.

Why then do they say you did?

We was in the swamp, me an Mas Johnson. He a overseer. When I wouldn't go with him peaceable he drew his pistol on me an fired. On account of it jammed it sploded an took off half his face. He weren't dead when I left him an there was people there to care fo him, so. He shrugged again.

James Rose nodded, accepting Cyrus' account, it seemed, for the moment at least. And you were running from the Tyler estate?

Yassuh.

If you were headed north, you were misdirected.

I was – lookin fo someone.

A loved one?

Cyrus looked up at that and met James Rose's eyes, and it seemed to him then that, unlike others, this white man could not penetrate his mind unless he, Cyrus, in some measure permitted it; and that lack of presumption, if Cyrus' understanding of it was correct, was in itself a sort of liberation. Yet there was something else there too: an undertone; a sense, perhaps – and he could place it no more precisely than this – of some obscure familiarity that was more, or other than, a simple though unexpected revelation of shared humanity. My brother, he said, because it was easiest. He named Abednego.

He run too?

Nawsuh. They was a bad harvest on Tyler last year, an Mas Tyler, he was force to make economies. He selled some of his people off. Bednego one of those got sold. I was hopin to find out where he sold to.

No doubt here is where they would have been brought, James Rose said. There is a monthly auction of human as well as animal stock, and gentlemen come from all across Welt County, and even from considerably beyond its borders, to carry on trade of every sort. The inland river markets have grown considerably since the cessation of the African trade. When Cyrus did not respond, James Rose added, You must have had occasion to notice the lack of additions to your workforce in recent years who were not native to these shores?

Yassuh, Cyrus agreed reflexively as he picked through the white man's words, though on reflection it struck him that what James Rose had said was true: those with any direct knowledge of Africa had grown older and diminished in number over the years. He had not until that moment considered why this should be so; had felt it only as a falling away of something that mattered yet was not easily expressed; that both symbolized and embodied a diminution of the possible influx of new experience, even by proxy, and connection to what was lost.

You have a wife?

The question jarred Cyrus. Nawsuh, he said. Then, to forestall further questions about himself, he dared one of his own: You from here, suh?

I was born in an adjoining county, James Rose said, and passed my early years there, so I am indeed a child of the South, like yourself. Thereafter for some years I travelled about, in search of – well, let us say experience.

He looked intently at Cyrus as he said this word. Cyrus looked back at him blankly.

My funds falling short, by way of earning a living I secured employment as driver for this mail-coach line. The company is owned by a distant relative, hence my connection; though there being so much competition in delivering of late I do not know how much longer it will be in existence.

His raising of money matters, and frank declaration of fear for his income, renewed Cyrus' uneasiness as to the white man's intentions toward himself, and so he attempted to divert him from such talk by asking a question that might also yield information useful to himself: You been north, suh?

It was a question both factual and in the circumstances coded, and James Rose evidently took it as such, for, while keeping his eyes on Cyrus', he answered on the oblique: In the course of my travels, he said, I came to a view concerning our peculiar institution that was decidedly unfavorable, though for reasons of social ease I largely keep my opinions to myself.

Cyrus nodded, wondering if, and how far, he could trust this man – this white man who would himself be punished, and with severity, were he caught harboring a fugitive slave; yet who could exonerate himself by the simple expedient of claiming to be not harboring but returning the unlucky captive to his lawful owner for the proffered reward – for which purpose, and no other, James Rose could maintain he had, in anticipation of financial advantage, concealed Cyrus from the slave-catchers who had lately been so hot upon his heels.

What's your name, friend?

Billy, suh.

Well, Billy, I have business to attend to now, and must leave you for a time.

Yassuh.

If I can spare the time, I shall go down to the auction-house and attempt to discover to whom your brother was sold, though of course you will know that he may well have been sold on to some third party since that initial purchase.

Yassuh. Thank you, Mistuh Rose, suh. Bednego his name. Abednego.

A good biblical name.

We had us a Shadrach too, but he died diggin the canal.

James Rose stood. Cyrus attempted to stand too, but the white man put a hand on his shoulder and prevented him from doing so. You rest up, Billy, he said. I'll lock the door after me, so you need fear no intrusion.

Yassuh.

Cyrus watched James Rose unlock the door and open it just

enough to exit through. Keep away from the window, he said as he went out. He closed the door behind him and Cyrus heard the lock turn. He took a breath, held it, then released it. In all his years he had never been in company with a white man for so sustained a length of time, save on terms that were wholly abusive; nor had he ever in his life been touched by one with seeming kindly intent. The experience was both disquieting and exhausting, and made the more so by Cyrus' continuing uncertainty as to James Rose's motive in helping him.

He a Bolitionist fo sho. But the thought seemed insufficient. A Christian, then, as he had said? But was not every slave-owner, every overseer, every patroller a Christian? He thought of the Reverend Mister Oglesby, owner of the plantation adjoining Tyler, a man known throughout the county for the capricious viciousness of his temper, and the relish with which he mortified the flesh, provided that flesh was black or brown or yellow; and even when it was the generally acknowledged fruit of his own loins he laid the cow-hide on personally and with great vigor, as though to expiate and wash away the sins of fornication and adultery with blood. A regular visitor to the big house at Tyler, Bednego told Cyrus the Reverend Mister Oglesby always led the prayers at table, and was considered by Mas and the Misses Tyler a model of piety and propriety. No: a white man professing himself a Christian meant nothing.

With care he unlaced his boots and worked them off his feet, then put them under the bed. Gingerly he unwound the bloody lengths of calico bandaging and set them aside. Though he valued his boots intensely, it was a relief to spread his bare toes on the cool boards and give the mashed blisters on his heels a chance to dry out and crust over. Having nothing else to do, without removing any of his clothing except for his hat, Cyrus lay back on the bed on which he had been sitting, careful to keep his feet extended past its end, so as to spare his wounded heels abrasive contact with the blanket stretched over it. The mattress sagged in the middle, but it felt good to lie unconstrainedly at full length after his long hours in the trunk. He wondered if James Rose's mail-coach went on beyond De Bray's Town, or only back and forth between the town and the farms and plantations he, Cyrus, had already traversed. If the former, he could perhaps once more be smuggled in the trunk, awful though the thought was, and in that way be transported a good distance in comparative safety, at the least putting many miles more between himself and Tyler. If the latter he did not know how best to go on – though unless James Rose could discover where Abednego had been sold to, Cyrus would have no option but to abandon his attempt to find him and return to his original plan of heading north.

Though he felt it would be wiser not to sleep, his belly was full, and his eyelids became heavy as he lay there doing nothing but staring up at the ceiling. Two oak beams ran across it, and in between them was lime-washed plaster much stained with candle-smoke. He began once more to ponder James Rose's nature. To ask a grown man if he had a wife was a wholly natural question, of course; and was, in the normal way of things, an appropriate prelude to the giving by a fugitive of a readily-understandable explanation as to why he, having escaped captivity, was not like a swift simply and determinedly heading north. Yet the white man had asked the question only after Cyrus had given the search for his supposed brother as his motive. Why? A random effort to draw him out, perhaps? – though nothing James Rose did or said seemed to Cyrus without a purpose. A simple desire to keep the conversation going, then, and avoid an awkward silence in an awkward situation? Perhaps.

Cyrus thought of James Rose's eyes on him, and all at once he suspected the white man of sharing his own desiring nature, and that the reason for his questions was as simple and complex as that. He wondered if that knowledge, if it was indeed knowledge and not mere projection, could be of any use to him; could be exploitable. To calculate in such a way was foreign to Cyrus' nature, however. *An even say we was the same, he couldn't of knowed it when he opened the trunk fo me.*

Cyrus considered that perhaps what rubbed against the grain in a man's nature in one way might give rise to other nonconformities; might encourage further rebellions against things as they were.

Maybe.

His hand searched for the packet Old Africa had given him, and found it resting on his breastbone like a cupped egg. He closed his fingers around it and the leather was smooth to the touch, and warm. Bird bones for flight, she had said, an never mind the rest. Sleep swept over him.

Cyrus woke to the sound of the key turning in the lock. The room was still daylit, though the sun's rays no longer struck the floorboards: it was, therefore, noon or later. He rolled off the mattress and fell clumsily to the floor, barely having time to grab his hat and scramble under the bed, and thereby conceal himself from at least casual scrutiny, before the door opened and boots he recognized as James Rose's came in. They turned and the door closed and was locked.

Billy? James Rose called softly.

Cyrus emerged from under the bed. His stiffened back and knees made his movements awkward, and James Rose offered him a hand to assist him in rising as if it were natural to do so. From being outdoors ungloved the white man's hand was cool, and, unroughened by manual work, smooth as polished wood; and Cyrus released it only once he was fully upright, and offered no thanks, fearing that to do so would draw attention to the unusual intimacy of the contact.

Come sit by me, James Rose said. I have various information. No, wait – conceal yourself behind the curtain. It's chilly: I shall have the fire lit.

Cyrus hid himself and James Rose opened the door and called for the maid, whose name was Agnes, and proved when she arrived to be the same who had brought in the breakfast earlier, but was on this occasion, likely on account of having been permitted to come and go unmolested before, easier in manner. Squatting before the fireplace she set a wad of lint in the grate and placed kindling over it. On top of this with slender fingers she positioned coals from a wooden bucket close by. That done, she went downstairs, leaving the door open, returning a minute later cupping a lit spill with which she set the lint ablaze, then used her skirts as a screen to set the fire drawing. Once the coals had caught to her satisfaction she withdrew. James Rose turned the key on her and Cyrus drew the curtain back. The room, being small, was quickly warmed, and only once heat arrived did he realize how cold he had become, how low the blood had pooled in his resting body.

James Rose sat on one of the beds and gestured to Cyrus to sit beside him. Not without awkwardness Cyrus did so, making sure, however, and by way of an experiment, to position himself closer to James Rose than strict necessity demanded; and he noted that the white man did not, as he might easily have done, shift along the bed away from him, either in irritation at being crowded or in repulsion at close contact with a black man.

Okay, then.

From within his jacket James Rose drew out a folded-over wodge of papers covered in tiny print. These he opened up to a large and unwieldy size, and Cyrus recognized them to be a newspaper, its engraved masthead a bird with spread wings, its head turned to one side, an eagle perhaps by the sharp down-turn of its beak. James Rose searched through the paper's interior pages until he found the one he sought, whereupon he folded it back on itself, then folded it a second time, then a third, so as to isolate a single column. It was made up of headings and text, and boxed in with thick black lines. James Rose smoothed it over the curve of his thigh with both hands, and his palms came away as blackened as Agnes' fingertips from picking coals.

This edition of the Welt County Times, he said, I took from the smoke-room as I came back in. Can you read?

Cyrus hesitated, then shook his head, though the admission, he knew, at once put him in James Rose's power so far as the transmission of information went. Yet he could not read, and saw no immediate benefit to himself in claiming otherwise; and indeed a possible future disadvantage in professing a skill a slave was forbidden under pain of harsh punishment, even death, to possess.

Nawsuh.

Still he found himself looking at the page on the white man's lap as intently as if he were indeed a lettered man, and he now saw that each of the many headings in the column was flanked by a small pair of human figures, a dark-skinned man and woman, turned towards each other, almost as if they were partners in a dance.

It is titled Two Hundred Dollar Reward, James Rose said, and he read: Ranaway from the subscriber on the instant of the eleventh of this month, Cyrus, a Negro male belonging to the Tyler Estate, approx. six foot in height and thirty years of age, dark-complected, markedly Negroid in facial features and strong-muscled, clean-shaven about the face and with short hair, numerous scars on the back, a skilled picker. Wanted for the heinous murder of Mister Richard Johnson, overseer on the Tyler Estate, and dangerous, he is considered to be lurking in the neighborhood of Willett's Farm. One hundred dollars will be paid for the conviction of any white man harboring him. Two hundred dollars reward will be paid for the capture and confinement of said Negro in jail so I can get him, and ensure justice is done – W. M. C. Tyler.

It weren't murder, Cyrus said. I tol you. Then: What's heinous?

An act that is particularly vicious in intent.

A coal popped in the grate, a noise like a tiny pistol-retort. The room seemed to Cyrus suddenly too small and too warm, and the ceiling pressed down on him as if it was false and being lowered by some tightening screw-mechanism concealed above. Impulsively he tugged off his scarf and struggled out of his coat and set them aside. After just a few nights without shelter but free he felt his nature had changed; that he had become a wild creature, and that, in his brief removal from what was claimed as civilization, he had also, and paradoxically, become more completely a human being; and that wild things and authentic human beings alike chafed at confinement.

Staring at the advertisement in the newspaper, he tried as best as he could to weigh up his situation. There were, he knew, not only patrollers on the roads between places, but also, in towns, white men who might seize any black man or woman on the street, not caring if he or she was free, even if they had papers; nor – and this was deemed the worse crime by the larger society – that that person was the lawful property of another, for the purpose of selling them away, almost always further south and therefore likely into worsened circumstances, at a handsome profit to themselves. Only now did he consider the possibility that he had fallen in with such a man.

It was not difficult to imagine a posse of other white men coming into this prison-cell, as he now could not but part-

consider it, overpowering, disarming, binding and collaring him, leading him out helpless in irons to some waiting cart, all the while secure in the knowledge that he would be unlikely to try and extricate himself from their grasp by insisting on being the property of another, given that other was the very owner from whom he had been so urgently attempting to escape.

He had no knowledge of how numerous such men were, or how bold; nor how far the tales he and the other hands had heard were untruths purposely propagated by their masters, in order to seed within the enslaved the thought that such was likely the fate of all those who ran and were not returned; at least those whose deaths were not reported. Lies or exaggerations, perhaps; yet since those tales were told by white men about the dishonesty of other white men, he was inclined to believe them.

He was struck then by a phrase in the advertisement James Rose had read to him: One hundred dollars will be paid for the conviction of any white man harboring him. Any white man, he thought. Not slaved or free black, but white. To harbor was to offer a place of safety in a stormy sea, and it seemed such a thing could and did occur, else why name both a penalty for its commission and a reward for its exposure? So Bolitionists is real, he thought.

There are numerous others listed here despite the inclemency of the season, James Rose said, for Cyrus had lapsed into inwardliness. Two Negro men together; a mulatto youth of fifteen; a Negro woman with a young child, a girl of twelve. Another Negro woman, said to be sassy. Each attracting a reward of but fifty dollars to your two hundred.

Cyrus shrugged and said nothing: no good attached to his price being higher than the others'. He wondered if the woman who had run was just possibly Esther, and for a moment considered asking if the advertisement said she was off of Hart, but did not, as he did not wish to imply to this white man that he had made acquaintance with, and therefore possibly been helped by, anyone on any plantation other than Tyler.

Once my errands were performed I found time to visit the auction house, James Rose said, setting the newspaper aside. Cyrus' heart leapt, but before the white man could say more there came from the street outside the sound of the tramping of booted feet, men in considerable number, marching in unison; and stentorian orders were given. The garrison is nearby, James Rose said, and he got up and went over to the window. Cyrus remained where he was, and watched the white man as he looked out at the passing company. I fear there will be war between the states, James Rose said.

War, suh?

War is a terrible thing.

Yassuh.

The soldiers were evidently now directly in front of the hotel, for Cyrus could hear the clatter of hooves and jangle of horse-harnesses as well as the unresonant clump of the marching feet. The sounds conjured a vivid picture in his mind, for he had a number of times in the past two years seen companies of white men, gray-jacketed and with gold braid epaulettes upon their shoulders, marching along the road past Tyler with rifles smartly shouldered, led by white-gloved officers on horseback wearing plumed helmets on their heads and sabers at their hips; and it struck Cyrus that those incidences had grown more frequent of late.

Despoliation, devastation, ruin, James Rose said, his back to Cyrus. And this war, this looming inescapable war, likely to set brother against brother, father against son, and send all to the graveyard, should any remain alive to bury them.

That sounds mighty bad, suh, Cyrus said, forcing dullness into his eyes when the white man looked round surprised, as if in his reverie he had forgotten Cyrus was there; and Cyrus pushed down the excitement that quickened within him at the thought of some vast and all-consuming conflagration, an apocalyptic hell that would be manufactured neither by the Almighty nor by Satan, if either of them in fact existed, but by the greed and spite of white men in competition with each other for profit, and yet might provide, by providence or chance, some reckoning for all the evil they had done. To see those fine houses toppled, the names incised in gold on marble monuments cast down, shattered and lost as those of his remote ancestors had alike been lost and scattered upon the ocean; to see all that was cultivated beneath the lash grow wild and the black weevils consume the white bolls and expel from their glinting abdomens more weevils, and more, and give issue to nothing generative of income or return, ever, but only an abiding hunger: that would be something.

James Rose wandered over to the fireplace, took up the poker that leant next to it, and in a preoccupied manner jabbed at the coals. Resting one arm on the mantelpiece he lent his head against the chimney-breast and looked down at the flames, and his hair fell forward in shiny black shards. Cyrus guessed him to be no more than twenty-two years of age, maybe as young as eighteen. His profile was regular, his ruddy lips full for a white man's.

To fight for freedom from a tyrannous overlord, James Rose said, that is one thing, for the enemy can be driven off and wholly removed from a territory. There can be such a thing as victory. But this. He gave the coals a further jab and they subsided in the grate in a sort of abrupt collapse, and a spark leapt onto the floorboards beyond the hearthstone but quickly turned gray. This hotel burned down three years ago, he said, the fugitive spark leading his thoughts in a new direction. It was rebuilt at some cost, and to much the same design as the old, and still they provide no guards for the fires. Is there a lesson in that, do you suppose?

Cyrus did not reply, preoccupied as he was with how he might best return the white man to the subject of his visit to the auction house, but wary of attempting too bold a redirection; and so he sat on the bed and James Rose stood by the fire, in silence and as it were in tableau, until the marching feet and the shouted orders that accompanied them had altogether passed from hearing, and the more usual street-sounds had reasserted themselves. It occurred to Cyrus the white man was perhaps considering that he might have a duty to put on one uniform or another; to fight for one side or the other; to obey or defy the dictates of his own conscience; and that he was answerable to that conscience, and that that was a part of being human, and free.

I chose to run, Cyrus thought. I fought an I will fight. Fo freedom. Fo Bednego.

To fight in that way, as an individual, he understood. But the thought of war made him uneasy, for just as when the flood near-ruined Tyler and the resultant hardships fell not on the white but on the black, would not a war, even one between white men, likely produce much the same disproportion of consequences, and on a scale more cataclysmic? And what were to be the terms of this war? What did either side intend? He thought vaguely of the Choctaw and the other Indian tribes, now just skulls in the ground and spirits in the woods, or wholly driven off, starved out and pushed west; and he thought of the rumors he had heard across the years of insurrections attempted and cruelly put down, and he thought too as to how slave-revolts might blossom on the twining vine of war.

I reckon it'd be worth it, he thought. My skull an Bednego's, side by side, an we did it fo us. But he said nothing.

James Rose sighed and returned the poker to its place by the scuttle.

Cyrus cleared his throat. You was at the auction-house, he said.

What?

The auction house.

Ah, yes. James Rose came and sat by Cyrus once more, neither unduly close nor away from him, pushed his hair back, and produced from an inside pocket a small note-book. I recorded some particulars.

Excitement crowded Cyrus' throat, and it was with difficulty he choked out, Particulars, suh?

It is a well-run enterprise, its records in the main well-kept, notwithstanding fire-damage five years ago, in which many papers and bills were consumed, which led to its being rebuilt in more enduring brick and marble.

An you got give some news bout the sale, Cyrus broke in, caring nothing for old conflagrations or prudent restorations.

The main part of the Tyler Negroes were sold as a job lot to a party by the name of Torrington, who, from the information I was given, is in the nature of being a broker of some sort for a consortium of planters, most of whom reside in the remoter parts of Mississippi and Louisiana.

Main part, suh?

Excluding only, so far as I could determine, the elderly and infirm, of which there were several.

An this MistuhTorrington, he live close by?

I assume not. The only address I could uncover for him was a room in a hotel across the way from the auction house.

You go there?

There was no need, for I soon discovered through the assistance of a helpful clerk that within a week he had made a series of resales of the lots he had purchased at auction, which included not only Negroes but also livestock and horses, for which he and others deposited bills of sale at the records-house, which, being public, I was permitted to examine. I imagine those purchasers to be mostly members of the aforementioned consortium, with whom I suppose him to have been in regular contact by letter, with skilled pickers being for the most part sent off at once to Louisiana and Mississippi. Those who had a trade were mostly sold nearer by, and some of these were straightaway hired out locally. And fancies – is your brother a fancy?

Fancy?

A house-servant pleasing in appearance, practiced in manners, groomed to serve at table and suchlike.

I don't know bout that, suh, Cyrus said warily. I know he brung food an drink to table fo the master an they dressed him up some.

Is he mulatto, quadroon or octoroon?

Nawsuh, he mostways full black. Just a lil lighter than me.

James Rose nodded. From here we must proceed by guesswork, he said, for the bills of sale lack particulars, and allow only that three unnamed Negro fancies, two girls and a male, were sold on to a Mister Robert Abigaile.

Cyrus nodded. Okay, he said, to be saying something.

Had your brother a trade?

Nawsuh. He skilled, but not like that, not to get hired out.

That being so, and his health presumed satisfactory, either your brother was sold off as a picker or as a fancy. Mister Torrington's bills of resale mention only general types and approximations of ages, and do not give names, so it remains uncertain as to which category he might fall into; and at near six month's remove the clerk had no memory of any of the sales, nor had he witnessed any auction in person, just stamped and filed and registered payments.

I reckons he sold as a fancy, Cyrus said. The word grated on him, for it implied a want of manliness, a lack of resilience and robustness and purpose in the world, but what did that matter?

Abednego's purpose was his own, and not the worm-blind white folks'. Excitement rising in him, Cyrus went on, I can't think of no other hand off of Tyler it could be. It *gots* to be him.

It seems likely so, James Rose agreed.

An this Mistuh –

Abigaile.

Mistuh Abigaile. He writ where he lives on them papers?

He did. James Rose consulted his notebook and read: Robert F. Abigaile of Saint Hall Estate, Blaze County; the nearest town is given as Amesburg.

Saint Hall. So Mistuh Abigaile, he ain't the owner?

I suppose not. A factotum, perhaps; or he might have married into the family. I know nothing concerning the Saint Halls except they are considered notably wealthy, and in the business of cotton on a grand scale, and are known for using the most modern and innovative methods of production.

An this Blaze County, it far?

A considerable haul from here, not less than one hundred fifty miles south-west, inward and downward by the map, though owing to the numerous intercessions of rivers, mountain-ridges and gorges, no road runs there directly.

Cyrus' heart sank. You ever go that way with yo deliverin?

James Rose shook his head. My route runs to the northeast of De Bray's Town only, and my schedule is of a tightness that precludes me from making any diversion.

Cyrus rubbed his face. Though its warmth was welcome, the fire had dried out his eyes, and his eyelids felt swollen as though inflamed about the tear-ducts. His heels pulsed, and the distance and difficulties ahead seemed barely surmountable.

An what if I do it an Bednego been sold on from there? What then? Only gots me so much luck.

James Rose closed the notebook and returned it to his inside jacket pocket, then took from under the bed the unused chamber-pot and went and stood in the corner, turning his back on Cyrus but not troubling to draw the curtain round before unbuttoning his fly and urinating for what seemed a long time. To not have to go outside to do this was luxury to Cyrus, yet to have your waste sitting in the room with you afterwards was not, and a sour tang quickly filled the close air and his restive nostrils.

Placing a cloth over the bowl, James Rose carried it back, kneeling on one knee to slide it under the bed. As he straightened up, as if out of a need to steady himself, he put a hand on Cyrus' shoulder and Cyrus neither rose to nor repudiated the contact. James Rose sat by him close then and said, I suppose you are puzzling over what is best to do?

Inward an downward, Cyrus thought, and not falling, no: that would be way too easy; a stone could do it; burrowing laborious in the smothering dark, near blind, a mole. He was it seemed being driven along a road that was in some way, however level it appeared to run, a descent into all that was filthy and intestinal. But Bednego, I'm gon do this. Fo you. Fo us. Believe.

Well, the white man said.

Can I ax you somethin, suh?

What?

You a Bolitionist?

James Rose gave Cyrus' shoulder a final uncertain pat, then removed his hand. It seems I have become one, he said, and his expression was both melancholy and opaque.

Zat why you helped me, back there on the road?

After a fashion.

Fashion?

It was owing to there was once someone I did not help.

Sometimes you wants to but you can't, Cyrus said.

I could have and I failed to. It has weighed on me since, a debt, a promissory note waiting on its chance for reclamation – for restitution – and now, it seems, receiving it.

He kin, this someone?

No blood relation. But for a time we were as brothers.

The color rose in James Rose's cheeks as he said those words, a heat within made visible that Cyrus had until that moment associated in white men only with rising anger, and it surprised him. Like David was to Jonathon, he said. In the Good Book.

Somewhat like, James Rose said, avoiding Cyrus' eyes.

What was his name?

Let me call him David, then, James Rose said. He was a mulatto and my uncle's – well, it was known by all thereabouts, if by none acknowledged, that there was a connection of blood between the two. But then, is not all known behind the mask of manners?

When Cyrus, who had only rarely seen that mask worn, made no reply, James Rose continued: He was fair-featured, honey-skinned and strong-framed, overall well-made and perhaps a year my senior, though the date of his birth was uncertain. And his eyes – well, his eyes could see. They could see me. That is something: to be seen. So few are.

An you was – friends?

Close as can be and closer besides, for the single summer I resided on my uncle's estate.

What they raise?

To Cyrus the question was natural, almost organic, the fundamental meaning of a place. To James Rose it was extraneous, for he replied, I forget: indigo, perhaps. I recall some rice-fields in the riverward parts. I was mostly in and about the house, and there was an air of prosperity – French crinolines, Dutch lace, Chinese water-silk. My sojourn there followed my mother's sudden passing from influenza, which was a dark time for me, my father having died two years previously, of small-pox, leaving me young to be alone and adrift in the world, hence my uncle's invitation – my mother's brother, and fond of her, I think. In the autumn I was sent away to pursue my education, which consumed the remnant of my small inheritance, but for that one short summer David was my light. Owing to his antecedents my aunt loathed him with a passion, as you might expect, and sought in small but malicious ways to bring him misery. Some of her wilder accusations I assisted him in evading; occasionally I even took the blame for some fantasized transgression, as I knew my punishment would be mild or nonexistent. David's mother she had had sold away south a decade before, and he knew nothing of her whereabouts, or even if she still lived, and had no way of discovering it.

Cyrus nodded slightly but said nothing. Though the viewpoint was as if turned inside-out, the white man's tale was in its general lineaments as familiar to him as his own, and stirred no particular feelings within him.

For me it was an endless summer, James Rose said, of willows trailing their weeping branches in the languid creek, of bougainvillea heavy with blossom and foraging, barely-wakeful bees, and a melancholy idleness that was greatly sweetened by David's friendly presence, for despite my aunt's resentment my uncle kept him much about the house and set him few tasks, and so he was available to be my companion whenever I wished it.

Cyrus watched James Rose as he talked, almost holding his breath, partway intrigued by the notion of unconcealed, unpunished idleness, something he could scarcely imagine; and partway repelled by eyes that saw only beauty, unstained by the toil that maintained it; that saw another man's presence in his orbit as untainted by compulsion, by dread of the lash. And Cyrus glimpsed then, for a brief robin's egg-blue instant it seemed, how white folks saw the world.

David seed you, he thought, an did you see him?

On one of those long, mint julep-moistened afternoons of idle talk he told me he was going to run; that my aunt's conduct towards him was of an exponential viciousness. James Rose sighed. Even during the few short months I was there I could see he told the truth, and that my uncle did nothing to check her, out of shame, perhaps, or guilt – all the while declining for some reason to send David beyond her influence.

He was gon run an you told? Cyrus asked.

No, no, never that, James Rose said quickly, and his face flushed redder. I didn't tell anyone, I didn't betray him, I just – I just failed him utterly.

He jumped up and crossed to the fireplace, reaching once more for the poker to trouble the coals.

I could have given him papers better than he could scratch out himself – passes, letters of conduct: I did not. I could have given him money – I had money then, and could have suffered a part of its loss easily enough: I did not. Once he set off I could have arranged to meet him in my uncle's fly along the way, passed him off as my driver, seen him onto a steamboat making for a northern port. I did not. I did none of these things. They would have cost me no more than a reprimand – the laws for assisting runaways were less harsh then than now – yet I refused it. I took his hands and looked him in his golden eyes and told him I was all for him, but in my heart I wanted him to endure his worsening sufferings and stay, for me. At the time I did not foresee my uncle and aunt sending me away, but even had I known of their intentions, still I would have wanted him to stay. I did not want him to fail in his flight, you understand; I dreaded to see him caught and brought back and punished; I just – it was selfishness, pure and simple. Love is selfish, you know, or it can be. Love is pure, but like the purity of wild animals: they follow their own natures, regardless.

An he run?

He did. At the commencement of autumn. And he was caught in the woods just three days later, lost and hungry. They flogged him till he couldn't stand for near on a week. And on the insistence of my aunt they cut his string, hobbled him. I feared to visit his cabin then: I felt the other colored people knew, and would somehow blame me and expose me to my uncle and aunt, even though I had done nothing to aid him. He recovered, mostly, but he never looked at me again: he knew how little I had done to help him, and he knew why. He was a slave but I proved myself the lower man.

Then what?

Once fit enough he was sent to the fields, whilst I, owing to my aunt disliking my partiality to one she loathed, and in consequence urging my uncle to be rid of me as soon as possible, was sent away to complete my education at a private college, where a place had been secured me on account of the family name, and I went, though I lacked the means to live as a gentleman thereafter. Hence my current employ. That was – he considered a moment – six years ago. I was seventeen, near on eighteen. Such was my pain of spirit I never once looked back, nor corresponded with my uncle or aunt thereafter; nor have I heard further news of – my friend – since. I call him friend still, though I doubt he would acknowledge me, and I suppose I do not have the right.

An then I come runnin.

James Rose smiled slightly. Like a prayer unuttered that is nonetheless answered, he said. Or the chance gathering of the threads.

Cyrus looked at James Rose then as if for the first time, and felt an unexpected kinship to his loneliness, his endless riding and round. Never before had Cyrus had reason to consider a white man apart from the generality of white men; indeed it had not occurred to him until hearing this confession – for confession it surely was – that a white man might feel – or even be capable of feeling – shame for his mistreatment of a black man; and to the extent of being moved to take positive ameliorative action as a consequence, and even in the course of that action put himself at risk. Cyrus wanted to say something about how this, now, was the proof that what he, James Rose, had called love had truly been love, or if not love then, if selfish desire then, that it had through his deeds been transformed into love now.

It will end, James Rose said, before Cyrus could formulate his thoughts to his own satisfaction.

What?

Slavery.

How it gon end?

Every day machines are being devised by busy minds. If there is no war – and I believe there will shortly be a war which may in any case destroy everything – but if there is not, those machines will quickly render slavery unprofitable, for each will do the job of many men, and require neither food nor lodging nor clothing; and will do so faster and cheaper and without needing to be urged on by the whip, and so without troubling the consciences of those who have a conscience as concerns how their profits are made and their fellow creatures treated.

Cyrus said nothing. He thought of the one machine he knew well, the gin, and could see no way such a relentless and insatiable mechanism would ever do other than raise still higher the demand for enslaved men and women to toil in the fields, to raise the crops to feed its whirring tooth-combed rollers, and by their labor keep it turning far into the artificially-lit night; and through it, like some creeping contamination, the entire world would, he foresaw, become one vast plantation under the lash until at the last the soil was wholly denuded of nutrients and all died.

He don't know nothin bout nothin, he thought.

But James Rose's eyes were bright now. Why do you consider the northern states are in the main free of the institution of black slavery?

Cyrus, having no reason to advance an opinion, nor any habit of doing so, offered no reply, instead encouraging the white man to provide his own answer with a dully-asked, Why, suh? – though in truth he was passionately interested in any analysis of the standing of the states which he intended to be his final destination.

Because, James Rose said, due to the nature of their manu-factory it is not in their economic interest to trouble with it. Though there are good men and women in this world who detest slavery loudly, it is a perceived unfairness in business competition that is the predominant motivation for disliking its continuation. Undoubtedly it suits them to pretend a greater morality, for who does not desire to look down on his neighbor, but this is merely a pretence – and this venality is the schism the clashing flints of which are likely to provide the spark that lights the fuse of war.

If you says so, suh, Cyrus said.

A little way off a bell began to toll, a mellow sound that contrasted pleasingly with James Rose's talk of greed and turmoil, and connoted, it seemed to Cyrus, the eternal, un-changing nature of things, and declared sonorously that that nature was benign. He became aware then that the room, which was lit only by the fire, had fallen into gloom. He looked over at the window, beyond the glass of which the sky was deepening towards indigo, and yawned.

That the call fo church, he asked, as the tolling continued past the count of hours.

Curfew, James Rose said.

Curfew?

For all Negroes and colored, excepting they be in the com-pany of a white man.

Oh.

Cyrus looked round at him then, and in the face of James Rose's indifferent stating of this fact the delicate, dewy connec-tion that had been established between them shriveled like a cobweb in a candle-flame. David seed you but you dint see him, he thought. You can't see me, see us. Not now, likely not ever. Leastways, not clear. He himself had, he now understood, been misled by the white man's talk of lazy summers by cool creeks, by the warmth of the fire a fellow slave had built and lit; had been seduced by the illusion of privacy in a room he had not paid for, and by a mutuality of the forms of their attraction.

A sense of being delayed flared up in him then. They's things I need, he said as roughly and abruptly as if he were once more threatening with the knife.

James Rose nodded, and went and called for ink and paper from below, and after supplies of both had been brought, along with further food and drink and candles, not this time by Agnes but by an older, heavier woman with a brisk, near-pugnacious manner that belied her station, James Rose pulled round one of the beds so he could sit at the chest-of-drawers, and wrote, and Cyrus, having emerged from behind the curtain once the door was locked again, went and rinsed the lengths of bloodied calico in the washwater bowl, wrung them out and draped them over the lid of the trunk, turning it toward the fire so they would dry. Then he sat quietly on the bed and watched James Rose dip clinkingly into the ink and scratch with the pen on the hotel stationery, and Cyrus wished he had some way of confirming that what the white man was writing was what he claimed to be writing.

Can you recognize this letter of the alphabet, James Rose asked after a while, showing Cyrus the first of several sheets he had written on. It is a B.

Yassuh.

And so this letter concerns Billy from Hart.

Cyrus nodded. After some consideration he had decided to use the name of Esther and Emory's estate as his own, reckoning it far off enough that its hands would not be known south of De Bray's Town. What's it say?

James Rose read: The bearer of this note, Billy, groom and stable-hand on the Hart estate and my property, is trusted by me, and has my permission to make his way to Blaze County, to collect and return with a stallion I have purchased from the stable of Mister John Jones of Amesburg of that county. Please allow him to pass unhindered on all roads lying between De Bray's Town and Amesburg. Signed and dated, Arthur Hart. I give the date three days before today, as that is when you would likely have set out.

Cyrus asked James Rose to read out the note again, his memory sharp enough that he could tell there was no difference in wording of the sort that would arise from a misleading improvisation away from the true text. Through his deliveries

James Rose had learned the Christian name of Mister Hart's oldest son, hence was able to add that additional touch of verisimilitude to the pass.

Cyrus took the paper, folded it and put it away in his coat, which lay beside him on the bed. He had already asked the white man if he could make him freedom papers, but accepted his answer that these needed official stamps and suchlike to be convincing evidence of manumission. Nonetheless James Rose wrote him another letter, again as if from Arthur Hart, and cosigning it with ironic intent as having been witnessed by local magistrate W. M. C. Tyler, to the effect that he, Billy, was free; and though knowing it to be entirely a forgery, even to hear the words read out – *the bearer of this document is a free man* – sent a strange, crawling thrill through Cyrus. And then his mind went back to the tavern kitchen, to Etta, and how she, though wholly deserving, had been cheated of just such a document, and his face and his heart hardened.

An unsupported letter of this sort will likely be questioned should you produce it, and quite probably see you jailed, James Rose said. But it may buy you time while its legitimacy is investigated, during which you might discover some possibility or means of escape from your situation. The quality of the paper is good, and that is a help, though being from the same quire, presenting these supposedly disparately-written pages all together is best avoided.

He then wrote a third letter, informing Cyrus that it was from Arthur Hart to the entirely fictitious John Jones, introducing Billy as the groom to whom John Jones should release the thoroughbred, and requesting good treatment for him. After reading it to Cyrus twice he sealed it with a dab of candlewax, marking it on the outside with a large J.J., so as to avoid confusion.

A fourth letter of conduct stated that Billy was travelling between the Hart estate, Welt County, and the Saint Hall estate, Blaze County. Make use of this when you near Amesburg, James Rose said, as for all I know it is small, and anyone familiar with it it may know at once that there is no such stable as I wrote in the other letters. He waved the paper in front of the fire to dry the ink before folding it and passing it to Cyrus.

Yassuh, Cyrus said, as if he was taking orders in the usual fashion. Outside the temperature was falling fast, and the room felt less warm than it had earlier. You wants I should put mo coal on the fire?

James Rose nodded, turning back to his task, and Cyrus did so, stirring up the last few embers until the fresh coals caught. Then he gathered up the supper-plates and stacked them on the tray. A piece of bread was left over that he was minded to slip into his knapsack for later but did not, out of fear of punishment for theft. Even after realizing that in the circumstances his fear was perverse, still he left the bread. He sat back down, feeling curiously as though the letters, the instructions he had been given were real and not lies.

Come dawn I must be on my way, James Rose said. My duty to the mail, and my paymasters' command. But I shall arrange for breakfast to be brought to our room before I set out. Your best road follows the Nooseneck for a way, running south-west. To move forward by water you would need to obtain passage on a steamboat, which seems to me too great a risk to take while you are still so close to a place where you are known, and which you are known to be near.

I won't risk no steamboat, suh, Cyrus affirmed, not least because his unfamiliarity with the ways of steamboat travel – the purchasing of tickets, which parts a Negro was permitted entry to and suchlike – unnerved him, and any misstep would be dangerously exposing. Gots to be at ease to not get seed in plain sight.

I'll take the road, he said, then go in the woods first chance I get. This brought him round to the looming worry of walking the streets of De Bray's Town by day – and the curfew-bell had told him that indeed it had to be by day. How I leave the hotel, he asked.

I shall call a boy to assist with my trunk in the morning; you will simply already be here in my room, waiting to take one end and help carry it down while I bring the coach round from the yard, and then you simply walk away. Here.

James Rose passed him a soft leather purse that clinked as Cyrus took it. Inside he found nine dollars in gold, a silver half-dollar, and several much-used copper cents and half-cents, the embossed profiles worn to gestures. Thank you, suh, he said.

He put the purse in the outside pocket of his coat that did not contain the knife.

There being nothing more to say or do, they sat in silence. James Rose produced a pipe, a long-stemmed brier with a tortoiseshell mouthpiece, and a tobacco-pouch from a pocket, filled the bowl and lit it with a spill from a dish on the mantelpiece. He puffed for a while reflectively, then offered the pipe to Cyrus. Cyrus took it from him and drew on it. The tobacco was in every way milder than what he was used to, and as such the echo of an experience rather than the thing itself, but even so it took him back vividly to the camaraderie of the cabin on Tyler, and thoughts of Zeke and Solomon, Nate and Joe and Lil Joe sitting about companionably at the end of a day. So co-extensive had their spirits been that at times he felt almost like a limb that had lit out on its own, rather than a whole man. Yet he was a whole man.

Leastways, with Bednego I'm whole.

He finished the pipe, knocked out the ashes on the grate, and returned it to James Rose.

By then the hour was late. We might lay down a spell, James Rose said, and he removed his jacket and waistcoat, and with an effort pulled off his boots, and for a moment Cyrus expected to be instructed to assist him in their removal, but was not. James Rose unhooked the suspenders from his shoulders and unbuttoned his pants and shucked them off. Now he was wearing only a long linen shirt. His bare legs were pale and strong. Moving the calico strips aside he draped jacket, waistcoat and pants over the trunk, pinched out the wicks of the candles on the mantel, pushed the coals down in the grate so they could not spill, and, returning to the narrow bed which had in the course of the day become his, turned back the blanket and slid in under it.

Cyrus, who had felt obliged to watch, to as it were attend on James Rose's disrobing, now removed his own pants, folding them and setting them on top of his boots and bundled coat at the foot of his bed. Unlike the white man he had no drawers to shield his private parts, which now seemed bulky and present in a way he did not wish. The tapes having dried, he retied them round his blistered heels in order to protect them from the roughness of the bedding, and then got into his bed.

In the fading firelight he could see James Rose watching him.

Chapter Eleven

J ames Rose turned to the wall, hunching his blanket to his shoulder. Cyrus watched him by the fire's fading glow until he was fairly sure the white man was asleep, then lay back and reluctantly closed his eyes. The building seemed alive with furtive creakings, but despite these and the occasional stirring of the white man in the bed across from him, and movements to and fro along the passageway outside, eventually he drifted into sleep.

He awoke confusedly from dreams of shaky, spire-high ladders and precarious ascents to banging at the door. They comin for me, he thought as he sat up, looking about him in a panic. The fire was out, and save for a slice of lamplight discing in below the door, and a shaft of moonlight from the window cutting across the other bed, the room was in darkness. White man sold me out. I'll cut his throat befo they takes me though. He groped about for his coat, forgetting where he had put it.

Mister Rose, a voice called from the corridor. Open up, there.

Cyrus now saw that James Rose was sitting up as straight as he was, his chest heaving, his pale features, caught in the moonbeam, registering alarm. His eyes met Cyrus' and were dark and wide, and the thought came to Cyrus that perhaps in some ironic reversal the white man had committed some crime for which he was being hunted: that that was his betrayal.

The handle moved sharply up and down, and then the key, which had been left in the lock, as though possessed of a will of its own, began to wiggle, and, after an interlude, fell to the floor. Mister Rose, I'm usin the master key and comin in, the voice outside announced.

At those words Cyrus snapped to. He scrambled out of his bed and hastily concealed himself beneath it, retaining sufficient presence of mind to pull his boots, pants and coat under with him, hugging them to him, his throat constricting as he heard the lock turn. His knapsack hung out of reach on a knob of the chest-of-drawers and his hat sat next to James Rose's topper by the water-pitcher, both items blaring his transgressing presence as the door swung open and lamplight spread in like a revelation. Too late now.

Mister Rose, this here is Mister Albany. The hotel bein at capacity, I ask he may impose on you and occupy this unused bed.

The proprietor's manner was such that Cyrus knew the request to be a nicety that would not brook refusal, and indeed before James Rose could reply a pair of muddy boots clomped into the room and a carpet-bag was dumped down beside the bed he, Cyrus, had so recently vacated. Where is your nigger with my bags, the man demanded in a voice thickened by drink and loud for the lateness of the hour.

He'll be up presently, Mister Albany. I had to rouse him.

And get this bed made up, Mister Albany said, it's an infernal mess. No, don't trouble, hang the bed, get that whisky brought up instead. And he sat down so heavily the zinging springs dove down close to Cyrus' ear, and Cyrus, who had been lying on his side, had to twist his shoulders round sharply to avoid being pressed down upon, thereby alerting the man above to his unyielding presence below. A servant, male and bare-footed, came in then, backwards, dragging two bulky leather bags which he pulled round to the foot of the bed; a second, female, her long skirts brushing her bare feet, followed him. She crossed to the chest-of-drawers and from his hiding-place Cyrus watched her set down a tray with on it a lit candle on a tin dish, a liquor bottle and two tumblers, and leave.

You, boy. My boots, the drink-thickened voice commanded, and Cyrus could tell from the position of their feet that the male servant was straddling the white man's leg, his buttocks towards the white man, bending forward and tugging off first the right boot, then with further grunts and complaining the left, exposing ham-shaped and -colored calves.

They right muddy, suh, the servant said. You wants I should polish em up?

The white man said nothing but must have nodded, for the young man took the boots with him when he withdrew a moment later. The hotelier squatted down to pick up James Rose's key where it had fallen to the floor, and for a heart-stopping moment his ruddy face, lit lividly by the lamp he held, dipped into Cyrus' view just two feet from his own, and though he was concealed by the shadows beneath the bed, and the hotelier's attention was all on his task, Cyrus cringed back and put his hand over his mouth to stifle his breath.

The hotelier's stubby fingers closed round the key and he straightened up with a grunt. I'll be leaving you gentlemen now, he said, and he and the lamplight left the room, and the door closed. Throughout all of this James Rose had neither moved nor spoken, though he could hardly have been easy about the unexpected imposition.

The other man shifted about on the bed and the springs pinged and pulled apart. Come sir, he said, struggling up to further complaints from the bed-frame, and padding in his bare feet over to where the whisky-bottle glinted in the candle-light, added, Join me. By way of an apology for my breaking in on you.

I thank you, sir.

The proprietor said your name was Rose?

It is, sir. And yours I believe is Albany?

Just so. Mister Albany poured two large measures and re-turned to the bed with the tumblers. Your health, sir, he said.

And yours.

Glasses clinked. A shift in the direction of the wind sent a funnel of air down the chimney, puffing coal-dust out into the room. Cyrus clamped both hands over his nose and mouth as Mister Albany and James Rose coughed and hacked and cursed.

Hang it, said Mister Albany, where is the screen?

They do not provide them, James Rose said, then hawked and cleared his throat several times in succession.

A most inferior establishment, the other said as Cyrus watched James Rose go over to the grate to spit. Though I'll allow this whisky is of a standard.

Shall I call the maid to open the window?

I'd rather choke than freeze, Mister Albany said as Cyrus rubbed his stinging eyes and tried silently to hawk phlegm up into his mouth. What is your business, sir?

Deliveryman and stage-coach driver for the North-East Brigham line.

Does it pay?

It is a living, despite the growth in competition lately.

What is to the customer's benefit is often not to the employee's.

True, sir. And yours?

I am a seeker-out of neglected commercial opportunities.

The wind moaned in the chimney but this time was not channeled down. Cyrus rubbed his nose fiercely in an attempt to reduce its itching. The maid had not brought the second chamber-pot back, and should Mister Albany grope about under the bed for it he would be sure to quickly discover Cyrus, and his manner of speaking made it clear that, drunk or not, he had his wits about him.

Have you come far, James Rose asked.

Up from Louisiana. The other man sneezed, and sneezed again. Confound this dust. Coal's a dirty thing.

And so their talk went on, with Cyrus in an agony of suspense under the bed. Clearly the white men did not know each other. Or was it clear? Once again the fear of conspiracy and being sold away grew in him. Even if they were strangers to each other, still he could at any moment be discovered, and should he be discovered, even if James Rose had the will, he could hardly protect Cyrus from capture. And this man sought, he said, neglected opportunities: what did that mean? It seemed to Cyrus a code for something illicit. The man suggested a game of cards. James Rose demurred and their conversation, by fits and starts, continued. In it business matters predominated, and, knowing little of either geography or manufacturing, Cyrus could follow little of what was said. One exchange stuck with him, however, for it seemed in its way emblematic of the whole.

There is no situation, Mister Albany said, which cannot be made to yield a profit for a present-minded man.

Even the worst, James Rose asked.

Worst, sir, is nothing but an incorrectly-considered point of view.

And what, then, is the viewpoint you would call correct?

Why, sir, to see an opportunity.

Even in war?

You ask, sir, for examples?

I do.

In war – munitions.

In dying?

To make things right, Mister Rose. With family and with God.

Their talk tailed off into silent sitting, and in due course the bottle was done. With an effort Mister Albany got up, went over to the chest-of-drawers and filled the bowl from the pitcher, in the low light not noticing the stain of pink in the water already in there, from when Cyrus had wrung out his bloody wrappings earlier; and splashed his face, huffing and puffing – for the water was cold as indeed the room was now cold – before cleaning his teeth with plump fingers and spitting into the grate. Taking the candle to light him to his bed, he sat heavily once again, blew it out and set it on the floor by Cyrus' head, then raised his hefty legs and lay down. In a little while he was snoring.

Stealthy as a spider, and with his possessions bundled as close to him as a spider's egg-sack, Cyrus slid out from under the bed. James Rose watched him in silence as he got to his feet. Cyrus kept his own eyes locked on Mister Albany, a quivering, dark and gelid mound beneath the blanket, as he slowly pulled on his pants and then his coat, retrieved his hat and knapsack, and, lastly, slowly and carefully worked his feet into his boots. The floorboards creaked as he stooped to tighten the laces, but only slightly. What now?

Kill em both an run.

Naw.

He stood irresolute. The moon had gone down hours ago: in the gap between the window-curtains a gray and lambent strip presaged the dawn.

Get back in the trunk, James Rose said, in a voice that was weightless and empty of emphasis.

Nawsuh, Cyrus said thickly, keeping his own voice low and his eyes on the other white man. I gots to go now.

James Rose made no reply. Pushing away his blanket, he swung his legs round and placed his bare feet on the floor. Come with me into the passageway, he said quietly; and, careful to make as little sound as possible, he crossed to the door, took hold of the handle and opened it. The hinge whined like some small, shrill and resisting creature but the sleeping man did not stir, nor did the pattern of his mucous-heavy breathing alter.

Cyrus followed James Rose out, gently pulling the door to behind him, but not so far as to cause the snib to click. In closing it made no sound, as if to prove that leaving was a right act. In the dim passageway, which had only a small window at its far end, and that curtained, he could barely make out the white man's face, and he supposed his own to be even less visible. The rest of the house was in silence, no servants having risen yet, it seemed.

Go down to the jetty, James Rose said. Follow the road up-river. Should you need to ask directions the first stop along your way is a hamlet called Honeycomb, in Gin County, so it is the Honeycomb road.

Honeycomb?

Named for the calciferous limestone upon which it is built, which has been much hollowed out by the actions of subterranean aquifers upon its fissures. The waters are said to be beneficial to the health, and above the hamlet is a spa hotel.

Yassuh, Cyrus said, thinking of bees, and summer flowers, and hives.

The Nooseneck curves back on itself to the west of the town, briefly appearing to head northerly, so at first you may doubt your way, but it and the road soon enough turn south-west again, near doubling back on themselves. Past a ridge of land, road and river divide, the river flowing west, the road south-west, which latter is your direction. Honeycomb is fifty miles from De Bray's Town. Here. James Rose caught Cyrus' hand in his, and pressed something coolly metallic into his palm. My compass, he said, closing Cyrus' fingers around the object. Held level, the arrow will always point north.

Yassuh. Thank you, suh, Cyrus said, and he was at once sincere and performing gratitude in the usual artificial way. The compass was on a fine chain that pooled in his palm, and he lifted it awkwardly over his hat-brim and head and tucked it away inside his shirt, where it hung on his breast-bone next to Old Africa's charm, two ways of knowing and being conjoining there.

Just then there came the sound of someone climbing the stairs towards them, the brisk sough of skirts, and Cyrus and

James Rose, caught by indecision, could do nothing but stand there as, holding a candle aloft, the second of the maids who had brought victuals the day before rose up in front of them, her flat face as inscrutable now as it had been then, and to Cyrus as much as to James Rose. James Rose let go of Cyrus' hand, and they watched the maid, and she watched them as she rummaged one-handed in her apron-pocket, took out a fresh candle and set it in one of the sconces that lined the corridor, lifting the smoke-hazed glass cover in order to do so, lit it with the candle she was holding, then replaced the cover.

I'm sending my man on an errand, James Rose said, attempting to diffuse with this everyday statement what surely must have had to the maid the appearance of some villainy in the course of its commission, the more so as their faces were caught in the flicker of a flame that, held at hip height, underlit their features grotesquely and cast dramatic shadows upwards.

Yes, sir, she said blankly.

Please ensure he obtains readmittance on his return.

Yes, sir. She moved to the next sconce, this time taking a moment to lever a remaining stump of wax from its socket. Now she was no longer looking at them.

What's your name, James Rose asked.

Mary, sir.

Thank you, Mary.

Yes, sir.

Mary moved along the passageway, continuing with her task. James Rose looked intently at Cyrus, and what was behind his eyes Cyrus could not tell. The young white man reached back and opened the door behind him. Snoring buzz-sawed within; the room was all in shadow. James Rose stepped back into that shadow. The door closed cryingly.

Cyrus was now alone with Mary. She stopped what she was doing and looked him over.

I'm Billy Hart, Miz Mary, he said.

Front door's locked, she said. I'll take you down an let you out. Mas Willett don't rise early.

He the owner?

Mm-hm. Wait a moment.

Cyrus looked about him as she replaced the last few candles. He had seen nothing of the hotel except the room he had been brought into while inside the trunk. Save for boots and shoes waiting newly-polished outside closed doors, a small window at one end and stairs at the other running up and down, it was featureless. What's it called?

What?

This place.

The Cypress, on account of there was cypresses out back, till the fire took em off.

You was there for that?

Mm-hm.

She lit the final candle and set the glass over it, adjusting the bowl briefly so it sat straight, demonstrating the pride in work that is impossible entirely to suppress even in extremes of exploitation. He found he wanted to ask her questions, she and all the black folks who lived so closely with the white ones as Abednego had done; ask them what that proximity revealed; but, doubting she would be able to express it, not having had his or any other experience by way of a contrast or a frame, he did not. She made her way back to the stairs and started down, and as he followed her she said, You can eat fore you go out: fire's lit in the kitchen.

He wavered. Thank you, Miz Mary, but I best get bout this errand. I gots to go down to the water.

I'll point you the way, she said. Fog's thick off the river this mornin: can't hardly see past a foot in front o yo face.

Zat usual?

Mm-hm.

From elsewhere in the building Cyrus could hear the sounds of servants quietly commencing their chores as Mary led him to the front door. It was large, and above it was a window, a semi-circle of stained glass illustrating some Bible tale, Cyrus guessed, though he could not identify it; and Mary had a key on a chain at her waist, which she used to unlock the door. It opened inwards, and the fog outside was drawn in over the threshold as if by some desire to enter and transgress, and beyond all was opaque white. Mary moved to one side and Cyrus stepped out onto the verandah, and it was wide and extended off to left and right into milky nothingness, and was bounded at waist-height by a wooden handrail. He crossed over to it and looked out. Mary followed him, her candle lighting only the fog around the flame, a weak nimbus that made the rest of it seem if anything denser. The smooth wood of the rail was damp with dew and chilly to Cyrus' hand.

Thas your way, she said, pointing to their left. Down them steps, then straight down Main Street past the courthouse. It ain't far.

Thank you, Miz Mary, he said again, and something in his manner revealed him to her, it seemed, for she touched his arm gently and said, Good luck, Billy Hart.

Before he could look round she had gone back in and the door was closing behind her.

The air was still and the fog was cold and clammy, and a shudder ran through him in the depleting predawn chill. There was nothing to see as he looked about him, excepting directly opposite there hung in the whiteness the spider-leg branches of some black tree, beaded with dew as a web is beaded with gum. He descended the steps to the invisible street and turned left, following along the side of the hotel, the fingertips of his left hand brushing the rough boards, reassuringly physical in a world that threatened to fail to exist. Reaching the wall's end he abandoned the known structure and made his uncertain way towards where a light on a tall pole glowed high overhead like gathered fox-fire, a beacon marking, as he realized when he reached it, one of a grid of intersections, and he crossed under it, keeping on straight. On either side of the wide street buildings stood, dark and surely solid, but, owing to the hazing effect of the fog, indeterminate; though here and there soft-edged yellow squares – lamps lit by servants behind blinds or screens, and set on sills – suggested their proportions.

He crossed a second intersection, and sounds from up ahead began to reach his ears: hales and halloos, barrel-roll thunderings and the thuds of lading and unlading, cart and carriage-wheels turning and creaking, clopping hooves and chinking harnesses, doors banging, all noises rendered unresonant by the enveloping fog. He crossed two more intersections, a lamp floating high above each, and continued on, keeping to the middle of the street. To his right the buildings were now more imposing: of stone, not wood or even brick; and with broad steps and pillars and – barely visible above – porticoes on which motifs were carved in bas-relief. To

Cyrus they had the quality of tombs, for at that early hour no lights showed in any of their windows, and he looked away from them. On the opposite side were what seemed private homes, of clapboard in the main or less commonly brick, square and of two and three stories, some with railings before them, and gates; and trees were planted on that side, the lower branches pruned so the trunks rose up slender and elegant. These gave way to more hotels, or so Cyrus took them to be, for they were set directly on the street, and were flanked by what were, by their smell, stable-yards; and a little way along were stores with painted signs above large windows, and blinds pulled down within those windows. In the window of one store that was without blinds stood bottles of different-colored glass, prettily arranged. Now there were people in the streets, not hurrying but moving with purpose and in the direction he was going, bundled up in coats and scarves and hats against the damp and cold, and in the fog their skin-color was indiscernible, and Cyrus was thankful as it meant his was too. He passed a long, low tavern, its lit windows an uneven oblong row, and glancing in saw white men and women of various classes and stations in life, most with baggage piled about them, some wearing heavy coats and hats they had not troubled to remove, being served breakfast by bustling black men and women. From a way off came the melancholy hooting of a steamer, twice repeated, and at the same instant the cool, sour smell of the river reached his nostrils.

Behind the tavern was a row of wooden warehouses, and beyond it lay an expanse of flat, frosted, muddy nothing, marked only by the occasional chopped-about black tree-trunk, a charcoal streak in the fog, and here and there the orange glow of braziers, around which dark figures huddled, warming themselves, maybe heating soup in cans as they awaited the steamboat's arrival and the commencement of their labors.

Cyrus found himself drawn to the water, needing perhaps to reach a boundary within the formless indeterminacy of the fog. He passed among slow-moving carts and wagons, their drivers hunched in their seats, as they made their way towards the unseen shore, some empty, waiting to be filled; others laden with goods for the arriving steamer, and came to a wagon that had collapsed on its axle. Seemingly abandoned, it had a melancholy air, and he took care to pass it by on the right side. Flaming pine-knots marked out the landing-stage, and Cyrus kept away from that, making his way to the water's edge a hundred yards or so along to the right. He came on it unexpectedly, for there was no noise and there was no bank. It was oily and rippled only slightly, and in the fog there was no clue visible as to how wide it was, just a rank, raw smell of mud, and he wondered how far up it rose during the rains; whether it had flooded the streets of the town; whether buildings had collapsed; whether anyone had died. Somewhere a tern piped, and was answered. Up ahead the sun breasted the milky horizon, a pale red half-disc that was without force and illuminated nothing but itself; and from its position he realized the streets of De Bray's Town were angled on the slant, not true to the points of the compass, and that in order to run south-west from here the river must all but loop back on itself, rather than merely curve round the town as he had assumed it would, and then he thought of its name: the Nooseneck. He turned away from the water, wondering if it might be to his advantage to wait for the steamer to dock and its passengers disembark, and find safety in the dispersing, multifarious crowd.

Maybe. Only if the fog sticks around, though.

He wandered over to one of the groups standing round the braziers, and once he could see for sure they were all black folks, he approached them. Wordlessly they moved round and made room for him to warm his hands. A drop of condensation formed on his nose, and he wiped it away. Someone else hawked and spat.

Empress'll come in late today, someone, a man, said.

If it come in at all, said another.

Why's that, then?

On account of they don't wanna run aground in this.

River's high though, an the stage is lit.

They could come in. Pilot knows the channels pretty good.

Snags snag, though, an sandbanks shift.

Thas true.

Mos likely they'll wait out the fog.

Uh-huh. An then we gets a scoldin for bein tardy gettin back.

That Mas Klein a motherfucker fo sho.

Uh-huh.

Cyrus made his way from brazier to brazier, listening to the talk, of which there was generally little, and saying nothing himself. The fog thinned in the lightening upper sky but remained a milky blanket down below. The steamboat, drawing closer, hooted again, and after a while he could hear the thud of her engines and the creak of her paddles, and see two chimneys poking up in parallel out of the fog, straight and black and gouting smoke; and it seemed that, as those waiting had predicted, she had come to a halt midstream, the pilot content to burn fuel so as not to be carried backwards by the current until the dangerously obscuring fog-layer dispersed, and so the engines continued to pound.

As he drew nearer to the jetty, which he had to pass to be on his way, Cyrus saw by the light of the pine-knots set about it that adjoining it was a row of single-story wooden huts. In their windows lamps were lit – offices he supposed, and therefore white men would be inside; and here carts, wagons and carriages were assembled, and more were arriving, in the main going at a crawl to avoid collisions in the fog. A large, hand-somely-equipped coach, pulled by four dappled grays, blink-ered and with high white plumes bouncing on their foreheads, rolled by faster than most, forcing him to jump back or be knocked down. He crossed quickly behind it, and was passing into the pale formlessness beyond when a voice, a white man's voice, called from another direction, You boy, and he could tell as if struck between the shoulder-blades that the voice was aimed at him.

Cyrus forced himself to turn without any trace of hesitation or reluctance, slackening his features and emptying his eyes as he did so. Yassuh, he said. He saw only a vague dark silhouette.

Where you goin, the shape demanded.

Call o nature, suh.

The man came a few steps forward, revealing himself as thin and of middle height. He wore a bowler hat, gray gloves and a checked brown coat that hung to mid-calf. A long gray scarf was wrapped around his neck, and in his hand was a stout, iron-shod hickory with a lead knob for a handle that he held head-down like a club. His gray eyes were red-rimmed and his lips, beneath a nicotine-yellowed walrus moustache, pursed in distaste at Cyrus' answer. Behind him stood a cart on which goods were piled high and roped down beneath a canvas cover. Two strongly-built black men of around Cyrus' age stood by the cart wearing only cotton shirts and pants, their shoulders hunched against the cold, though glancing down Cyrus saw they at least had shoes to wear, and one had a short red scarf knotted round his neck.

Confound your nature, the white man said. Whoever heard of a nigger with propriety? Help my boys get them hogsheads off and bring em to the jetty quick-smart.

Gots to get back to my fly, suh, Cyrus said. My massah spectin me to be waitin fo him when the boat comes in, an the mare needs humorin or she acts up.

God-damn your idle hide, the white man said, and God-damn your mare. It won't take but a quarter-hour. Then, in a more placatory tone he added, It'll be done before they dock, easy. Your master won't miss you. I'll see you don't get whipped fo it.

Yassuh, Cyrus said, trying to appear content to help with the unloading of the wagon. The other two were already untying the ropes. The white man stood to one side and took out a cigar-stump but did not light it, watching as Cyrus helped them tug off the cover to reveal hogsheads and tobacco-barrels packed in tight together, maybe thirty in number and stacked two high. It took two men to lift each hogshead down – they were filled with cider, one of the other black men told Cyrus – but thereafter one man on his own could rotate it on its iron-rimmed base the short distance to the bottom of the steps that led up to the jetty, the farther end of which remained lost in the fog. The barrels of tobacco were smaller and could be lifted singly, then wrangled along in the same manner.

After about half the load had been brought down to the jetty the white man wandered over to one of the offices and disappeared inside. The moment the door closed behind him, one of the men Cyrus was working with, the one without a scarf, turned to him and said, Go.

What?

This ain't what it looks like. Next is he'll get you carryin them barrels on board. Then down to the hold. An then the Cap'n'll lock you in, an fore you know it you'll be pickin cotton way down south an dead in a year.

Cyrus nodded, wrestled the hogshead he had been struggling along with round so it stood lined up with the others by the jetty-steps, and headed back towards the wagon as if to collect the next barrel. The other black man was waiting there and watched him as he reached the wagon and kept going, but said and did nothing. The instant the curtains of the fog had closed behind him, Cyrus began to run. All before him was white opacity, however, and he had gone barely fifty feet when he heard up ahead a hissing rumble and then a heavy thud. Perplexed, he slowed to a walk, peering into the frustrating obscurity, wary but determined to keep going. There were no lights or fires on this side of the jetty. To his left a spikily-wooded, mist-tangled and steep-sided hillside emerged, and directly ahead something large and black and angled loomed up in parallel to it, barring his way: a great black flume, or that was the nearest he could come to naming it, though through it no water flowed; but as he watched a great canvas-wrapped bale came slithering down fast, making a dry snake-belly sound, slowing somewhat as the gradient gentled; and it passed in front of him and disappeared in the direction of the river.

The pressin mill, he thought. Here arriving cotton bales, and, he supposed, bales of other things such as tobacco, were compressed still further, so as to take up less space in the holds of the boats. Drawing nearer, he saw the flume was propped up in segments by a procession of timber frames and cross-beams, buttresses and braces, but that there was space enough beneath them for a man to get through. With only a little awkward clambering he passed under the flume and went on, keeping the shore just within view to his right. Several other bales rumbled down behind him, and he heard fog-muffled voices calling to each other, and supposed the bales were being received and wrangled aside, in anticipation of the riverboat's arrival.

A little way on he came to a fence bounding what he took to be a rice-paddy, for though it was at that season nothing but muddy and bare, it ran away at a level slightly below that of the river. Cyrus followed the fence along, away from the unending curve of the Nooseneck's shore, heading back inland. After passing several fallow fields he reached a road that by its width, and the depth of the wheel-ruts sliced into its surface, was of consequence, and therefore surely the one he was seeking. Away from the river the mist was less dense, though it still lay thickly among the underbrush. Somewhere a rooster crowed – tardily, for it was now an hour past dawn. Looking round, Cyrus saw the road ran back between two hills; the rivermost one, topped by the pressing mill, seeming to be a sort of headland or bluff, its taller inland neighbor the beginning of a ridge; and as he looked the crowns of both were struck by the rising sun and gleamed amber and gold, and the sky above was a clear, pale blue.

Cyrus turned his back on the town and the hills and went on. Emboldened by the letters of conduct James Rose had written for him, and having no knowledge of the surrounding country, he decided to keep to the road, which at that hour, likely due to the delay in the steamer's docking, was wholly free of traffic, those coming to meet the ship having arrived already, and none yet departed. The road ran flat and straight for close on a mile, and here and there, on both sides and set back among the trees, were single-story farmhouses of rough timber. There were lights in their windows, and in their yards fowls squawked. Somewhere a pig squealed and grunted; an unseen someone was chopping firewood with an axe. Cyrus passed orchards of tidily-pruned pecan and apricot trees, in this season bare-branched and fruitless, and thought of summer, and plenitude, and lack. By a barn with a door that hung loose on one hinge he saw a mound of frost-ruined, wrinkled pumpkins, and the mist was thin enough now that the sun brought a sparkle to their orange rinds, and to everything above ankle-height, and a pastel world of ochres, umbers and cadmiums was revealed to him, and the cloudless sky above seemed soft and without cruelty. His stomach told him it was time to eat, but he kept on, wanting to get away from the habitations of men before breaking his fast. The farmsteads grew more infrequent, and the last, though he did not realize it was the last until he had gone a good mile farther on, was derelict and overgrown: an outlier, reclaimed by the relentless woods. But to Cyrus the crowding trees held a wild welcome.

In another hour or so he was amongst forest so wholly un-cultivated that only the road asserted the existence of man and

his works. Here his compass told him it turned a shade south of
west and began to slant up a steep hillside thick with cedars. He
had left the last of the mist below him, and everything now had
a glinting sharpness and seemed preternaturally hard-edged, as
if cataracts had been abruptly sliced from his eyes.

God's cataracts, he thought, taking a moment to look up at
the endless azure nothing above him. Fog an cloud an swamp
vapor.

An what do He see?

An what don't He see?

A world without mercy.

A world without end, amen.

Sound now carried with a clarity that had been lacking
lower down, and this was reassuring: even the hooves of a lone
horse would be audible long before it reached him. Above him
the bone of the road bent back on itself like an elbow, then a
wrist, zigzagging up the hillside at an angle he guessed would
be barely tolerable to carriages, though it continued well-
maintained, its outer edges here and there saved from slippage
by split rails driven in in upright rows. At one of the hairpins a
spring tumbled among emerald-mossed rocks, and by it a fallen
oak made for a pleasant seat, so he drank all the water in his
flask, refilled it there, and sat and rested a while. Afterwards he
went a short way into the woods and opened his bowels; then
he went on. Though there were, he did not doubt, patrollers on
this as on every road, they would have no reason to be searching for him – the killer runaway, Tyler's nigger – here; and the
passes in his pocket gave him a name to go by, a face to wear,
and a claim to walk the road by day unmolested; to ask for
directions should the need arise, even of white folks, for his
name and face were doing the white man's work.

Still, when he heard a carriage on the road above him, rather than risk being seen, he withdrew beneath the cover of the
trees and crouched low among the ghost-weeds, re-emerging
only once it had gone by and turned the bend below him, and
vanished from sight. It had been a stagecoach much like James
Rose's, gloss black and yellow-trimmed, with bags and cases
piled unsteady high and tethered on its roof, though the driver
had been a Negro, light-complected and wearing a derby hat.
By now the sun was high, and flashing through the bare crowns

of the cypress trees. Its brightness lifted Cyrus' heart and he felt hope, and it seemed a fine and natural thing that once upon a time men had worshipped the solar orb, though he considered it surely futile to ask anything of it: to pray to it as if it might care; as if it might be kind any more than burning coals are kind. The frost was gone from things now, though there was in the immobile air no warmth, the glinting sun proving no more generative of heat than gems in a white woman's tiara.

Three slanted hairpins later he reached what was evidently the brow of the hill, for here, though the crowded trees contin-ued to obscure his view, the road began once more to run straight and principally level – albeit with dips and undulations – even slightly downhill; and so he knew he was looking along the backbone of a declining ridge, and that his way now ran like a spine's groove between the brown-ribbed woods. Seeing a greater distance was at once a reassurance and a source of anxiety to Cyrus, for just as he could see others farther off, so too he could be seen; and for a black man to be observed leaving a path as a white person approached would be a clear trigger for suspicion and inquiry. And so Cyrus went on faster than before, with frequent glances behind him, and a gathering anxiety.

He had gone only a little way when a cart that had been concealed in a dip in the road rose up before him. Drawn by two mules, its wheels turned slower than the passing seasons. The driver was a thin, elderly black man with white stubble on his narrow lower jaw, dull, rheumy eyes and stoved-in cheeks denoting toothlessness. A straw-flecked gray blanket was draped around his hunched and spindly shoulders. Next to him sat a fleshy, ruddy-faced white man in a dull blue top hat, a dull blue overcoat and shiny black boots. On the back of the cart a large boar was penned in a wooden cage, facing forwards.

Cyrus felt the white man's eyes on him sharp as chisels set against soft wood, awaiting the mallet blow. Reckoning it would be wisest to face the man's suspicions down, when the cart drew level with him Cyrus stepped aside from the road, took off his hat and, holding it before his breast, bobbed his head and said as innocently as he could manage, Good day to you, massa.

The white man gestured to the driver, who flicked the reins, and the mules dawdled to a stop. The old man took not the slightest interest in Cyrus: his occluded eyes were almost crossed, and if focused, focused only on the mules' backsides and no further: the limit of his twilit world and its fading possibilities.

His jaw moving cuddishly, the white man looked Cyrus over, tobacco-juice staining the corners of his mouth in glinting brown threads as he did so. One of the mules' ears twitched and swiveled, and it flicked its tail, and the boar grunted in a satisfied-sounding way.

Could you tell me how far it is to Honeycomb, suh, Cyrus asked. My massa sent me on a errand an I'm spose to be there by nightfall.

A fair step yet, the white man said. What is your master's name?

Mistuh Hart, suh.

And he trusts you to roam about so?

I spose so, suh. He gave me a pass, Cyrus said, not producing it.

The white man looked at him – into him – and continued to chew. Cyrus tried to keep opacity from his eyes; to seem transparent, and conceal from the white man that he had over the last few days become less penetrable, less knowable, even if he himself scarcely understood the transformation he was undergoing; just that it was somehow to do with being on the right road, and was in part the consequence of an accretion of allies in the face of what the world seemed to be; what this white man and so many white men and indeed white women wanted it to be. And too he kept his mind away from all thoughts of the knife in his pocket, and the shallow grave he might improvise in the woods nearby; and how the cart's driver would continue to sit as though carved of bone, an effigy for his master's tomb as Cyrus bled the white man out like a hog at slaughtering time.

His eyes locked on Cyrus', the white man turned his head slightly and spat on the ground close to Cyrus' foot. Droplets bounced up brown from the impacted dirt (not easy to dig in, then, and Cyrus had no tools) and speckled his pants-cuff. This stretch is known for bears, the white man said. You seen any?

Nawsuh.

You ever seen a bear?

Nawsuh, I never did.

They look clumsy but they can run faster'n a man. Or a nigger. An they can climb trees. Best keep to the road an go hasty.

Yassuh. Thank you, suh.

Hart's nigger, huh.

Yassuh.

The white man's eyes crawled over Cyrus' face like beetles, seeking in the way of burrowing things an entrance. After a long study he nodded as if satisfied, though perhaps he had merely reached the limits of his interest, and the driver twitched the reins once more, and the mules and, with a slight jolt the cart, started forward.

As it passed him by, the boar eyed Cyrus in a sly sidelong way, as if the spirit of its owner was in some way inside it; a familiar, as it were, or a tumorous extrusion of its master's fleshly excesses that had acquired a measure of independence. It was bristly and, save for random patches of dusty charcoal, white as lard, and its testicles were large as twin udders.

Cyrus replaced his hat on his head and went on, resisting the urge to look back in case he should be observed doing so and by such an action excite suspicion. He wondered whether there were indeed bears in the woods around him, uneasy as he had not been before about the possible presence and proximity of wild and predatory animals, for even dogs, he knew, could in sufficient numbers take a man down. And he pictured the white man in the blue coat turning the pages of the newspaper in De Bray's Town that evening and jabbing a plump finger at the description of Cyrus in the Runaways Wanted column, though he had no reason to think that was the man's destination; indeed it was likely not, for surely he was either going to, or returning from, a nearby farm for the purpose of breeding a well-considered sow.

A number of coaches and carriages passed him as he trudged along, going in both directions, driven by coachmen white and colored, and each time he stepped aside from the road and removed his hat and waited to be addressed, but being commercial conveyances, and their drivers and passengers wishing no delay, they did not so much as slacken their speed, instead spinning past him as fast as the condition of the road allowed. Cyrus alone was on foot, and this began to trouble him, suggesting as it did that the next town, and therefore the possibility of food and shelter, was a long way off yet.

The road stretched out before him wearisomely, running on level and with no end in sight, and his legs felt heavy, and his heels, which had until now done no more than ache, began to pain him again. On either side of the road tracts of tussocky grass and underbrush began to push back the gray-brown walls of the forest. Eventually Cyrus turned aside and, finding a stump to sit on, removed his boots and retied the calico strips, which had worked their way down so as to form an uncomfortable ridge and permit the crudely-finished leather interiors to once more chafe his raw and blistered skin. This readjustment eased the pain some.

The sun was brushing the tree-tops as he made his way back to the road, and the temperature was beginning to fall, so, tired as he was, and despite the lack of any visible destination, he made himself go on. Now no vehicle passed. A mile further along a harsh cry made him look up: ahead and off to the left he saw, circling above four pine-trees as it were columnarly, three buzzards, and the pines rose up through the bare-branched cedars that surrounded them like church-spires above a skeletal town, and the buzzards it seemed were being drawn down slowly, as if they were the answers to prayers, welcome or otherwise.

Only mean one thing, Cyrus thought, but when he came level with the pines he found himself unable to resist turning aside to see what there was to see. At that pellucid, chilling hour all was hushed and still, and wading through the brittle weeds as he descended the sideways tilt of the hill his awareness of the crackle of his footsteps, of the fabric swish of his thighs against each other, and the popping catch of brambles on his coat-hem, was heightened, and he thought of foxes' ears pricking, rabbits' noses twitching. There was no track here of any sort, just last season's dead growth, packed close in nature's baling, and though the pines implied a focal point, they did not in fact mark a clearing or any place in particular.

Yet, as if waiting for him, there it was: a body, lying on its side. One of the buzzards was perched on its shoulder; another stood on the ground nearby, its wings spread out flexingly before it, flight-feathers displayed like tobacco leaves on the drying board, and both birds were larger than any Cyrus had ever seen. At his approach they turned their heads in unison, and their watchful, unblinking profiles made Cyrus recall the masthead of the newspaper James Rose had shown him, the newspaper in which runaways were listed, and rewards, and punishments for their assistance posted; and there was in their cycloptic eyes no more of feeling than in that printed masthead, and certainly no fear; and so Cyrus at first made no movement to drive them off, but only observed.

The body was that of a black man, severely emaciated, in rags barely protective of decency, and locked around his head was an iron cage, and from the neck of the cage extended spikes a foot in length, one at each cardinal. At the back of the cage, for the dead man lay on his side, a padlock was visible, and at the front a metal spike that had been welded to the frame on its interior surface was wedged into his mouth. Around this, dried blood had clotted black. Though the cold had doubtless slowed the spoiling of the flesh, he had died not long ago, it seemed, for though the birds had taken his eyes he had been little mauled by critters: his toes and fingers and even his penis and testicles were still intact. Cyrus could not guess his age: younger than he had at first glance seemed, perhaps; maybe only in his twenties: but the stomach below the ridged hoop of the rib-cage was tautly convex, a subsided grave within the boneyard of his body, and the skin pale brown, inelastic parchment.

Starved, Cyrus thought. Ran an got lost an starved.

No: starved rather'n go back.

In a sudden fury he looked about him, picked up a broken length of branch and threw it at the bird that perched on the dead man's shoulder. It hop-flapped off, but a few feet only; the other did not move at all. Defeated by their indifference, and knowing there was no sense in expending his living energy on the dead, however strongly he longed to at the least free the man's head from its cruel and degrading constraint, Cyrus left them and returned to the road. Dread was now thick in him again, and the weight of his mission heavy upon him; and the fear that Abednego had met such an end, that all this was futile, gave rise in him to the sudden thought, I could turn back. Head north. The night gon be clear: the Star be up there bright; an by day, or if clouds come, I gots me a compass. I knows some of the land round Hart now, an where the north road is from there. An I gots me a pass.

But still he went on; and the sun sank slowly behind the fretwork of the trees, and the road ran dully on as the woodland grayed about him, and the sky paled, and the stars began to prick as through a sere blue cloth cast over the glass globe of a lit lamp, and the road continued deserted. He drank the remaining bottle of cider as he walked, and its sweet fermented warmth gave him encouragement even as the temperature sank with a rapidity that was palpable and his breath turned to mist and the tips of his fingers grew numb. There was no sight of any human habitation: no bounded fields; no lanes; no build-ings; no distant chimney-smoke or far-off glow of fire or lamplight; just the road, vanishing rapidly into obscurity. How far had James Rose said it was to Honeycomb? Fifty miles, Cyrus thought; and how many of those fifty miles he had now walked he had no way of knowing; nor did he in any case know how accurate James Rose had been in his reply. The tempera-ture continued to fall.

Gon freeze.

The thought came upon him sudden, as undeniable as reve-lation, and so did its corollary: Gots to find me some shelter, or make me a fire, or die. An there ain't no shelter. Thas bad. But it means ain't no-one out here to see no fire, nor smoke neither, an that's good; an the brush is dry enough up here to make a blaze an not a smother.

To his right the land rose on the slant, and where the furze beneath the trees seemed less dense he struck out in search of something that might approximate a clearing out of sight of the road. Soon enough he came upon a shallow dip beneath an old, dead cedar from which he could clear the brush with little difficulty, shoving it to one side and gathering it into a springy heap that would serve him for a mattress, in doing so laying bare a round of earth sufficiently large for him to set a fire that would not spread. Dry-rotted fragments of branches were readily to hand, and above fistfuls of hastily-snapped twigs he built a shaky structure of them, into the midst of which he pushed twists of dry leaves, and in the face of rapidly-rising desperation, for his fingers were now so numb it was hard to strike the flint, and the air, though still, was cruel and turning crueler, he eventually managed to get a spark to catch. He cupped the tiny, tentative, yellow flame like a new-hatched chick, blowing on it gently as if to warm it, husbanding it until the twigs around it caught. Then he could take a breath on his own behalf, straighten his back and push cramp from his chest. With a craftsman's care he added more branches here and there, and the fire blazed and the cedarwood popped and crackled and warmed his hands and face and the front of him, and he could feel the cold deepening at his back like some dread thing drawing near.

He took the knife from its pocket and the hen from his knapsack, slit the bird open below the breastbone and drew its guts, scraped a hole in the dirt with the heel of his boot, dropped them in and covered the hole over, then roughly plucked the feathers. Lastly he cut off its head, and then he set the body to roast among the burning branches, where by chance they wigwamed to form a supporting tripod. In an afterthought he pushed the two wizened sweet potatoes into the glowing wood-ash, to bake overnight and be ready to eat on the road tomorrow. He sipped a little water from his flask and waited for the bird to cook. There was no wind, and he heard and sensed the presence of no animal, large or small, in the woods about him. He tilted his head back and looked up at the orange-underlit, interlocking cedar-boughs and judged the main bough to be climbable, which was some comfort, though the white man had said bears could climb and too it might be brittle and break beneath his weight; and beyond them the stars were sharp and pure against the black night sky, and he breathed deeply, filling his lungs with a mixture of the clean but bitter and the woodsmokey warm, and pushed out his chest and, exhaling, arched and stretched out his back.

Sparks an stars, he thought: the unity of all things.

Once he judged the chicken cooked he hooked it from the fire and ate it so hungrily that the clear and spilling liquid grease burnt his lips. After gnawing the carcass close, cracking the larger bones and sucking out their marrow, licking the now-gelid grease from his fingers, and urinating at the cardinals to deter predators from approaching while he slept, he built up the fire and, huddling on his bed of brush and twigs, closed eyes now twitching from tiredness and woodsmoke. Lying facing the flames he felt the heat on his eyelids and forehead, on his nose and cheeks, and as the sweat beaded there he loosened his scarf.

In the dream he was elevated higher than any building he could conceive of, and was looking down. It was a lambent hour, dawn or dusk, he could not tell, without direct light but somehow luminous, and tiny black figures were making their way across a snow-covered terrain, all moving in one direction, not hurrying but determined; small and slight as bird-prints, vulnerable but resilient, and in the dream he knew they were nearing the borders of some free state, and that two of those figures were Abednego and himself, and somewhere close behind were pursuers with torches.

He woke to a frosted dawn and cold ashes. A mist tangled in the branches above his head like gauze veils around the heads of horned and black-boned brides. Every joint in his body had seized up in the night, he was twisted like a cripple, his fingertips were filled with burning ice, his throat and nostrils were parched and raw, but he was alive. The sky, which seemed little higher than the misted tree-tops, was serried with gray rows of cloud, and in the air was a dry, cindery smell that told him snow was on its way.

After raking the now-cooked sweet potatoes out of the ruins of the fire with a stick and putting them in his knapsack he stirred about in the blue-white ashes till he found an ember winking in its sleep. This he fed with crumbled dry leaves until he got a small but bright blaze going. The little smoke it made brushed up into the dun sky and would surely not be seen even close by. He warmed himself before it until his hands were once again his own and the worst of the aching had left him, hawked and spat and drank some water from his flask. Then he kicked the fire apart, heeled earth over it, and returned to the road.

As on the previous day, to begin with it was wholly deserted, then stages began to pass by, first towards him, then overtaking him from behind, and as before there was no interest shown in him, a lone Negro, trudging along in plain sight on some errand for a master too hard-hearted to supply him with even a mule. There was little wind, and the sky above was a colorless fallow field reflected upwards, as it were, and to a fieldhand as burdensome and crowding to the spirit. The road, having run for some time level, began once more gently to head downhill. It curved eastward in what eventually revealed itself to be a long loop, and after perhaps an hour Cyrus was afforded, for the first time since he left De Bray's Town, a panorama.

To the right of the road, to the west, deep woods predominated, gray and brown, running unbroken into what may have been hills or equally low-lying cloud, for there was no clear horizon, just a formless, uneasy admixture of the two. Nearer to, a lead-colored lake quivered dully, and beyond the lake a wide river ran, whether fast or slow he could not tell, for he saw no craft moving on its surface, nor evidence of human presence of any sort. He thought of the tribes whose land this once was, who had fought the white invaders and been killed or driven off, forced ever further south and west, declivities hellwards as it seemed to him then, and the strange insight came to him as he stood there looking out that there was a revelation in that: that things do not ever remain unchanged; that nothing is fixed, good or bad; and all things end except perhaps the turning world itself, and that in that truth there was hope, however high the bodies were piled, however loud the gaping skulls cried out for restitution: savage hope, yes, but within it the pitiless possibility of overturning everything that seemed fixed and eternal.

As he scanned the skyline he heard, a long way off, rifle-shots: hunters, he presumed. He listened intently for a while, but no more shots came. He thought of the man with the caged head and the dull knife-blade in his mouth, and of Abednego, and Abednego's hand in his, and then the first snowflake kissed his cheek, dry as ash, and a breeze began to blow. He looked up: overhead the sky was shifting fast, the white scumbling over the gray and there were undertones of ocher too, curious soil-echoes. He turned from the view and went on, disquieted.

The snow at first blew drily about him, and stingingly into his eyes, and seemed disinclined to settle, and the road once more sank among the trees, cutting off a view that was in any case rapidly being swallowed up by the descending whiteness. As it snaked its way down through the vanishing landscape cedars gave way to oaks and then pines, and the wind was funneled behind Cyrus as if he was in a corridor, and the snow continued to not so much fall as swirl about him in intensifying flurries and soon he could see no more than thirty feet in any direction. Now no carriages passed, no carts, no riders; no patrollers, and the wild beasts too would surely keep to their lairs and burrows, and still there was nothing of the works of man about him, though he was uneasily aware that these need be set back only a little way among the trees for him to miss them, for the snow, which was by this time beginning to cover the ground and drift lazily around his ankles, might obscure smaller and unposted paths and turnings aside. His feet were leaden and his pelvis and the sockets of his thigh-bones ached. He had come across no stream since drinking the last of his water and his mouth was dry, and any snow that blew in seemed disinclined to melt and more likely to catch at the back of his throat and make him cough and choke. Under his breath he muttered, One mo blow, lift that hoe, one mo blow, trumpet blow, daylight gone, day's work done – a field-holler, and he felt the other hands with him then, Zeke and Lil Joe and Nate, Solomon and Samuel and Joseph, the living and the dead, and was lifted up some, and the wind hard at his back drove him on also.

How many hours had passed beneath that lightless sky and in the tiring confusion of the blowing, cinder-dry snow he did not know when he saw the figure up ahead, black and swathed and barely discernible, and he determined he must catch it up. Even as he reached his decision it vanished behind a striating white flurry of especial violence, then, as he squinted anxiously, emerged again, and at sight of it he tried to run in its direction. The snow was by now lumpy on the ground, six inches deep, a wearying drag on each lifting of his feet; yet that would be as true for the person he was pursuing, though of a certain unless they too were lost they would be less tired than he and might yet get ahead, and so he stumbled onward hastily, his heart thudding, his throat tightening, once again aware his life might depend on this. But despite his best efforts the round, bundled figure did indeed vanish into the white opacity ahead of him, and Cyrus, feeling the whole landscape about him disintegrate into a disorientating, rotating kaleidoscope, fought back sudden tears, and despair lanced his heart. Head down he plodded on, because to stop was to die. Must of come from somewhere, he muttered to himself. An close to, to be on foot that way. But had the figure turned aside without him seeing? Had Cyrus missed the turning and was now blundering on along a road that would end only in death? Then the thought crept up on him: the shape weren't right.

That weren't no man.

Maybe it was a bear.

There was nothing to do but keep going. The road now seemed to be cutting downwards on a slant, and steeply. After a time the wind swung round and Cyrus sensed rather than saw the trees and hillside fall away to his right, exposing him to its increased velocity. There was a depth to the whiteness that told of vast spaces, and somewhere within it, low down, was a dirty yellow smudge that, past the plummeting ocherous switchback of the road, and way out beyond briefly-glimpsed ink-etched pine turrets, might have been the dying sun. As Cyrus looked it closed its eye and was gone, and the world shifted and sank down, and, sensing a sudden presence looming behind him, he turned sharply.

Chapter Twelve

The building was large, tall and white, clapboarded, peak-roofed, and fronted by a broad, balustraded verandah reachable by a short flight of wooden steps, below which the brick foundations were boxed in with lattice-board to which were tethered snow-burdened briars. Its windows, each the height of a man, faced the whirling, skirling abyss, but were shuttered, and no light was visible within. Regardless, and regardless of the spasm of unease he felt at approaching directly an entrance through which he would expect to be forbidden to pass, Cyrus climbed the steps and hurried up to the front door, the decorative porch of which extended forward sufficiently to offer some shelter from both snow and wind. Within the porch benches were set on either side, and finding the most shielded corner, Cyrus dropped down onto one of them to catch his breath, taking a quick moment to brush the accumulated snow from his shoulders and hat as he did so, to prevent it soaking through, resistant though it seemed to melting in temperatures now surely below zero, and his body heat, such as it was, withdrawing to his core. Beyond the porch the snow swirled and eddied, but little of it was carried in over the threshold.

Contemplating the door, Cyrus saw it was solid and solidly-framed, plainly not easy to force or break down; and he could not risk cracking a shoulder-bone or foot or ankle in the attempt. Flanking it were leaded, gothic-arched windows inset with red stained glass, but these were too narrow for even a child to climb in through. He looked out at the snow grimly, wondering if it was worth sitting a while longer in hopes it would start to fall less heavily, or even stop, before he began what would have to be his next task: working his way round the outside of the building in search of a possible point of entry; for to remain outside would be death. He reached out and scraped some snow from where it had accumulated like a sugar-cone on the end of a handrail in order to moisten his mouth a little, then ate the remaining sweet potato, in small bites and without pleasure, swallowing being uncomfortable, and the snow making his back teeth ache. It was disquieting how rapidly his body was deteriorating, and this despite his having had some luck with food while in the company of James Rose: his meals at the inn had been better by far than the slave rations on Tyler. He thought of the leftover bread he had been too timid to take from the dish, that had been carried away and likely fed to hogs, and irritation and self-loathing spasmed within him.

Above Honeycomb is a spa hotel, James Rose had said, and perhaps this shuttered building was that hotel, and the hamlet of Honeycomb somewhere below, lost in the confusion of rushing snow and rapidly-descending dusk. He wondered whether the healing waters were to be drunk or swum in, and considered that, if swum in, the hotel might be shut up in the winter months, for who would choose to swim in icy water? Yet surely there would be a watchman set against thieves, even so. Perhaps the watchman was not in residence, instead living nearby – in which case he would likely not come up on such a night as this.

Could go on down, Cyrus thought. But if he was wrong, if there was nothing but more road below, and wind and snow and the swallowing dark, he would be worse off by far; and if he was right, to knock on the doors of white-owned farms was another sort of peril, pass or no pass, and his passes were, after all, forged. No, he would not go down, not without trying to get in.

Snow ain't abatin none.

He forced himself to stand and leave the shelter of the porch, and as he stepped out onto the verandah the wind cut across him like a knife.

Be less fierce round back, maybe.

Descending the steps, he turned left and made his way along the front, keeping close in, the wind buffeting his back. The house was built on a jetty-like base-frame, and across the road the ground fell away steeply: evidently it stood on a bluff. The hillside rose up behind, invisible but he could sense it.

Back'll be easier for gettin in windows.

Turning the corner he worked his way along the side of the building. Though he was confronted by nothing but more shuttered windows, the rise of the land meant they at least became easier to reach up to the further back he went. The wind blew as harshly here as it had out front, for the hotel looked out across the country on this side too, though there was no verandah or balcony from which to take in the now-hidden view. The track Cyrus traversed was narrow, and at one point a near-snow-buried flight of stone steps descended steeply to his right, and he glimpsed, perched on the hillside below, a small dome supported by stone pillars. Open to the elements on all sides it offered no shelter, and so he kept on, reaching up to tug at shutters as he passed them, but none yielded.

Rounding the next corner he finally escaped the direct line of the wind. The back wall of the hotel was without windows at ground level, and the pines crowded down from the hillside above and pressed in close against it. There were no outbuildings here, though surely the place must have a stable and storage sheds and suchlike somewhere, and a back door for servants – perhaps round the other side, or further along, through the trees and set back from the main structure. Snow-obscured rubbish was heaped along the wall; beyond, the pines blocked his way.

And then the back of Cyrus' neck began to prickle. He peered forward, squinting through the blue-gray confusion of falling snow and onrushing dusk and saw that, yes, something was there, in amongst the close-packed black trunks, something dark, round, large and now bounding towards him: a bear, coming on fast, scattering snow from the laden lower branches in percussive bursts as it struck them. Cyrus turned and ran.

This was a new sort of terror. He was already bone-weary, and his little knife would be of no use even if his numbed fingers could hold it, and the threat of it had no power to deter a brainless adversary. There was no way into the building on this side, and perhaps not on the other side either; nor time to force his way in, even should there be a chance to do so. Yet leaving the hotel offered no hope or advantage, and so he ran back the way he had come, hackles high as those of a hound lanced through with lightning, stumbling, his thudding heart and gasping breath and sloughing feet in the snow obscuring all sounds of pursuit, and he wanted to yell and so he yelled and did not even throw a glance behind him as he recrossed the front of the building and, refusing the trap of the porch, staggered round the far corner and along the left-hand side to find at first only more shuttered windows and no point of ingress.

In panic, and from the sudden thought that noise might deter his pursuer somewhat, he thumped the clapboards with his fist as he ran; and then all at once he was passing between the side of the main building and another wooden structure, staggering along an alley narrow enough to perhaps at least briefly slow the bear, then banging through a high plank gate without latch or lock or bolt. Now in a yard enclosed on three sides by windowless single-story sheds, and on the fourth by the hotel, and slithering on snow-covered cobbles, trapped maybe, Cyrus followed the next turn blank-minded.

Rounding the corner at full tilt he barreled fast and heavy into a man standing there holding up a lamp, the light from which the falling snow had obscured, and they collapsed in a tangled heap with a cry and the lamp shattered, flinging burning oil across the cobbles and spattering their coats with flames, and both men rolled impulsively in the snow even as Cyrus shouted, Bear! They's a bear! And the other man understood at once and quickly he and Cyrus helped each other up, brushing at each others' coats to ensure the flames were extinguished, at the same time darting looks in the direction Cyrus had run from, and there it was, black head angular, designed for its business as is a tool or weapon, looking at them round the corner of the main building, held back perhaps by the scattered, burning oil, though that was already guttering in the melting, puddling snow.

Up the steps, the other man said thickly, a black man and that was all Cyrus perceived of him then; and Cyrus followed him in a breathless scramble up a narrow side-stair to a screen door six feet above, and they crashed through it onto a small external balcony, a raised porch as it were, and Cyrus turned and watched the bear round the corner and pad toward them, its head down and wobbling from side to side as if it could not see but only smell them, and the other man dug in his pocket for a key to the door that would let them into the building proper. He got it out but dropped it and cursed and fell to his knees. The bear reached the bottom of the steps and looked up with black eyes devoid of emotion: instinct and appetite embodied. Nearer to, Cyrus could see it was large, heavy as eight men maybe. Hesitantly it placed its forepaws on the first step, and Cyrus watched the black claws extrude like knives pushed through fabric, and he felt the weight and strength of it. Its fear of a habitation of men would not last long, he thought, and even as the thought came to him the bear heaved itself up another step. He moved back and swung the screen door closed, flimsy though it was, and leant against it while the other man scrabbled about for the key in the shadows. Cyrus glanced about him for anything that might be a weapon, but there was nothing.

God damn it, the other muttered, but now he had the key, and a moment later the inner door was unlocked, and they hurried over the threshold into the enveloping darkness within, and the man slammed and locked the door behind them, and the lock and the door were solid and the frame seemed sound. Their chests heaving, they stood in the dark and listened, but did not hear the bear come any further up the steps. After a while the screen door creaked and banged, but that might have been the wind, and was not followed by any sound of furtive moving about, or snuffling, or clawing.

It break it down, Cyrus asked once he had mastered his breathing, keeping his voice low.

Naw, the other said. Can't get the run-up. At this Cyrus relaxed a little. Looks like we stuck here fo a bit, the man added.

I ain't got nowhere better to go, Cyrus said. Not in this. You the watchman here?

The other nodded. He was bundled up in a bulky coat and a coonskin cap, the tail of which switched as he moved about the shadowy room, rummaging in drawers for a candle and tinderbox, and he was evidently familiar with the placing of things, for he soon found them. Once lit, the candle revealed a spacious kitchen with pots, pans, ladles and spoons hung up orderly on hooks, crocks on dressers, two ceramic sinks, a large and dully-gleaming black-leaded stove set in a brick fireplace with a full coal-scuttle nearby; and in its middle a long, well-scrubbed pine table with eight plain chairs set about it. The cold air was still and there was no smell of cooking, nor of foodstuffs, nor coal or woodsmoke: evidently it had not been in active use for some months.

I'm Plowman, the man said as he squatted on his haunches to set a spill amongst the heaped lint and kindling that waited orderly in the stove's grate.

Thas more of a task than a name, Cyrus said.

My task till a mule took the blade over my foot, Plowman said, and Cyrus realised then that his movements, though confident, were lopsided. Lost half of it an I gots to keep one boot part-full o wood so's I can walk. This all I can do now: watch. Come over by the stove.

Two settles of carved walnut waited there. Plowman unbuttoned his coat and underneath it were layers of waistcoats and shirts, and as he shrugged them off Cyrus realized he was lean rather than stout, as he had seemed at first glance. Cyrus unbuttoned and took off his coat too, and removed his hat. Plowman kept his cap on. Head gets cold, he said off Cyrus' look, tipping coals into the stove-belly with a scoop. What's yo name, brother?

Billy. Off of Hart.

Plowman didn't seem to know the name of the plantation, nor did it interest him, and he gestured to Cyrus to pull his chair closer to the stove, which was now beginning to warm the cold, still air. His eyes were hazy, and his dourly handsome face long and angular. The wind outside set the shutters rattling.

You come up from Honeycomb, Cyrus ventured.

Uh-huh. Weren't gon bother, but Mas Elsten said he'd tawse me if I dint, blizzard or no blizzard, so I come up. Lucky for you.

Cyrus nodded. They a inn open down below?

Naw. Mas Elsten lets rooms out in his house, though, an thas big enough. He run the general sto an grog-shop too.

An this place his?

Uh huh. Pine Bluff Spa it called. Eighteen rooms fo guests an down below they's hot springs. Closed up fo winter, though.

Cyrus' fingers burned as the blood forced its way back into their tips like spring shoots through frozen soil, and Plowman watched as he bent down to clumsily unlace his snow-clogged boots and with a grunt wiggle them off his wounded feet.

Lost yo mule?

Died on me, Cyrus said, not liking to lie but wary of doing

more than mirror Plowman's assumptions until he had the measure of him, and Plowman nodded. As other discomforts receded Cyrus' thirst grew on him powerfully. I spose the well out in the back yard, he said.

Plowman nodded again, but drew a bunch of keys from his pocket, moving them round on the hoop like prayer beads on a string until he reached the one he was looking for. Beer cellar, he said, a gleam in his eyes and a small smile twitching his lips. Taking two pewter mugs from one of the dressers, he crossed to an inner door in quick, uneven steps, unlocked it and went through, and Cyrus heard him descend wooden stairs. His toes were thawing now, and his heels pulsed unpleasantly, but at least no part of him had died, as he had heard might happen once you froze right through, and was said to happen often to runaways wandering the northern states – the which rumor, taking it for propaganda, Cyrus did not believe. Plowman returned with the mugs brimming and handed one to Cyrus and, after relocking the cellar, joined him by the stove, and the two men sipped and warmed themselves, and outside night arrived and the snow continued to fall.

You been in Honeycomb long, Cyrus asked.

Since I was maybe fourteen, fifteen. The Bretts what owned me got took down by liquor an gamin, an I was sold on to Elsten bout ten years back. Ruth got – Plowman cut himself off: to talk of mothers or wives or daughters, of loved ones torn away and sold, was both futile and a pain beyond articulation, and in any case mutually understood without the raveling out of it in words. Plowman shrugged, and Cyrus did not ask more of this man, perhaps ten years his senior, who, unlike him, could not run, however driven he might be to do so. The wind rattled the shutters with especial forcefulness then, making both men look round, and Cyrus shivered even though there was no draft. They settled back into their seats.

Gots to get me to Amesburg, Cyrus said, staring at the slots in the stove-door as he had so many nights in the cabin back on Tyler, and that seemed years ago. Thas in Blaze County. An then on to a estate call Saint Hall, you heard of it?

That's a ways, said Plowman, and he was looking at the stove too. Ninety miles, I reckons, maybe mo. This here is Gin County: we right on the border. Down in the valley you in

Cleaver. An then south o that is Blaze.

I hear there ain't no road.

Thas right. River'd serve you better.

What river?

Stone River.

It wild?

Naw. Wide an slow. Lotta craft on it. Take you all the way to Blaze.

Amesburg on the river?

Plowman shrugged. I reckon so. White folks what's got money come up from there in summer an they always complainin of skeeters, an skeeters mean water. Bloodsuckers complainin they gettin they blood sucked, he added, chuckling mirthlessly. Ain't that somethin?

Cyrus supped his beer. It was cool and warming at once. How I reach the river, he asked.

Down below they's a watermill on a stream. A couple miles along, the stream joins up with the river, so all you gots to do is follow the flow – they's a track on the mill side; can't miss it. They gots a landin down there, where the barges bring they goods to load onto the steamers. Get yoself there an you can follow the current on down.

Plowman did not ask why Cyrus had no proper directions, nor why he was heading south, and Cyrus volunteered no explanations: even in a closed-up house otherwise devoid of inhabitants, such talk seemed best avoided.

How'll I know Amesburg?

I never been, Plowman said. But they's a big foundry there. You hear of Amesburg rifles?

Cyrus shook his head.

Some o the best in the land, they say. Look fo smoke by day an fire by night an you won't go far wrong, I reckons.

Cyrus nodded. His stomach gurgled audibly. Plowman smiled and got up again, unlocked another door and went in – a cold store or larder this time, for he returned with a smoked ham. This he carried over to the dresser, from which he took out a tin dish and placed the ham on it. From a drawer he produced a carving knife and cut them generous slices, which he heaped on a china plate and brought over and set between them on the hearthstone. Cyrus reached down quickly and ate hungrily. Plowman ate only a little. Et earlier, he said in response to Cyrus' questioning glance.

You wanna see, Plowman asked, once Cyrus had finished, and was wiping his greasy fingers on his coat-hem.

See what?

This place. Plowman tilted his head in the direction of the hotel's interior, and Cyrus, fed and beer-warmed, nodded. Plowman drained his mug and went and found a second candle, which he lit with its fellow and set in a wooden candlestick. This he handed to Cyrus, and together they left the kitchen, Cyrus barefoot, and, holding their candles aloft, passed into a gloomy but clean passageway paneled to waist height. At the far end a door opened onto the grand hall, and the air was so still their candle-flames barely shivered as they entered it, and it was empty, and in the rooms beyond, the furniture was draped in white sheets and all seemed dreamlike. As they moved about, Cyrus and Plowman now and again caught the nimbus glow of their candles reflected in the dusty surfaces of curlicue-framed mirrors larger than doors hanging above outsize and pallid marble fireplaces; and Cyrus thought of tombs, but without unease, for here the living were merely absent, not transformed. Not resident souls. Before one of the mirrors a gilt-and-ormolu clock sat, its face the size of a dinner-plate, silent and still. To Cyrus it was an ornament, without purpose.

I'm spose to keep it wound but I don't, Plowman said. Cyrus nodded, not understanding. C'mon, now.

Plowman led him back to the hall, and Cyrus now saw that the kitchen-passage emerged from behind an imposing, red-carpeted staircase that rose to a broad balcony a full story above. Reaching its foot they looked up.

We gentry now, Plowman said, grinning; and reaching back as if to take Cyrus by the hand, but not quite doing so, in a gesture both romantic and childlike, he started up the stairs, and Cyrus followed him. The carpet was plush and soft underfoot, and the brass runners and splayed, curving handrails glinted in the candlelight as the two men ascended to the balcony, which was as wide as the hall. At back of it were four glass-paneled doors, contiguous, and on either side of them the stair split and doubled back on itself, going up to another floor, but Plowman and Cyrus passed through the doors and wandered the corridors beyond, peeping into rooms as they passed them, and finding in the main bedrooms and sometimes private sitting-rooms, their furnishings shrouded as those below had been, and one was larger than the rest.

Bridal suite, Plowman said as he opened the door and went in.

What's that, Cyrus asked, following him, thinking he meant 'sweet'.

They found themselves in a spacious sitting room. Opposite were double doors painted a pale green and beaded in gilt, and Plowman set down his candle on a dustsheeted surface and threw them open to reveal as if waiting for Cyrus and himself a vast four-poster bed. The heavy uprights were carved walnut corkscrews, the fabric of the canopy above and the bedspread below glinted with gold thread, and pale green predominated throughout the room. And Plowman did not explain, and did not need to explain, for Cyrus understood by the bed's width and grandeur that this was where those who were treated as human came to celebrate their love and their desire, and to have that love and that desire honored by the fineness of the furnishings and fabrics around them.

Grinning at him, Plowman turned and threw himself backwards onto the swelling eiderdown at full stretch, innocent and childlike and old and defiant and furious all at once as the yielding mattress took him in, and Cyrus set down his candle and fell back onto the bed beside him, and both of them looked up at the embroidered green canopy above, and neither of them spoke, and perhaps as Cyrus' thoughts went to Abednego Plowman's thoughts went to the long sold away Ruth, and the sag in the mattress's centre tilted them towards each other and neither resisted it, finding the pressure of shoulder against shoulder companionable. Cyrus wondered how often in the months the hotel was closed up Plowman came to this room and lay on this bed and dreamed.

Anyone else come up here, he asked, and suddenly sleep was sweeping over him.

Just us, Plowman said, and he too sounded drowsy.

The candles, Cyrus said, unable to make himself struggle up from the enveloping mattress to attend to them.

Uh-huh, Plowman said, but he didn't move except to pat Cyrus' thigh in a vague, reassuring way. Then with a sigh he got up, and through shuttering lids Cyrus was dimly aware of him, still in his coonskin hat, snuffing the candles with the palm of his hand, then climbing back onto the bed next to him and drawing the curtains closed about them.

Cyrus woke with a sour mouth, a full bladder and cold feet to a pale green glow, and at first was uncertain as to where he was, but then he saw Plowman lying on his back beside him, snoring softly; and saw that the glow was the curtains gently backlit all around; and he reached over and tugged the one nearest to him back. The air beyond was chillier, and white light filtered in through shuttered windows on two sides, for the room was a corner one.

Yawning like a cat he rolled to the edge of the bed, sat up and lowered his bare feet to the floor, and a rug he had not noticed the night before welcomed soles anticipating cold boards. Standing with a grunt, raising his arms high he stretched out his spine, and behind him Plowman stirred and set the bedsprings pinging. Cyrus went over to one of the windows and peered down through shutter-slats at a landscape in which nothing moved and there was no color save white. What little he could see of the sky was milky gray and yielding not much light, though what there was was thrown back brightly by the fallen snow.

Snow's stopped, he said.

There was the sound of curtain rings being slid along a wooden pole and a creaking of bedsprings as Plowman got to his feet. Les go eat, he said. Then I gots to lock up an go back down.

What about the bear?

He'll of moved off most likely: they don't hang around where people is. We be okay long as we keep a eye out.

Before they left the room they pulled and straightened the eiderdown and counterpane, finding themselves oddly clumsy as they performed this woman's task; and somehow making the coverlet smooth was laborious and hard to achieve, though at other things their hands were deft and skillful. Perhaps too there was something within them that sought to defy the erasure of their presence, of their claim on this bed, on this room, if for somewhat different reasons. When all was restored they made their way downstairs, closing any open door behind them as they went, and were encouraged to find that, though the stove was out, the kitchen held a little residual warmth. Plowman cut them more slices from the ham before wiping the knife on his sleeve and returning it to its drawer, and this time he ate as hungrily as Cyrus. He took the ham back to the larder and relocked the door while Cyrus retied his foot-bandages and slid his feet carefully into boots, which were, to his relief, after a night before the stove, dry. Then there was nothing to do but put on their layers, and Cyrus his hat – Plowman had worn his even while sleeping – and leave.

Plowman opened the kitchen door a crack and peeped out, then, evidently seeing nothing deterring, opened it wider and stepped out onto the screened-in balcony. Cyrus followed him. The wind had dropped and the air, though cold, lacked the bite of the night before. Looking down the snowy steps as Plowman locked the door behind him Cyrus saw no sign of bear tracks. He descended one slippery step at a time, gripping the handrail tight. Glancing up at the sky he reckoned it maybe two hours past dawn – late, that was, though he doubted anyone would be outside today unless compelled by need. He crossed to a corner of the yard, the snow cottony-crisp beneath his feet, and urinated steamingly, and Plowman emptied his own bladder nearby.

They made their way round to the verandah-skirted front of the hotel, and for the first time Cyrus had a clear view of the countryside about him, though the snow, which seemed to have blanketed the whole of the visible world to its horizon, concealed details, and rendered all, the swampy and the stony, the wood and the plain, deceptively uniform in aspect. Directly below him, at the precipitous hillside's base, a village was laid out along a single road, with on its far side several larger houses, and past them, set among fields, bigger houses still, about which were clustered farm-buildings and slave-cabins. Plantations, then. From the chimney of every house large or small smoke rose, and the road, discernible despite the snow owing to the trees and bushes planted alongside it, zigzagged down steeply from the bluff where Cyrus was standing. To the left of the village a wide stream ran blue-black, and built out over it atop a sluice was what Cyrus took to be the watermill, though from that angle he could not see the wheel; and around it were sheds and barns, all white-roofed, like loaves that have expanded past the lip of the tin in baking, and owing to the snow, by the stream no path was visible.

Plowman was already tramping off, and, seeing the tracks he left, Cyrus became conscious of his own: pursuers would be impossible to evade in this, and would need no dogs to track him. But there was nothing to be done, and so he hurried to catch Plowman up at the turn and descend. He had never experienced snow this deep before, but sensed by the slump and sag of it beneath his feet that it was barely holding its shape. This encouraged him, for if the temperature held steady it would soon commence to melt.

A half hour later they were at the bottom of the hill. Still no-one was about. They trudged on, and soon they were among houses, smallholdings, each sitting on its own patch of land. In the front yard of one of these fowls hopped and clip-wingedly fluttered about, intensely brown and orange against the white, pecking at grain that had been flung from the porch; in another two young black women in gray caps and aprons emerged from a woodshed, hauling between them a basket of split logs which, owing to its weight and size, they let drag in the snow, their slender arms stretched and straining. One noticed Plowman and attempted a wave, earning a cross look from the other, and he waved back as they staggered lopsidedly off towards the farmhouse.

I'll point you to the mill-path, he said. They's a lane to the left.

They had gone forward only a little way when up ahead a horse appeared, coming slowly toward them, its rider bundled up in a heavy brown coat and broad-brimmed flat-topped hat.

Mas Elsten, Plowman murmured to Cyrus, and his voice was tense. The horse, a mare, dark-brown, and with a coat that needed clipping and a white blaze down her nose, stepped daintily and snorted, uneasy in the snow, and Mister Elsten's leather-gloved hands were tight on her reins. Gathered up with them was a leather tawse, its haft weighted with brass. His progress was slow but still he came on. The two black men dawdled to a halt.

Where you been, Mister Elsten asked Plowman when he reached them.

Up at the Spa, suh, Plowman said, coming closer in the manner of a supplicant. They was a bear. This boy's mule up an died on him, an he was passin, an he saved my life, an we had to hide up an wait fo the bear to go.

Mister Elsten looked Cyrus over with glacial, red-rimmed eyes. His white walrus moustache was yellowed with tobacco-smoke and his skin was crazed with burst blood-vessels, and what was pale was shadowed purple, and he sat as heavy in the saddle as a barely-balanced sack of meal. Inert he seemed, yet the movement when it came was sudden as a moccasin's and as vicious, and the heavy brass weight in the base of the tawse struck Plowman's temple with the sound a shoemaker's hammer makes shaping the leather round the iron foot-template beneath it, and Plowman's head moved sharply sideways but his neck did not, and he fell to his knees like a collapsing stack, then tipped over in the snow, and his mouth moved once, emitting a creaking sound from deep in his throat that did not match what the lips were attempting to say, and his eyes opened wide and stayed wide, pupils locking mechanically, and his forehead where it had been struck was cratered in the best part of an inch.

Cyrus had flinched at the blow, and as he looked down on Plowman – on Plowman's body as it had become in no time at all, in the moment between a heartbeat and its cessation – he couldn't keep from shaking his head, and his jaw moved but no words came, just an aching grinding, and his shoulders hunched bullishly and he tried but could not keep from sliding a hostile glance at the white man on the horse, on whose face was readable nothing but irritation, and the white man saw the way he looked, and his eyes sharpened as shudders ran up Cyrus' body that were a different sort of cold, pushing his chest up and out, wild energies surging. You, stay, Mister Elsten said.

I gots a errand, Cyrus said, forcing tonelessness, swallowing horror and rage. Fo my massa. He waitin. He'll beat me if I'm late.

I'm magistrate here and you will stay or I'll have you flayed.

Plowman's body lay unmoving on the snow between them.

There was then no god and no meaning.

Gots that ring in my nose, Cyrus thought, though to rip out a ring was only painful; it could be done if a man could bear the pain, risk the disfigurement. Yassuh, he said. I'll stay with him. With Plowman. And the emphasis he placed on the name was a rebellion, and read as such by the white man, who might have said more, but magistrate or not, no-one else was there to witness the exchange, and so he pulled on the mare's reins, turning her, and thumped his heels against her sides. She broke into an uncertain canter that almost unseated him, taking him back the way he had come. Cyrus watched, hoping he would fall, but he did not, and the instant a bend in the road took him from sight, Cyrus ran. His view from above had shown him where the lane to the mill would be, and he took it confidently, palming tears from his eyes as he went. In his turmoil he had no thought of attempting to cover his tracks; all his need now was to get out of sight, get gone: flight now, thought later, if there was a later, and all force was kinetic, bursting out from the blow to Plowman's skull, propelling Cyrus forward, as a boat lifted up on a flood.

He ran full-pelt into the mill-yard. Though it was deserted, the snow there had been churned to muddy slush by the passing back and forth of feet in commission of some task now done. The mill loomed up ahead, round-arch-roofed, three stories high, and in the gap between it and an adjacent ware-house there had also been a passing of feet. Towards this gap he headed, his own prints merging with the rest as he plunged through: the start of the riverside path, he reckoned – rightly, for a moment later he was there. Close by, a flatboat was tethered, to which planks had been laid across; and four black men in coats thin for the weather were unloading bales of winter feed, two on the barge and two on the shore, slinging and receiving in pairs, and singing as they did so, and though it was early the song was of the day being done, and toil and perhaps life being done too:

Oh, dark gonna catch me here
(Dark gonna catch me here)
I won't be here long –

The caller, who seemed by his bearing the lead man also, looked round as Cyrus came hurrying forward. Hey, he called, before Cyrus could pass by.

Mas Elsten kilt Plowman in the middle of the road! Cyrus shouted breathlessly, and he kept on going as behind him the men threw the bales down and moved in a body toward the millyard, breaking into a run as they went, and though he had shouted without purpose, with only the need to say it and have it said, he knew they would reach Plowman before the white man returned with other white men, and black men to heave the body, and their feet would obscure where Cyrus had turned aside from the road, and he hoped Mister Elston would not at once wonder how they came to hear the news so fast and draw the inevitable conclusion.

The mill path was easy to follow, the reed-lined stream on one side, and on the other a running boundary-fence, and on both sides of the stream were snow-covered fields and, distantly beyond them, white-gray woods. By a lone, wind-twisted cedar Cyrus took a minute to catch his breath. Looking to his right, away across several fields he saw a large, two-story house surrounded by outbuildings, and some way farther off a row of slave cabins. Several figures on horses were moving about in front of the house, and others were gathering on foot around them.

White man'll try an put the blame on me, Cyrus thought, and he was glad he had hollered the truth to the bargemen, both for its own sake, and because it meant they would be less likely to betray him when the false accusation was made, as it surely would be, the lie being more convenient than the truth, and the only witness to it being both the accused and a non-person. He glanced back at the hill, and the hotel halfway up it, and now in its shuttered whiteness it seemed to him as it had not before, a tomb.

Chapter Thirteen

C yrus turned his back on the hill and the hotel and went on, and an hour later had left the estate behind him. Ahead lay a low expanse of uncultivated scrubland, dotted with clumps of swamp-oaks whose presence implied a bogginess the snow concealed, and now the path ran level with the stream, which here and there extended dark fingers across it through the snow. By one of these he squatted and filled his water-bottle, drank, refilled and stoppered it. He now had no food and felt about inside his knapsack for crumbs, but there were none. Shoving his hands back into the pockets of his coat he found the coin-purse, reminding him he had resources, useless though they currently were.

Gold and silver; dull copper discs with holes in.

He thought of Plowman's drilled, locked eyes and once more blinked back tears. Shoulda closed the lids. Shoulda tried. But there had been no time.

Though the sun remained concealed behind the clouds, the sky lightened as the day wore on, and the air grew milder. Snow perched on branches slipped and fell in soft lumps, and the tinkle of ice-water dripping from twigs merged with the rippling of the stream. Hidden among the snow-topped, yellow-brown reeds that lined the bank as dense as thatch, birds cheeped. Behind these natural sounds Cyrus was alert for those of pursuit, though he supposed it just possible that he might have been thought to have returned the way he had come, and he had, thankfully, said nothing of his destination to the white man. It was possible too that Elsten and the other white residents of the village imagined him to be skulking about in the vicinity, hoping to rejoin the only road out after night had fallen, and would not think of the stream path, though he could count on none of these things. He did not think the bargemen would betray him, not unless the white man could convince them that he, the stranger, had killed Plowman.

It was mid-afternoon when Cyrus reached the jetty, though he did not see it until he was almost upon it, for there the stream looped round on itself, and the path left it to drive in a straight line up a low, tree-topped rise, an earth bank as it were, that cut off the sound as well as the sight of what lay beyond: the confluence of the millstream with the mighty Stone River, a hundred yards or more wide, and yellow-brown with silt and therefore, Cyrus presumed, in the main shallow. The variations in its coloration suggested deeper channels here and there, and one such channel ran past the head of the jetty, which was of wood, sturdily-built and well-maintained, around thirty feet long, and the snow coating its length had been trampled to slush.

Next to the jetty stood a shabby cabin with a small window and by it a door, to the front of which had been appended a poorly-constructed porch with a snow-freighted and sagging shingled roof. In front of the porch was a rail for the tying of horses and mules, and over the rail a hide, that of a deer Cyrus reckoned, had been draped to weather; and nailed to the wall by the window were several moss-stained sets of antlers and one that was cleaner than the rest, and bright: an entire skull; the home of a hunter, then. An unlit lantern hung on a hook by the door, smoke rose from the narrow tin chimney, and fish – two bass, a bream and a small pike – hung from a length of twine strung at chest height between the posts that supported the porch's dipping roof, meaning that whoever wanted to exit or enter the cabin would be compelled to duck down to pass under it. A similarly poorly-built, open-sided shelter stood beside the cabin. Under it logs were stacked, and behind it a small skiff and a larger rowboat had been pulled up onto the snowy mud, just far enough out of the water to not be tugged away by the current. The rowboat's painter was tied to an iron ring bolted to one of the struts of the jetty; the skiff was untethered. From a distance both seemed in good repair.

Cyrus hung back under the cover of the trees, considering what to do. He had heard no sound of pursuit since leaving the village, and there was no way a message could have reached this place ahead of him. He had his pass and the pass stated he was tasked with going to Amesburg and Saint Hall by as direct a route as he could find, and this was, so Plowman had said, the most direct route, and he had money for his passage. All this meant he could personate a legitimate traveler, yet to wait here for who knew how many hours for the coming of a ferry on which, owing to the color of his skin, he might not be permitted to ride, was surely to place himself in great danger; and in any case it seemed wisest to him to travel as far as he could unremarked upon, ideally unseen by any white man, and his mind went to taking one of the boats. Though he was no oarsman, steering it downriver seemed a task he could manage well enough, in daylight at least, for he had in his time punted rafts and pulled as one of a team on a flatboat and knew something of currents; and on both sides of the river the trees crowded down to the banks and overhung them, and their branches, though bare, were densely twigged enough to offer quick concealment from other craft by day, should the need arise, and easy mooring for the night.

Take one of them boats an snatch them fish, he thought, though the latter would mean standing before the window, visible to anyone within.

At that there came from the trees to his right and only a short way off the ringing metallic clap of a rifle shot followed by the clatter of bird-wings, a gruff call, and a hound barking in response, and within the cabin a baby started to wail. Time compressed abruptly and his thoughts blurred and sharpened all at once, one set as it were inside the other, and he started down the bank.

Just as he did so, there came to his ears the sound of hooves pounding along the stream-path behind him, not far off and coming on fast, and his chest heaved with the rhythm of their coming though as yet he could not see them, for the wooded rise lay in between, and the hooves to one side and the gunshot to the other pincered him, and the searching nostrils of the hunting-dog rendered any attempt at concealment futile, and after all there was the snow, and his tracks. The boats, then. He hurried down and crossed the open space in their direction.

You, boy.

Cyrus turned to see standing there among the trees a scrawny, lantern-jawed white man in bib-overalls, a heavy coat and a slouch hat, with by his side a brindled, yellow-eyed and watchful hunting dog, a duck bloody and floppy-necked in its jaws, and in the white man's vein-wormed hands was a rifle, and the rifle was aimed square at Cyrus' chest, and the man was old and his eyes were watering in the cold, but his grip was firm, and there was no more and no less than forty feet between them. Cyrus raised his hands palms facing forwards and moved slowly backwards.

Stop that fidgeting, the white man said. Ettie, he called, shooting a glance at the cabin. Ettie, you safe? The baby safe?

They safe, suh, Cyrus said, but his words served only to return the huntsman's eyes to him, and they were at their centres black as the bore of his rifle, and as unhuman. I gots papers, suh.

Damn your papers, boy. I didn't ask bout no God damn papers. Fact, I dint ask you bout nothin.

The horsemen – there were two of them, white men with rifles slung across their backs – topped the rise then, and they were young and ruddy-faced and bright-eyed with the chase. Seeing Cyrus at gunpoint with his hands up one of them called to the old man, Shoot the nigger, what you waitin for; but his command drew the huntsman's eyes away from Cyrus, and in the momentary breaking of that connection Cyrus turned and bolted for the shore. Well, shoot, the young man yelled, frustrated and excited in equal measure, foreseeing perhaps a game of cat and mouse, with all advantage belonging to the white men, as was their right. Cyrus tore past the front of the cabin, grabbing the line of fish as he went and ripping it away to the accompaniment of a cry from within, darted round behind the woodpile and scrambled down to the riverbank, in that way briefly escaping the old man's line of fire, for the cabin now stood between them.

The skiff being untied, he chose it. As Cyrus dragged it round hastily on the slush-slippery, snowy shore a shot rang out from the direction of the rise and red pain exploded ringingly inside his head and his hearing was deadened on one side. He could feel blood running down his neck, but he struggled on, throwing in the fish as he bent forward and, with arms and shoulders straining, shoved the boat out prow-first into the river, clumsily jumping after it as it slid away from him, almost falling into the water but by good fortune not, and the boat wobbled perilously and one toe-cap and the edges of his coat dipped beneath its surface as he pulled himself forwards, and after a tense, counter-balancing moment in which he might have fallen back he was safely aboard and on hands and knees scrabbling for the oars and fumbling them into the locks, and the blood was hot and cold and wet on his neck as he turned and sat and braced his legs and began frantically to pull away, half his first few strokes missing the water entirely, others chopping in too deep and threatening to snap the oars and wrench his shoulders from their sockets, and a second shot went wide.

As he pulled more confidently, his back to the wide river ahead, the merciful current drawing him forward, the two horsemen came cantering down in search of a clearer vantage-point from which to fire at him, one unobstructed by tree-branches as their view from the rise had been, and both of them wore bright blue coats and bright white breeches and black boots; and as they reached the cabin a thin, bare-legged white woman in a gray shift and shawl came round the side bearing a wailing baby in her arms and stood there staring after Cyrus with lightless eyes and a slack mouth. Kingdom, she called over her shoulder to the old white man, who was coming up on her now at a fast limp, the hunting dog at his side, the broke-neck duck still in its jaws, glossy green and black and white. Kingdom! A nigger's thievin our boat!

The old man stumped to a stop beside her, raised his rifle to his shoulder, peered along the barrel and fired, and whether he was aiming to shoot Cyrus dead or, through scaring him, compel him to return the skiff, Cyrus did not know, but the shot struck one of the boat's locks glancingly, making a spark fly but doing no harm; and leaning back till his shoulderblades brushed the hull he redoubled his exertions with the oars.

Kingdom, that nigger's stealin our boat, the woman repeated in a dull fury, standing there in the slush and mud, thin pale hair lank around her colorless face as the old man fumbled to reload and the baby wailed, an emotionless animal tone. Do somethin, Kingdom. That boat's ours. Do somethin.

Next to the ill-matched couple the horsemen dismounted fast, one almost falling from catching his boot in the stirrup, and raised their rifles to draw a bead on Cyrus.

Do somethin, the woman begged them. He's old. He ain't

no good. Do somethin. That's our boat.

Further out now, and trusting to the current to carry him past their range without further exertion on his part, Cyrus pulled in the oars and lay back catfish flat on the ribbed bottom of the boat so as to make as small a target as possible. His injured ear throbbed lancingly, as though the hearing-bones were splintered on that side, and grinding against each other, and the nerves caught in between, though each pulse of pain reminded him his heart still beat. The skiff rode little more than a foot above the waterline, and that and its faded, blue-gray paintwork made it a poor target for the white men on the shore, it seemed, for a shot cracked out and the ball struck the water some yards away; the next Cyrus thought went high, for there was no sound of impact anywhere at all, and by the time the third shot came he had been carried a long way out, and in a short while more the skiff was caught in the faster current of one of the deeper channels and Cyrus was sped away from the cabin and the jetty and swept round a bend, the little boat spiraling along on the river's swollen surface like a sycamore seed.

For a time Cyrus lay there unmoving, staring up into the empty sky, and the ringing in his head sweetened to a fiddle-string, thinned to a mosquito whine, emptied out and was gone. Experimentally he moved his jaw. Pain shot from his bloodied ear, flaring behind his eyes as if a skewer had been inserted. He clamped his teeth together to keep his jaw still, and the pain grudgingly receded. Once it was at a bearable level he began tentatively to explore the injury to his ear, beginning at the undamaged top and delicately moving his fingertips down the curve of gristle towards the aching lobe where he could feel the worst of the destruction had occurred, both wishing for and dreading the thought of a looking-glass. To his relief he found the lobe still there, and, though stingingly shredded by shot, not reduced to some dangling piece of meat held in place only by a scrap of skin; not likely, then, to die where it hung, and require amputation or risk sepsis. Something hard was in there, and pinching it between his thumb and index finger, he wiggled forth a small lead ball, breathless as he did so from the burning pain, but then it was done and he flicked it over the side of the boat and lay back flat again, and now he could hear the sound of the water unmuffled.

Flanked by the oars as though upon a bier and cold as the dead he began to shudder then, and found himself crying uncontrollably. He let the sobs come loud and long as they needed to, and his throat burned and his chest jerked as his eyes overflowed and would not stop, as floodwater will not stop when the levee ruptures, and, overwhelmed, he wailed, and the river bore him along, a small thing amidst vastnesses of water, woods and sky, lamenting for the living and the dead, and he thought he would go mad.

And then, suddenly, as such moments are always sudden, and as though the tears and snot and hawked phlegm were spirit extrusions and their source exhausted, he was empty, and, if not calm, for that implied a resignation beyond what even the dead could get to; or balanced, for in his life, the world being as it was, there could be no balance, he was blank; blank as a newborn, and though thoughts would return later, and with them the halfway-welcome burdens of self-awareness and self-determination, for now he was a will-less part of things, a vessel within a vessel, and it was a mercy.

Bednego born with a caul coverin his face, he thought. Caul to veil to shroud. No veil for us, though, or only a veil unseen.

Dusk was coming on. Cyrus sat up and looked about him. He was midstream, and on either side the gray-brown, snow-burdened forest crowded down to the water. The river was considerably wider here than it had been back at the jetty, and both banks seemed to him a long way off, and nothing was visible beyond the treeline. There were no signs of habitation: no landing-places, no chimney-smoke; and no other craft were on the water, the old man's woman evidently having failed to persuade the slave-catchers to pursue Cyrus in the other boat. The air was damp and his bones ached and his teeth ached and his wounded ear ached, and the sense of being a motherless child came upon him powerful strong and once more tears fell from his eyes, though this time, needing to see more than he needed to weep, he resisted them and palmed them away.

Shifting his position to ease his buttocks, he became aware of the soaked, cold weight of the points of his coat where they had dipped into the water when he first scrambled into the skiff. Pushing a hasty hand into a pocket he brought out the papers and letters James Rose had written for him, now sodden and pulpy, and bleeding a bruised yellow-black as the constituent elements of the ink separated out. He tossed them down in front of him, unwilling to discard them all at once, though they were surely beyond salvation, or resurrection: only the money remained, irreducibly metallic.

It's all on me, he thought: somehow he had known it would be so even as he sat watching James Rose dip nib in ink in that close room back in De Bray's Town; that the white man's words and works would not be his liberation.

Twisting round to survey the river ahead of him, which was rapidly sinking into the tawny obscurity of the dusk, and seeing here and there spars jutting up like spears braced to impale the hull of his little boat, Cyrus decided to find a spot to rest up for the night. Taking the oars, he pulled for the bank that was opposite the one on which the jetty had stood, miles behind him though it now lay. The air was still, and all was quiet save for the slop and ripple of the water and the clink and creak of oar in lock and scoop of blade.

He was in no hurry now, and such little light as remained was wholly gone from the sky by the time he drew near the tangle of trees that lined the western bank. Here there was little current. Willows mingled with oaks and cypresses, their branches overhanging or even trailing in the water, making a curtain of twigs and boughs; and Cyrus steered a stately way among the upturned branches of the drowned trees that were for some reason particularly numerous here, eventually reaching up to take hold of the lower-hanging willow-branches overhead and pulling himself and the skiff, hand upon hand, altogether out of sight beneath them. Above and below, they held the little boat in place like a cradle and, due to their profusion, on the ground of the bank beneath them no snow lay, only a carapace of dead leaves dense as reptile hide, and Cyrus thought of the fish he had snatched when he ran, and of making a fire, and weighed the risk that might come from the fire being seen by passing craft.

None of the larger vessels would make a detour to investigate such a fire, he was sure of that, their passengers' business being too pressing for such unprofitable time-wasting, as with the stages that had passed him by without a glance between De

Bray's Town and Honeycomb. Yet any boat heading downriver might be carrying news of him – surely would be if it had called in at the Honeycomb jetty – and the pilot, seeing a fire at night, might make a note as to where, and inform patrollers further downstream. But would patrollers row upriver at night on a pilot's say-so? Cyrus had no idea how far downstream the next town was.

River's full of spars regardless. Greedy or needy, no slave-catcher gon run that by night, not with no moon. An where I pulled in there weren't no landmark anyhow.

Cyrus decided to risk a fire, if he could get one going in the damp air. Holding onto a branch overhead he stepped from the trembling boat onto the matted shore, squatted down and scraped the driest of the fallen leaves into a small, aereated cone. Reeds stood in the water nearby, their sheltered heads untouched by snow. He broke a couple off and crumbled them for tinder. This time he could be calm and methodical, for the cold was not severe enough to kill him, and he wasn't fighting the wind. Even so, it took him several long minutes of striking steel on flint to get a spark to catch, and then the leaves were resistant to combustion, preferring to smoulder and make a smother. Eventually, however, he had an adequate fire going, and after feeding it with willow-twigs he gutted the fish, dropping the entrails into the water, regretting as he did so the lack of a hook with which he might hope to catch any predator that came to eat them. Sliding a longer twig inside each fish, he held it in the fire until it was cooked and ate it hot. Food and warmth cheered him, and the desire to sleep came on him fast once the last fish was consumed. After taking a heavy-lidded moment to ensure the skiff's painter was securely hitched to an overhanging branch he lay down on his side, facing the fire and keeping his wounded ear, which now pulsed dully and slowly enough to not prevent sleep, upwards. The leaves gave little more beneath him than would wet sand, but were at least tolerably dry, and the branches above would shield him from the worst of any snow that might fall while he slept.

Leaving the fire to burn itself out, and leaning on his arm for a pillow, Cyrus closed his eyes.

He woke to cold ashes and a pale sky striated by hanging

willow-branches. His ear ached drearily, and when he drew a breath pain stabbed him in both lungs as if something had torn inside, and stabbed again when he coughed, then hawked up phlegm and spat. He struggled to his feet and went down to the water, squatted, cupped his hands in it and splashed his face. Removing his hat, he rubbed his wet hands fast over his scalp, then replaced it. The skiff waited and there was nothing else to do, so after emptying his bladder against a tree he untied the rope and stepped back into it and pushed off with an oar. Soon he had worked his way out from under the trees and was on the open river again, pulling for a current to carry him forward.

At first there were no other craft on the water, and the woods – soon wholly free of snow, no more having fallen overnight and the weather continuing mild – ran on dense and wild along both banks, but the Stone River, which flowed through Cleaver County, where he now was, and then Blaze County, his destination, proved to be a busy trade route and thoroughfare for travellers, and soon Cyrus had more than enough company to make him uneasy, though what came upriver troubled him far less than what followed on behind.

Here and there he saw small, often dilapidated landing-stages, and these he avoided, keeping midstream or pulling towards the opposing bank, hoping that at such a distance – for the river continued broad – his race would be impossible to discern. Twice as the morning went on he was passed by great timber-rafts, moving faster than him because steered by men – black men – far more adroit than he was at finding the faster currents, and unimpeded by any need to conceal themselves from others. The rafts had at their fronts lamps hung on poles, now extinguished, and, erected at their centers, tents. Outside one such tent, on the second raft to pass him, two white men sat on folding stools playing cards, and one had a rifle leant against his thigh. Since rowing required Cyrus to face backwards and look upstream he saw both rafts in plenty of time to steer away from them, abandoning the faster middle current and drawing closer to one or other of the banks. Each such course of evasive action consumed energy, and he had woken hungry.

Turning to watch the second raft go by, and also to check what was up ahead, he found he was gaining steadily on a large flatboat the best part of one hundred feet long and twenty wide, on which stood, facing forward, perhaps thirty head of cattle, black and tan in coloring and, bar the odd flick of a tail or ear, still as tar-barrels. At the rear of the flatboat were piled bundled hides, atop which stood a man in a heavy coat, his race obscured by the hat set on the back of his head. His mittened hand rested on the great curved arm of the bladed rudder-pole, one of three by which the craft was steered, the others being at that time tilted up out of the water.

The flatboat was following a current close to the bank, so Cyrus took to his oars and headed out into the midstream. His arms ached in their sockets, for though he was strong the movements in their exactness were new to him, and worked parts of the muscles in his shoulders, arms and back that neither plowing, picking nor hauling had developed, and the base of his spine burned. As he drew level with the flatboat he saw it had at its front a small, windowless covered section in which a stove-chimney was set, and smoke came from the chimney; and also that the man at the rudder was white. Three black men perched on one of the boat's boxy sides, their backs to Cyrus, hunching against the cold in heavy cotton shirts and no coats. No white man other than the steersman was in evidence, and he was keeping his eyes on the strip of water between the boat and the bank, which was congested with sunken branches, and paid Cyrus no mind. Still the sight of him, and the curled whip that lay beside him on the piled hides, made Cyrus pull harder.

At that point the river curved round to the south, and there came a thrumming in the air and, checking over his shoulder as he passed the flatboat, Cyrus was alarmed to see dominating the midstream into which he was now being carried fast, and bearing remorselessly down upon him, a great steam-launch, its twin chimneys pumping vigorously as its engines pounded within. Two stories high, and with a small pilot's cabin on the upper story at the front, its woodwork freshly-painted white and its iron fretwork crocus yellow, it came on like a mansion lifted up on a flood. At its prow, and at the front rail on the upper story, passengers, crowded together, white, and prosperous by their dress, looked out with, as repeateded glances round told Cyrus, rising alarm on their rapidly-nearing faces as he pulled about desperately and the pilot sounded his hooter again and again and the current drew him directly into the oncoming steamer's path.

The muscles across his back burning and tearing, Cyrus managed to wrench the skiff's prow past that of the steamer, but so barely that, as if magnetized, the rowboat was pulled into the launch's side, wood clonking hard against wood, the little boat tumbling along the speeding steamer's length, and it was all Cyrus could do to pull in his oars and save them from being smashed as he spun. His disorientation was markedly added to when, as he bumped and rotated along the steamboat's flank, a passenger – Cyrus glimpsed a flushed white face, dark green coat and top hat – lent over the rail and landed two vicious blows on his head with the weighted knob-handle of a cane, to the accompaniment of drunken laughter from those around him, men and women, and only his hat spared Cyrus a split skull, and beer was flung over him as he threw up his hands to ward off further blows. But he was already past the man's reach, and no-one else attempted to assault him; and he had just alertness enough to snatch up one of the oars as he neared the steamer's stern and, with a lung-tearing yell of exertion, push the skiff away from the enormous paddles that churned at its rear. For a terrible moment they loomed barn-high above him, blades rising, skeins of glittering water scattering over him, their motion pulling him towards them, and then, in obedience to some natural law of forces and distance and kinesis, the sucking water let him go. Had he failed to shove off as hard as he had done, he would certainly have been pulled in and at the least capsized, or, worse, caught in the rotating paddle-blades and hideously mangled and then pushed down beneath the boat and drowned; and even had he been somehow flung free, he could swim only a little, and the current was strong and the river wide and no-one on the larger craft would have even tried to help him.

Dazed by the blows to his head, and tossed about in the steamer's wake, his arms strained and at that moment will-less as ropes, Cyrus could do little but sit fearfully gripping the skiff's edges, trying to keep it steady as with heaving chest he watched the stern of the larger vessel draw away. Its rear upper deck looked out over the rotating paddle-wheels, and children and youngsters had, it seemed, run back to see what had happened to him, for they leant there on the rail elbowing each other, and some were laughing.

Once the steamer had disappeared around the bend upstream Cyrus turned and looked forward. From here the river ran straight a long way, and though small rowboats moved about, keeping close to the banks, belonging to fishermen he supposed, to his relief there were no craft of any size in the midstream up ahead. Too exhausted to row, he let the current carry him along, and for a while he trembled, and then the trembling passed from him. After an hour or so he steered the skiff into a more minor channel, and the rest of the day went by without further incident, though later on he had to steer away from a second steamer heading upriver, and another passed him coming down.

Though his hunger was growing, recalling the events at the Honeycomb landing he passed by several smaller jetties where he might have tied up and gone ashore, and as night fell he once more drew in where the trees overhung the bank and concealment was easy. This stretch of the river seeming still to be wilderness, once again he risked a fire, and its warmth was a mercy, though his grumbling stomach began to torment him, and his sleep, when eventually it came, was broken. His head was tender where he had been hit, and his ear remained sore, occasionally burningly so, and his coat and hat smelt of the beer that had been thrown on him.

The morning that followed was brighter than the one the day before, though cloud still hazed the sky and leached it of color. Dourly Cyrus punted the skiff out from among the water-brushing willows, rowed until he found the first current that would pull him along, and straightaway drew in the oars to conserve his waning strength. All his thoughts were now of food.

First landin I come to I'm a chance it, he thought. Who gon stop at them small places an say I'm comin their way? No-one, thas who. An I even gots money if it comes to it.

But there were no landings along this stretch of the river, indeed no habitations of any sort: here it seemed to pass through nothing but raw forest, and for Cyrus the hours inched by in cramped, damp hunger, and he drank and drank to fill his stomach but it did no good, and each time he stood up to urinate over the side of the little boat, which was often, it wobbled worrisomely, and he felt himself shrink as his body's dwindling heat withdrew and hid itself within him like a dying ember. Now and again he took to the oars to pull away from any boat that seemed it might draw near enough to take too great an interest in him, but in the artery of commerce along which he was now passing all were concerned with their own business and little else, and his efforts that afternoon were directed predominantly toward the avoiding of spars, which in that stretch became once again numerous, the water being shallower here than it had been upriver; and as dusk drew on he passed the tilted, ash-gray skeleton of a steamboat that had run aground on a sandbar. The rear portion was charred black, its ribbing and decking curiously expanded and splayed, the blossom of a boiler-explosion he guessed, having heard talk of such things, and seen kettles left too long on stoves. He wondered if people had died when it blew, or had had time to jump and flounder to shore.

A little way along he happened upon a densely-wooded is-land. It rose up directly ahead, and he let the current carry him to it. Like flotsam the little boat was drawn into an eddy and with a gentle bump and jostle caught on the wide, shallow shore that hemmed it. Disembarking with an awkward jump that at least successfully spared him wet feet, Cyrus turned and pulled the skiff up the shore until it was concealed among the bushes that massed beneath the trees, which were in the main pines, and quickly explored the island, squaring the territory before all light left the sky. It proved small and low-lying, with a slight rise at the center, a hundred yards long and half that in width, and bore no evidence of the presence of man. His cramped stomach was now aching from the muddy river-water he had been drinking, and when he made his camp he set his bottle upright in hopes the sediment would sink overnight, and that he might get clean water to consume, providing he sipped with care. Though he heard the occasional pipe of a river-bird he caught no sight of one, and in any case had no way of setting a snare. There were no traces of rabbits or other animals, not even rats or mice, though twice he heard the hooting of an owl.

Again he chanced a fire: in the middle of the island he

could be confident the many intervening trunks and heavily-needled boughs would screen it from view, and as he sat there, warmed but consumed by hunger – that soulless demand of the pitiless, mechanical flesh wherein the craving intestine consumes the very musculature of the body that supports it – horror crawled over him, for in his mind's eye his gut became the caved gut of the starved boy with the caged head and the crow-stolen eyes; his bruised and swollen temple the living inverted mirror of Plowman's stoved-in brow.

Feelin it worse on account of I'm alone, he thought, and his hand found its way to the charm around his neck, but now the leather pouch was cold, as if depleted. Maybe thas my luck gone, he thought, aware Abednego would laugh at him for his too-ready belief in charms and haints and hoodoo.

But what else we got, Bednego?

Our wits.

Ourselves.

God damn this stomach.

It was with difficulty he did not punch himself there.

To attempt to sleep seemed futile, for his belly squirmed and cried and his restless limbs twitched like deer-heads, and suddenly he stood up as if there was action to be taken, which there was not, and he longed to shout, but did not.

Far out now, he thought. I'm all the way out. And he was so light in his hunger and tiredness he believed he could rise and soar, spirit and body as one transcending, and a calmness came over him then. Breathe, he told himself, breathe, and the fire was to his back.

Still he was not ready to lie down, and, after throwing a few more branches onto it, for he dreaded it failing in his absence, he went down to the shore to look out at the night. There he watched a log-raft big as a paddock float sedately and silently past, a lit lantern on a pole at its front end, beneath which a white man in a gray coat and bowler hat sat on a barrel and peered into the blackness ahead; and toward the back of the raft stood a tent that glowed from the lamplight within, and inside it dark forms were visible in silhouette. The lookout tilted his head back and a bottle glinted in his hand, and Cyrus was glad the island had so little about it to draw the eye. He drifted backwards into the deeper shadows of the pines and watched until the raft and its lights were swallowed by the night. Then he made his way back to his campsite and lay down by the fire and stared into the flames, his mind empty, resting his body without trying to make himself sleep, and so sleep eventually came upon him.

He awoke with a start and the uneasy feeling he was no longer alone on the island. Day had come, smoke was drifting upwards from the remnants of the fire and likely had been doing so for some time, and perhaps had drawn someone's attention. His hackles rising, Cyrus surveyed the dense, surrounding wood. Could a bear have swum over? Nothing moved, and there was no sound, save on all sides the stir of the unseen river. Stifling an urge to cough and hawk, Cyrus rubbed his face, pushed his hat down on his head, picked up his water bottle and, without tilting it, stealthily made his way back to where he had concealed the boat, casting wary glances about him as he went.

The boat was waiting for him as he had feared for no good reason it would not be, and he braced his chest against its prow and slowly slid it back to the water. At that early hour sounds – the shuff of keel on pebbles and mud; his grunts as he pushed the little craft – seemed magnified, the still air conductive, betraying. There were no footprints on the wide, muddy bank save his own arriving, and yet he did not feel reassured, not even when he had pushed off and got the skiff turned about and once more in the current, and he kept his eyes on the island as he was carried away from it, a spikily-canopied black mass under a milky sky beyond which was a premonition but no more of a golden sun, yet nothing burst forth, and no rifle-shots came.

And so with fading strength and will he went on, his hunger a violence, or so it seemed to him then, engendered by all that was against him, though in the return of the sun he sensed a primordial shift that was empowering: the resurgence of that heliotropic energy that feeds all life and growth. Even so, he was now struggling to concentrate, and felt a decline in his ability to weigh matters and make decisions wisely, or at all; and when the sun broke through the thin, ashy membrane of the sky the glint on the water made his eyes sting and feel tired, and so he closed them, remembering the butterfly-wing brush of Abednego's lips against their lids, then opened them abruptly: something had bumped the boat; a small log, it transpired, but it made him think of alligators as he had not before, and wonder where they went in winter, for in winter they were not seen; and the thought came to him that the eye he had felt upon him on the island had been perhaps not a human but a reptile one.

His third day on the river passed in much the same way as had the preceding two: drifting as much as he could to conserve his strength; taking up the oars to avoid spars and sandbanks when he had to; keeping his distance from other boats and rafts. Come midday, to his left the forest gave way to miles of fields belonging to a series of large plantations. Each estate had its own jetty, and around each jetty were clustered well-appointed mills and barns and sheds, and black folks moved about them at their tasks, but Cyrus clove to the opposing bank, preferring to starve rather than risk attempting to go ashore on the plantation side. Flatboats were more numerous here than previously, passing slowly up and down, servicing the jetties, and there were in addition many small rowboats, all on the plantation side. From some of these men and women were fishing, and Cyrus felt an insanity of hunger descending on him as the day drew to its draining, irresolute close.

By this time there were plantations on both sides, and there had evidently been a concerted effort to clear this portion of the river of spars and dig out sandbars, for it ran shimmering smooth and even and unobstructed. Keeping to the midstream, Cyrus chanced carrying on into the blackness of a night in which for the first time in what seemed like weeks stars pricked gauzily. These he first saw reflected in the river, and to begin with he thought them spirit lights sunk impossibly deep in the shallow water, and only afterwards looked up at the sky, and one star shot, and then another, and another, and his heart was in his mouth with wonder and their silence was absolute.

The corollary of a clear sky was intensifying cold, and Cyrus' bones ached. For all their beauty the stars gave little light, and there was thus far no sign of any moon. Just when he had decided that, regardless of the risk of capture, he must pull in or chance being capsized by, or running aground on, some unseen obstacle, he heard the dint of hammers ahead, metal ringing rhythmically on metal, DINK dink, DINK dink, their massed and metronomic strokes underscored by flatly-bouncing echoes, and led, it seemed, by a call and a response.

Chapter Fourteen

C yrus sat up and listened, and the song of the anvil was almost magical to him then, and at once beautiful and appalling. Up ahead an orange light radiated like a second sunset, one where the solar orb could not sink below and rest, but had been trapped and tethered on the ground. The skiff was now approaching a bend in the river, and the interposing east bank was lined with oak-trees, their topmost branches silhouetted by the light beyond. The boat bumped bottom, and as the hull grated on the pebbles below it, Cyrus started in alarm, but before he could think to take up an oar to push off with, the current caught the little craft and carried it forward, by chance drawing him into a deeper, faster channel.

Using an oar as a rudder he sat back and guided the boat as best he could, staring ahead, and within a few minutes was rounding the bend, and the source of the light and the song was revealed to him as by the slow drawing back of a curtain from its farther end: a great iron foundry, all shadow and blaze; and had he not heard the men singing before he saw it, and known them to be men, he might have thought it a vision of Samuel's hell, a hell in which he himself had never believed, no worse being conceivable to him than what already was, and no further hell required beyond the extinction of the body and spirit in slavery.

First he saw the tops of five great belching chimneys, each fifty foot or more in height and made of brick, and feeding a canopy of smoke above, the underside of which was lit orange by the blazing forges below, and the chimneys were arranged in a crescent around a central yard that ran down to the river. The yard was dominated by a large, open-sided rolling mill, behind which a vast water-wheel turned. A short way up the stream that served the mill were moored, barely discernible in the dark, a procession of flatboats awaiting their loads. The pitched roof of the rolling mill was supported by pierced iron columns thirty feet high, ornately latticed at their crowns, and at back of it twin furnaces roared, and in front of these, black men stripped to the waist and gleaming with sweat guided with heavily-gloved hands iron sheets the size of cabin walls through huge slitting-presses, and the huge, water-powered rollers slowly and screechingly sliced them into rows of rails that another crew of black men lifted and swung and set clangingly upon the ground in stacked crosswise grids.

Behind them yet other black men rhythmically shoveled coal from heaps into the furnace mouths, and white men moved back and forth among them in open shirts and no coats and hatless, such was the heat generated, their whips hanging loose in their hands, and as Cyrus watched, one of them struck a man bent over his task on the shoulder for no apparent reason than ill temper, and the man bore the blow as he would a rotten branch falling from a dead, storm-struck tree: a natural event without meaning or morality. To the right of the rolling mill stood a two-story clapboard building with lamplit windows, most likely offices, before which stood a black and yellow handsome with between its shafts a plumed and blinkered white stallion, its brasses glinting red; beyond, further inland, were a great number of sheds and warehouses, at that hour sunk in darkness.

All this was revealed rotatingly to Cyrus as his boat round-ed the bend: first what was farther off, then what was closer to. Now he saw a large, rectangular brick structure, its longer side facing the shore. Its wooden doors were almost the width of the building, and folded back on themselves, and furnaces and forges were visible within, and twin smoke-stacks rose up behind, and it was before this building that the singing men, a dozen of them, worked at their anvils, beside them braziers, and each strike of the hammer on the glowing, tong-gripped and turned metal sent sparks scattering on the impacted earth, and the men wore leather aprons and cloth gauntlets but their arms were bare, and one man led the song and the others answered him:

Pharaoh was a proud man
(Ring, hammer, ring)
Chained up Moses' people
(Ring, hammer, ring)
Now, Pharaoh had a only son
(Ring, hammer, ring)

And full of sinful pride he was
(Ring, hammer ring)
Though they faced the river, and the same light that silhouetted them from behind surely revealed him to their eyes, in the
main they were bent upon their tasks and did not look up. Any
who did gave no sign of seeing Cyrus as he floated by. The
hammers struck dink DINK dink DINK dink DINK, and the
rhythm with which the men raised their arms and brought
them down was it seemed to him then, echoed as it was by the
clanging slinging of the rails within the slitting mill, at once
torn between the heartbeat and its son the song, and the
dominance of the mechanical, the relentless and the imposed.

The yard where the blacksmiths worked ran down to the
water's edge to make a wide and shallow shore but there was no
landing-station there; however a little way beyond it and past
the slitting mill Cyrus saw a stubby jetty at which several small
rowboats were tied up. The jetty was set between two water-
front warehouses, and was, Cyrus saw, at that hour encourag-
ingly shadowy and unattended.

Needing food above all else, and sure this must be
Amesburg, Cyrus now took up both oars and, with many a
glance over his shoulder to ensure he was on course, sculled
over to the jetty, maneuvering the skiff round to pull in on its
downstream side, and next to a wooden ladder he had noticed,
around one of the lower rungs of which he looped the painter,
and up which he climbed, pausing hunkered down at its top to
peek over. Seeing no-one, he quickly clambered up onto the
jetty and, keeping low, made his way to the riverbank. After so
many hours and days afloat it was a relief, but also strange, to
have solid ground beneath his feet, as if he continued to in
some way undulate while it of course did not. He had not felt
this on the island, or in his other mooring-places: perhaps his
increasing hunger magnified the effect; certainly the simple act
of standing now made him light-headed. He made his way
quickly into the shadows between the two warehouses, tension
as well as hunger gnawing his gut.

I'ma make a mistake here, he thought. What I oughtta do
next?

A harsh brass horn-note cut through the foundry-din. The
hammers rang, and rang once more, then they and the work-

song ceased. The slit-press screeched on till the slicing through of the night's final sheet was concluded, and then came the clanging of furnace doors being closed, and of rails being set down, and shouting, and the cracking of whips.

Their workday done, surely the slaves would now be permitted their evening meal, and Cyrus considered whether he might attempt to join them, though to do so would of course place him in great danger of capture, as they would doubtless not be allowed to come and go as they pleased even about the foundry-yard, never mind beyond it, and his presence – that was if the others did not at once expose him as an interloper – would soon enough be discovered by the overseers. As he made his furtive way along the length of one of the warehouses he heard, somewhere up ahead, horses' hooves. At the corner, however, he saw ahead of him, barring his way, only a row of windowless sheds, mostly built of wood, though one – that closest to the yard – was of brick, and its door was of iron, iron-framed and heavily chained and padlocked. Cyrus took a moment when he came to it to see if there was any gap through which he might peep in, but there was not.

Keeping to the deepest shadows he now looked out on the yard. The smiths had gone back into the forge, and pairs of workmen were pulling the folding doors closed, shutting in the light and leaving the black iron anvils lined up outside like sacred carvings, horned like faraway night-beasts or, had he but known it, Legbas awaiting their sacrificial offerings. As Cyrus watched, the men started to emerge from a side-door, their gloves and aprons set aside, pulling on shirts against the cold air as they made their weary way towards the slitting-mill to join their fellows. Their procession was overseen by three white men on horses, the oldest and most corpulent of whom, who wore a heavy black frock coat and wide, flattened, silkily-gleaming top hat, held open before him a large leatherbound book with gleaming oily-gold edges, and, resting its weight on the gaily beribboned neck of his bay, he declaimed, Slaves, obey in all things your masters, not with eye-service as men-pleasers, but in singleness of heart, fearing God. And whatsoever ye do, do it heartily, as to the Lord, and not unto men; knowing that of the Lord ye shall receive the reward of the inheritance: for ye serve the Lord Christ. But he that doeth his master wrong shall receive for the wrong which he hath done. So sayeth the Lord. Amen.

The white men flanking the preacher said Amen loudly, looking about them with hard, bright eyes, and their utterance was, though unframed as such, a command, and the black men murmured the word with bowed heads and a tense, tired reluctance that ensured the saying of it brought neither peace nor resolution, but the old man closed the book as if satisfied, as indeed he was, for the intention, as all present knew, was to demonstrate the dominance not of God but of man, of pale skin over dark. Pinning the book awkwardly under one armpit so he could gather up the reins, the preacher turned his horse around and urged it into a trot over to the office-building, towards which two young colored women in aprons and kerchiefs were now hurrying with heavily-laden trays of food and drink; and the sight of that wrenched Cyrus' mind round to his immediate quest: victuals.

Food must come from somewhere. Yet this was a place where all seemed bent towards manufactory and nothing else: there was nowhere in sight, as there might usually be, any garden or vegetable patch; nor were there detectable the sounds or smells of hogs or cattle or poultry. Over all lay the particular odor of what fed the furnaces alone: stone coal, or anthracite, an odor different from that of the bituminous coal used in the small smithy Cyrus had known on Tyler; cleaner somehow yet also bleaker: industrial, though that was not a concept Cyrus' mind could yet encompass. Even so he intuited something of its absolute and reductive nature, a presentiment as it were, that added to his unease as he crouched there hungry as a large-eyed wild thing in the dark.

The slaves, a workforce perhaps fifty in number and all men, made their way in a straggling line toward a long, low flat-roofed and shingle-sided shed, in the small, square unglazed windows of which light showed weakly. Along its longer side ran a verandah that was in reality just a row of planks laid on dirt, at the far end of which hogsheads were stacked; and from the shed's squat, tin cone-capped chimneys smoke rose. There were two doors, and these, Cyrus saw, functioned as entrance and exit respectively, and between them stood a barrel raised on bricks into which a downpipe ran from the guttering along the roof-edge, and chained to the barrel was a tin ladle, and as each man emerged with a plateful of food and a tin mug he filled the latter from the barrel. Some would then pass inside again; others preferred to sit on the rough planks of the verandah and eat outside, needing perhaps to counterbalance the swelter of the furnaces and the coal fumes with cold, clean night air, or perhaps in rejection of the confinement of walls, the constraint of unneeded talk.

Cyrus too had often sat alone.

He considered then that there might be a white man inside, supervising. Though likely not: why would any white man care how slave rations were prepared or apportioned? And what white man would put the nourishment of his or his employer's property before his own?

None, that's what.

Lanterns were brought out and hung from the guttering, lighting the scene and giving an illusion of the picturesque. Though his stomach was now gurgling frantically it seemed to Cyrus best to wait: for the men to be done eating, for the stove within to be bedded down and the lamps doused and taken in, and the hands gone to whatever cabin was assigned them, and then attempt an entry in darkness. If there were women sleeping inside, as seemed likely, they might help him, though there was a risk his sudden appearance might cause them to panic and raise an alarm. The two girls he had seen taking trays to the white men's building did not return to the slave canteen.

Reckoning it would be good to get closer if he could do so unobserved, Cyrus doubled back and made his way round a row of smaller sheds, eventually coming out by a large coal-bin that stood near the canteen on the angle, from the shadow of which he could without being seen watch what was going on both there and in the yard beyond. Lacking the strength or resolve to do anything more, Cyrus first squatted, then sat on the cold, hard ground, leaning against the side of the bin, and watched the men eat what closer to he saw were meager rations, and by their look meatless; and, after eating, some of them played dice, and small items he could not make out were exchanged, some of which glinted.

Perhaps he dozed; perhaps he merely closed his eyes a moment. But in any case he became abruptly aware that a fight had broken out between two of the dice men. Those inside the canteen came crowding out, plates in hands, in response to the raised voices of the onlookers, and one of the men cut at the other with a blade of some sort and was urged on by some in the circle that was quickly gathering about the pair, and both men were wild-eyed. While this was happening, as if by prearrangement, two of the others who had been shooting dice moved to opposite ends of the planking verandah to keep watch, though each, reluctant to miss out on the sport, cast regular glances over his shoulder at the furious combatants, and Cyrus cursed, for he did not want the attention of the overseers drawn here.

The circle shifted and distended as the onlookers at one point drew closer and at another pulled back from the slashing blade, all the while keeping both men penned in. All at once the unarmed man broke away, shoving, almost leaping through those around him, and to Cyrus' alarm came sprinting directly towards him, the knife-man close on his heels, and all eyes followed them. Cyrus drew in his feet and clasped his arms around his knees, making himself as small as possible, a heaped bundle of rags and debris, and lowered his face as two sets of feet pelted past him in the direction of the warehouses and the jetty. Glancing back at the canteen from beneath his hat-brim Cyrus was relieved to see no-one was following them; indeed in the main they were settling back to their food and talk and gaming as if nothing had occurred; as if once swallowed by the night the two men had vanished from the world and so from their thoughts. From the direction in which they had run no sounds came, and since to move seemed riskier than remaining where he was, Cyrus did not move.

After a while the unarmed man, who was the slighter and shorter of the two, emerged among some sheds from another direction, having apparently evaded his pursuer and made his way round in the dark. Cyrus saw the back of his shirt had been slashed, though was unstained by blood. The man crossed the yard in quick, nervy steps, darting glances to right and left, and disappeared into the canteen, avoiding as he passed them the mostly indifferent looks of those of the men who still sat on the verandah, the others having gone back inside.

As the door closed Cyrus became aware that someone had

silently slid up on him, and looking round and up sharply he found the knife-man standing over him, his blade, an open clasp, held loosely in his hand, ready for instant use, and he was looking down on Cyrus in near silhouette, the stars outlining his head, and Cyrus could make out little save that he was dark-complected, burly and tall; that the musculature was overt on his bare arms and heaving, curving chest, and that his head was shaved so close it glinted, but this was enough: Cyrus recognized him as the smith who led the hammer song.

Who the fuck are you, the man said.

Name's Cyrus, Cyrus said, working to keep his voice level.

The man moved his jaw and Cyrus made out a toothpick there and sensed something that might almost have been of all things laughter. Well God damn, the man said, and he stepped back a little, so as not to be looming so entirely over Cyrus, folded the knife into its antler handle and slipped it into a pocket in his bib-overalls, and extended a hand. Cyrus took it and it was warm and calloused and strong, and he let himself be pulled upright, and just to stand was good. Off of Tyler, he added, though he scarcely knew why, but something began to rise in him then and he straightened his back and pushed out his chest and looked the other in the eye. The two of them were, it transpired, the exact same height, and much the same in build.

I'm Bale, the other said. And then he spelled it: B-A-A-L Bale. I'm guessin you hungry.

Starvin, Cyrus said. Been days since I et.

Stay there. I'll get you some fixins.

Cyrus nodded and watched Bale amble away, from behind broad-shouldered, bullnecked, block-buttocked. Before, Cyrus would have been as strong as Bale, but not now, not after days and nights of his gut devouring the meat of his muscles; and he had no sense of how far, if at all, he could trust him. God damn, Bale had said when Cyrus told him his name. Why?

On account of he knowed it already. An that means – Cyrus pushed hope down: Don't be no fool, now. Could mean a lotta things, an most of em bad.

The men on the verandah moved aside to let Bale pass as they had not troubled to for the other man. He disappeared into the canteen, and while he was in there, for what seemed to

Cyrus an unnecessarily long time, his unease began to seethe. What was he up to? Reconciling with the man he had fought, maybe; or being refused more food; or plotting Cyrus' betrayal, for money or some other advantage?

They's those that gets lost in the white.

Just when Cyrus was feeling he must at least move to another patch of shadow, Bale emerged from the canteen with a loaded plate and a mug he dipped in the barrel as he passed it; and ambled over to where Cyrus waited, a lit cheroot between his lips, and a few men looked after him but most did not.

There's a place, he said as he passed Cyrus by, and Cyrus, after a wary glance back at the lamp-lit canteen-front, fell in beside him.

They passed among sheds and outbuildings meeting no-one and in a little while came to the foundry's edge, beyond which all was mud and diggings, earthworks, with here and there the beginnings of foundations laid in pits, and further off, past the mill-stream, a dark mass of trees. To the right of it was the river; to the left, at a distance, lights showed: a town.

That Amesburg, Cyrus asked. Bale nodded, and led him by a path that ran alongside the excavations and came to a round brick building that at its apex tapered to a low, squat chimney-stack. Into it was set a wooden door.

Kiln-house, Bale said, opening the door. Wait here.

He vanished inside. Cyrus peered after him into the darkness. A stove-door at ankle-height was hooked back, revealing glowing embers sleepy within, sickling Bale orange as he bent over and lit a spill, and with the spill a candle, and, setting it on a shelf, he gestured for Cyrus to enter. Cyrus did so, closing the door behind him. There were no windows, and the air in the room was close and blessedly warm, and smelt of damp clay and dry dust. They's sacks, Bale said, handing him the plate and mug and a wooden spoon, and Cyrus sat on two full and dusty sacks that proved unyielding as rocks, and Bale leant against the wall and smoked his cheroot and watched him eat hungrily. Go slow or you'll choke, he advised, and Cyrus nodded and ate more slowly. It was a thin mush of cornmeal mixed with a little sour milk, without a trace of meat or any seasoning; nonetheless his shrunken stomach was grateful, and he had to fight to keep the tears from starting in his eyes, so great was his relief.

The room was twelve feet across, shelved two thirds round, and here and there unfired pots and bowls sat waiting on the shelves. The remaining circumference was taken up by the entrance-door and, facing it, an iron door the height of a man set into the curving brick above the low stove. This was the oven for the firing of the clay, and it radiated a gentle heat. In the candlelight Cyrus could see numerous shiny discs on Bale's bare forearms, and keloid scars on the domes of his chest, and he thought of the sparks flying each time the hammer came down, and of years spent amongst forges and white-hot metal, and now he saw a suggestion of dull blueness in Bale's right eye that might be some old injury.

Look out fo smoke by day an fire by night, Cyrus said, by way of opening a door in the silence between them. He told me.

Who?

Jus someone I met. He said see that, an you at Amesburg. He right.

He dead. Off Bale's non-response Cyrus asked, You know a place call Saint Hall? Big plantation hereabouts?

Uh-huh. It bout twenty-five, thirty miles downriver. Why? You goin there?

Maybe. You know what it like?

Ought to, Bale said. Lived there most my life.

But now you here.

Got hired out.

They lets you keep yo earnins, Cyrus asked, aiming to move the talk away from himself.

Bale shrugged. Some.

You lookin to buy yoself?

Maybe, but we all seen how that goes. But even if they cheats me I rather be here than there.

How come?

Here look like hell, Bale said. There is hell.

Cyrus was fumbling for another question when Bale cut him off with a sharp gesture and tilted his head, listening. With a tightening throat Cyrus listened too. Stuck in a room with no window, he thought, an only one door in or out. But he heard nothing, and it seemed Bale was mistaken, for he exhaled. Don't go by road, he said. They's patrollers all over. More all the time, an more vicious. You gots a pass you still gets a beatin jus fo being black an movin about. Get yo hide cut or worse. You a woman you get used. Harsh. They was a boy weren't even a man yet he come home with nothin but a meat rose between his legs. They doesn't even care bout wreckin what they calls valuable property now, thas how crazy they is. They the snake eatin itself. Shit drawin tight like a noose, can you feel it? Judgment Day comin, an when that trumpet plays we all gon dance. We all gon dance, Cyrus off of Tyler, but some of us gon dance with our feet off of the ground.

Bale's stare was intense, and deep and shallow all at once.

Cyrus sipped his water. His eyes slid to the door. What you make here, he asked.

Gun-parts, Bale said. Barrels, stocks, bolts an pins, everythin, an we assembles em too. More an more orders comin every week, fo rifles, pistols, revolvers. We gots us a regular armory now, locked up tight, just waitin fo use.

Cyrus nodded, remembering the brick building with the heavily chained and padlocked door he had passed earlier, and noting the use of the word we, though there was in Bale's voice no misguided pride when he spoke: no fantasized convergence of interests. What else you make, Cyrus asked: Bale and the other smiths had not been working on gun-parts when he passed them at their anvils.

Just now rails is big, Bale said. Railroads spreadin out west, where gold is, an north, where cities is; an they comin south too: they gon reach here soon enough, tie it all together. They the future. And so is the guns. Thas two futures, an only one can win through.

You reckon war comin?

Cataclysm.

Cattyclysm?

Bale nodded but did not elaborate, instead bending low and spitting into the stove, making a soft sizzle, then hooking the door shut.

Did you see me come by befo, Cyrus asked, on the river? Bale shook his head. It safe fo me to rest up here? I'll be gone by sun-up.

Bale shook his head. Overseers come in here an warm theyselves when they do they rounds. That starts bout midnight. I'll take you someplace else. And with that he reached over, pinched out the candle-wick and sank the room in darkness. Cyrus braced himself for a sudden attempt to seize him, but a moment later the door opened, black within black, a rectangle of chill air. Cyrus shivered: he had not realized how quickly he had become accustomed to the warmth inside the kiln-house. Plate and cup in hand he followed Bale out.

Bale led him back a different way to the one by which they had come, and Cyrus struggled to orientate himself to the one location that mattered: the jetty where his boat was tethered. At a crossroads between the rows of sheds Bale pulled up sharply, reaching back and putting a hand on Cyrus' chest as two men passed in front of them no more than six feet away, both young, one, white, shouldering a rifle; the other, light-skinned, holding up a lamp and carrying a coiled whip, and at his hip a pistol was holstered; and there was about them, in the brief time Cyrus saw them, surely a confraternity.

Ain't no such thing as a nigger too valuable to whip, the white man was saying. You just got to know where to put it on. Cut up the bits ain't worth nothin, you won't get no complaint off of the owner. For instance: a nigger don't need a nose to use a hoe.

An wenches, the other asked.

Cut the back. You don't look at the back, so that don't matter.

Me, I don't like the front, the light-skinned man said as they passed from view. On account of you see they eyes when you doin em.

Tell em keep em closed or you'll put em out with a cigar.

Harsh.

They got two; they only need one.

Like titties?

After waiting a minute, warily Bale and Cyrus went on, and soon Cyrus recognized the warehouses that led to the jetty, and Bale led him to one of the larger sheds nearby. Its door was unlocked, and Bale opened it and gestured for Cyrus to go in. Passing Bale the plate, spoon and cup Cyrus stepped uncertainly over the threshold and into pitch-darkness. Extending his hands before his face he touched cold metal objects that, from the way they turned and clinked and floated, were hanging from the roof-beams on chains.

They's a heap o straw fo packin to yo left, Bale said quietly. You can lay there amongst the crates. Fo sho ain't no-one gon come in here, not fore dawn.

Before Cyrus could thank him the door was closing and Bale was gone.

Cyrus groped about to his left, and soon enough found the heaped straw and the crates. Lowering himself carefully onto the straw he felt for the walls, which were wooden and splintery, as were the crates. Chill currents dribbled in through gaps between the boards, but it was better than sleeping in the open, on hard ground and damp soil, the more so on this night when, due to the clearness of the sky, the temperature had fallen considerably; and his stomach was comparatively full. Rather than lying down at once, for a while he sat with his arms about his knees, leaning against one of the crates and considering what was best to do. Bale might bring him food before dawn, or might not. He – Cyrus – might skulk about in search of supplies and opportunities, and then return to this shed, if he could find it again. Or – assuming he was not discovered by the watchmen – he might leave straight away, once more risking the river by night. Or he could do as Bale advised, and stay till dawn limned the sky and leave just before the horn sounded.

Twenty-five miles downriver was Saint Hall: the journey of half a day. He was so nearly there, but then what? He regretted Bale had told him so little about it. A hell worse than hell, he had said, or something like, and the worm of madness had been squirming in him as he spoke, fed by not only what had been done to him and to others but perhaps also, it came to Cyrus then, by what he himself had done to others.

Thas why I dint ask him bout Bednego, he realized. Somethin he done: I felt it. Even though he helped me.

He decided to risk a few hours' sleep, trusting his attenuated nervous system to wake him before dawn broke if Bale did not return. His ear no longer pained him, but nonetheless he avoided lying on the side that would press it into the sharp whistles below. His wrists and ankles ached distractingly from the cold, but one benefit of the long days he had spent largely immobile on the water was the healing of his blistered heels, and his feet had warmed a little in the kiln-house, and that and a full stomach helped sleep to come.

As had happened nearly every morning of his journey Cyrus woke abruptly, unsure as to where he was, and with a profusion of images jumbling through his head. Sitting up and looking about him he found himself in a storage shed lit dimly by pale, predawn pearls that beaded like resin through the chinks that peppered the board walls. There were no sounds outside, and though the clangor of the foundry was surely soon to recommence, Bale had not returned.

Now Cyrus could see what had been hidden by the night, and he understood why there had been no lock upon the door; why no-one would come in: for here, suspended above him on hooks like drying squashes or the disjecta membra of butchery, were all the instruments of the cruelty that white men inflicted upon those with darker skins. It was on such instruments, Cyrus realised, that the smiths had been working the night before, and he did not wonder at their blindness and disconnection from their task, and even from themselves, as they hammered and sang. Here, hanging above Cyrus' head, were shackles, chains, clamps, mouthless metal masks; iron collars, some with spikes extending outwards from their cardinal points, others with nubs or short blunt spikes on their inner surfaces intended to abrade the skin; blunt-ended objects that might be forced into a person's body; a neck-brace with a metal hoop arched over it on which small bells hung for the unavoidable detection of the wearer; and knives, peelers and cleavers, perhaps intended for innocent culinary purposes but guilty and collusive here.

His skin crawling, Cyrus quickly got to his feet and left the store-room, brushing a set of shackles with his shoulder as he did so, sending them turning and clinking; and the bells, jostled by the shackles, shivered, a treacherous silver tinkle.

Outside all was gray and no-one was about. In the cold air Cyrus' breath misted and his eyes ached and twitched. To the east, between the two riverfront warehouses, and beyond the massed oaks on the opposite bank, a hint of pink presaged sunrise, and Cyrus headed towards it, sensing the imminence of the work-day's commencement: he would empty his bladder and bowels once he was away from this place.

The horn sounded as he reached the jetty. Hastily he found the ladder, turned and scrambled down it, slipping and almost falling as he did so; checked and slowed himself; then stepped carefully into the tremulously-waiting boat, tugging the painter loose with chilled fingers the moment he had found his balance. Bracing his shoulder against one of the jetty's uprights he pushed off, then sat and took up the oars and, glancing over his shoulder, made for a channel that seemed to stir the gray-brown water more muscularly than the rest.

There were at that hour no other craft upon the water.

Facing backwards as he pulled away, after some minutes he saw a figure come out along the jetty, though at that distance he could make out no details, neither of race nor even sex. Smoke was rising from the stacks beyond, and even before the jetty and its lone spectator were swept from Cyrus' sight a rhythmic clanging began.

Chapter Fifteen

P ast Amesburg the forest reasserted itself, running wild on both sides, oak mingling with cypress, and here and there and further back, pine. In those first pellucid hours there was no traffic on the river, which for a stretch ran deeper, and was faster-moving than before. Once established, Cyrus drew in his oars and let the current carry him, reflecting as he floated along on the particular pain and insult of being compelled to use one's skill to create devices intended, for that was all their purpose and no other, to hurt one's skin kin: how that would warp the spirit and destroy, as did not all slaved work, but here to a greater degree, any joy or pride in excellence. Better do a shoddy job. Better incompetence. Better dishonesty, shirking, sabotage and theft, an inverted morality for an inverted world that seemed beyond salvation. Cyrus found he did not believe a war was coming, or at the least not one in which all would be resolved, and the right men hang: not as the steely threads of trade drew ever tighter; not as more land was cleared south and territory claimed west; as the cotton-fields spread, devouring even swamps and marshes, and the manufacturers grew ever greedier for the labor of colored hands and bodies. How could all that ever end? In favor of what be overthrown? The lion laying down with the lamb, Samuel had said, quoting Scripture and claiming prophecy.

The more Cyrus saw, the less possible it seemed.

One man seeking one man and then going: that he could encompass.

The sky was clear and cloudless that morning, and, as it brightened, the blue above contrasted with the coppers, rusts and chalcedonies about him in a manner that was pleasing to the eye; and the sun, though bestowing little warmth, was bright and encouraging. By a small, choked inlet, into the mouth of which driftwood had eddied and gathered, he put in and stepped ashore to make his ablutions, hurrying back and pushing off hastily when only a minute later he heard the crack of rifles and the barking of dogs nearer by than was reassuring:

to encounter an armed white man here, without papers or sufficient knowledge of local geography or personalities from which to fabricate a story, was to be caught for sure, and he labored over the oars until a sweat broke out on his forehead despite the cold.

Once when he was a boy he had seen a black widow kill a cardinal, a fledgling that had tumble-fluttered from its mother's nest down into the spider's web, carrying both web and itself to the ground below; and as the bird's scarlet breast quivered and then stilled, and the lacquered arachnid was busy at its neck, he had felt there must be a lesson there. Perhaps that what is natural is not kind, nor order beneficial in itself.

That was, he thought, before his father died.

As on previous days the river became busy with traffic: heavily-laden and slow-moving flatboats and barges, and many skiffs and rowboats, the oarsmen black, and sometimes the pilots too. In the main these kept close to one bank or the other; midstream, following the deeper channels, broad-beamed steamboats breasted. Their decks were habitually crowded with passengers, and these, owing to previous experience, Cyrus took particular care to keep a distance from.

The banks rose up about him steeply now, remaining thickly wooded at their shoulders but bare below, the sides having fallen away to expose slanting transections of yellow-ochre limestone and shale, for over the long years the river had worn its way through the hillside and caused collapse, present action thereby cutting into and laying bare the remote past. Shortly after noon he came upon a small island. Lying midstream, it was little more than a tall stack of rock around which a sandbar had accreted, and was crowned by a grove of twisted cypresses. There was at the rock's base sufficient scrub in which to conceal the skiff, and so he put in. Hunger and particularly thirst were once again troubling him, the river persisting muddy and barely drinkable, but the rock had called to him, for, despite the enclosing riverbanks, it offered the possibility of a wider view of the unknown countryside about him.

It was perhaps fifty feet high and at first glance on all sides deterringly sheer, but here and there the obliquely-layered and tawny stria had split and slumped so as to create small handholds and ledges by means of which, after an initial leap and scrabble for purchase, he could climb up, and thereafter work his way along and round in an uneven spiral ascent, and soon enough he was hauling his chest onto the small summit, followed by one bruised knee and then his hips and crotch and thighs. The summit was wholly covered by the stiffly writhing and interlacing roots of the six cypresses that crowned it, for there was no soil in which they could bury themselves to gain a purchase, and so the trees, blown here long ago as seeds, were held in place only by the myriad stringy cilia that ran down from the roots' undersides into small fissures in the rock beneath them. In time their penetration would, Cyrus knew, cause it to fracture and collapse into the yellow water below, and had they not died by then, the trees would fall with it, to their ending.

Crouching low, for here as elsewhere there were a fair number of craft on the river, and the bare trunks and leafless boughs offered little concealment from any who might chance to glance up as they passed, Cyrus took in the landscape about him. His views to right and left were in the main cut off by the hill through which the river now clove, atop whose last remaining sentinel he stood, a sentinel that was, of course, no taller than what it once had been a part of, and he would not risk climbing one of the tenuously-rooted trees to gain a higher vantage point. He spared no more than a glance at the land through which he had already passed: all his focus was on what lay before him.

The bisected hill was, he saw, part of a range that ran off equally to right and left, east and west as his compass told him, in a declining crescent, the densely-wooded horns of which curved slowly southwards, encompassing a great plain through the center of which the river ran wide and straight and glittering, and the entirety of that plain – beyond an intercession of woodland fading into scrub and perhaps swamp that ran on for a mile or two beyond the hills' feet – was turned to cultivation: one vast plantation it seemed, and this was surely Saint Hall. Fields spread out as if they, and therefore the plantation, had no ending, and in those fields, small as ants, teams of black men and women slowly followed plows, breaking up and turning under the dead growth from the previous season, some behind mules, some oxen; the least fortunate forcing the plow through the iron-cold soil and fibrous, matted mass by main strength alone, the toil as wearying to watch as that of an insect struggling in resin; and to see that, even at such a distance and with so little particularity of personality, made Cyrus heartsick, and the men and women numbered in their hundreds. Dotted here and there on horses were overseers, mostly in pairs. He counted sixteen, and thought of rifles, and wondered over what distance they could drop a man.

Though the fields held dominion on both sides of the river, excepting a handful of sheds all the buildings of the estate were on the left bank. There stood the great house, dominant, a vast white colonnaded edifice set among orchards and sheltered by windbreaks of pines. From it a tree-lined avenue, maybe a mile in length, extended inland, leading to a main thoroughfare that ran parallel to the river, along which a black and yellow carriage was now moving, bright as a beetle and like a white child's toy, and it was pulled by black horses. The pitched roof of the big house was tiled pale green, and near to it, on a grassy rise, a small white-pillared rotunda had been erected, positioned to offer a river view, its cupola the same pale green, and something golden glinted atop it: a weathervane perhaps, caught by a breeze and spinning. On that side of the house was a broad terrace, from which a lawn ran down to the river: there there was a small jetty, next to which brightly-painted rowboats were pulled up and turned over; and extending over the water there stood a boat-house. Adjoining the main house Cyrus could make out a walled stable and carriage-house, a large vegetable garden, glinting glasshouses, storage sheds and animal pens, and, lining the river-bank, a number of white-washed clapboard cabins, for house-slaves, maybe; or guests or their servants.

Set considerably apart from the big house and its dependencies, and inland, a good way past a whitewashed chapel from the center of which a small spire rose, sprawled, on either side of a wide dirt track, rows of gray, shingle-roofed slave cabins. In the midst of these the track widened to make a sort of communal yard, and here, seemingly unattended, bonfires burned, and smoke rose. Between the cabins and the great house stood an intercessionary row of cottages, whitewashed and green-roofed, each set in its own modest garden, and these were surely where the overseers resided panoptically. Nearer to where Cyrus stood, on the river and at a considerable distance from both the slave cabins and the big house, and served by a jetty larger than that which served the latter, stood a congeries of buildings, the largest and tallest of which was a mill. Before this stood a long-armed cotton press larger than any Cyrus had seen before, and around it were arranged barns for storage, and outbuildings he took to likely be a sawmill and a smithy, and sheds that he did not doubt housed all that was needed for the processing of the cotton crop from boll to bale. Flatboats lined the bank by the jetty, awaiting their cargoes. There were also sties for hogs, a smoke-house and a milking-shed, and in an adjoining pasturage thirty or forty black cattle stood, all facing north.

Not so different from Tyler, then, excepting in scale, and there was a simple triangulation of elements: the slave cabins, overlooked by the whip-crackers; massa's house, dreaming, as James Rose had in inadvertence revealed to him, its dream of itself as glory achieved without exploitation or degradation; and the processing, trading and storage area where the business of the plantation was carried on. By night this latter would doubtless be watched closely by the overseers, so as to guard against any slave who might have the temerity to attempt to claim a portion of the food he had raised with his labor; and on the main road would be patrollers, both those in the employ of the planters and free-lancers, their motivations money, order and the ecstasy of cruelty.

Further off there were other buildings, though at that distance Cyrus could make nothing of them except they were large and seemed to be on the river; but whether they were part of the Saint Hall estate he could not determine. More usefully, at what appeared to be the plantation's northern border, and so nearest to him, he could make out another, again small, jetty serving a scattering of shacks and sheds that appeared to be near-buried amongst encroaching trees, and this seemingly neglected spot suggested itself as a place where he might tie up, and from which he could explore in comparative safety.

A steamer's hooter sounded, bringing him back to himself. Not there yet, he thought, and once it had passed he commenced the climb back down, lowering himself cautiously feet-first over the edge and following as best he could the route of his ascent, clinging anxiously higher up, finding it easier as he got lower, but then slipping and slithering down the last ten feet in a panic and landing awkwardly amongst the scrub below. In a little while he was on his way again, not hurrying, for he considered it best to arrive at the estate's border at dusk, when the eye was most easily deceived, and all would be keen to get indoors, and shut out the night and the sharpening cold.

He was passing close to the left bank when, noticing a stream tumbling among mossy rocks, he drew in to refill his water-bottle and drink deep. Hydration lifted his spirits, and though the water was tooth-achingly cold, he set his hat and coat aside, stripped to the waist, and, leaning over carefully so as not to cause the skiff to dip, plunged his arms and head and torso into the freshet. He pulled back shuddering and gasping but with dust and dirt and staleness washed away, and as he rubbed his hands briskly over his bare skin he wished for something to oil himself with that would add a gleam. *Don't want Bednego clappin his eyes on no ashy thing.*

Hold on, now. He mayn't be there.

But Bale said –

Bale dint say much.

Bed might be sold on, or dead. He might have run and be lost to Cyrus for good, having no notion Cyrus would come for him, as why should he. Cyrus tried to prevent his mind from running to the punishments Abednego's boldness might have brought him to – the violence and violation that twists what is within or snuffs it out entirely; that causes a tangle that cannot be unskeined; a lamp that cannot be relit – or, worse still, those cruelties resulting from nothing but white caprice, against which no servility, no self-abnegation could safeguard; and which could not, therefore, be evaded by either wit or prudence. Though refusing to allow them explicit form, for a time Cyrus let these thoughts play on the fiddle-strings of his mind, the pain their contemplation caused him just enough, he hoped, to head off any divine punishment he might have otherwise incurred for his audacity; for the slave's crime of hope.

The sinking sun was once more blooding the sky as he pulled his shirt and coat back on and continued his journey, sculling slow and keeping close into the bank, and the woods, now running low and level, thinned to scrub and the scrub sank into gloom as the solar embers cooled to lunar ashes. Mist began to seep up miasmatically from the mud and water, and roll out across the river's surface. Above, the blackening sky was ice-clear, and a tilted sliver of moon slid up and perched upon the dying horizon. There were few vessels on the water now, lampless black shapes pulling home late, vague in the gloom and the rising, thickening mist. In that low country the river's banks were delineated only by the palely-massed reeds, and beyond these all was shadow. Sounds were muffled, distances distorted. Some way off he heard oars dipped in unison, and men singing in call and response:

Knee-bone when I call you
(Haul, Lord, knee-bone bend)
Bend my knee-bone to the ground
(Haul, Lord, knee-bone bend)

Their voices were deep and low and carried in their timbre the day's dying, and for a while he matched his stroke to theirs, until they had drawn beyond his hearing and been wholly swallowed by the night. The fog was thick about him now, damp and chill and catching in his throat. He drew in his oars and turned and faced forwards, for the spars along this stretch were once more numerous, and often he saw them only yards or sometimes feet before he reached them.

Can't head out further, though. I do that, I'd likely miss the jetty in the dark.

Hunger and rising anxiety commingled in his gut growlingly, threatening to distort his judgments. Keeping facing forward, he let himself drift, steering using one oar for a rudder, with the other pushing his way round the jutting, sunken branches as he came to them, a wearying, interminable-seeming business that kept his eyes focused on what was close to.

It was only when, perhaps a half-hour later, needing to stretch his neck, he looked up again, that he saw, some way ahead, the light.

Keeping a wary eye on it as he drifted slowly forward, he judged it to be on the nearside bank. He looked about to see if there were any trees nearby among which he might pull in and conceal himself, but there were none, not even scrub bushes. Since his skiff rode low in the water, and was now almost entirely swallowed by the still-thickening fog, Cyrus considered he could chance drawing closer with little risk of being detected.

In a little while he was near enough to make out that a blazing pine-knot had been set on a pole at the end of the small jetty that marked the plantation's northern boundary. It was, he now saw, in a state of partial collapse, its planking twisted and subsided in a sagging loop, and there were no lights in the windows of the neglected shacks he could dimly discern among the grown-up trees nearby. Yet here was this knot, flaring, sputtering and dripping resin, a summons it seemed, yet surely not for him, and if not for him then for who, and why?

Reaching the jetty, he turned the boat and sculled as silently as he could along its length, into the waiting reeds. There the skiff's hull brushed gravel and the prow nosed the bank. By the jetty's rotting struts he prodded about experimentally with one of the oars, trying to figure out where water ended and land began. Setting the oar down, with the painter in one hand he stood and chanced an awkward leap, landing in sucking mud, but stumbled forward quickly enough to neither sink down into it nor lose his boots, and then he was on his hands and knees on solid ground, though this was as hidden by the fog as the water and quagmire had been. He stayed crouched there for a time, listening, but hearing nothing save the stir of the river. Winding the painter round both hands, with his back to the land he pulled the boat in just far enough, he judged, to ensure the current, which here was sluggish, would not carry it off.

There was nothing to do now but go on, and all his senses were electrostatic in the chill, still air.

Knife in my pocket.

Before him were tumbled dwellings, single-story shacks with slumped roofs, some reduced to nothing more than free-standing chimneystacks and breasts, the wooden parts having fallen wholly into desuetude; and nearer to, he recognized the trees about them as plum and peach, sloe and pear and walnut, all grown wild, and the ground was tussocky underfoot, forcing him to step carefully as he advanced. Way on downriver a few lights showed where he took the mill and barns to be, toil for some continuing on into the night, the massed buildings cutting off any view of the Great House further along.

From somewhere close by there came a whistle made by lips, sharp and eerie in that tenantless terrain, a call and not a tune; and Cyrus' disquiet intensified when another whistle came, in evident reply to the first, and then a third, shorter, sharper.

Signals.

Cyrus crouched low. They were on three sides of him, these unseen whistlers in the dark, and his back was to the river.

In the middle of somethin, he thought, I'm in the middle of somethin, and his heart beat hard and his mouth was dry.

Book *Two*

Chapter Sixteen

It took Abednego several long, nervy minutes of striking steel on flint to get the lint to catch in the damp, foggy air. The distinctiveness of the sound added to his tension, for to be outside the cabins after dark was a lashing offence, no excuse allowable, and in any case he had none. He dipped the knot-head into the fragile flicker and held it there, and the glistening pine-resin caught just before the lint was wholly consumed. Glancing about him in a darkness deepened by the proximity of the firelight, he made his way quickly down to the jetty. The fog was thickening on the water.

Keeping a careful hold of the handrail, and lighting his way with the knot, Abednego made his tentative way out onto the slumped structure. On the railless side it tilted and sagged down into the fog and water, and the wood of the rail was clammy, and here and there spongy to the touch, threatening to give way if any weight was put upon it and send him and the torch slithering down into the hidden river; and it was with relief that he eventually set the burning knot into an iron ring on a pole that marked the jetty's end. Its crudely-hacked base was slightly too thick for the ring, but he forced it through, dots of resin falling stingingly on his hands as he did so, and the flames flared excitedly, and his chest tightened. All over the Saint Hall plantation, it was beginning.

To be near the flame, the lure, was dangerous; would soon be, perhaps, the most dangerous place of all, and so he made his way back to the shore without delay, moving now with the speed and confidence of a tightrope-walker, one hand lightly on the rail, looking ahead. A minute later he was passing among the abandoned shacks where ten years ago victims of the flux, men, women and children, all of them black, had been brought and left to die amidst their own bloody vomit and excrement, without even water to drink, or so he had been told by Diver; and Saint Hall had called it an experiment, though in proof of what thesis none could say nor dared to ask; and had announced at table that he considered it more than worth the price in lost stock and returns on outlay.

Once he adjudged the infection passed, Saint Hall had ordered great cauldrons to be taken to the cottages, and had had the bodies lifted in and the flesh boiled from the bones. Like fowls, Bed had been told; like stock, the dead sitting crouched in the cauldrons, lolling heads bouncing about on the roiling water as the fat rose up slickly, and some had brought herbs against the sickness, and the bruised leaves added to the cookhouse smell.

An if you hadda go outside an heave up, Diver said, you got a whippin.

Once the rendering was done, Saint Hall had the bones polished, varnished, wired together and stood in glass cases in his study, and it was rumored they were posed as dancers; that the only intent was comedy. On moonless nights their haints were said to shriek and groan and tear about the rotten shacks in which they died in such great agony, a tale at first spread among the hands by the overseers for the simple pleasure of inducing fear, but greatly ornamented thereafter by the hands themselves, and many believed it, for why should those who died in such distress not continue to suffer beyond the grave? To think otherwise was sentiment.

Bed did not believe in haints, and in any case the night was not moonless but silvered, but it was nonetheless a place of negative associations; of bad luck, and he did believe that the luck a person had could be poisoned by contact with the luckless, and so he hurried on.

Abednego believed in his own luck; always had, even in the face of circumstances that seemed likely to be nothing but bad; had believed in it despite being selected along with seven others from the Tyler main house to be sold after the flood. For he had seen in old man Tyler's expressionless face as he moved along the line, struggling to find a few words to say to those who had lived on the most intimate terms with him and his family, some all their lives, neither engagement nor compassion; had seen in those lead-shot eyes only the mortification Mas Tyler felt at being compelled to sell away the main part of the fancy niggers whose adorning presence demonstrated his prosperity and social standing. To leave that house, that family, was a sort of luck, then, however little hope there was of a better situation resulting, and however much reason to fear a worse.

Miss Tyler joined her father that morning, and burst into fretful tears at having one of her maids torn from her, working herself up so excitedly her ivory cheeks were blotched incarnadine, and declaring in breathless tones, in the midst of a faint that required the strength and present-mindedness of her two remaining maidservants to prevent her slumping to the floor in a billow of pink silk hoopskirts, that she simply could not do without Lissa, who alone, she cried, understood her hair. Thus overwhelmed, she did not trouble to intercede a minute later, when Lissa had her dress pulled up exposingly by Mister Olsen, and was belabored savagely around the bare buttocks for her inability to stem her own hysterical sobbing at being torn from her little girls, big-eyed twins short for their age, and thin, for her milk had gone to a white boy on Oglesby whose mother struggled to breastfeed, finding the sucking pink mouth too painful for her delicate pink nipples.

Such a to-do! Miss Tyler said to Tuny, one of her two remaining maids, as the keening twins were pulled away by another servant. She will soon enough have more, and she knows her girls will be well-raised here. And then Miss Tyler added, I never did care for their names; I shall change them.

No, Bed could not regret leaving that household, which was not, and never could be, home; but what tore his heart was to be taken without a parting from Cyrus, for with Cyrus he had found home.

Though talk of Tyler folk being sold away had been circulating ever since the failure of the second planting, indeed since the flood itself, on the deceivingly bright morning the selections were made no time had been allowed for farewells. Those fallen out were shackled at the wrists and ankles and collared into a coffle, and as papers were exchanged between Mas Tyler and the dealer, set to shuffling up the drive. The very young children, of which there were four, and Louisa, one of the cooks, now so infirm with rheumatism as to be able to do little, and at times dangerously forgetful in her habits about the stove, were suffered to ride on the back of the black-clad dealer's mule-cart, along with supplies for the journey. Though Bednego looked about him as he shuffled with the others, he caught no sight of Cyrus in the fields, and the edge of the collar cut sharply into the soft skin of his neck, and all meaning fell away from him.

The pain of parting he was compelled to bear in secret, for he knew it could not be spoken aloud. Cyrus had never really comprehended Samuel's bible threats but Abednego had: One word bout them cities on the plain, he said to Samuel once, when he caught the preacher giving him the side-eye, an it won't go well for you. Think on salt an walk away. And Samuel had flushed and turned from him and stalked away not looking back, his shoulders hunched, as in anticipation of a blow.

Abednego did not look back at the big house, and would not have done so, even had the iron collar about his neck not made it painful to do so.

The road to De Bray's Town took three days to walk, and the shifting shackles tore their skins at wrist and neck and ankle, then chafed the raw flesh revealed below. It was as if the eyelids of some strange sleeping creature composed entirely of hurt were slowly opening to reveal pink optical mush below, and it became increasingly painful to move, or even just sit or lie down: this and only and ever this, it whispered; and their spirits sank and their eyes dulled. The weather at least was mild and dry, the leaves, though bled of green, still thick on the trees, and there was little wind. For two of the nights they slept outside, and on the third in a barn, by prearrangement with the owner. The field hands talked little of where they might be sold, beyond a hope it would not be further south; the house-servants – when they were permitted to pause to eat, ablute or rest – of nothing else, for they greatly feared demotion to the fields. Abednego alone of them did not, and never had – though he hoped by shrewdness or good fortune to avoid it.

At nights, when the neck- and wrist-shackles were removed and only their legs were constrained, he thought of holding Cyrus, and Cyrus holding him, and of the particular heat that is generated between two men who desire each other – or men and women, he supposed, though he had never felt it; or women and women, no doubt: that heat that overrides all social regulation, all orthodoxy of mind; that deep crying of one spirit to another that for him no woman had ever answered, though he had – briefly – known many in his twenty-seven years. And then Cyrus had all unknowingly called him, in the angle of his neck and flare of his back, in the planes of his profile as he turned his head when he wrestled the plow round – flat nose, full lips defined as if edged in iron, cheekbones like hammer-heads, delicate ears, strong brow; in the boat-rib curves of his thighs and twin barrels of his buttocks; the broad set of his shoulders, the left one always slightly dropped; in the strength of his hands and the deep brownness of his skin, smooth despite a lifetime of laboring, save of course for his back; in what slept and woke between his legs; and in the dark depths of his eyes, eyes that even when he dipped his head shyly, avoiding conversation, seemed always hunting for something, and in Abednego finding it.

Still, the kiss had been as great a risk as anything Bed had ever done. He had not planned it; had had in mind rather talk of some sort that might over its meandering and scattered course be gathered like threads into something purposive and implicitly revelatory. But no words had come: instead body had called to body, lips to lips, mouth to mouth, a physical law as primary, as ineluctable as something dropped falling to the ground, and all around them the spring growth had been wild and vigorous, an encompassing violence of green, and where the myriad stems thrust up against other and split, sap leaked down, and Abednego's heart opened like a seed splitting in Cyrus' dark, hot soil and truth spilt out.

Bed studied the drivers, three white men. Two were of the overseer class, younger, strongly-built, habitually drunk and coarse in speech; one was older, more cultured. The others grudgingly deferred to him, and Bed assumed him to be in the employ of the auction house. Several of the more muscled male hands and two younger women of pleasing appearance were sold to estates along the way, so either he was authorized to make side-deals, or was defrauding his employer. On the whole being sold to estates closer to those they knew was seen by the slaved as desirable, so whether the dealing was honorable or otherwise concerned them not at all. Bed doubted it was: he had heard much bragging concerning sharp practices as he placed plates before guests at the Tyler dining-table; had heard the relish with which one man cheated another, and sometimes he saw all white men as clockwork mechanisms, with profit the key that wound them, and the search for it their entire motivation, suborning even the satiation of desire.

Bed had not been permitted to return to his room before being collared, and so had lost the eight dollars he had saved up and concealed among the corn-husks of his mattress. Since such an amount would have been insufficient for a bribe, even supposing the drivers corruptible in that way, he did his best to feel no way about it, hoping only that another enslaved person would discover it, and so benefit by what he was no longer able to.

Soon enough he and his fellows retreated inside themselves, a defense against the removal of all privacy – evacuation, defecation, menstruation having all to be managed while no more than three feet from one's neighbors, and under the presuming eye of one or more of the white men – this excepting the night in the barn, when Lilibeth was unshackled and taken away and later brought back sobbing, for at twelve years of age she was not yet properly formed, and bleeding before her menarche; and old Louisa had held her and stroked her hair with a tremulous, vein-wormed hand and fingers slanted with arthritis. Too young to fall pregnant, was all she could say by way of consolation, and the white man had looked ashamed when he brought Lilibeth back, and cold rage had flared up in Bed then: to see that performance of humanity, but only when done.

If I'd a rock in my hand I'd of –

The next morning two hours' stumbling along brought them to a hotel on the edge of De Bray's Town frequented by planters, brokers and dealers; adjoining it a high-walled courtyard like a stable-block, in which were sheds containing cots. This was the seasoning house, and here they were to rest up prior to being offered for sale. They were closely watched but not shackled, for torn skin and inflamed and weeping wounds did not make a slave attractive to a purchaser; and were provided with pork, and more varied vegetables than some of them had ever tasted before, and the means with which to cook them, a diet intended to induce a healthy appearance as rapidly as possible. They ate their improved fare pragmatically and without pleasure, and through those blank days of torpor lanced through with the tensity of uninformed anticipation –

for no indication was given them of when the auction might be held – Bed thought, over and over, Me and Cyrus should of run. Should of chanced it. Both of us was strong and fit, and tween us we knowed enough to get north; leastaways get underground: hear that railroad whistle and get on board. He saw now a certain paradox to the power of love: that having found a small cascade of joy had deceived him into believing that happiness could be achieved even in hell; that the intrinsic nature of hell would not consume it.

For the worm, the moth, eats the cotton too.

They said grace before meals, though the words of gratitude were empty or else grotesque, and prayed each night as they were locked into the sheds, now separated, in a parody of decency, by sex – though each morning the women were more silent, more closed in on themselves, and there was no need to ask the reason; and the children, who were housed with them and therefore saw much of what occurred, more skittish and fearful. In their unbearably wounded eyes he saw himself reflected back, for once he had been such a child, torn from his parents at the age of four or five and sold for, as best as he could subsequently reconstruct it, their punishment, though at the time it had seemed his own.

Bed could remember nothing of where he was born, his memory beginning only when he and his mother were sold to another estate when he was perhaps three years old, though even of that he recalled little save a general impression of the cabin, and that for some reason always at night. The name of that estate was Auger, and his father, who had been compelled to remain behind, becoming frenzied with love and loss, was caught repeatedly by patrollers attempting to visit his wife, though the distance between the two plantations was more than a man on foot could go and come back from in a single night, and so his task was unachievable. Yet he tried, over and over, and despite the increasingly savage whippings inflicted on him as a consequence, such was his strength of feeling, and in that Abednego knew he was his father's son. Central to his memory was a single image of his father's face, leaning over the crib and looking down on him, dark and strong-featured, with strange feline eyes that were both kind and not, and beautiful and not, perhaps on one of his rashly-attempted night-visits –

but Bed knew the memory was uncertain, for it had about it a dreamlike aspect, with branches and a moon behind his father's head as though outdoors, and a suggestion of reflection as in a dusty looking-glass. Dreamlike too were his impressions of his mother as somehow a body without a head: breasts, stomach, thighs radiating cinnamon warmth; hands that touched kindly, and above, an indeterminacy that was strange but did not alarm.

When he grew old enough to ask and have a question answered he tried as best he could to find information concerning his parents, for in the quieter seasons Mas Tyler hired hands out all across Welt County, and they heard news and brought it back. Bed knew his parents' names – Simeon and Sarah – and that of the estate on which he and his mother had lived until at the age of four or five he was sold away – Auger; but he could discover nothing beyond a rumor of the subsequent selling south of his father, his back scarred as a wrought-iron gate, someone said; in the end gelded, said another, to quell his heat, but that Bed strove not to believe; and his mother, doubly bereaved, and considered an excellent picker and therefore a valuable property, had also been sold, though no-one knew to whom, or even in what direction; nor whether either of them still lived. She might have had other children, or that might have been someone else, and there the trail went cold and even an Indian could have gone no further.

He had no memory of voice, neither of his mother's nor his father's, and that seemed to him emblematic of some larger silencing.

They were a fortnight in the seasoning house, during which time Lilibeth cut her wrist deeply with a peeling knife and was taken away and did not return. A bucket of water was brought, and the spilt blood sloshed away, and no trace of her remained, though after that, to the white men's chagrin, Louisa's talk was wholly without sense, reducing her already minimal value still further. Then a morning came when they were ordered to undress all together in the yard, and, once wholly naked in the chill air, instructed to oil themselves head to toe from a basin that was brought in, which they hastened to do, the younger women in particular, rather than be forcibly oiled by the white men, and they assisted Louisa, whose buckled fingers were unequal to the task, and who cried as they lifted her empty breasts and the loose skin around her belly, and Bed looked away and blinked tears back too.

They were then given clean cotton shirts and pants or shift dresses to wear, and some attempt was made to ensure these fitted pleasingly to the eye. Those such as Abednego who wore shoes were permitted to retain them; the others went barefoot. Then they were led in a double-line, thirty of them, collared, linked by chains at the neck only, through the bustling streets of De Bray's Town, down to the auction house. To most the proximity of so many white people was a new experience, and a disturbing one, for though subordinate they were used to being by far the numerical majority, and to some the revelation that white men and women were so numerous was in itself alarming. A number of the white folks were dressed worse than they were, and that added to their confusion.

Bed, who had occasionally accompanied the Tyler grooms about the county and twice been to town, saw clearer; and his experience of waiting on the family and their wealthy, or wealthy-seeming, guests had developed in him a sense of the social status conferred by cuts of coats and heights of hats and resplendencies of bonnets, by trims of capes and varieties of fabric. Nonetheless, used as he was to being next door to invisible, to being an unconsidered eye assumed to lack a brain, a floating pair of hands, Bed found being paraded before these white men and women as an object, a beast or bauble, and experiencing their eyes drifting over him, with hazy indifference or bright, penetrant curiosity, made his skin crawl, and revealed the truth: they will always strip you back to this.

The chained men and women were led round the back of an imposing building on the main street, marble-pillared at the front and brick at the rear, into a large yard where other passels were waiting with the traders who had brought them in, passive as oxen, nervy as fowls. The yard was split into two pens, processing and receiving, and auctioneers passed among the black men and women, inspecting them – an act that routinely included the dropping of the men's pants, even the most elderly, and the exposure of the women's breasts, even those long past child-bearing; the examination of teeth and sometimes the back passage. Details of height and build and age and work-history were called out and recorded in ledgers, a slip was made out to the trader who had brought them in, and a number written on a scrap of paper was pinned to the breast of the examinee's shirt, who had then to pass through to the second pen, which led to the auction-hall. Despite the briskness of each invasive and humiliating inspection, the administration of the process was by its nature slow and bureaucratic. Bed had no memory of any such experience from when he was sold as a child, though at the age of four or five all would have been confusion to him, incomprehensible, and the absence of his mother what mattered, not the rest.

During his inspection he looked down as they all looked down, and so had not even the impression of a face as his pants pooled round his ankles, just a cold hand jabbing roughly at his genitals, an exploration so forceful it seemed intent on causing an injury to his testicles; then being bent over and a finger forced partway into his back passage, and a voice said, No piles, and that same finger went sour into his mouth and that same voice said, Teeth good. Not much rot, and he was thereafter permitted to pull his pants back up, and all the women saw this.

What skills you got, boy, a voice asked close behind him, breath aromatic with chewed tobacco.

Waitin on table, sir, Bed said. So discreet massa don't notice I'm there, thinks the fine food just appears by its ownself. Carvin the joint so no scrap gets missed. Carin for silver and china and glassware and fine leather so it looks good as new. Better, even. Polishin wood so it gleams good. Servin wine and spirits how they meant to be served; cuttin cigars fo the gentlemens, doin small mendin of buttons and such with needle and thread, keepin clocks wound. I can saddle up a horse and brush him down so he don't get a chill; tighten a harness so it don't chafe.

Can you read?

Nawsuh, can't read none, Bed said. Don't need me none o that. Had any slave ever lacked the guile to answer otherwise? A girl began to sob behind him so breathlessly she seemed likely to lose consciousness but he didn't try to look round, for there was here no gesture of solidarity, of reassurance, to be made, and in a while she quieted, managing quavering umhums and nawsuhs to the questions put to her concerning her competencies. Ten, she said, an seven dead. Three livin still. Though she had mastered herself, moans and tearful sounds continued to escape anguished throats around him as those to be sold became overwhelmed, and the auctioneers continued their assessments as if sobs were as brainless as the rasping of locusts, tears as without emotion as sap dripping from split stems.

By the time all were processed and assigned numbers and transferred to the inner pen the sun had grown bright overhead and their shadows were tight beneath them. Empty troughs lined one wall, and into these maize mush and grits were tipped from cauldrons brought in by pairs of colored girls in service at the auction house, and from these troughs Bed and the others ate by hand, though with little appetite, their nerves now at such a pitch that many at once vomited up what they had just consumed. The girls who had brought the food returned with straw, which they threw down in handfuls over the freshly disgorged stomach-contents, sopping them up somewhat, though the acid smell remained. A water-barrel was wheeled in, from the lip of which depended several ladles, and they were permitted to drink, and those needing to ease themselves were directed to a fly-infested outhouse in one corner of the pen, set above a hole that stank so strongly the air seemed dense to Abednego when he went inside to empty his bladder. He had eaten some of the slops and avoided vomiting, but in the outhouse it was all he could do to keep his stomach down as he urinated.

Then the time came for potential purchasers to pass among those to be sold and examine the stock before the auction commenced, and the same degradations and humiliations were repeated, yet now far more frightening and indeed repellent because the auctioneers, however invasive their actions, were not looking to own the human beings whose bodies and dignity they violated. Here, however, there was the direct engagement of personality, the grotesque need to charm, to appear pliant, while at the same time frantically attempting on the scantiest evidence to judge whether this owner was likelier to be kind than that one: an impossibility; and in any case all knew of kindly-seeming owners who, either through credulousness, or out of some sort of obligation, or in revelation of their own true natures, employed overseers of especial viciousness, and all white men, Bed knew, lied.

Beneath their feet the straw-scattered yard became orna- mented with brick-red lines and loops of expectorated tobacco- juice, and studded with trodden-out cheroot-ends and cigar- butts, and the inspection continued wearisomely, and with, on the part of the slavers, owing to the heat and glare of the sun above and the lack of any shade, growing ill-temper, until at one point tankards of beer were brought round on trays for their refreshment, and with the arrival of these their mood grew merrier, and the remarks thrown between them concern- ing the merchandise bawdier – until a bell was rung within, and at that they grudgingly withdrew.

You'll notice how some of em come for this part only, an older auctioneer close by where Bed happened to be standing said to a younger, as he passed him a ledger to add to the stack already in his arms.

How so, Mister Pendleton, the youth asked. He was pale as milk, copper-haired and freckled; the older man was thin and stooped, his mouth a turned-down slit.

There's a class don't never buy nothin. Dress like they got money but they ain't. Likely can't afford even a old nigger for show. Come for kicks and free beer. You'll get to know em. I told that one there – the older man indicated someone behind Bed with a jerk of his thumb – Sir, this ain't no place of idle diversion, this is a place for the transaction of business. Ruby pin in his cravat or no ruby pin.

Nine, maybe ten white men spoke to Bed that day, though none with a ruby in his cravat; and in his replies Bed stressed always that he was being sold as a result of his master's financial difficulties owing to the flood and then the early frost, misfortunes well-known locally, and not through any business shortcomings, mention of which might imply a judgment concerning a white man's character or competency on the part of a black man – expressing as he did so solicitous regret for Mas Tyler's losses, and at the same time the hope that the fine upstanding gentleman before him might offer him the chance for modest betterment within service. At such performances he had become adept, though always he more than half-suspected that the white men, some of whom were undoubtedly shrewd, knew them for what they were, as how could they not? Yet in a strange way this did not matter, for they suppressed that knowledge; kept it at all times pushed below the waterline of their conscious minds: because to face it, Abednego concluded, would compel them to confront what lay behind every such performance, and those of them who were not wholly depraved could not bear to do so, for any such confrontation would morally oblige its corollary: the end of what they veilingly called the Peculiar Institution.

There were up north, he knew, white men and women who had done this: who had faced themselves in the looking glass; had seen that the same hearts beat beneath different skins and accepted all that that implied; had seen themselves in the other, stepped through the mirror's surface, and seen it from the mercury-poisoned side without which it could not reflect, but that day those white folks, who had evoked such fury and fear around the Tyler dining-table as Bed moved about the Tyler guests silent as a shadow, refilling glasses before their emptiness was even noticed; who were dismissed as race-traitors, and defiers and defilers of both Christ and the natural order of things, were as unreal as dreams, and the north as beyond his reach as those Caribbean islands of black men and women where, after many uprisings, another nation, Great Britain it was called, had ended slavery.

The conversations in the pen, those as it were auditions, were for Abednego the day's real climax, the auction an afterthought – though not for those hoping to keep families together, or at least somewhere close by; those who begged that a failing relative be bought along with them so he or she might be cared for, the desperate pleading more often than not acting as a repellant, inducing greater callousness amongst those who bid, for would not any emotional connection made, precisely and scientifically prove the shared humanity they most needed to deny? Better to loudly laugh it to scorn. Yet how could those standing before them, lamplit as though on a stage, as indeed in another way they were, not plead; how not cry?

You die ahead of time, he thought, as over and over he witnessed tears met with laughter, and he wished for a stone in his hand to dash into those flushed pale faces, impotent as the wishing was, and did not they realize his impotence, and did not that add to their excitement, even their virility.

For all his endeavor to charm as an individual, Bed was sold in a job lot of field-hands and house servants to a broker named Torrington, about half of whom, including himself, were then, as the consequence of some sort of side-deal, at once sold on to another man, Robert F. Abigail, who it transpired was purchasing for the Saint Hall estate, a vast cotton plantation several hundred miles to the south. Such plantations were for all a source of dread, for it was well known that they were unmatched in harshness and brutality; that life on them was in all respects miserable, and life-expectancy cruelly foreshortened. Five years was the figure most often mentioned, meaning: if you were placed, as most would be, in the fields, you would be worked to death in five years. Yet Abednego retained the hope that he might be given a position in the big house, at the same time resolving to seize any opportunity that might offer itself for flight.

Get back to Cyrus, maybe, catch him by the hand and run with him. Follow that North Star. Follow the Dippin Gourd.

He and thirty-five others, twenty-nine men and six women, overseen by six white men, five on horses, one on a mule-cart, began their journey at sun-up the following morning. Those purchased were once more collared and chained together, but their wrists and ankles were left unshackled, and at first and under the bright sun the chain did not feel too burdensome, though over time the endless erratic tugs on it as the person ahead or behind stumbled, or merely walked faster or slower, became exhausting, and the iron rims quickly began to chafe. The chain was at no time removed, and short of a total revolt in which all six white men were simultaneously overpowered, Bed, despite having early taken note of which of them held the key to the padlock that kept the chain looped over at its end, could see no possibility of escape so long as it was in place.

At first he entertained a thin, mean hope that one or more of the women would be taken away, necessitating the removal of the chain, and the possibility of the rest of them rising up, but the man who held the key, Mister Abigail, who was older and in authority, shook his head whenever one of the other white men suggested such a thing. Read your bible, he said, read them commandments, though whether sincerely or in mockery Bed could not tell.

Mister Abigail rode ahead of the coffle on the mule-cart, onto the back of which had been loaded sacks of meal, tubs in which mush could be prepared, and cured meat, cuts of which were of course reserved for the white men; and Bed took note of where the carving knife was stowed. The other white men sauntered on horses as the chained-together black men and women trudged on foot. Once they came upon a clump of wild walnut trees that overhung the road, and were permitted, under the overseers' watchful eyes, to gather some of what had fallen. This task was carried out in haste, for no reason other than the inducing of anxiety in those performing it, a restatement of the white men's power, and several were belabored about the shoulders by the crackers' tawses as they grubbed. The nuts were put into a sack – a stoop-shouldered girl near light enough to pass receiving a vicious kick in the small of her back for attempting to secrete a couple in a pocket – and doled out by Mister Abigail over the days that followed, a few at a time, adding a little virtue to their dispiriting diet.

After five dreary days' march, and under graying skies, they reached a village above which a closed-down hotel perched on a bluff. There they rested the night, in a barn at back of a large house that doubled as a hostelry in the off season; and a further day's trudge alongside a millstream brought them to a river and a jetty at which large flatboat was tied up, waiting. There papers were looked over and exchanged, and after some disputation concerning ownership of the chain and collars – Mister Abigail eventually conceding the point and, when given a receipt, the key – Bed and the others were led on board by the pilot, another white man, though the three crewmen were black.

Rain began to fall shortly after they boarded, compelling Bed and the others to crowd into the low-roofed, open-fronted but windowless cabin that took up the rear two thirds of the boat, and stand there like livestock. Atop the cabin, sacks, bales of feed and hogsheads were piled, and within it was a stove, and by the stove the pilot sat hunched over on a stool, chewing and spitting tobacco, attended now and again by one or other of the crewmen, and the chained slaves watched him, all talk among them stifled by his presence. Their presence stifled him too, however; and soon enough wearying of their persistent requests to be unchained so as to be able to step outside and micturate or empty their bowels over the side of the boat, grudgingly he removed the chain that tethered them together, though he left the collars in place.

Don't none o you go gettin no ideas bout goin for a swim, he said as he dragged the chain over to a corner and threw it down. Weight of them collars, they'll pull you under fore you reach the shore, take you down by the head straight into the mud, like plantin a bulb. That's if the gators don't get you first. If you're lucky one of my boys'll hook you out. If we see you in time. And then I'll open yo backs.

Bed touched his collar. The bolt fastening it about his neck had been wound into the screw tighter than any fingers could turn it back without the assistance of a wrench or some other tool. The weight of the iron was less lethal than the white man claimed, he was sure, and Bed was strong, but he could swim but barely, a crude splashing about, and that in a swimming-hole, not even a stream, and in high summer; and he knew rivers hid currents that could draw even a confident swimmer down, and the water at that season would be exhaustingly cold. Were there really gators here? He had seen none, but knew they would be hard to make out in the river's muddy, ocherous swirl. And so he was obliged to content himself with looking out and taking note of the terrain through which they passed, though standing at the cabin's open front he was exposed to rain and wind and the more general river dampness, and on the second day he began to cough and feel a stabbing in his lungs each time he did so, and a curious sense of fibrousness lingered within his chest for several weeks after.

Alone of those who had been bought in De Bray's Town he struck up conversations with the three black oarsmen, whose names were Tilt, Billy and Hutch, and over the long days of passing downriver was able to learn from them in their less occupied moments a little about the plantation that was his destination. At first their words were guarded, but over time became less so.

Phelps – he chief overseer at Saint Hall – he put a boy in a press fo runnin, Tilt said on the third day, after throwing a glance at the pilot to ensure his attention was elsewhere, as indeed it was, the white man being preoccupied with staring moodily at the stove in between pulls on a whisky bottle, and suffering no doubt the agonies of spirit endured by those who are terminally idle yet in authority. The rain had stopped; Billy was manning the great tiller-oar that arched back from the stern as grand in scale as the spine of the whale that swallowed Jonah; Tilt and Hutch were at the prow, smoking their pipes, and Bed had joined them there.

Gators in the swamps an patrols all round the place, Hutch said. Isolatin.

Thas the only work white folks do bout here, Tilt said: patrollin.

Thas how comes he got caught.

These days, you runs, you gets caught an drug back fo sho.

Thas what they want you to believe.

You know anyone who dint, Tilt said. Hutch shrugged, but Abednego sensed this was a conversation foreclosed because he was a stranger to them. Tilt continued: How it went was, one of the overseers – he black, thas why they put it on him – they made him turn the screw on Varlet. One mo turn every day.

He screamed like a cat in a bonfire, Hutch said. It weren't – he shook his head.

Hands be bringin in the tail end of the crop for weighin, an there's the press right there an him inside it. They all heard Varlet beggin an beggin, Mas Saint Hall let me out. How old was he, Hutch?

Fifteen, sixteen, maybe. Bertha's boy.

Wound down on, an crushed like he was – Tilt looked down at his hands, and anger thickened his voice. Yeah. Like that.

It took a week, Hutch said.

Longest week I ever knowed, Tilt said.

Zinnie saw in when they opened it up, Hutch said. On account of she had to clean it out after. Zinnie's my wife, he added, to Abednego. Lost her breakfast. An a piece of her soul.

Bale lost his mind.

Who?

Who they made do it. He hired out now. To the forge.

Devil to the fire.

Abednego said nothing; Hutch tapped the ash from his pipe.

Looking back along the flatboat, at where the pilot sat hunched by the stove, flask in hand, Bed said, He drinkin to get drunk.

Uh-huh, Hutch said. He do that.

Man that drunk could fall over the side, Bed observed.

Uh-huh, Hutch agreed. He could.

Fact, Tilt said.

I'm surprised it ain't happen already, Bed said.

Even pullin with every oar we got, the load we bearin we'd struggle to get the boat upstream of here, Hutch said. Tilt nodded.

Load could fall overboard too, Bed observed.

It could, Hutch said.

They were passing now through wooded country, and the leaves, though drained of their chlorophyllic life-blood, still crowded the trees, pale yellow, copper and ocher; and the rise of the banks, which here were steep on both sides, meant there was no wider view to be had, and as Abednego looked about him and wondered, the river, like some great vein, drew him – drew them all – toward a chamber of that terrible southern heart, and he feared it was already too late.

Well then, he said.

But even as he spoke he felt unwelcome eyes upon him, and glancing round he saw Billy the oarsman watching the three of them close from atop the cabin, and with no particular expression on his flat face.

I best relieve him, Hutch said, and he slipped his pipe into the breast-pocket of his woolen vest, clambered up onto the cabin roof and made his way aft. He and Billy exchanged a few words, Hutch tucked the tiller under his armpit, and Billy came forward and joined Tilt and Abednego in the bows.

Looked like the three o you was holdin a regular colloquium, he said.

Bednego here axin bout Saint Hall, Tilt said.

Why, Billy said. You be seein it soon enough.

Dint you ax when you was bought, Tilt said.

I was born there, Billy said. Dint ax nothin when I come out my mama's belly, dint even cry. None o them others talk, he

added, looking over at the cabin under which the rest of the
newly-purchased men and women stood in silence.

They cowed, Bed said.

An you ain't? How come?

Bed shrugged. Billy was strongly-built and moved agilely
about the boat. His sleepy-lidded eyes were watchful and he
most often of the crewmen huddled with the pilot by the stove.
Now he picked up and took the glass from a lamp and, producing a haft-knife, trimmed the wick – a practical task, for they
set lamps at the bows and steered on a while past sundown in
hopes of reaching and putting in at some jetty or other, but
done now to intimidate, and to remind both Bed and Tilt that
he had in his possession a weapon. Only on the first night had
they not reached a jetty and been obliged instead to tie up on
the riverbank; and that night the pilot chained the new purchases together again, indifferent to any call nature might
make before morning.

At each of the jetties where the boat stopped, as by prearrangement white men waited with torches, supervision was
constant, disembarkation forbidden; and the waiting white
men were armed with pistols as well as whips and clubs, and
some carried rifles. This left only the days on the water during
which escape or insurrection might be attempted; yet, long as
these felt, there were few moments in them when there were no
other craft nearby from which an alarm might be raised, and
those moments could not be predicted. Moreover, the pilot's
presence made the conveying of any plan Abednego might have
formulated with Hutch and Tilt to the huddled others all but
impossible; and in any case he did not trust his fellow men and
women to as a body and without debate follow it, and division
would likely lead to failure, and he did not doubt that in that
event their punishment would be savage, and for some lethal.

And so the spirit of revolt bubbled, brimmed and sank back
seething, and on the evening of the fourth day they reached the
Saint Hall estate, and nothing had been dared along the way.
All that long, slow final day they passed between endless-
seeming cotton-fields in which many hundred men and women
were toiling bent near-double, ripping with fingers tougher
than leather the last of the unbearable whiteness from the bolls
as it expectorated from the now-browning, finally-expiring

plants, and oh, how those picking with burning spines longed for that expiration as they waddled forward ungainly as skunks, backsides high, heads low, made dizzy by the weight and pressure of their own blood; and then it was sunset, and orange flamed across the empty sky, and they put in at last at a jetty that served the estate mill and were brought ashore and their collars were removed.

Before the mill stood a great press, into the hopper of which a line of hands were tipping sacks of cotton, after having had it weighed, Bed did not doubt, in one of the adjoining sheds, and seen punishments assigned for those whose pickings fell short of quota by reason of infirmity or illness, both of which conditions the white men considered nigger idleness; and Bed looked up at the central pole black against the flaring sky and the inverted V of its iron arms, and wondered if it was in that press, around which lamps had been set against the encroaching dusk, that Varlet had been crushed until his bones broke and his interior parts split open: a mechanism of evil, then, masquerading as useful; as did not this entire plantation. And beyond its bounds were swamps, and in the swamps gators. They throw em stillborns, Tilt had said. Nigger stillborns, he had added, needlessly. They wants em to get the taste.

Those standing in line and those performing other tasks about the place took little notice of the newcomers as they disembarked and assembled in two lines before the silent white overseers awaiting them. These were on horseback and were four in number. Once papers had been exchanged with the pilot, two ahead and two behind they led Bed and the others away from the river along a wide dirt lane that ran through fields the farther bounds of which were lost in the deepening gloom.

Bed had assumed that he and the others would be taken to the slave quarters and assigned cabins but they were not; instead they were led wordlessly on until, after maybe a mile, they came to a long, tree-lined avenue. Looking left he saw, a considerable way off, and at that distance tiny as two chicken-bones set upright in the dirt, white stone pillars with spheres atop them. These marked where the avenue joined what Bed took to be a road bounding the estate, though the fields ran on beyond it, and so perhaps it merely transected, rather than marked the limits of the plantation. To the right the avenue ran die-straight to the Great House, as distant that way as the pillars were the other. The black folk dawdled to an uneasy halt beneath the trees, and the overseers were obliged to bring their horses in close and herd them forward. The avenue was graveled, and as they stepped onto it, hesitant as hens, the chips of amber stone crunched crisp beneath their feet.

With his whip one of the silent overseers now pointed in the direction of the Great House and as one they turned to look. The intention, plainly, was to awe them, and it succeeded. On both sides of the wide avenue huge oaks, ancient as the land it seemed, and draped with Spanish moss, arched inwards, forming high above their heads an elegant tunnel of writhing branches, and at the far end of that tunnel, a full half-mile away, the Great House stood bathed in the twilight, its vast white marble pediment and eight marble pillars, each greater in circumference than three men could reach around with arms outstretched, glowing as if somehow energized from within, and seeming almost to float above the emerald lawns that spread out lush and lambent from its foundations, and between the marble pillars lamps that had been lit within the building flared gold on a myriad of panes of glass, creating an illusion of iridescence. Four times the size of the main house at Tyler it was, a carven rectangular block of sugar, of crystallized wealth, and here all talk of change, of ending, of war seemed futile; doomed, as the primordial trees announced it must be, to remain talk and nothing more; and even as Abednego knew that all he saw was constructed to create in the minds of those who looked upon it exactly that impression, still it was as unavoidable as arousal is unavoidable when a man is confronted suddenly with the object of his most passionate desire.

At that hour all was hushed, anticipatory, and what was seemed what would always be: the great house, solid as a church, eternal as a tomb, at the heart of things; and about it the cabins and barns and mill and press and boats upon the servile, ever-flowing river; the mile upon mile upon mile of the cotton-fields; the unseen roads beyond as ceaselessly-patrolled by the white men as by any predator marking its range; and out past them nothing but the swamps the reptiles ruled.

Reluctantly they followed the overseers' horses forward, and the white men's silence implied reverence, a ritual ordering in which what was done was done according to a tradition without a beginning and thus implicitly without an end, now or ever, world without end, amen.

Yet no-one was waiting for them when they reached the Big House.

Chapter Seventeen

T heir part in this, they understood, was to wait upon, and so they stood before the Great House passive as oxen, facing it in a loose crescent, and the tails of the overseers' horses switched, and now and then a restless head-toss set a bridle clinking. From the graveled, semi-circular drive twin stone staircases swept up to a first floor that was elevated a full half-story from the ground, curving in towards each other as they climbed so as to meet on either side of the central portico in the form of a heart; and between the sugar-white pillars supporting the pediment, which were as tall as the building itself, stood great double-doors made of some dark wood, paneled, and with brass handles that gleamed. These now opened noiselessly inward to reveal a great space beyond in which a vast chandelier was suspended, glinting and twinkling, with, high on the walls to either side behind it, tall, gilt-framed paintings showing scenes that were maybe Biblical, for thin gold circles haloed the heads of the men, and they were robed.

Looking up from below, the enslaved could not see who were the inhabitants of this room. Two footmen came forward bearing lanterns, brothers for sure, twins possibly, light-skinned, green-eyed and dressed identically in white breeches, ruffled shirts and green velvet jackets, and as one with white-gloved hands they set the lanterns on the central balustrade and took up their positions behind them, and it was done neatly as a quadrille, and they looked not down on the new arrivals but out and beyond, as at what was eternal, and they locked their hands behind their backs and thrust out their chests and were thereafter still as painted statues.

Then at last, at a stately pace, they emerged, Mister Saint Hall and his wife, and those assembled were unsure as to whether they should look up openly and visibly perform being awed at this first sight of their new master and mistress, or whether, as when Satan came beguilingly to Christ in the wilderness, the proffered spectacle was rather a temptation that, yielded to, would lead to instant punishment; and so, their minds clogged with uncertainty and fear, they hung their heads and performed submission, risking only oblique peeping as Saint Hall and his wife came to the balustrade and looked down on them, and as one the overseers removed their hats.

She was slender and wore a deep green dress of watered silk, its spreading skirts a layered dome that brushed the ground in a whisper or hiss as she moved, and her feet made no sound. Her waist was cinched in like an insect's, so tiny and compressed as to be beyond what seemed possible for a human body to bear, and diamonds and emeralds depended flashing from her ears as the moss hung from the great oaks that lined the avenue. Her pale shoulders were bare, her powdered breasts pushed up by the bones of her corset till like heaped curds they came near to overflowing its bounds – whales hunted and hauled from the sea for that, Bed thought, for he had heard tales of the great fishes of the world, and of the catching of them, and the using of every part of them – and her soft, pale flesh was shored up by a tide-line of frothing ivory lace. Her auburn hair gleamed in the lamplight, and was set in curls that framed her face to the cheekbones but no lower, and on the back of her head a circular green silk bonnet was set like a profane halo. Her features were small and hard, her eyes dark and unrevealing, livid spots were painted on her colorless cheeks, and she wore emerald gloves. She looked to be little more than twenty years of age. None expected her to speak, and she did not. Bed thought little on seeing her, for kindly or cruel appearances were as often deceiving as representative, though he did not doubt that, malignant or benign, she taxed her maids to the utmost.

It would be Mister Saint Hall who mattered.

A tall, broad-built man, he wore a black silk frock-coat, faun britches that fit his solid-looking thighs closely, glinting black riding-boots, a green silk vest ornately embroidered with gold and silver stitching, a white silk cravat pierced with a diamond the size of a pig's knuckle, and a gleaming jet top hat in an extremity of fashionable style that added close on a foot and a half to his height. His chest was broad, his yellow-kid-gloved hands were large, his ruddy face slab-like, prognathus-jawed, and his eyes, under heavy brows, were gray, their lower lids heavily pouched. His teeth were large and white. He looked to be in his late forties, and the sideburns that slanted down both cheeks to join the curlicued moustache that adorned his upper lip were black and luxuriant. He put to his mouth a cigar a foot long, and the valet to his right lifted the glass from the lamp before him on the balustrade and offered his master the flame. Saint Hall inclined his head slightly and, underlit in a macabre fashion, puffed on the cigar until it was aglow and he himself was wreathed in smoke. The gesture of dismissal he made was minute, but the valet was acute enough to pick up on it without seeming to so much as glance in his master's direction: he set the lamp down, replaced the shade and stepped back.

All this Abednego recognized for what it was: the setting of a tone.

Mister Saint Hall studied his new acquisitions as the dusk deepened about them and the aroma of the cigar drifted down to their nostrils. Stars commenced to prick, and bats to flit about the trees, so fast as to be barely visible, caught only at the tail of the eye, seeking autumn insects. Moths began to flutter about the lamps on the balustrade, bumping the hot glass bowls shielding the flames over and over until they became dizzy and dropped onto the gravel drive below, and their distracting movements broke the moment, and Saint Hall placed one gloved hand on the flawless-seeming white marble balcony-rail and at last he spoke:

When my great-grandfather came to this place it was nothing but a swamp, he said, and his voice was strong, though his overbite blurred his sibilants, and his manner was sermonic. My great-grandfather was not a wealthy man, but he had a strong right arm: he came to this unnamed, untamed tract of land, this purchase, with nothing backing him but God and self belief, and with these two things, and with his main strength he wrested it from the mosquitoes, the Indians and the alligators. He drained it and ordered it, made the soil fit for cultivation, and the Good Lord smiled upon his works, and he prospered. And my grandfather, his son, built this great house before which you stand in awe today, for himself and his wife and sons and daughters, and for their descendants, in righteous perpetuity; and as his father had cultivated the soil, so my grandfather, and then my father after him cultivated the lives of those about them, creating gardens garlanded with flowers, greenhouses of twining vines; bestowing churches and institutions for the arts; raising above all else an ideal of gracious living, and that ideal I continue today, and will continue, and my children and their scions will embody: gracious and elegant living.

And Bed recalled as Saint Hall paused to drag on his cigar moments he had snatched with Cyrus, moments of hard-earned and sweaty joy that were as soon clawed back by the demands of just such gracious and elegant living – hot kisses hurriedly broken off upon hearing the voice of one or other of the housemaids searching for him in a panic, calling him to rush back at once – tugging up his breeches, tucking in his shirt and awkwardly hefting his desire-heavy crotch as he went to attend to this or that critical need of Mas Tyler or his aged father or spoilt son or sister or daughter: the brushing of a coat's shoulders; the piercing through and fastening of a wayward cufflink; the picking up of something that had slipped to the floor from listless fingers – a book of verse, a handker-chief, a sheet of writing-paper, an unraveled spool of ribbon; the carrying through of a pear upon a gilt-edged plate; its brisk transection with a pearl-handled silver knife – Bed's fingertips touching only the stalk so the flesh would remain unsoiled by contact with even the pinkest parts of his dark-skinned hand, all the while knowing those fastidious white men were not so fastidious about the placing of their private parts inside black female bodies; did not require even acquiescence, their hog-parts squealing and squirming beneath the silk, maggot-hungry, forever eager for release.

And Abednego recalled Cyrus' hand slipping inside his shirt, rough-palmed but gentle against his hot side as they lay below a drift of bees and tumbling apple-blossoms between the orchard hives; kissing the curved domes of Cyrus' chest, teasing his nipples with tongue and teeth; the hot, dark smoothness of Cyrus' skin electrifying against his lips; the mercy of Cyrus' strength.

He put his big arms round me, held me so close my rib-bones spread, and crotch against crotch he lifted me up; I was uplifted, as by a song. And I do believe I lifted him, and was not that grace.

A bee had landed on Cyrus' hand, and Bed had watched

him as he studied it with bright dark eyes, a living jewel adorning him like royalty, scattering gold-dust pollen as it foraged about on the brown petal of his skin; and after a while it flicked away and Bed kissed the hill-range of Cyrus' knuckles where it had been, and they were shiny-smooth with scars from toil, and there was a fury of love inside him, and then Deborah's voice came shrilly: Bed, Bed, you needed.

He will come, Abednego thought, and impossible though that seemed, he found he believed it.

Cyrus.

He will come here.

You all are now a part of my family, Saint Hall said. Part of this great and enduring work. I would ask you to look upon me as a father, and I would say this: do right by me, and I and my men will do right by you.

At these words Abednego and the others risked looking up at the white man more directly than before, for there was not one among them who had not learned in the course of their journey south that this plantation was viewed as a site of especial dread and horror; and each of them, needing so desperately to have hope that he or she would allow its possibility even here, was at the same time judging himself harshly for opening his heart even a crack to what would likely prove merely another manifestation of the million-faced Prince of Lies; or if not that, if that was too spiritual a conception, then the ineluctable functioning of the mechanisms – made by men and yet inhuman – determining that all be done for the maximizing of profit, as if profit could be in and of itself an end: just that; and so they berated themselves for that endlessly-betrayed faith in possibility without which life was nonetheless unlivable.

And my men.

Abednego now attempted to take a measure of the white men sitting silent on their horses, for they far more than Saint Hall would determine the quality of his life, and were the reality behind the façade that he adorned, not a realm of justice or even functional order, but – Bed had no doubt, for why would it not be so? – a zone where vicious caprice would be allowed full rein, and cruelty rule. For the illusion to which Saint Hall and his line had dedicated their lives could never be made real; could never be filled in from behind and below; would always be a glittering bauble filled with eager abuse. And Saint Hall and his wife, and Mas Tyler, and every owner of darker-skinned men and women knew – all being known, or so Abednego believed – of the hollowness at their core, and so over all they had achieved there lay a desolation of spirit, an awareness of some future catastrophe that could not be averted; and whether they articulated it or not, this knowledge filled the hearts of even the most elevated, elegant and gracious with rage and terror; and the energy they poured into the maintenance of their delusion, as is the nature of all energy, multiplied the complexity of its forms thermodynamically, accelerating it towards the point of kinesis and violent fragmentation, and in all directions cruelty grew and was thrown off as by a centrifuge.

Mister Phelps will direct you, Saint Hall said, and without another word, as if he was now bored with his own performance, or had realized it made no difference to them or to himself, he turned and, hand in hand with his wife, went back inside, followed at a respectful distance by the lamp-bearing valets, and the doors soundlessly swung closed behind them, shutting off the glittering chandelier, and a shadow fell across the faces of those watching.

Returning his hat to his head, one of the white men pulled on the reins of his roan and turned her about so he was facing them. I am Mister Phelps, he said, chief overseer here. These – he indicated the other white men, who were bringing their mounts around to form a line alongside him – are Mister Hale, Mister Skelton and Mister Darnell.

Bed looked up and took in their faces, though were they not in truth all the same face. He knew well enough that just as all bodies however finely clothed shared intestines for the pumping out of excrement, so all plantations shared a certain type of man who suited the role of overseer, and these four were no exception, merely slightly better dressed than those on Tyler. Coarsened by their function, and made vicious by it if not by their intrinsic natures, constantly vibratingly aware they were despised both by those above them and those below, their souls were distorted not only by the power that was thrust into their hands, but also by the knowledge that it was they who kept the business going by acts so base the despite was wholly earned. Perhaps – and this was a sort of faith on Abednego's part – on some primal level they knew that, just as Original Sin was both universal and yet nonetheless sin enough to send every man, woman and child in this postlapsarian world to burn in hell for all eternity, this too was sin: a crime of near-inconceivable enormity; a moral obscenity for which they would surely be called to account come the ending of all things and the forcible resurrection of the rotting dead for judgment. And if they did not know this in the conscious mind, as it seemed many did not, it surely stained their souls as poisons stain the flesh, a syphilitic contamination against which ignorance or denial could be no prophylactic, as equally it was not in sexual life, the which Bed knew from Mas Tyler's son rotting from the groin inward, and passing on the rot to Deborah, the issue seven months after, proving a cretin that keened mindlessly and died within a day of its emergence; and both Mas Tyler's son and Deborah commenced to lose their eyesight shortly thereafter.

Was all this, then, Original Sin? This world of horror? Bednego could not believe a just God would allow it so; would permit so unequal a visitation of suffering upon the sons and daughters of Ham, the sons and daughters of Africa, for no reason but the color of their skins and the texture of their hair, for the width of their noses and the fullness of their lips; and since they were, after all, for the Bible told them so, His creations, made in His image, how could these tiny things displease Him so? Always Abednego was returned to this simplicity: there is no God.

Turn about, Phelps said. He was florid-faced and yellow-toothed and smoothly fat, and beneath his faun frock coat a scarlet vest forced his flabby frontage upwards as Mrs. Saint Hall's corset had done, though inelegantly, and in the manner of a rooster's breast, and his blue eyes were cockerel-bright.

Shufflingly Bed and the others obeyed him, and the overseers led them back the way they had come. At a divide in the lane they took a fork that led not toward the mill-yard and jetty but away through the unending fields, and another mile or so along they found themselves at the row of cabins in which they were to be domiciled. By now night had fallen and evening meals were being prepared, in the main outdoors and over open fires, and Bed was struck by how thinly and raggedly-dressed the gathered hands were; how many were bare-footed, and the weather was not warm; how scrawny even the young girls were, how ashy their skins; how neglected the windowless cabins, the graying boards of which had never been so much as lime-washed, and were here and there gappy owing to slippage – time, energy and nails being evidently in short supply; and all eyes were averted from the overseers as they led the newcomers in, four white men cowing over a hundred black, men, women and children, a perverse miracle of power.

You, Diver, Phelps barked at a strongly-built, dark-complected man in his thirties who was just then coming round from behind one of the cabins with an armful of logs.

Yassuh, Mistuh Phelps, suh, Diver said blankly,

The white man gestured with his whip to where Bed and the others stood waiting. Get em parceled out.

Yassuh. Right away, suh.

Phelps looked at Diver as if his servile promptitude might be in some way ironic and therefore insolent; then, evidently deciding it was not, said, It's dark. Light me a pine-knot.

Yassuh.

Diver disappeared round the side of the cabin, returned with a knot, thrust it in one of the cook-fires until it caught, brought it over to Phelps and handed it up to him. Phelps took it and turned his horse about. Without a word the other overseers followed suit – Bednego realized then that he had not yet heard them speak – and as they cantered off into the night the atmosphere shifted, an effect akin to the slow decompression of unbaled hay. Both men and women stood more upright now, their shoulderblades spreading like the wings of waking birds, and their shoulders lowering, the ropes within the muscles of their necks slackening even as they bent to their tasks, and the dull thudding of the hooves of the white men's horses faded away.

Following the shrinking marshlight of the torch Bednego saw the overseers had gone in the direction of the millyard, not the Great House, and it struck him then that the vast scale of the plantation could in and of itself enable secrecy of action, for each part of it formed a separate island among the mile upon mile of ocean-flat fields. It was true the desiccating cotton-plants offered little cover by day, being no more than waist-high; yet even under the exposing glare of the noon sun the dense, spiky twigs would offer a crouching or crawling man concealment. He thought of blue eyes squinting and wondered how many overseers there were, and how their duties were divided.

Past the cabins, maybe a third of a mile distant, and on a slight rise that stood between the slave-quarters and the Big House, lamps hung in porches, illuminating the whitewashed fronts of a row of cottages, ten or so in number, and these he took to be the homes of the married overseers, though whether they formed a single line behind which was nothing more, or were but one side of a larger compound, he could not tell.

Before lighting the knot for Phelps Diver had set down the logs he was carrying next to an elderly woman tending to a cauldron hung on an iron tripod over one of the cookfires. He placed a log among the flames for her, then came and looked Bed and the other newcomers over. There was an assurance to his movements, and he at once picked out Abednego as someone who was alert in a way the rest were not.

In this Diver's judgment was correct, for over the weeks of travel the others had indeed fallen into passivity, and those of them Abednego had known from Tyler had become somehow strangers to him. It was as though once their roles were thrown into doubt their personalities seemed equally to cease to exist. In vegetable quiescence they waited, to be pricked out or espaliered in another place that would not be home as the Tyler estate had not been home: just where they were, and where they suffered, more or less, and endured, more or less; that and nothing more, and so they became mindless as gourds. They could not be called friends, these men and women Bednego had known on Tyler; just he knew a little of their histories, should anyone be interested, as he supposed they knew a little of his. Only Cyrus, who was absent, remained a concrete personality and presence in his mind.

What's yo name, Diver asked.

Abednego. Diver grunted and held out a hand and Abednego shook it. Bed to my friends, he added.

You got Big House hands, Diver said. Soft.

I ain't countin on that here, Bed said. An they ain't that

soft.

The other man shrugged. Wise not to count on nothin here.

What you go by, Bed asked, what that white man called you?

Yeah, I'm Diver, the other man said. And he did not need to add that he was lead hand; nor that he was so not only because the white men wished it but also because the black folks accepted him as such, for it was evident in their easy, unforced deference.

You swim, Abednego asked, keeping his eyes on Diver's, and they were penetrant and wary, and yet seemed to him warm.

Dived in an pulled a boy out the swimmin hole, the old woman said before Diver could reply, and his chest tensed visibly. Went in headfirst. Saved his life that day or he'd of drowned. Boy named Varlet.

Hush, Miz Mary, another man who was standing nearby said, and his eyes were sad, and though he spoke gently, with an arthritis-slanted hand she covered her mouth, and her blue-calloused eyes looked scared.

The firelight played on Diver's face, which was now a carven mask, heavy-featured and, it struck Abednego, in its way handsome; and beneath each of his eyes Bed saw small symmetrical scars, flesh tears or knife kisses or sad clown maquillage; and he was clean-shaven, and his head hair was cut close to the scalp save for sideburns angled sharply down his cheeks, and he stood a few inches taller than Bed, and was in build and coloring much like Cyrus. His agate eyes twitched and the flames from the cooking-fires were caught in their shattered-jet pupils.

Thas somethin to carry, Bed said.

Diver looked him over again. You'll bed with me, he said, and Abednego nodded.

Then Diver divided up the rest of the newcomers, setting the women and young children apart from the men. None of them were coupled, so Abednego did not that evening learn what, if any, accommodation was made for the married – though was to discover soon enough that the answer to that question was none, the performance of morality at Saint Hall being reserved for the white, and not permitted the slaved.

What next, overseer Skelton remarked of a black child recently arrived to a piously-inclined mother, in a conversation Bed would overhear a week later, baptizin a sow's litter?

The cabin assignments made, tin cups were dipped in bubbling pots and kettles and handed round, each newcomer receiving a meager few mouthfuls of cornmeal porridge in which, judging by its taste, there had been dissolved just a dab of pork fat, and that likely rancid; more than nothing, but an amount plainly insufficient to sustain a body through a long day of hard toil. Though scant interest was taken in the new arrivals as they joined the Saint Hall hands at their respective cook-fires, this sharing of food was done with a stoic lack of grudging that signaled all had common cause, and thus constituted a welcome of sorts, and was, it proved, a prefiguration of all that lay ahead.

By a brick-edged well halfway along the row sat a wooden bucket with a length of drawing rope tied to its handle, and there was much going to and fro with smaller buckets, which evidently served to store drinking or washing water in the cabins. Filling and carrying these consumed the last of the hands' energies, and there was not, as there had been on Tyler, any postprandial smoking on porches or idle talk, just a defeated retreat to the windowless cabins in hopes of the brief respite of sleep, though all knew that merciful extinction was but a prelude to grim awakening to, as Abednego was quickly to learn, not only toil and fear, but unending hunger.

Diver's cabin housed twelve men including Bed, and each had a husk-filled sack to sleep upon, and the floor was impacted dirt. Being a leftover, Bed's sack was the least well-filled, and was somewhat too short for his length when he lay upon it, and the blanket Diver handed him was moth-holed and for some reason smelt of burnt hair. Though pitched, the roof of the cabin was low, and at the far end was a small fireplace with no fire in it. By the light of a single tallow candle-stump set upon the rude mantelpiece Bed found a space in which to lie down among the others. The cabin smelt of sweat and male closeness and earth, and once the candle was extinguished the scuttling of mice or rats became audible, and the colder air outside slid in through gaps in the unevenly-clapboarded walls.

For much of his adult life on Tyler Bed had been accustomed to the more comfortable conditions in the cabins of the house-servants – a cot raised off the ground, doors that fit, scrubbed plank floors, rag rugs, glazed windows and even curtains, albeit cut and patched from cast-offs – and yet he did not miss them now, for he felt he had at once been drawn into the orbit of a man at the center of what was important here; and whether he himself was set to labor in the fields or assigned to serve in the Great House he had always despised the preoccupation with small comforts and fripperies that predominated among so many house-servants – house slaves – as if to be among the fine things of others was to have a grasp on them; as if they believed themselves entitled to comfort through mere proximity.

Holdin a rich man's purse don't make you rich.

Once more he thought of Deborah, young and rotting inside and with calcifying eyes, who had thought young Mas Tyler's attentions might bring her some advantage; might mean something more to him than the putting on and pulling off and discarding of a glove when the stitches split, so desperate was she to believe her desirability might be parlayed into privilege, or at least protection, rather than becoming as it had, a mere sluice for the white man's degradation.

Having done little more that day than stand about and walk a few miles, Abednego was eager to talk, but the other hands were dead from toil and lay down without a word of conversation or even a prayer. Diver told Bed their names – Simon, Peter, John and the rest, names in the main but not entirely biblical – but there were too many to take in; too many to match to faces whose predominant characteristic was a drawn weariness that made them seem all the same face, and they gave him no more than guarded, candle-lit chiaroscuro nods before Diver pinched out the wick.

Bed lay on his side, cradling his shoes to his breast. His hip-bone jutted uncomfortably against the ground beneath him, which was hard as brick, though at least dry. He sat up and shoved the husks about inside the sack to make it more even, then lay down again, pulled the disintegrating blanket to his shoulder and closed his eyes, and as he did so he held in his mind the memory of Cyrus curled close behind him, Cyrus' crotch against his buttocks, the hot rigidity there; Cyrus' arms around him, his hands locked over Abednego's heart like a talisman.

If I can't go then he will come.

He will come an I will be here.

This, faith.

Something – rat, squirrel, possum – scurried over the roof.

Someone cleared his throat, then turned over with a shuffling shift of husks.

Chapter Eighteen

Bed was woken in the small hours by sounds outside the cabin that were muted but particular: the clinking of harnesses; low laughter; and yellow light, glinting through the chinks in the walls, cycled spoke-like through the lashes of his narrowed eyes as the lantern and the laughter moved along the row. The men around him did not stir, and so Bed supposed that this was not what he had been expecting as he lay there waiting on sleep: the sudden appearance of white authority, the random calling out intended to remind the slaved that uncertainty was now and forever the governing principle of their lives.

A horse whinnied and there came the sound of a hand slapping a flank. Listening hard, Bednego found he could make out a little of the talk, though he did not know the white men's voices then, excepting Phelps, and he was absent, or did not speak. There seemed to be three of them, maybe four.

You got the clap, you shouldn't dip yo wick is all I'm sayin, one was objecting.

She ain't agreeable, she don't get wet. The drippins stand in, make it easy.

...works its way up an rots the brain.

You takin the mercury?

Thas poison.

You sayin my brain's rotted?

Damn your brain.

Nigger wenches don't need no brain.

Niggers need partways of a brain to be of use. Bout on the level of a ox.

They all used up fore the rot occurs so it don't matter none.

You give every wench the clap they won't breed good. Saint Hall –

That's Mister Saint Hall to you. Ain't you got no respect –

He makes calculations, an the clap ain't a factor.

God damn his calculations. I'm goin first is all I'm sayin. Fore you anyways.

Half the bucks rottin out too, I reckon, on account of the wenches pass it back to em.

They mostly too tired to fuck.

Fo a man it's work, that's true. Less you lay back an she rides.

Calculations, I'm tellin you.

God damn.

There was the liquid sound of expectorated tobacco-juice and with that the white men passed beyond Abednego's hearing, though a short while later he heard the sound of a door opening, followed by colored female alarm and white male vexation, and an absence, an existential vacuum that was repressed black male shame and fury. Later came sounds of muffled upset; and as he lay there Abednego felt the consuming rage of the powerless storm up in him, a rage that was of necessity wholly split off from those other parts of the spirit that sustain a man in his humanity, and are buried in the earth of his flesh deep as a coffin: tools for survival.

It was only after this cruel variant on a tensely-anticipated event had occurred, and because sufficient time had elapsed without any attempt on the part of his cabin-mates to harm him, that Abednego was able finally, and despite the rats that like his thoughts scurried restively in all directions, to drift off to sleep.

The hoot of a conch jerked him from chaotic dreams. It was the lightless hour before dawn, and the other men were already putting aside their blankets and pulling on shirts and pants. Bed joined them as wordlessly they took turns to dip their hands in the bucket by the door and splash water on their faces, then sleepily stumble out into the gray, bleak morning to empty their bladders behind the cabin. No overseers awaited them in the cold silence as yet unbroken by the crowing of any cock, the lead man or woman of each cabin being tasked, it seemed, with rousing and ordering the hands. No escaping the fields, then: no selection; no exemption. All would be broken in, and those removed later would be grateful, and the more biddable for having been put for a time to the lowest and most punitive form of labor. For was it not everywhere the same, this manipulation, this breaking of the spirit? – and yet no more resistible, for all it was so clearly and nakedly known.

We gets anything to break the day on, Bed asked a man he thought was named Peter.

They brings it to us out in the fields, the man said. We works a couple hours, then breaks. Get gived maybe a quarter hour to eat, drink, shit.

Bed nodded. A cold gold drop of sun showed between the cabin-rows, throwing a weak, yarrowflower-yellow dazzle across the dead grayness of the morning. Beyond, and a good way off, the overseers' cottages sat prettily, each freshly whitewashed and with its own small, well-tended garden. Autumn berries scattered bright colors amongst deep green clumps of leaves, and lamps began to show at windows, implying cosiness within, and that cosiness and picturesqueness mocked the hands, for it called to them Aspire even as it flung pepper in their eyes and blared, This is never for you. And as Cyrus, while watching James Rose gaze from the inn-window at the passing troops, had visioned the devastation of total war, so Bed too saw in his mind's eye the demolition of those cottages by gunpowder, a bursting out he took to be like a stove exploding, and he had seen that as a child, and a red-hot metal splinter had scarred his right thigh.

Once all the hands were assembled they went to the fields, walking fast, and there was some jostling. An open cart waited at the top of the first row, and from this each man or woman took a long, umbilical sack and went to join the line of other pickers, taking the first unoccupied row he or she came to, those arriving later having as a consequence to walk further, thereby losing picking time. By and large the new hands picked alongside their cabin-mates, and there were altogether several hundred of them, and the rising sun revealed to Abednego an unending expanse of relentlessly splitting and yielding bolls that seemed undeterred in their fecundity even by the wiry, immobile death-throes of the plants on which they swelled and burst like sores.

To a stranger the sight might appear beautiful.

Bed's muscles soon commenced to ache and tear from the unaccustomed labor, which followed on from days of inertia on the flatboat, and weeks of using only his legs for walking. He had picked in his earlier years, before being selected to work in

349

the Tyler big house, so the doing of the task was not unfamiliar to him, though Diver had not been wrong to note the softness of his hands. The perversely protective spikes of the cotton-plants repeatedly pricked his fingers, and his blood reddened the soft white puffs as he thrust them down the insectile abdomen of the picking sack. He at least knew, as some of the other former house servants did not, that to break a branch on which an unopened boll waited would bring the whip down on his back: many were lashed on his first day for that and other plant-husbanding infractions.

Diver led the holler and Bed soon picked it up, and his line and the other lines worked in unison, breaking twice, briefly, for food and water. This was brought to the fields on wagons by the older women, so as to minimize the time wasted on re-freshment. The overseers, some of their faces familiar to him, others not, arrived mid-morning, and thereafter watched over their charges burdensomely, enforcing a pace to the work and controlling needlessly the way in which it was to be performed, and Bed soon saw that a shrewd person could work less while appearing to work more, which technique he at once adopted. The food – once again maize meal – was flavorless and inade-quate in both bulk and nutrition, and Bed now noticed through the open shirts of the men the too-prominent bone-stripes of ribs splaying out from sternums where pectoral muscles should have covered them meatily; the stringiness of the biceps and excessive vascularity. Whenever the hands gathered at the food or water-wagon the overseers would move their horses near to them to forestall talk, and so incommunication hung over the day, lowering the spirit in a way that was only partly relieved by their singing.

They worked on into the dusk, and only when it had grown too dark to see were they permitted to drag their burdensome sacks the more than a mile to the weighing-scales, which, flanked by overseers like high priests, waited for them in a barn next to the mill. When he disgorged his pickings into the basket Bed was relieved to find that he had scraped in just above the minimum weight to avoid the lash, as none of the new women had done: after going and tipping their sacks into the great press that loomed like a gallows in the middle of the yard they were lined up, along with some of the more elderly or infirm men, and ordered to turn away and bare their backs, a task they did voluntarily so as to avoid having the fabric torn down by the white men, and they were whipped as the others stood in line to empty their sacks into the hopper, and the women sobbed and screamed and some soiled themselves, and Bed and the others moved like the dead, slow and empty-eyed, and each scream was a splinter slid under the skin, and the white men whipped until their arms were tired and then quit, and that haphazardness added to the grotesqueness of the punishment.

Back in the weighing-room Bed had noticed that the top picker in the line ahead of him was not a man but an older woman, hunched but strong and deft in her movements and possessed of sinewy forearms. Her face, while certainly not pretty, was perhaps handsome, save for a pale scar running diagonally across her forehead and down one cheek; and her hair, he saw when she pulled off her kerchief to mop her brow, was cropped close to the scalp, save for a white tuft at the front.

Thas Durance, the hand behind him said, when Abednego asked what was her name. Best picker here. An that means likely anywhere else too, he added, factually and without pride.

Could pick mo, the man ahead of Cyrus said, but she don't. Don't want to make no-one else look bad.

The cotton unloaded, and the punishments carried out, the hands left the press to be wound down tight by a crew of men tasked it seemed solely with the job of baling, and in straggling lines made their way back to the cabins. The overseers, mounted on their horses, stood along the way like sentinels. That day Bed counted at least fifteen, and did not doubt there were more of them about the place and, beyond its bounds, patrollers.

Few cabins had lamps showing in their open doorways, oil being beyond their means, but the older women – many of whom were not as elderly as he had at first assumed, their bodies less buckled with age than wrecked by excessive childbirth and too-quickly-resumed hard labor – had the fires going, lighting the pickers' return for a final, impoverished meal at the day's end; though before sleep there were chores to be done, principally the chopping of wood and the pulling up of more water from the well.

This was the pattern of their days in those final weeks of picking: insufficient sleep, relentless toil, inadequate food, little talk; and soon enough all were in a perpetual state of weariness and depletion. No-one came down from the Big House; no-one – no hand – went there. No-one brought news of even the most local sort. Only the overseers were connected to what occurred outside, and their world extended little further than the fields, the mill and their own cottages; and they shared no news with those of darker hues, and even had they done so, it would not have been believed.

Marooned in the horizon-wide brown-and-white sprawl there settled upon Abednego, as upon them all, a sense of absolute isolation, a timelessness that denied any experience save this, now. Had he ever been someone else, somewhere else? It became hard to believe so; and were it not for the memories of Cyrus he held so close to his heart they were a part, a defining attribute of it, a chamber as it were within a chamber, he would soon enough have lost himself. Even the work songs in which he joined, and without which the monotonous task would have been wholly unbearable, were a seduction into loss of self, their willed defiance perverted as a matter of course into serving the interests of those wielding the whip. His repeatedly-pricked fingertips ached, became leathery, sealing sensitivity within, severing inside from outside, and his muscles and even the placing of his bones shifted in conformity to what he was being made to do. *You become this.* An overseer named Skelton whipped him about the back of his head for alleged slowness one afternoon, and on the third strike the tip of the lash flicked round into Bed's eye and he screamed in pain and staggered and fell, and Skelton yelled Quit shammin, but the eye filled with blood and the sight of it alarmed the white man and in the mirror of his fear Bed felt fear too, though of a mercy the vitreous sac had not ruptured.

The blood cleared slowly over the weeks that followed; and when Phelps chided Skelton for his carelessness with another man's property Skelton replied, A nigger only needs one eye to pick, and Abednego saw the world through a crimson lens then.

Hunger quickly came to preoccupy him as it did them all, for they were given no more than a peck of meal to grind each week, along with now and again a few bacon rinds or a smear of rancid lard. One man in Bed's cabin, Strawson, had lost fingers at the start of the year attempting to haul a snapping turtle the size and weight of a millstone from the swamp.

It et an I dint, he said with a hangdog grin, gesturing with a hand that was missing index and forefinger, a brown crab pincer.

Bed learned that to the north-east of the estate there was an incursion of scrub that split the swamp and ran on into woodland, and there was salivating talk of the hunting a man might do for possums, wild pigs and deer, though to go there in search of game would earn you a whipping and a splitting of the ears or amputation of the nose if you were caught, for it was not only ten miles of fields away, but across a well-patrolled boundary road, and was thus a transgression that could be deemed that worst of all crimes: attempting escape.

An past that, Bed asked.

Simon, the sad-eyed man who had corrected the old woman Miz Mary on Bed's first day, shrugged.

They's a railroad, Diver said, and the energy in the cabin shifted, and Abednego detected it and asked nothing else, and shortly thereafter Diver put out the candle.

Day after day, week after week, the picking went on, until at last it was done: whiteness was reduced to brownness, and all was wholly stripped and dead. That task concluded, they were at once put to plowing those of the other fields that were to lie fallow the coming season and be seeded with clover to restore the soil. This was back-breaking work even with mules to do the pulling, and foreshadowed the plowing under of the mile upon mile of dead cotton plants that lay but a few weeks ahead, consideration of the endlessness of which induced in them all a longing for the restfulness of the grave; and the cold and the damp worsened their hunger until the rats grew wary of them.

As winter drew on a still worse task fell upon them: the clearing of a stretch of uncultivated land in a far-flung part of the estate. To get there was a two-hour trudge, and as a consequence they were roused a half-hour earlier each morning, so as to offset somewhat the work-time lost. This rousing was done by overseers bearing flaring pine-knots yelling and kicking doors, and, the task falling upon them as normally it did not, and having been forced from their own beds some hours earlier than was their custom, the white men's rage and venom was intense. But the land they were to clear lay on the estate's north-eastern border.

It was a bleak expanse, flat and wide and lonely, dotted here and there with pines and oaks, its only boundary, way off, a gray-black wall of trees: the wood in which some dared to hunt by night, beyond which – somewhere – Diver said the railroad ran, and at first Abednego listened for the sounds a train might make, though he did not know what those sounds would be, but the gruelling nature of the work and its danger-ous aspects soon compelled his full attention. The scattered trees were first cut down with axes, and then their fallen trunks were sawn into lengths by pairs of men operating great band-saws. Both these tasks took care: one time an axe-head flew from its handle and would have crippled or killed anyone it struck, which by chance it did not, falling, however, near enough the hooves of an overseer's horse to earn the unlucky axe-man a lash about the shoulders and a rebuke for damaging a tool.

The resultant logs were wrangled together and piled up, along with the undergrowth that grew all about them massed and thorny, entangled as mattress-springs and as hard to pull apart. Logs and undergrowth were then burnt together in great pyres that blazed on into the night and were often still smolder-ing the following morning; and the flames and smoke could be seen all the way to the cabins. By and large the men chopped and sawed and the women grubbed, and mules were brought along to assist with the most arduous task: the wrenching up of the stumps, the root-ball's tangled reach beneath the ground being little less than the extent of the branches overhead, a wearisome symmetry; and the roots of the ruined trees, though dying, necessitated much joint-jarring chopping about with spades to amputate and excise them from the increasingly frozen soil, and much tearing of muscles was required to force it to disgorge the resistant, clinging stumps. This work was more exhausting than picking, but the hands' rations were if anything less, and at the dying of every wretched day all returned to the cabins dizzy with hunger and weariness. Week after week this went on.

Dimly Abednego became aware that Christmas was draw-ing near. Always on Tyler there had been some gesture towards festivity: a half day off was permitted, provided the needful chores had been completed; the provision of a few barrels of cider and strips of pork-belly, and the making of a cheery speech by Mas Tyler bright with Christian pieties set a holiday tone, as did the granting of a larger than usual number of permissions for those enslaved to visit family on neighboring estates, or to receive visitors on Tyler, the usually sharp curfews softened by the knowledge it was a day on which few patrollers wished to be out checking passes; a camouflage of civility that was for the white folks also a self-deception and, it seemed, a sincere one; for Mister Tyler, like Mister Saint Hall, called those who were his slaves his children, and had not meant by that those of color who were indeed in part his issue.

Bed assumed there would be no such festivities on Saint Hall, where brutality was at all points more naked. But in this he was to be proved wholly wrong.

He had by then made friends of his cabin-mates, chief among them Diver, their undoubted leader; then came watchful, sad-eyed Simon, and the lanky and likeable Strawson, whose adventure with the snapping turtle suggested a toughness of spirit that was more than confirmed when Diver added that Strawson had returned from the swamp that night only minutes before the conch; had wrapped his mutilated and still-bleeding hand in a rag and gone straight to the fields with the others to pick. No overseer had noticed his wound, and despite it he had picked enough that day to stave off the whip.

There was a man of twenty-five or so who could not speak but only make a creaking noise in his throat, for his Adam's apple was a scarified indentation, the bite, as it were, in place of the fruit, and he went by Crawfish on account of his skill in catching the crustaceans in the creeks about the place, but was called Crawford by the overseers. Then came twin brothers Richard and Robert, coltish lads who in better circumstances would have been full of fun and mischief, and were the youngest in the cabin at seventeen; a man stringy and bony and strong, and at fifty the oldest among them, Emmanuel; and four others, biblically-named: Matthew, Mark, Luke and John. Another hand, Earnest, who was silent and struck Bed as particularly watchful, had been assigned elsewhere by Diver at the end of Bed's first week.

Too busy with his lookin, Strawson said when Abednego asked why.

Too busy with his tongue, Diver added.

For all the hands were in a state of perpetual exhaustion, some evenings after eating Diver would visit with Durance, her name, Bed learned, a compression of Endurance, and it was a name put on her, as all their names were, but one she had claimed, for it was apt, and Strawson called Diver's visits courting and no-one, not even Richard or Robert, laughed. On his return Diver would be thoughtful, and often as he collapsed onto his mattress he would ask Bed to tell of his journey from Tyler, and Bed obliged, veiling behind tale-telling and attempts at humor the passing on of information; and at back of those evenings, in which the passing of time was marked by the dwindling of the cabin's single candle and never extended beyond its natural extinction, there was a sense of dark water rising; of an approaching convergence of things; for all knew the skeletons beneath their skins were becoming daily more visible, were becoming who and what they were. We will be bones an nothin else. And Bed thought of Ezekiel, of the resurrection of the Children of Israel, and of the vengeance of the dead.

Twined in with talk of Tyler, its geography and its people, Bed spoke of Cyrus, at first without intending to and with, in his weariness, little passion, but thereafter more fully, for to think of Cyrus was to feel a rising within him as of bread-dough in the pan; and to speak of him alleviated Abednego's sense of loss through the simple restatement that it was real, and one evening as the candle guttered low he said, We gon be together again. I know it.

How, Strawson asked.

Don't know how, Bed said, but we will.

Thas a powerful friendship, Diver said, and he smiled a lopsided smile.

Crawfish nodded, touching his fingers to his concave throat.

That's faith, Emmanuel said.

You prays to him, Richard asked, and he too smiled, shyly, and by his smile it seemed to Bed the youth saw more than the older men.

I prays fo him, Bed said. An give thanks.

To God, Richard asked.

When Bed shrugged Robert said, God ain't hereabouts, thas fo sho.

Preacher say He everywhere, Matthew said.

Same as He nowhere then, Diver said.

Emmanuel hawked, opened the door, and spat outside.

Bednego preachin on Cyrus, Robert said.

He testifyin is what he doin, Emmanuel said, and the others nodded. To hear one man speak of another with such passion and conviction of future possibilities kindled something in them, for all they could not understand the depth of it, but in their aching bones and hearts they felt the mystery, and the wick slipped down into the transparent slick of molten tallow and the quivering flame died.

Christmas week arrived, though it was to the Saint Hall hands of far less account than the close of the picking season, and that had been marked by nothing save the darning and folding of the sacks for storage, and the replacement of one wearisome task with another, worse one: the clearing of the land. Nonetheless, wreaths of holly and mistletoe, red berries and white, twisted by Miz May and the other older women, appeared on the porches of the overseers, hung on nails, and many more were sent up to the Great House. They pagans up there, Emmanuel said, and spat.

Two nights before Christmas Eve, Richard and Robert were taken away without explanation by overseers Phelps and Hale, and the drunken merriment of the white men sank stones in the hearts of the black, who lay down disquieted, avoiding speculation. The two youngsters were returned shortly before dawn so beaten and bloody they could barely speak, and Richard could not stand; and both had lost front teeth. The door was kicked open by the overseers, jarring those within from sleep, and outside was a mule cart, and the boys were carried in, first one, then the other, by the two white men, who threw them down like sacks and left them crying on the floor, and flinching when Diver and Bed tried to tend their wounds.

They been in the arena, Emmanuel said sadly, his brows puckering as he touched Richard gently on the shoulder.

Arena, Bed asked.

Emmanuel shook his head and didn't answer, and no-one, not even Diver, would explain. Later it transpired that Richard and Robert had been forced to fight each other for the white folks' amusement until one was rendered fully unconscious, and had been given hammers as weapons, and had, when they attempted in their youthful ebullience to refuse the hammers, been threatened with a knife between the legs, and had not doubted the threat would be followed through on if they did not fight; and the gentlemen guests of Mister Saint Hall had crowded round a cleared space in the dining-room to put money on the outcome: on which boy would win; on how long the fight would last; and Abednego had had to fight back the tears when he saw their beaten faces clear and surgical in the raw morning light.

Boys been made to fight dogs up there, Emmanuel said, and his eyes twitched. Boys young as eight. One time they dragged in a gator an a young buck had to fight that. They gave him a knife though.

How you know they gave him a knife, Matthew asked. He was wringing out the rag he had been using to wipe blood from the boys' faces at the door, and was haloed by the pallid light beyond, and his voice was thick.

One a the houseboys told me after. He was bringin whisky an rum fo the gentlemens an he come in on it. Jackson tried to get the gator behind the eyes. They's a kinda hole back there a blade might get in. But he slipped an fell an it got his head in its jaws an shook him till his neck bruck.

Stone-faced and with burning eyes they met the morning, and in the empty air and in their tautening bellies they sensed an acceleration of things.

The overseers were later to the cabins that morning than was their custom, and ill-tempered from drinking so intemperately the night before, and possibly owing to losses from gambling, and were therefore more prone than usual to striking without provocation. Otherwise that day was the same as every other: the weary trudge, the long hours clearing the land, the laboring that ground on until the sky was dead and it grew too dark to see.

On their return that evening, a mule-cart piled high with

white cotton shirts, pants and shift-dresses came creaking along the cabin-rows, and Mister Phelps sat up front, and he ordered Diver to instruct the hands to leave off their domestic tasks and assemble at the wide central part of the road, the square he called it, for the disbursement of the year's new clothing. The weave was coarse, the cut basic and general and the fit consequently poor, and the stitching had been done with little care, but that was true of the dirty and ragged clothing they currently wore, and so they took what was handed them without remark. No shoes or boots were offered, and Abednego had already been obliged to knot rags around his, for the soles were coming away from the uppers, and there was available no awl or leather-needle with which to mend them satisfactorily.

Standing among the heaped clothing on the back of the cart as the hands gathered round him, Phelps announced, Yall gon be workin extra to pay for this – his mood soured, perhaps, by the niggers' lack of gratitude. Mister Saint Hall got to make his profit, he added. Thas only fair. His face was flushed and he took a swallow from a silver flask.

None made to complain, for the practice was usual: a technique whereby the encouraging of slaves to perform extra work in their minimal free time through the exciting, empowering novelty of being able to earn money, ensured that same money was soon enough returned to the owner through a grotesque parody of contract and commerce. And so it was that any impulse to industry was twisted round and exploited to extract further labor from the industrious, and burden all hands with yet more toil, and, Abednego supposed, amuse the mercantile, mercenary minds of the white folks. And so they took the new clothes and returned to their cabins to put them on, setting the old aside for rags or patching. Some would stitch the outworn clothing into shoes of a sort, or make pads for kneeling work. Bednego thought of traveling clothes, but said nothing.

Later that evening several sacks of bones, of pigs and oxen and possibly several mules, were carted over from the slaughterhouse by the mill, to be distributed and boiled in soup.

At conch-call the following morning, having assembled, they did not at once go about their tasks but instead, according to some pre-arrangement, remained in the lane, awaiting the overseers. It was Christmas Eve, and cold, the air was damp, and they stood shivering beneath a dun sky scumbled dirty yellow at its margins. Crawfish repeatedly touched his fingers to his indented throat, swallowing awkwardly, and Diver gripped him by the shoulder. Abednego's skin prickled beneath the new cotton shirt. If I could, I'd never wear cotton again, he thought, futilely.

Four overseers, Phelps, Skelton, Hale and Darnell, came cantering down the lane, and those waiting braced up and deadened their eyes, and their skins were ashy as corpses', and the horses of the white men were pale and snorted steam. Somewhere along the line a newborn wailed without seeming to draw breath, Dinah and Terrance's child that had come two nights earlier, the birth both premature and difficult; the wail a tearing sound unnatural in its base purity, hunger evacuated of reason and restraint, and the sound of it made the waiting men and women afraid: they will see that we are this.

Every bone had been cracked and sucked and scoured of marrow.

Tonight, Mister Phelps announced, as is tradition on the Saint Hall estate, there will be a masked ball. And as is also tradition, our neighbors, and the best families of Blaze and Cleaver counties will be attending. He turned in the direction of the now-screeching infant. Quiet that brat or I'll drown it in a bucket.

The wailing was quickly smothered, a turning-in that was not a comforting.

Mister Saint Hall is known not only for the extensiveness and progressiveness of his estate, Phelps continued; not only for its innovations in modern techniques of management and cultivation; for the elegance of its great house and the gracious traditions established therein; but also for the much remarked-upon contentment of his dusky children.

Phelps paused and looked about him, his eyes – small, sharp, blue – searching for defiance in brown eyes that were in spirit sclerotic, and their pinned irises were retreating, the true black revelation shrinking, shielded. When he considered no opposition was offered, he continued his address. It will please Mister Saint Hall to see his servants line the avenue this evening in their freshest, gayest dress, in order for them to, with heads bowed in modesty, honor the arrival of his guests, and by their smiling presence bear decorous testament to the temperate humanity of their master's regime. Each tenth man or woman shall bear a lighted pine-knot, so as to create a bright and welcoming spectacle pleasing in its symmetry. And there will be singing –

Crawfish touched his concave throat again, and swallowed and emitted a creaking sound. Caught not singin cheery enough, Simon murmured. Skelton took the pliers an took out his apple. Made Bale an another fellow hold him down while he did it. We all sings out lusty after that.

There will be singing and music, Phelps said. Jig an fiddle. And in the turnin drive befo the front steps, a merry show of dancing to delight our guests.

Phelps remained on his horse; the other overseers dismounted and passed up and down the line, indicating for the more handsome boys and prettiest girls to step forward, which, hesitantly, and with downcast eyes, they did. Robert and Richard were passed over, for their faces were still frog-swollen and asymmetrically distorted, their mouths damaged and their eyes wounded in a way that would defeat any kindling of merriment. Eight of each sex were selected, and were led away by Mister Darnell to practice dances with fiddle-players hired in, Bed learned later, from a neighboring estate. Meantime he and the other hands were set to practicing a song of welcome, and to sing together, even in circumstances such as this, gave them heart, and they could not hold back from expressing something of their true spirits; and as they at first hummed and then sang they grew in power and sonorousness, and some voices soared above others, one of them to Bed's surprise belonging to Durance; others switched back and darted through the melody like swifts, and their song was sorrow sweetened with a rising joy in their own suddenly-awakened humanity, a humanity they sometimes, separately and privately, feared had been wholly extinguished, but was reignited in their doing of this all together; and the white men were moved, visibly, for they rose up in their saddles as though lightened and something shifted in their features, and so they cut the singing short, for to be stirred in that way – and worse, to be seen to be stirred – was to admit the truth of things, and that they could never do, not and allow the world to continue as it was, and Bed saw Skelton's red-rimmed eyes land on Craw-fish's gaping mouth and move on fast.

In bright mansions above, they sang.

Lord, I want to live up yonder
In bright mansions above
My mother's gone to glory
I want to go there too
My father's gone
My sister's gone
My brother's gone
My Savior's gone –

That'll do, that'll do, Phelps said hurriedly, and he cracked his whip and they fell silent, but their chests were lifted up and pushed out, and they were at once inspirited and inspired, and the cold air continued to vibrate as if inhabited by something living yet unseen, and Dinah's baby no longer cried.

Get to your tasks, Phelps said. Cabin leaders, assemble your crews and have em ready for two in the post meridian. I'll send down a bucket of oil. Get you shines shinin. Get outta yo new clothes now: Mister Saint Hall don't want em spoilt.

Diver and the other leaders called out their Yassuhs, and the hands returned to their cabins and changed back into their dirtier, more ragged shirts and pants and smocks. Today they were not led out to the scrubland but were set to commencing the plowing-under of the cotton plants in the fields near to. Work was curtailed by the sounding of the conch shortly after noon, and they were allowed time to wash and change and oil their hands and faces so as to set their skins gleaming. At two they lined up before the cabins, and were briefly looked over by the overseers, then led along the lane to the Great House's avenue. No-one spoke. In their silence the overseers detected sullenness, and so they were ordered to sing as they walked, and it was Durance who led their song:

Mos done toilin here, she called out.

Oh, brethren, others chorused, and, Mm, Lord, and the response: I'm mos done toilin here.

I aint been to heaven, Durance sang.

Mos done toilin here

The streets up there are pave with gold

Mos done toilin here

Quit that, Skelton snapped, for it seemed the sentiment displeased him. Sing a happy song, he ordered, but he lacked the force of personality to compel them, and they sank back into silence as they walked along.

They reached the avenue somewhat after four and the lining-up took a further half-hour, by which time the sun was lowering in the sky, and Bednego found himself positioned not far from the Great House. He would rather have been nearer the gate-posts, for that would have afforded him a better view of the road and the land that lay beyond it, but had had, of course, no choice in the matter. A wagon heavy with pine-knots that had creaked along the lane behind them now pulled up between two of the great spreading cypresses that flanked the avenue. The two colored men driving the wagon had had the foresight to bring a brazier with them. This they set up and lit, in order to be ready to set the knots blazing when dusk descended and the first guests were due to arrive. To stand there doing nothing was preferable to dragging stumps or forcing the plow, and Bed felt, as did, he assumed, most of the others, a slight curiosity about what he would see, what the best families would amount to, though he was wholly bereft of anticipation, for what, in truth, would it matter?

Time dribbled by and they shifted restlessly where they stood, for the oncoming evening was cold: the sky had cleared, and such warmth as there had been earlier had tumbled upwards and was gone. A slight mist crept in, rising no higher than their ankles and prickling their toes and heels. The sun set behind the Great House, and as it did so the knots were lit. Four younger boys were tasked with running back and forth handing them out, and as the lamps of the first carriage appeared on the boundary road the order to hum was given, and they obeyed, and the stars pricked the deepening blue of the sky as though all creation was in service of this.

Smile, Mister Phelps shouted as the carriage turned into the drive, and Bednego thought of the grins of skulls and the rictus of the dead as he, as they all forced a smile and hummed. Phelps was now dressed in a black silk frock-coat and top-hat, and a mass of white ruffles exploded between the shiny lapels of the coat. His breeches were dove-gray, and his gloves and boots faun, and he kept his whip coiled and set back on his hip near out of sight, for tonight all was to appear as if uncoerced.

Cutting through the humming, to Bednego's right there came the sound of fiddles striking up, and the boys and girls who had been taken away earlier came dancing out from amongst the trees onto an oval of lawn directly in front of the Great House, around which the drive circled to permit the turning of carriages. The boys were in white shirts and pants, and over the shirts they wore red-and-black striped vests and on their heads straw hats, while the girls wore white blouses and full white skirts puffed out by layers of petticoats beneath, and on their heads black-and-red kerchiefs, and two fiddlers followed them, playing as they did so, and they wore bottle-green tailcoats but were barefooted. The dance was a quadrille, and the dancers' movements were both lively and precise, though would become less so as the hours wore on without an intermission.

Wreaths of holly and ivy adorned the elevated stone balustrade behind them like rosettes on a thoroughbred, and the doors of the Great House swung inwards, and the chandelier in the ballroom sparkled, and as that first carriage turned in the crescent before the house footmen in liveried uniforms hurried down the right-hand flight of steps to wait attendance on the guests with champagne glasses upon silver trays.

The carriage was covered, well-maintained, driven by a light-skinned groom in a heavy coat and bowler hat, and drawn by a pair of dappled grays, and it was lacquered black and trimmed in gilt. The groom descended from his perch, folded down a hinged iron step, and opened the door for those within. These proved to be an older white man, who emerged first, then turned to assist one then another white woman in alighting after him, wife and daughter judging from their similarity of features; and both women, struggling to control expansive and unwieldy ruched silk hoop-skirts, held back fearfully, feeling about for the unseen step with tentative feet, and the man wore a white domino that was already wrinkling and obscuring his sight, and the two women more elaborate eye-masks studded with gems, from which peacock and ostrich feathers rose up tremulously. Confronted by the extreme opulence of their surroundings the three seemed ill at ease, and the man – balding on top and with gray side-hair tied back in a black ribbon – was, it seemed to Abednego, overfull of bonho-mie as he led them past the footmen. As they began to make their way up the steps the older woman turned and reached back awkwardly to take with a white-gloved hand a glass from one of the proffered silver trays, drained its contents in a single swallow, then found herself holding an empty glass with nowhere to put it, and she looked about her like a nervous hen, all the while smiling inanely.

Other carriages came rolling up the drive, in the main cab-riolets and barouches, several dozen of them; and occasionally smartly-dressed young men came cantering along on horse-back, singly or severally, and, though he was by habit alert to, and fascinated by, white folks' performance of status, Bednego quickly lost interest in the minutiae of the many arrivals. His lower back had locked and his feet were cold, and he would have liked to urinate.

Torches sputtered out and were replaced from the heap on the wagon by the scurrying youngsters. After two hours one of the dancing girls fainted, and was quickly carried out of sight by two of the boys, who returned and carried on as though nothing had occurred, and Bednego was close enough to see their smiles were terrible.

In between receiving the arrivals with drinks, the footmen brought wicker baskets out to the overseers who had been tasked with keeping the hands in order, and the trace smells of chicken and bread from within the baskets were enough to make Bed's shrunken stomach gurgle, and his mouth water in an incontinence of hunger.

God damn, Diver muttered as Phelps tore a greasy wing from a roast half-chicken and the meat, dry white and shiny dark, was revealed beneath the prickled golden skin; and watching the white man eat was both sickening and exciting, and sent the minds of those gazing at his greasy lips and busy teeth to dark places.

Once all the expected guests had arrived, a process taking somewhat over three hours, the hands were ordered to cease humming; and, leaving the dancers, tortured marionettes, to their heartless, clockwork task, they began to file back to the cabins. As they were doing so three white men came up the avenue fast on horseback, and they were not dressed fancily in the manner of guests to a party, or masked; nor was there anything about their manner or bearing that suggested they were of the best families of Blaze or Cleaver counties. They rode up to Skelton and Darnell and without dismounting fell into muttered conversation, casting glances as they talked at the several hundred dark-skinned men and women passing by in silence and seeming docility, and rumors of an escape ran along the line like a shiver up a spine.

Back at the cabins, in a fever of hunger Bed, Diver and the others hunted and caught several rats, cut off their heads and tails, skinned and cooked and ate them.

They wondered who had run.

Chapter Nineteen

T he new year came and went and was celebrated up at the Big House: from the cabins the hands saw clouds of fireworks explode in the night sky; and childlike exclamations of joy from Saint Hall's assembled guests at each whiz and bang and fusillade were carried to them on the breeze, though to those enslaved the spectacle suggested not wonder, not innocence, but gunshots and baleful comets, cannon-fire and obscure prophecies.

The sight was not new to Abednego, for on Tyler every July fourth there had been fireworks, in celebration of a hard-won independence from tyranny, the irony of which was all too present in the minds of the black men and women who witnessed that explosion of gunpowder and patriotic sentiment, and the declaration of truths so self-evident they need not be acted on. The catching smell of ignited saltpeter and sulfur itched Abednego's nostrils as he looked out across the cabin-roofs at far-off evanescent cascades of rubies, sapphires and diamonds, and the distant crackle and rumble returned his thoughts to the war that at Tyler had appeared, to the alarm of the white folks, imminent, but here seemed impossibly remote. Out loud he said: War.

Diver, who stood beside him also watching the fireworks, nodded, and said, What don't come of its own accord, we gots to bring. And it seemed he too had spoken his thought aloud without intending to, for he wrinkled his brow and was silent a while. Then he said, I'ma meet Durance later.

Zat so?

Yeah. An you best come with me.

And so Abednego became part of the conspiracy that was to ignite the night Cyrus reached the Saint Hall plantation, though at first, despite the taint of gunpowder in their nostrils, the slaves' scheming concerned not rebellion but the provision of food. Their focus was predominantly on the possibility of night-hunts to the north-east, for the hog-pens, chicken-coops and grain- and other stores and barns about the mill-yard were patrolled all night by the overseers; lamps burned there from dusk to dawn, exposing any skulkers about the place, and a slave caught attempting to steal would be flogged near to death, and in their weakened state 'near to' could soon enough become the thing itself. And so, though it would involve a trek to get there, avoiding patrollers on the boundary road as they crossed it, and then actually catching game in the dark, going to the woods seemed to them the less dangerous path. The land-clearing had been abandoned for the season, but all of course recalled how to get there, and knew which paths ran straightest in the dark, and which ways least likely kept an eye on.

Over the years Diver and Durance had made connections about the estate to which Bed was not privy, and secreted in her cabin, inside a log that had been cunningly sawn in half, hollowed out and set back in place as if a part of the wall, were hunting and skinning knives, wire snares, a small bow – real Injun, she said – and a quiver of feathered arrows.

That first evening Abednego found it strange to sit before Durance in her cabin, for there by the fire she seemed somehow regal, sitting straight-backed on a stool into the legs of which large-eyed lizards – chameleons, she called them – were carved, and surrounded by the other women who slept there; and they were her juniors and she their senior, and they knelt in silence and looked up at her as at a ruler or perhaps a seer, save for the prettiest of them, a caramel-skinned young woman with hazy green eyes that caught the firelight, who sat at the older woman's feet and faced the others, and Durance's work-gnarled hand rested sometimes on the girl's shoulder, some-times on her braided head, and the girl looked at Abednego and the other men with an expression that was hard to read, and that he both recognized and did not, for he had known the power of love but had never been an acolyte. The logs smol-dered in the wide, sagging fireplace, and herbs hung from nails in the mantel above. Almost it could have been a shrine, but the talk was practical and unadorned.

We goes in shifts, Diver said. Else we be kilt by lack o sleep.

Durance nodded. No-one goes out more'n one night in three, she said. Knives an such come back here after.

Snares, Strawson asked.

Leave em if they empty, Durance said. Set em someplace

you can tell whoever goin out next.

Strawson nodded. Can't risk lights, Diver said. Not even a candle.

We hunts by moonlight, Durance agreed. Any night the sky's clear, people gots to be ready to go – like that, she added, snapping her burled fingers.

The fourteen or so hands Diver and Durance trusted to take part in these initial forays were divided into groups, and duties parceled out among them. They were in the main men, but five were women, including Durance herself; and it was agreed that anything caught on such a night-hunt would be shared out equally between the fourteen, and also that each individual might divide his or her share among favored companions – though only those of whom Diver or Durance approved, for not all could be trusted, and just as hunger bound the conspirators together in the quest for self-preservation, so it could drive others to bartering treachery. All agreed something be set aside for Dinah and Terrance and their baby regardless.

To take all this upon themselves was dangerous, and not only for those who went out, but also for those who remained behind, for there might be at any time an inspection by the overseers, and a head-count, which would at once expose any absentees; and the hands who shared cabins with those who were absent would be tormented to make them tell what they knew. The punishment for the ones caught returning would be vicious, and could be, as Abednego was to learn later that evening, executed wholly cold-bloodedly, for back at their cabin Strawson told him of a stable-hand who had been caught by Mister Skelton that spring picking up from the ground, and thereby stealing, a single egg that had been laid in a patch of grass away from the hen-house. Gus, a husband and father of two, had begged the enraged overseer, who was by then laying about his head and shoulders with a length of plank, to be allowed to speak with Mister Saint Hall and ask the great man, on behalf of all the hands, for rations sufficient to obviate the need for theft.

Unexpectedly overseer Skelton agreed and Gus, by now in some measure concussed, was taken up to the Great House. He returned a little while later staggering, his head split open, anointed as in some profane ritual with both his own blood and the yolks and albumins of a dozen broken eggs, and was at once handed a shovel by Mister Hale and made to dig a shallow grave. In this, when the digging was done, his wife and two small children were compelled to lie as he spaded the dirt back in, living until the soil wholly covered them and stoppered their screaming mouths, and Mister Hale made Gus tread the silent earth down upon them till it was flat, and would allow no marker.

Next night Gus went out to where they was buried, knelt down an cut his throat, Strawson said. I found him.

An the knife, Bed asked.

I gots it still.

Despite their knowledge of the vigilance of the overseers, and despite a terror of punishment that saturated their psyches to near-paralysis, their hunger was now so extreme that all were prepared to risk the night-hunt. They were, moreover, aware that to delay would weaken them still further, and thus make any search for foodstuffs the less likely to succeed; and they knew that as winter wore on the weather would harshen, the game would become thinner on the ground, and there would be no time to dig out the burrows of those that slept in the earth.

They's nuts too, Durance reminded them, the first time Abednego was to go out. A skirtful of nuts, thas somethin.

Bed nodded, adjusting the empty gunny-sack slung across his back. With him were Diver, Strawson, Crawfish and Robert, men he knew to be tough, commonsensical and indeed wily, and that was reassuring; another five, three men and two women, were to go out in a separate group a half-hour after.

None wondered aloud why their master did not feed them enough. All understood the cold calculation, the fulcrum-tilt past which buying new stock was cheaper than maintaining what was already owned. All understood no appeal to humanity was possible where humanity did not exist. All understood also that in that lack of possibility there was a brutal liberation: from misguided hope. They saw the reality of their situation, and so they planned without delusion. And if behind that reality lay an abyssal mystery, an unfathomable question as to how such pain and horror could be inflicted by one set of people upon another with no deeper justification or excuse than skin, they had neither the time nor the resources to attempt its penetration, nor even, then, the desire. For they saw that the attempt to understand was in and of itself the giving of a gift, and they had no gifts to give Saint Hall or his overseers, not as they starved and toiled in the white man's fields. Durance made two curious movements with her left hand over the candle-flame into which she had been gazing as if somehow seeing afar, and Abednego thought of Old Africa back on Tyler, and of knowledge distorted or lost, and Cyrus, who was, it struck Abednego now, more connected to the deep past than he was.

For all the fear that swirled chokingly about them, to creep out by night thrilled Bed. To not be overseen; to be moving voluntarily; to be attempting a self-appointed task, was to be alive, not a puppet, automaton or tool: a man, for he was a man; and also a human being. It made him, and he did not doubt them all, want to run and never stop, and the waxing moon was bright, and the dead growth in the fields was silver and the shadows were black, and they loped along the track in silence, alert as foxes for sight or sound or smell of overseers loitering in the dark.

What if we come up on one, Bed had asked earlier as they readied themselves.

Robert looked up sharply. His eyes were luminous, and his tongue-tip touched the gap where a front tooth had been.

Drag him down quick an – Diver drew his thumb across his throat.

Or take a rock –

We best bring a shovel, Strawson said, in case we needs to do some buryin, and Diver nodded.

You ever butcher a horse, Robert asked, and their stomachs grumbled at the thought of such a mass of flesh, and Strawson said, Hogs. I done hogs.

Now they were passing through fields. Abednego wished Cyrus was with them, not in suffering but as his companion, and Cyrus would catch Abednego's hand in his and they would run and pass beyond the horizon and be swallowed by the sun, and only in such a delirious extravagance of imagery could he picture freedom then. No-one spoke and the air was still.

An hour's jog more brought them to the area of land they had been, until recently, so laboriously clearing. It was now still more desolate, having been stripped of trees, and was pitted with root-holes; and, amongst black pyres of burned logs and scrub, charred and upturned stumps lay here and there like casualties from some strange war. The thickets beyond the area they had cleared, though low-lying, were dense and slowed their progress, and, while in their midst, to their alarm they saw upon the road ahead a light and it was moving. As one they threw themselves down among the clawing briars, and lay there still and silent until it had passed from sight. They waited some more, then struggled to their feet and went on, more warily now. Crossing the road Bednego felt something shift in him.

I could run, he thought.

His scalp prickled. A storm, nearing: a storm inside his mind; the tiny currents that run through muscles, the brain charging up the body; lightning flooding the soft tunnels that sat within the cradle of his skull.

But no, not like this.

Cyrus had taught Bed skills in trapping, gutting and skinning, but he had never put them into practice, and besides he had no plan; if he ran unprepared he would be caught.

An if I go an I'm gone when he comes –

A plan.

Eat.

Yeah, that.

Think about it later.

They passed into the wood, which was less dense than it had appeared further off and by day, when Bed had broken off to stare at it in speculation in between sawing trunks and wrenching up stumps, and was therefore more usefully penetrated by the moonlight than he had expected. Almost at once they came upon a rabbit. It eluded them, white tail flashing as it vanished among the undergrowth, but its presence implied a warren close by, and so they set snares. Counting on Strawson's confidence that he could find the place again, they went on, their mood now both feral and childlike, the two states after all close kin, their eyes straining scotopically, their occult senses attuning to the presence of those living things that move unseen in the dark; and to be keyed up in that way generated neuro-electric energy both within and between them, and discharged it in waves, and so the night wore on, filled alternately with watchful waiting and sudden surges of exertion. Diver spotted a raccoon, and they pursued it in a desperate, exultant but wholly silent chase, and Bed and Crawfish threw themselves upon it, and Bed knifed it repeatedly and excitedly as it squirmed beneath him, and it died. Diver looked at the sky and the position of the moon and said quietly it was time to head back.

On their way back to the road they found two rabbits jerking in the snares, and Diver broke their necks with brisk twists and thrust them into his sack. At the edge of the wood, while still concealed among the trees, they gutted the rabbits and the raccoon, throwing the still-warm entrails aside; then began their return journey.

It was as they drew near the cabins that the fear began to grow on Bed that in their absence an inspection had happened. All was in darkness and all was silent yet he was not reassured; and as they made their way down the track behind the row that ran parallel to the lane he sensed a willed repression in what struck him as a near-unnatural stillness in which the smallest sounds were clearly audible – the brush of cotton between thighs; the exhalation of held breath. He thought of the saucer eyes of owls, and, imagining Phelps and the others lying in wait, looked over at Diver and Crawfish, half-minded to share his fears, but they and Robert and Strawson appeared, so far as he could discern in the dark, unperturbed, and it seemed unlikely he had noticed something they had not. Were they caught returning they would have done better to run, however ill-prepared the attempt, but it was too late for that now. In the course of what had become their jog back the raccoon had become burdensomely heavy to Bed, and as they made their wordless way out into the lane he hoisted the gunny-sack from his shoulder, ready to fling it aside in the event of being caught, in hopes it might benefit someone from the cabins who happened across it, and not be taken by the overseers.

But there was no ambush, and they returned to their cabin without incident. As they concealed the raccoon and rabbits inside various mattresses Peter told them a party of horsemen had galloped through at around two a.m. The riders had not stopped, being on other business it seemed, but it was enough to make Diver uneasy, and though the sky remained clear, neither he nor Durance sent anyone out the following night. The meat, shredded into their mush over several days, nourished them sufficiently to make the expedition worthwhile; and the bones were cracked and gnawed and boiled out, then buried with care, and the skins scraped and secreted.

Travellin clothes.

Bed lay down to snatch a few hours' rest before dawn came, and dreamt of Cyrus nourishing him, of the heat of Cyrus' veined rigidity and Cyrus' seed hot in his mouth, and awoke to find he had ejaculated in his sleep, yet did not feel depleted, but rather energised.

And so things continued through the months that followed, though as predicted game grew scarcer and the weather progressively more hostile. To go out on moonless or overcast nights, or in a downpour, would have been counter-productive, and such nights were not uncommon; and so their minds turned to the thieving of foodstuffs nearby and its impossibility; and, consequently, to insurrection.

In Amesburg they's a foundry, Diver said one evening, when drips of rain penetrated the much-patched roof dishearteningly, and fell hissingly onto a fire which the damp had deprived of much heat, and from which, due to the direction of the wind, smoke puffed out intermittently into the windowless room, reddening the eyes of those who sat there, for they kept the door closed.

So? Strawson said.

They makes guns there.

Yeah. An chains an collars an cuffs.

An guns, Diver repeated.

You ever handle one, Bed asked.

Had a dog once, Diver said. Phelps saw I was fond of her. Made me shoot her.

With a rifle?

Revolver. Colt it was called.

Like a horse?

Name o the man who made it. They's others been took huntin deer: they knows how to use a rifle an can show the rest.

The principle ain't hard.

How far off, Bed asked, for it had been night and he had been under cover and dozing when the flatboat passed the foundry.

Twenty, twenty-five miles, Strawson said. Upriver, though.

Roads?

They ain't no good roads, not less you wants a long detour, Simon said. An you takes the road you gon meet patrols.

Rivermen help any?

Help with what?

Bed said nothing.

Diver ground his jaw. Saint Hall hires men out to there, he said.

Like who?

They's Bale.

Yeah, but he done gone crazy, Robert said. Richard, sitting by him, nodded.

Still an all.

We could take us a rowboat an –

How we do that? Overseers'd –

They's fo hundred of us, Emmanuel said, speaking for the first time: the others had thought he was dozing, for his eyes were closed. Now he opened them, and they were wakeful. Fo hundred of us, maybe twenty o them. They armed, but –

Twenty to one.

Uh-huh.

We could do it, Richard said: rise up; and Robert nodded, and he and Richard were eager and would have gone out with knives then.

Gots to be done in cold blood not hot, Diver said.

Richard seemed minded to dissent, but Diver kept his eyes on him until the youth looked down, muttering, Okay, okay. Cold. We do it cold.

It was not a plan, not yet; but none opposed it. And their brutalization in the fields continued, and their condition worsened, for their rations remained insufficient, and their eyes grew exopthalmic, and the decision made itself: uprising; and that single word once heard transformed the meaning of the work-songs that had sustained their spirits. Hollers telling of toil and tasks to come took on a glinting new significance, as did those more spiritual songs that told of a holy kingdom achievable on earth, and the imminence of judgment for all.

More prosaically, every possible conduit for communication between the different parts of the plantation was deployed. Every errand run for the white folks contained within it another run for the black. A broken plowshare dragged to the smithy for repair took with it questions, and brought back answers as well as a new edge to its notched blade; and Abednego came to learn there were networks that included even a number of those in the Big House: enduring a more intimate predation at the hands of Saint Hall and his scions, some felt common cause, as Bed himself had done at Tyler, with those in the fields.

He found himself appointed map-maker, for he could write somewhat, having taught himself furtively while a house-servant, and his mind could scale an image down proportionately. From what he knew and what others told him he pieced together a plan of the Saint Hall estate, drawing it out painstakingly on a sheet that one of Durance's girls had smuggled out from the Big House, wound round beneath her skirts. It had been discarded on account of the mistress's monthly bleed, and that rusty central stain which even boiling with boracic salts could not eradicate Bed marked as the Big House, and he worked outwards from there, adding details as he learned them. His ink was charcoal mixed with dregs of turpentine, his pen a reed split then burned after use so as to leave no trace or clue, slave writing of any sort being a criminal act viciously suppressed and violently punished when detected. About the estate's outer edges he added as best he could information concerning the territory beyond: rivers, canals, streams, towns, hamlets; the foundry; the railroad – the scale diminishing as he worked his way outwards, reaching at last as far as De Bray's Town, and then beyond that to Tyler and its neighbors, Oglesby, Sharp and Harrington, this last part drawn upon a ripped pillow-case, stitched roughly to the sheet's edge so as to allow an extension in that direction; and in that way a representation was created of the land about them, and a miscellany of facts assembled that at its outer edges shaded into rumor and speculation; yet each element added strengthened their resolve.

As their plans took shape their danger as well as their hunger and their weariness increased, for to dissemble and suppress defiance required an energy they more and more lacked; yet all knew it was crucial the overseers remained entirely unaware of their intentions.

It gots to come on em sudden, Diver said.

Durance nodded, staring at the map spread out on the dirt floor of the men's cabin, committing every detail to memory, her jaw moving as though reciting mnemonically beneath her breath. She cracked the knuckles on first one hand then the other. All the teeth in one mouth now, she said. Bale sent us somethin?

Atonement, Diver said, and that, Abednego said, was code for things of iron.

There were twenty of them gathered in the cabin that evening, and the air was dense with body-heat and sour-breathed with hunger, and the firelight flickered on their tense, drawn faces and in their hollowed eyes. They said few words, and no discussion was prolonged, for they feared detection; and above all, for it cut more deeply into what was still tender in them, betrayal by their skin-kin. The lack of windows, usually oppressive, was now beneficial, for it ensured no passer-by could by chance glance in and see what was occurring inside; and the door was closed, and Richard stood by it and Robert lent against it, and both held gutting-knives ready for use. Emmanuel sat on a stump outside, smoking his pipe and keeping watch, and if he knocked the bowl against the door as if to clear the ashes they knew someone was coming: two knocks black, three knocks white.

That night Terrance and Dinah's baby died. A perverse miracle it had lived so long, for others – grown folks – had been dying, one a fortnight or more, since before Christmas. Miz May was found cold and rigid the first morning of the new year, with concave cheeks, and mouth and eyes wide open as if surprised, which surely she could not have been, for her upper arms were by then thin as her wrists; others Bednego did not know even by name. Some fell in the fields, and those, once an overseer had taken the whip to their prone forms, lashing them repeatedly and even frenziedly to ensure they were not shamming, were left lying in the furrow where they had collapsed until the day's work ended. To carry them to the waiting cart with reverence was beyond the capacity of the exhausted living, and so they were dragged and slung like sacks, and both the living and the dead thereby diminished. A boy was consumed by fever, and all feared typhoid had come among them, and there was bible talk of plague and famine, death and war.

Rise up.

While we still can.

As if sharing some group mind they knew: Plannin done.

We begin.

Tonight. Pass the word.

Morning broke, cutting cold and clear, and as one and wordlessly they rose, washed, dressed, and assembled before the cabins to await the arrival of the mules for plowing. Dinah and Terrance waited with them, their faces impassive, their dead child left to bury once the day was done, and no white man noticed tiny Eloise was now silent and not slung upon her mother's back.

So docile were they in the fields that day that the overseers remarked upon it. Saint Hall's great experiment had succeeded, they said: the minds and spirits of those enslaved were at last wholly evacuated, leaving as was intended only the body and its autonomic systems, purified of aspiration and thus resentment at its exploitation; subordinate and dominant finally fused in a process that was claimed by those who dominated as symbiotic but was in reality wholly parasitical, with the parasite, through endeavor but acting as by divine right, lord over all as the mosquito ruled the swamp, and the tiny, brainless creature dwelling in its gut and mouthparts ruled the mosquito, all serving what was most purely exploitative, most reductive in purpose.

In the cabin that evening Diver nodded to Bed. Unseen energies coursed kinetically between them as from amongst the husks in his mattress Abednego rooted out the knives that Bale had sent, and passed them out to Richard, Robert, Strawson, Simon, Crawfish and the others.

All would go armed tonight.

We gon pray, Strawson asked.

This ain't prayin business, Diver said.

Book Three

Chapter *Twenty*

The first whistle, sharp and short, was followed by a second with a swoop to it; then came a third, low and level – an unseen triangulation floating in the darkness, and in the cold, still air the sounds were eerie, even mocking. Crouching low, Cyrus looked about him but could see no-one: just the tumbled, shadowy shacks rising from the milky mist, and beyond them, through tangled, bare-black-armed fruit-trees, furrowed fields, running away emptily into the night.

Did the whistles mean he had been seen? If so, by who?

Somethin goin on fo sho.

He looked back at the sagging jetty, at the pine-knot flaring, a rallying point, or, no: a lure.

Sliding his hand into his coat pocket he found Nate's knife awaiting him. He contemplated returning to the skiff and slipping away, withdrawing from whatever this was, but did not, instead remaining crouched down and listening hard. No more whistles came, nor other sounds: they had not been for him, then. Knowing he was exposed out there on the moonlit riverbank, Cyrus moved stealthily in the direction of the shacks, glancing all about him as he went. Most had at least skeletal roofs; a few were reduced to only a chimney-stack or a forlornly-buckling piece of wall; and around them, skeined in mist, rose to near waist height a snarl of undergrowth.

A short way in Cyrus came to a cottage that was almost whole, though its roof sagged so low it seemed a defiance of natural law that it had not fallen in entirely, and the doorless entrance gaped blackly. He went up to it, aiming to look inside, perhaps hide in there and watch, though he knew a place of concealment could all too easily become a trap.

As he hesitated on the threshold, for the impenetrably dark interior smelt cold and damp and sour, the blunt base of a corn-cutter clonked against the doorframe by his head. Cyrus started and whipped round and was confronted by a wiry-looking black man with wild hair, intense eyes and a gaping mouth, standing close to him as a lover, and from the man's mouth came not speech but creaking noises, and Cyrus saw his undulant throat was caved in, and that scars like dripped wax coated the indentation. His eyes fixed on Cyrus', the man jerkily shook his head, as if to indicate that to go inside was a bad thing; and Cyrus, while still grasping the handle of the knife in his pocket, allowed himself to be caught by the arm and held. Keeping his eyes locked on Cyrus', the man pursed his lips and whistled sharply. A soft answering whistle came from somewhere beyond the shacks, and, tugging on Cyrus' sleeve, the man led him towards it, and Cyrus did not resist.

Assembled where the shacks tailed off and melted and rotted down into the ground was a group of three: two men and a woman, standing silent among a clump of pear trees; and he did not see them until he drew close, for they were as unmoving as the trees, and their outlines were broken up by the black and silver dapple of shadows and moonlight. The man who could not talk shoved Cyrus forward so he was in their midst, and he turned on the spot to take them in: an older, mannish woman, short, with intent eyes and a thrust-out jaw that ground; the man with no throat; a rangy man with a well-trimmed beard and moustache, and hair that was gray at the temples; a shaven-headed youth missing his upper front teeth. There was about them a similarity that at first he did not understand, but later did: the taut cheekbones and exopthalmic eyes, the wiriness of build, were markers not of family but malnutrition, and perhaps his own hunger and depletion mirrored theirs, for he at once felt kin to them.

Who is you an what you doin here, the woman demanded in a low voice, and by her bearing and their deference he understood that she was their commander. He glanced down and saw she held a bow and a quiver of arrows, and also that the bearded man standing alongside her was missing two fingers from his right hand, and that mutilation, along with the boy's missing teeth and the other man's concave throat, added to Cyrus' sense that this was a place of especial brutality.

Name's Cyrus, he said.

The man with no voice gave him a look and made a rasping noise.

Where you come from, the woman asked.

Off a estate call Tyler, Cyrus said. I run – he thought a

moment – three weeks ago, I guess.

Naw, said the man with the missing fingers.

Hush up, said the woman, and, moving in closer, she looked up at Cyrus, and her eyes searched his intently.

But *he* said –

I said hush up, Strawson. Cyrus off of Tyler, why you come here?

I was runnin.

Long way to run, the younger man said, and his voice was blurry and oddly breathless.

Wrong way to run, said Strawson.

Why you run south, the woman asked.

Lookin fo my friend.

Friend?

Uh-huh.

He got a name, the maimed man asked.

Abednego.

God damn, the younger man said.

Hush now.

He said you'd come.

Who?

Bednego –

Cyrus' heart leapt.

He said it an we laughed, the youth went on, shaking his head and smiling lopsidedly. God damn.

He here, Cyrus asked in a voice that cracked.

You just missed him, the man with missing fingers said. He run back to the cabins.

Cyrus recalled from the view from the top of the outcrop in the river that these were four or five miles from where they now stood. Why, he asked.

Durance sent him.

Durance?

This Durance. I'm Strawson. Thas Robert – indicating the youth.

Okay.

Thas Crawfish. The voiceless Crawfish nodded. You was gon go in the shack, so he had to stop you.

Why?

They's sickness in there.

Cyrus' scalp prickled. Another young man materialized beside them then, the brother of Robert by their shared likeness. He glanced at Cyrus and said to Durance, They comin. Who this?

Not answering him, she studied Cyrus. We got us some trouble to manage, she said.

Trouble?

Overseers, said Robert.

An none of em can't get back to warn the others, Durance said.

Cyrus nodded. Outwardly he was calm, but inside his skull his brain was buzzing, neuroelectrical energies discharging downwards through his chest and earthing in his groin, and his muscles twitched, eager to be used. How many, he asked.

Five. On horses.

You gots somethin to fight with, Strawson asked him.

Knife.

You done use it befo?

Cyrus nodded.

Can't let em fire off they guns is the main thing, Strawson said. They gives the alarm an we done.

Less go, said Durance.

They moved through the trees in silence, skirting the ruins of the shacks on their southward side until they found a place among the weeds from which they could view the jetty while remaining concealed.

A track, wide though overgrown through lack of use, ran off in the direction of the mill-yard, close to and alongside the river, which from this point curved gently east. Along this track a posse was now cantering towards them, the rider at its head holding a lantern high to light the way. Durance muttered something to Strawson and hurried off across one of the fields, making as if to intercept them on the slant, a black shape bent so low it was near swallowed by the ground-mist. Crouching down the others moved forward, drawing closer to the track, and Cyrus' thoughts churned, excitement and anxiety surging through him in waves. To face patrollers not as a solitary fugitive but in a group, and armed, and with a plan: that was a wholly different thing to the terror of being pursued alone. And Bednego was there, and he was close: this had not been a delusion. And to find Bed, and thus himself, part of an uprising seemed to Cyrus as it should be: a drawing together of liberatory energies on many levels. He touched Old Africa's charm where it rested on his breast and it was warm, warmer, if that were possible, than the heat of his body, as if charged up with something, and the hairs on the back of his neck prickled and his chest was pulled upwards cosmologically as the moon lifts up the sea.

In a short while they came to a long, low, bowed brick wall that at its far end met the track, and there, at a gesture from Crawfish, they crouched in its shadow until the white men had cantered past, and they were, as the boy – Richard, Robert's brother – had said, five in number, and two had rifles slung across their backs, and two had pistols at their belts, and their jaws were set, and their eyes beneath the broad brims of their hats were dabs of tar.

Strawson leading the way, he, Crawfish, Richard, Robert and Cyrus emerged from their hiding-place and followed the riders, slipping over to a freestanding chimney-stack that pointed skyward like a rheumatic finger. The jetty was just twenty feet away, and from behind the stack they watched the white men thudding up to it. Two of the five at once dismounted and, one holding up the lantern to cast its light widely about, gazed out first at the still-burning torch at the jetty's end and then round at the shacks, and there was some low conversation between them that was inaudible to the watchers. Cyrus wondered how many other black folks were concealed about the place; how practical or how deluded was this action of which he was now a part; and he thought of his hidden boat. The riflemen remained on their mounts, and thus far neither had unslung his weapon. Not too fearful, then; not yet.

Won't be Saint Hall niggers, the man with the lantern said, raising his voice to include those up on the horses. They too scared to come here.

Spooks em, one of the riflemen agreed.

Still an all, said the other, the flux.

That's long past.

Says you. I ain't goin in there.

Maybe outsiders, the horseman without a rifle said. Abolitionists.

They everywhere nowadays, one of the others agreed. Spreadin their poison.

Ain't none a them in Blaze County, the man with the lamp said, grinning mossily. Last one showed his face got tarred an feathered. Claimed he was a preacher.

God damn.

We made him eat that bible page by page.

I heard he died, the younger of the riflemen said.

Let's get this done, the third man said, the one without a rifle, who was perhaps their leader, and so permitted to be fastidious in the bearing of arms, pistols being deemed more in keeping with an aristocratic bearing than shotguns or their ilk. I got victuals waitin fo me. Keep watch.

The riflemen nodded as he dismounted with a grunt, and with the other two began to make his way on foot towards the waiting, shadow-choked shacks, the man carrying the lantern taking the lead, and they went as masters, not warily, and with a swagger. They passed from sight among the grown-out trees and collapsed buildings, and for a time there was silence. Then came a thud, a smothered cry, a yell – of alarm or attack Cyrus could not tell – followed by shouts, from black throats and white, and white men's oaths, and crashing about and the fast breaking of undergrowth.

At the first yell one of the horsemen unslung his rifle; the other at once turned his mount about and urged it back along the track in the direction of the mill-yard, spurring it into a gallop as Strawson, Crawfish, Richard, Robert and Cyrus burst out from behind the chimney-stack, weapons in hands, attempting to block his way, but having to throw themselves aside to avoid being trampled, and horse and rider were past them and gaining speed. Cyrus' heart sank, for already it seemed disaster had overtaken their endeavor, but the rider had not gone more than six chains when he tumbled sideways from the saddle, and looking to his left Cyrus saw Durance standing in the neighboring field, limned by moonlight, the bow in her hand. But the horse galloped on and vanished into the dark, and Strawson cursed.

Muffled sounds of struggle continued among the shacks, but evidently the ambush had been co-ordinated well enough to prevent the drawing and firing of pistols by the white men:

now all the focus of those Cyrus was with was on preventing the remaining horseman from discharging his rifle and thereby sounding the alarm, and they came forward in a group, knives and corn-cutters held loose but at the ready, blocking the way; and the overseer, a young man, hatless and in a blue coat, had his rifle at the ready, and his horse moved restlessly under him and his aim wavered, for he knew – and knew they knew – there was but a single cartridge in the breech, and that once it was discharged, even if he killed one of them, he was done; and the gunshot would alert others, and the revolt might be put down, but he would be dead; and so he did not fire, wondering in an agony of indecision if the threat of being the recipient of that single bullet might play on the mind of each individual now advancing upon him sufficiently to deter that person from being the one to strike the first blow, and might thusly be parlayed into his survival.

Git back, he said weakly, waving the rifle at them, and he was not used to this, and had no courage for it, and no language either, for then he said, Go on back to your cabins now. Don't make no trouble now.

The horse, a piebald gelding, backed and filled and snorted, and the young white man's free hand tightened on the reins as the black men drew closer, and soon it was too late for the rifle, too late to decide which one among the five of them might be killed, for by then it would alter nothing, and Strawson took hold of the barrel and with a gentle tug pulled the weapon from the overseer's grip, and the young man let it go and his face in the moonlight was the color of old bones, and his flax-pale hair hung lank, and his eyes: confused.

If not at that initial contact – the brown hand closing coolly round the machine-bored barrel – then at its breaking, at the release, the white man realized his mistake and, perceiving there was left to him no course of action that would serve him better, he spurred his horse hard and it leapt forward, its forelegs kneeing Strawson and Robert aside, and Robert's corn-cutter flew from his hand. Cyrus with a sweeping movement of his arm rammed his knife into the overseer's thigh as he passed, and he screamed, and Cyrus felt the blade strike the bone within the flesh, then pulled it back out, and the man fell towards him in a reflexive compression of muscle, but his foot caught in the nearside stirrup and he was dragged away by the bolting horse, his head bouncing on the ground, arms flung out but not flailing, for he was either dead or unconscious. They watched the gelding go; and a little way on and of its own accord it slowed, then came to a stop, and Robert, reclaiming his corn-cutter, jogged off to bring it back. He made several hacking blows at the dark shape that hung from the stirrup unmoving on the ground, levered the booted foot free, rolled the body aside and returned, leading the horse by its bridle.

They now became aware that all had fallen silent behind them. Making their way back to the shacks they found a group of around fifteen black men methodically stripping the hacked-about bodies of the overseers of boots, coats, shirts and britches, though much of the clothing was too bloodstained to be worn; and also weapons and holsters. The men's movements were jerky, their eyes star-bright, shared glances and flashed smiles ecstatic, their manner, which was both feral and rational, suppressedly excited, a great collective yell of exultation rising in them that was of necessity held down; and whatever happened next, this had been worthwhile.

You gets the other two, one of the men asked Strawson breathlessly.

Strawson nodded. Mighta lost a horse though; Robert bringin the other.

Once stripped, the pallid, butchered corpses were slung like sacks into the sagging cottage Cyrus had been prevented from entering by Crawfish. That done they gathered by the jetty, and there the overseers' horses waited, Robert holding their reins, their restiveness at the smell of blood and adrenalin calmed by the skilled hands of a man who cared for them, and Strawson assessed their situation: a rifle and ten rounds, three pistols and eighteen bullets; four horses; and then Durance came up, riding the fifth horse, though awkwardly, and Crawfish aided her in a dismount made clumsy by her short stature and the second rifle slung across her shoulders. Ain't rid a horse in twenty years, she puffed.

The man you brung down, Strawson asked.

Rolled him in a ditch. He outta sight. We best get on. Richard, the lure.

Richard bobbed his head and made his way crabwise out

along the slumped jetty, threw the still-flickering pine-knot into the water, and came quickly back.

Durance surveyed the weapons and nodded. We know what we doin, she asked, and there was nodding and quiet agreement. We gon keep both rifles an one of the pistols; Richard, here's two fo Diver, an bullets.

Yes, Miz Durance.

Take two o the horses with you. Can you ride, she asked Cyrus. When he shook his head she shrugged and said, You can sit; he can keep a hold o yo bridle. Cyrus nodded as Durance handed the pistols to Richard, who pushed one down the front, the other down the back of his pants. Don't fire em, though, she cautioned. Not less they knows what we doin an there ain't no quiet way.

Yes, Miz Durance, Richard said; then to Cyrus, Come on then.

After a brief exchange with Robert, Richard chose the piebald gelding and a gray mare, placid in manner, into the saddle of which he helped Cyrus climb, a more difficult task than it had any right to be for a capable man who had, after all, ridden mules. The mare was higher, wider and more barrel-shaped and -sized than he had expected, and to sit with his thighs splayed made his hips feel queer. Probing with his feet, he awkwardly wiggled the toes of his battered boots into the stirrups as Richard swung himself up onto his mount as if born to it. He reached for Cyrus' bridle, and with a nudge of his bare heels against the gelding's sides, set both horses moving slowly off. A little way along they broke into a cautious canter, and Cyrus, one hand buried in the mare's mane, strove to remain as upright as possible while at the same time trying to move with her rather than against her, and he felt the life in her strong beneath him, and the experience was somehow wholly different from riding mules: the simple distance from the ground, perhaps, and the nature of the animal bending towards speed.

Where the others goin, he asked.

They gon watch the road, Richard said. Make sure any patrol comes by don't see nothin. We beginnin, Cyrus. We in it. We best hush now.

Where the track divided they took the fork that ran inland, and for a half hour rode through plowed fields, during which time they saw and met no-one, black or white, eventually nearing the backside of a long row of cabins, sufficient, Cyrus calculated, to domicile several hundred hands. Smoke rose from several of the chimneys, and beyond their pitched and shingled roofs was a glow, as of outdoor fires, and Cyrus could smell woodsmoke. They trotted along a narrow track that ran directly behind the row, ducking low-hanging branches, the dry weeds brushing the horses' bellies, and around halfway along Richard stopped and dismounted, then helped Cyrus down. The sight of the white man being dragged to his death ensured that Cyrus took care to free both feet from the stirrups before, leaning on the mare's neck, gripping the pommel and swinging his body round, he did his best to imitate the young man's movements as he dropped down, and Richard's hands were light on his hips behind him, and Cyrus managed not badly, not born, then, but growing into the correct technique.

After tethering the horses to a branch, Richard led Cyrus through a narrow gap between two cabins and out onto a lane. There another, equally long row of cabins faced them. These had no porches, but here and there people sat before them on stools, resting after eating, or working on some small task. The vast majority of the hands, however, were gathered at a wide spot in the lane that evidently functioned as a communal yard, preparing food or warming themselves around the cooking fires. Two thin-armed women came struggling along with a large wooden bucket swinging heavily between them, their elbows braced against their pelvises; a man appeared with an armful of wood. Though all seemed normal, Cyrus sensed a vibration in the air, as of the beating of a bird's wings in a confined space. His mind was blank as Richard led him forward: all seemed possible and impossible both at once, and he could not believe that Abednego was here.

As he passed among the fires eyes turned in his direction, yet no-one reacted, even though he was a stranger to them, albeit in company with one they knew. It was an unexpected and indeed unlikely disgengagement: a performance, then. He wondered how many of those gathered here were involved in what was plainly a revolt. All? A courageous few? Richard acknowledged no-one, and none hailed him. Gruel and grits bubbled dully in cauldrons and pans, the drifting steam almost wholly devoid of aroma, and once again Cyrus was struck by that similarity between them that was not kin.

Just beyond the yard Richard turned aside and went up to one of the cabins. He rapped three times on the door-frame, then, without waiting for a response, pushed the door open, and there was candlelight within. He stepped across the threshold, and Cyrus followed him.

The cabin was crowded, and instinctively Cyrus hung back, though behind him someone at once closed and moved in front of the door, barring his exit. The light was low – two candles in tin holders, positioned on a sheet that was spread out on the floor. This had been elaborately drawn upon, and around it the men – and they were all, or mostly men, it seemed – stood or squatted, their faces underlit and sickled black and yellow; and behind them a fire crackled in the fireplace, though their bodies blocked out most of the light it cast, and the breathless air stung from a clogged flue and leaking chimney-smoke, and the shadows danced in silence on the walls around them.

We on, Diver, Richard said breathlessly to someone Cyrus could not see, for the youth, though slender, was tall and standing in his way.

How many come, the man named Diver asked.

Five.

Thas a start. You get em all?

Richard nodded. Threw em in the flux huts.

Any noise?

Naw. We took em by surprise.

Good.

Miz Durance went off with the others. Lef a couple by the huts in case.

What you get?

Five horses. I brung two with me now, an a pistol an the bullets fo it. Miz Durance kept the rest: two pistols an two rifles. An they's this.

He stepped aside, revealing Cyrus, and all faces turned towards him. The man named Diver locked his eyes on Cyrus', and he was large-featured and, though gaunt, strong-looking, handsome-haggard in the way of older men, and he chewed on a wood-splinter, moving it from one side of his mouth to the other as he took Cyrus in with no particular expression on his face.

Says his name Cyrus, Richard said excitedly, and Diver raised an eyebrow as Richard added, Off of Tyler.

Well, damn, Diver said. Bednego?

One of the crouching men, who had silently straightened up while Diver studied Cyrus, now stepped forward.

Bednego, Cyrus said, and everything about him fell away.

Chapter Twenty-One

C yrus, Abednego said, and it was him. Less meat on his bones, but it was Bed, and he was radiant, his hazel eyes blazing bright, his build and proportioning pleasing still and somehow flawless; and his full lips broke into a wide, wide smile, the sort of smile rarely seen in that dispiriting place, and he jumped the map on the floor, making the candle-flames dance, and threw himself into Cyrus' arms, and they held each other while the others watched, surprised, amused and, as Cyrus would later realize, also in awe, for this was prophecy, this was hope embodied; and for Cyrus, and for Abednego, there was too a power in having their reunion seen, having it witnessed: this happened; this was done. And their bodies fit together like the restored halves of a shattered geode; like the river's current and the catfish; the bird's wing and the updraft; the sun and soil and the erupting seed, need answering need and yet all was a giving and not a taking; and they did not kiss, not before the others, but cheek was warm against cheek, and their salt-traced faces were wet with sudden tears, and there were no words, and nor were any needed.

After a time Diver cleared his throat, and Cyrus and Bednego broke off their embrace and turned to face him, standing side by side, their hands brushing knuckle to knuckle, gesturing towards an intertwining, neuro-electric energies sparking between them with each brief contact; and Diver's face was set but his eyes were kind, and their chests rose in unison and they stood tall as pines, and all seemed possible then.

Cyrus brung down Darnell's son, Richard said, and Diver nodded his approval. There was a sense among them all, it seemed, that his arrival augured well for the other things to be done that night, a perception – a memory, maybe – carried forward from long ago and far away that this thing between men might be powerful magic.

You welcome here, Cyrus off of Tyler, Diver said, extending a hand, and Cyrus took it and Diver's grip was strong; and

Diver did not ask and did not need to ask if he was in this, saying instead simply, It's time. And the other men – and Cyrus now noticed three or four young women – nodded, and those squatting stood.

Terrance, you an yo men go up to the cottages. You know what to do. They's two horses waitin back o the row – he glanced at Richard: Richard nodded. When you done, send two men an any guns you get yo hands on over to the mill: we gon need em. Keep a couple fo yoselves an go stake out the avenue. White folks can come in; no-one gets out.

A gentle-looking, toffee-colored man with a shaved head nodded. Cyrus saw that from his right hand a hatchet dangled. Les do this, he said to two men standing by him, and they went out.

Okay, then, Diver said. It's time, so I'm gon pray. Won't take long. As the others bowed their heads, he continued, Lord, bless what we do. Ancestors what come before, bless what we do. Keep our arms strong an our hearts stronger. Amen. And the others said amen, and the praying was done. Remember, Diver said as they moved in a body towards the door, we gots to go silent. An no lights.

They filed out into the lane, Diver taking the lead, Bednego at his right shoulder, and Cyrus by Bednego, keeping close; and as they went along each man and woman they passed wordlessly set aside his or her task and stood and joined them, and they were headed toward the mill, and like debris swept downriver come flood season they grew, as their numbers accumulated, increasingly dangerous. Up ahead Cyrus saw Terrance and eight or nine others peel off and take a track that curved away to the left, moving at a lope.

What they gon do, he asked Abednego softly.

Overseers' cottages is up that way.

How many you got? Overseers, I mean.

Twenty, twenty-two maybe.

Whereabouts?

In they houses; at the mill.

Over at the big house?

Some be creepin bout the place, no doubt. Most'll be at the mill, though, on account of that's where the foodstores is. The five you run into, they'd of came from there.

Cyrus nodded. Bed's way of speaking had shifted some, he noticed; had become more of the fields. As they moved forward in the dark there was the sense of a mass of people accumulating behind them but no noise save the soft, ambiguous brush of cloth against cloth; and the lane ran straight.

I knew you'd come, Bed said.

How? I dint know. Not when I started out.

I don't know how I knew, but I did. An here you is.

Cyrus glanced at Bed. You glad?

Bed smiled, and the moon caught his smile. Fool, he said. Then: Yeah, I'm glad. You?

Fo sho.

Even with all this?

Uh-huh.

From somewhere behind them and up to the left there came carried on the empty air the hard-edged sound of someone knocking on a door, and a high, urgent voice calling, Massa! Massa! Come quick! They's trouble!

Cyrus listened but heard nothing more, and since neither Bed nor Diver reacted beside him, he judged the voice to belong to one of Terrance's party, and not a traitor.

It was a strange thing to be amongst so many moving in silence and with a common purpose: dreamlike and not; latently magical and not; and the lane continued straight and level, and on all sides the furrowed fields ran away in black and silver lines that were swallowed by the night long before they could achieve convergence, and there was no horizon, just an eventual ambiguous swallowing of the lower stars by the formless dark.

At a gesture from Diver a group of four men came forward and jogged off into the darkness ahead, a scouting party as it were, or an advance guard.

They gon spy it out an report back, Bed whispered, and Cyrus found Bed's waist and put his arm around it, his hand resting on Bed's hip, and they went on in that fashion for a while, under a star-dense sky, the risen moon behind them, and the air was cold and getting colder but they did not notice it then. In less than an hour they came to a graveyard, and gathered among the stones to wait for news, from both ahead and behind. A steepled clapboard chapel, freshly whitewashed and in good repair, adjoined the graveyard and screened them from the mill-yard – now less than a half-mile distant, as Cyrus judged, for at a turn in the lane shortly before they reached the burying-place he had seen in that direction lights that did not move.

The headstones they stood among marked out the passage of time, those furthest from the chapel still sharp-etched; those nearer to, soft and rough with lichen: generations of Saint Halls, then, waiting on judgment; and what they dreamed justice might consist of as they slept below the ground Cyrus could not conceive; and the thought that they might in any way rise again disgusted him and lanced him through with horror and futility; and in a sudden rage he pushed against one of the older stones that was already leaning. It sheared off near the ground and fell with a muffled thud and puff of mist onto the grass. Cyrus almost fell with it, but Bed caught his arm and kept him upright. Where the stone had broken it showed raw and pale in the moonlight.

Don't believe in none o that anyway, Cyrus thought. Only reckonin's the one we make our ownselves.

From the lane behind them came the sound of hooves, and as one those waiting looked round, and unease passed through them as fast as a swoop of swifts, but the riders – a pair – were soon revealed as Terrance and another of the men who had gone with him, and they dismounted, and the other man took both sets of reins and waited with the horses by the lich gate while Terrance hurried up to Diver.

It done, he said in a low voice.

How many you get?

Three.

How it go?

We crept up on the porches. I made the sign an Billy there – indicating the other horseman – knocked and commoted. Three doors opened. Hale an Edgerly an Smith come out like cuckoos out a clock. They each got a adze in they gut an a hatchet in they head.

The womens an children?

Tied an gagged. One of em dead, though: got the flat of my axe on her head on account of she carryin on, tryna run.

You quieted her all the way down, Diver said.

Dint aim to, but I did. Phelps' wife.

Huh. You dint kill em all, then?

Aw, Diver, Terrance said. Naw. They tied an gagged, an we told em, We takin over. You gets free, stay put. Run an you be kilt.

How many was there?

Seven womens, eleven children, fo of em babes in cradles. We tied up the ones that was walkin. Locked em in if they was a room with a lock. All in they separate houses so none of em don't know what else goin on.

I don't like it, Diver said.

Well, it's done.

Send Billy back. We can spare him an he can watch em. Don't want no white womens runnin lose sayin we was gon rape em.

We wasn't, Terrance said. Okay, okay, I'll send Billy. Terrance made his way back to where the younger man stood by the horses.

Thas eight, Diver said. Then: Where the scouts at? They back yet?

Not yet, Bed said. It's not been but a quarter hour, though.

Diver looked in the direction of the mill-yard. Time bleedin, he said.

Their adrenalin surged as they waited among – above – the white dead; peaked, receded, surged again; and the sweat chilled on their taut, raised bodies, and their hands and feet prickled as the moon rode high above them, a crescent of ice it seemed then, a source of radiant cold as the sun is a source of heat, and the light it threw down of a wholly other order; and Cyrus thought of haints and what gave them energy, and what unseen system of power compelled them to appear, but there were too many of the living present there for any haint to dare to walk in the churchyard that night.

Twenty more minutes, he guessed, inched by in silence, during which time eyes met with were increasingly avoided, and heads lowered like dying sunflowers crowned with black honeycomb; and more and more Cyrus longed to be away from there and alone with Bed, though he knew his desire was disloyal to this thing of which he was now a part; and too he knew this truth: all struggles for freedom are conjoined, and so conditional. He looked at Abednego's face on the three quarter, cheekbones heightened by hunger, and thought of bones, and skulls, and stamped his booted feet against the cold.

Just then he became aware that the men in the advance party had returned and were passing through those assembled, making their way to where Diver stood waiting.

We counted seven, said their foreman, a skinny, dark-complected man with a shaven head and a wall eye.

What they doin?

Gamblin, gettin drunk, said the youth next to him.

An the hands?

We gived em the owl hoot like we agreed, the shaven-headed man said. They's one in the smithy mendin plowshares, an two butcherin hogs in the slaughterhouse, so they got knives an hammers handy.

An a flatboat just come down, the youth said. The press mens been put to rollin barrels.

Boatmen know what needs doin?

Sho, Diver said. Hutch an Tilt there?

The man with the wandering eye nodded. We gives em the sign an they guts the pilot, he said. They's fo gals from the kitchens brung victuals over fo the white men, an liquor.

Who?

Prudence an three others.

They put the stuff in?

Dint see, an they weren't no chance to speak, but Jackson flashed em a sign an I seed Prudence nod, so I reckon so.

You count the guns?

I seed fo rifles laid by, an they likely all got pistols.

They look worried the others ain't back from the landin yet?

Naw: they dicin an arguin amongst theyselves.

Well, we best move on em befo they do, Diver said. To Bednego and Cyrus he added: Pass the word.

They nodded and did so, moving among the others, saying in low voices, It's time, and soon all were making their way back into the lane. They advanced more quickly now, aware that their energy and thus their courage had sunk down, and that the white men might at any moment turn suspicious. Bed and Cyrus worked their way through the still-silent throng until they were once more alongside Diver, and Cyrus could not but ask him, keeping his voice low, You worried bout traitors?

Sho, Diver said quietly. Up in the big house mostly, on account of they get fed some so they don't look ugly fo the white folks, an they fraida losin that. Prudence solid, though. Not just them, mind: we left a dozen we wasn't sure of tied an gagged in the cabins. Hutch an Tilt dropped a man in the river last week. Okay, now. We here.

Diver extended his arms scarecrow wide and the men and women massed behind him, for they were now more than two hundred in number, bunched to a gentle halt. The backsides of the barns, sheds and other dependencies loomed up before them – smithy, slaughterhouse, smokehouse and hog-pens. Beyond them the mill's stack rose high, and past that, unseen, was the river. Close by stood a pair of elderly cypresses, last survivors, maybe, of the forest that once had covered all the land, their trunks twisted like candy canes and denuded of lower boughs, the uppermost branches fanning out skeletally above the mansard of the largest of the several barns; and some way past them, marked at regular intervals by slender trees of a type Cyrus did not recognize, the path to the Great House ran along the riverbank.

Lamplight spilled down the spaces between the buildings, and glimmered in the gaps between the boards of those that were lit within. There were on that side no windows, which was doubtless why Diver had had the uprisers gather there. In the centre of the yard, and viewable along one of the yellow-lit slots, as Cyrus saw when he shifted his position, was the mill. No water-wheel adjoined it, and he guessed it to be run by steam-power. The stack stood separate from the main body of the mill, perhaps for reasons of safety, and both parts were built of brick. At that hour it was in darkness, the doors were closed, and from the stack's head no smoke rose.

At a sign from Diver the men and women divided into groups that by their orderliness had been predetermined, and, maintaining their silence, spread out behind the buildings in both directions. Diver led a phalanx to the right and Abednego, following, caught Cyrus' hand and drew him after. An odor like burning hair, at that moment disconcerting and uncanny, caught in Cyrus' nostrils, and from the direction of the yard he heard voices raised: the white men, he presumed, for the talk was boisterous in manner and interspersed with oaths and unguarded laughter. He followed Bednego as Diver led them in single file along a narrow path that ran behind a line of sheds and storehouses, and they moved as by peristalsis, for each man paused at the corner of every building before slipping shadow-quick across the revealing strip of light the lamps in the yard threw out. There came then a delicate sound, a hammer tapping gently on a nail-head, and Cyrus guessed the sound and the smell of burnt hair were from the shoeing of a horse, though glancing down the gaps as he passed them he saw nothing and no-one.

The sheds gave way to hog-pens and chicken-coops. Through gestures that Bednego copied, and Cyrus echoed down the line, Diver indicated that those following should crouch on their haunches and spread out amongst the pens, and in that manner work their way forward. The sickle moon was bright above them now, and as Diver glanced back and drew his corn-cutter Cyrus could see a gleam in his eyes that was in Abedne-go's too; and was also, Cyrus did not doubt, in his own as he followed Bed between two hog-pens. Slow an easy, he thought as one of the inhabitants grunted in a way a listener might construe correctly as curiosity. Bed like Diver was armed with a corn-cutter, and Cyrus drew his knife. His mouth was dry, his senses were alert, his muscles loose and ready.

The hog-pens fronted onto the yard, a large rectangle about which several lamps were placed. The surface of the river beyond was still vaporous, a reminder to Cyrus that not much time had passed since his arrival, a lifetime though it felt to him then; and a large flatboat was tied up at the landing. This was being unloaded, the men on board – five in number – swinging up barrels, bales and hogsheads that were caught, hooked and pulled onto the jetty by a line of men at the rail, of which there were seven, more being required for this latter task owing to the awkwardness of leaning over, and the weight of the goods being swung up. There were lamps on the roofed rear of the boat and hanging from poles on the jetty, and the work was being done rhythmically, though without song, and, judging by the amount of cargo piled up on the river-bank, was almost complete.

A pair of wagons, each drawn by a team of three mules, stood waiting to be loaded with what the boat had brought, and at the head of each a skinny, drawn-featured black boy held the reins of the lead mule and looked ahead dully, and the boys were perhaps older than they seemed, starvation, as it does, retarding growth.

The center of the yard was dominated by the great cotton press, the screw of which rose up like some featureless totem, a god with no face flanked by arms without embrace, and before the press four white men sat on barrels with a pair of lanterns at their feet, drinking from bottles and jugs, picking at food from trays that had been set on bales of straw for their convenience, and playing at cards; and coins glinted among the cards that had been set down. Nearby, and under their nominal supervision, a blacksmith wearing a leather apron was indeed shoeing a horse. By him stood a small, conical brazier in which coals showed so red they at their hearts were almost white, and the smith had the horse's rear right leg up between his thighs as he affixed a nail to the smoking shoe with neat, brisk taps of his hammer. The horse, a chestnut gelding, stirred, whinnied. The smith locked his thighs about its fetlock, resisting a stagger.

Do it right, one of the white men said without looking round, or I'll split your ears.

Yassuh, Mistuh Phelps, suh, the smith said around a mouthful of silver nails. The teeth of something old in the world they looked, and savage; and his face was sweaty and he held the hammer in a way that made the muscles and sinews of his right arm striate and the veins pulse, and for a moment he looked at the back of Mister Phelps' head with an expression it was as well neither Phelps nor the other white men saw, all their attention on the cards, and Phelps half-turned his head towards the smith but brought it sharply back, saying with a belch, What you doin there, Skelton? I see you. You cheatin me?

He ain't cheatin you, Phelps.

Says you, Darnell.

You doubtin my word?

Play your hand, Phelps. That's all there is. Play your hand. Damn it, I'm drunk.

Me too. Drunker'n I oughtta be.

Can't hold your likker, the third man said.

God damn woman.

Go squat then.

With gentle care the smith tapped in the final nail and set the gelding's foot down. At the same time, and as if co-ordinated, the last hogshead was handed up from the barge, and it was heavy and took three of the boatmen to heft it first to their shoulders and then, straightening their wobbling arms with difficulty, raise it up to the men on the jetty receiving it. Cyrus now noticed there was a white man on the barge, heavy-set and flush-faced. He was swilling from a jug and looking over at the other white men, no doubt wishing to be with them and not supervising niggers who plainly knew how to get a job done but could not be trusted to refrain from idleness with no white man present, whip at the ready.

There came then a sound that was very like, but was not, the hooting of an owl, low and twice repeated. It went unno-ticed by the white men, but the smith slipped the hammer into a pocket at the front of his leather apron, spat the nails in after it, and tugged out and put on a pair of thickly-padded leather gloves; and on the barge two of the hands moved silently into position behind the unnoticing white man. The women who had been mentioned earlier were nowhere to be seen: perhaps they had been sent back to the Big House, though they had left the trays behind. Cyrus' fist tightened about the handle of his knife as he watched the smith grip the brazier in his padded gloves and lift it up, arms tensing as he held it out in front of him and away from his body, and crossed at a fast stagger towards the white men. Bent over a fresh deal of cards they were absorbed in their hands, and looked up only in illuminat-ed confusion as the smith raised the brazier high, inverted it and dumped the red-hot coals onto their heads, sending them jumping, stumbling, crying out in pain and confusion, hunch-ing, jerking, kicking and flicking the burning coals aside. Simultaneously the pilot on the barge was knifed repeatedly in the lower back by the two men behind him and tipped back-wards over the side, and those uprising poured forward from between every building, and the men on the jetty and the men in the boat joined them in rushing upon the four panicked overseers.

They's more though: dint he say seven, Cyrus thought as he dashed forward with Abednego and the others into the yard, knife at the ready, and at that moment a fifth white man, by far the fattest he had yet seen, emerged from an outhouse next to what he guessed to be the slaughterhouse, buttoning his fly and looking sick and then startled. Without so much as attempting to draw his pistol the man turned to flee, showing dark stains marking the back of his pants – the results, perhaps, of Prudence's ministrations – only to find himself at once confronted by two burly black men in blood-soaked aprons, who had emerged from the slaughterhouse and now set about him methodically with cleavers, though Cyrus saw their pragmatic butchery only peripherally, for his main concern was the men who had been gambling.

The card-players yelled and cursed confusedly as the massed uprisers closed in around them, silently, for their purpose was sure and no debate, no demonstration or cranking up of passion was required: this was to be done and would be done; and no shot was fired, for the white men had been too caught up in shrugging off and avoiding the burning coals and hot ashes tipped over them to draw their pistols. In a moment all four were down in the dirt, and Cyrus joined in stabbing at arms and hands that reached and clutched, and there was much kicking and stamping until the work was done and breathless they stood back and looked down on it.

Can't hardly tell which is which, a youth said in a tone of mild surprise. Huh.

He wiped his hand across his mouth and there was blood on his knuckles, as there was on Bed's, on Cyrus' own he saw as he glanced down, and on the hands of many of the others; and the young man laughed nervously as the boatmen – Hutch and Tilt, Cyrus guessed – came up to Diver, and their chests were heaving and twitches pulled at the corners of their mouths, and Cyrus could feel his own features doing the same dance.

The smith joined them. Two of em rid off to the flux shacks, he said. Bout a quarter hour ago.

Diver turned to Cyrus. Durance leave people there, he asked.

Uh-huh. A couple. She gave em a pistol an a rifle.

Ain't likely they be comin back then, Diver said.

What if they gets away, Hutch asked.

Durance done reached the road by now, Cyrus said. Them crackers won't find no patrols to save they backsides. They won't give no alarm.

An the Big House, Tilt said.

Diver looked along the riverside path. Yeah, he said, though it was both too far off and too screened by trees along the way for its lights to be seen. Now for the first time he raised his voice sufficiently to be heard by all: Okay, we knows what we doin. We knows who doin what. We on a schedule. If you unsho, come to me.

What's goin on now, Cyrus asked Bed as the men and women once more broke into groups.

Diver's goin upriver with as many as the boat can hold, Bed said. He gon raid the foundry at Amesburg, get us fire-arms an munitions. Durance can only cover the road to the north, so the rest of us is goin the other way. First off we gots to keep watch on the avenue, make sho the Big House is cut off.

What if someone comes?

They gets let in; they don't get let back out. We gots to keep Saint Hall cut off till morning after tomorrow: that's how long it gon take Diver to get back with the guns. Then we cuts a swathe back up to Amesburg, a free black army on the move, more'n three hundred black folks, all armed. We bringin war, Cyrus. Bednego's eyes were bright. Overseer to undertaker, we doin it.

We goes in the Big House, Cyrus asked.

We goes in like a crawfish pincer closin, Bed said; cut em off on all sides, an then – he was breathless, and his chest was heaving, and he kissed Cyrus full on the lips, and if anyone noticed, in the wild extremity of the moment they said nothing.

Diver now called for the breaking open of barrels, boxes and hogsheads, and for the breaking in of sheds where provisions might be stored. We gots to supply the men what's goin upriver first, he announced. They needs all they strength to row twenty miles against the current an then fight. Keep it quiet, he added, for a hubbub was building as doors were wrenched open or, if locked, shouldered in, and lamps hurried inside.

An if Diver don't come back, Cyrus asked Abednego quietly.

We scatter, Bed replied. Whole plantation worth, all of us, all at once. Some'll get through. Come on —

Chapter Twenty-Two

All set about their tasks with purpose. By their attack they had gained four more horses, and maybe ten of them could ride with confidence; four more pistols and two rifles, and a good many of them knew how to use a firearm. Those who did not were armed from the toolshed with hoes, pitchforks, sickles, spades and scythes, and as each hand gripped a tool, strength flowed from the waking wood and iron into the muscles of the man or woman who received it.

Though the thought set their mouths watering, it was agreed there was no time to dress and cook the butchered hogs that hung from hooks in the slaughterhouse, but in the adjoining shed they found winter apples stacked in straw crates, and shelf upon shelf of canned and bottled quinces, peaches, plums and walnuts, many of which were easily opened; and the smokehouse yielded four hams, three of which were carried over to the boat and stowed as supplies for the rowers, who would, more than any of them, need protein for their task. The barrels and hogsheads were prised open, and were found to contain lamp-oil, tobacco, cider and other, more luxurious items of the sort that could not be manufactured on the plantation. A large tub revealed embroidered silk, satin and velvet dresses, shirts, jackets and underskirts, and the more practically-cut of these were hastily distributed and pulled on against the harshening night. Needing nothing Cyrus took nothing, and it was strange to him to watch these starving men and women transformed by external finery into – what? Not masters, nor even a parody of masters; not freedmen or women either: those were not made by clothes. Bed passed him an apple and he bit into it, and it was shriveled but crisp and sweet, and it set his mouth watering and his cramped stomach pinging, and his teeth felt strong.

Diver took charge of the cider-barrels and set them on the back of one of the mule-carts, directing the two young drivers to gather up the white men's mugs from where they lay on the ground and disburse a cupful of cider to each man or woman who asked. One draft an no mo, Diver announced. We can't get drunk. We gets drunk, we done fo. The boys' eyes brightened as they bent to their task.

The bales when cut into proved to be in the main hay for animal feed, and much in the storehouses could not be quickly or easily prepared – sweet potatoes, sacks of corn that needed grinding, sacks of rice. Several tore the sacks open regardless, and Diver had to quell the desire rising in many of them to delay moving out in order to light fires and cook, for the sight of foodstuffs brought all minds back to their hunger, the unbearableness of which had, after all, pitched them into this desperate action.

Listen up, he said. We can't cook now. You all know why. We gots to go on up an hit hard, no delayin. We delay, we gon lose. We set fires, they be seen. Don't want no white folks comin this way with guns drawn an minds full o suspicion. Can I get a amen?

Grudging amens were murmured, and preparations continued with. Cyrus mentioned to Bed that he had been inside the Amesburg foundry, and Bed hurried him over to Diver, and Cyrus shared all he knew, marking out as best he could recall the placing of its buildings with a scythe-point on the ground, drawing particular attention to the location of the brick-built weapon store; pointing out the ways that seemed to him least visible from the central yard and foundry office; and telling of the routines and movements of men and overseers he had observed there.

Seems like you was fated to bring us this, Diver said, once Cyrus was done telling.

Maybe so, Cyrus said. That Bale, he gived me a look when I tol him my name like he knowed it already.

Everybody knowed bout Bednego sayin you was gon come, Diver said. I guess Bale heard too. Dint none of us believe it, though.

I guess it ain't about belief, Cyrus said.

It gived him heart, though. Helped him through.

Maybe I heard his call, Cyrus said, an dint know what it was. Just I hads to up an go.

Diver put his hand on Cyrus' shoulder and with a grunt pushed himself up from where they had been squatting. Tilt, he called, you ready?

We ready, Tilt called back.

Okay, then. It's time.

From about the yard the men appointed to the journey up-river broke off from what they were doing and came and gathered about Diver. Once they were assembled he led them to the flatboat where, assisted by Hutch and another boatman, they clambered in, those who Cyrus supposed had never been on the water before uneasy in their movements, and supplies were briskly handed over and stowed away.

All this had taken perhaps thirty minutes. The mist had cleared from the river, which now appeared wholly black, with a shiver of stars scattered across it. Abednego approached the boat and exchanged a few quick words with Diver, who was now aboard, then stood back as the oarsmen pushed off from the jetty, and soon it was turning in the current, with no lamps lit a low black rectangle barely visible in the blackness of the night, and it commenced to move upriver creakingly, a low-hummed song keeping the oar-strokes even.

Wasting no time watching it go, Abednego now addressed the others, standing on a barrel to gain their attention. Okay, he said, we goin up to the Big House now and we gots to be quiet about it. We goin in two teams. The first gon stand guard along the avenue so can't no-one get out. They can come in, long as they don't see us, but they can't leave. We gots rifles an pistols but we can't use em less it's life or death: once a shot goes off the white folks'll know there's trouble an be on they guard, an try getting news out an goin fo help. There's seven crackers left, maybe mo, an we don't know how many Saint Halls is home, nor how many guests visitin. We gon make a slow pincer, first the avenue – that's half of us; then the rest skirts round on the river side, makin sure no-one sneaks out that way an runs south. Then we goes in through the back. Where's our riders?

Three men Cyrus had not seen before came forward, leading the horses they had liberated from the overseers.

Joe, Lexander, Nathaniel, you gon run between us like the mail-coach, carryin news. I wants you goin in a loop an goin fast so we all of us gets any information soon as we can.

The men nodded as one. Abednego then directed the sicker

and frailer of the assembled hands, those who could not fight but had come along anyway, to stay behind and load as best they could any foodstuffs that were readily edible onto one of the mule-carts. Thereafter they were to follow the faster-moving main party to the avenue, and hand out comestibles, to maintain morale during what were sure to be long, cold and anxious hours of watching and waiting, for the vigil would have to be kept up for the whole of the next day and the following night at least. There'll be food in the main house fo the rest of us, Bed concluded.

Bed took one of the rifles for himself; the other he assigned to Terrance, who was to lead the avenue team. The pistols were divided equally between the two parties, which were equal in size, and each numbered over a hundred. Terrance's party moved out first, and he was accompanied by two of the horse-men, for only once the avenue was known to be secured would the second team, led by Abednego, move to cut the house off on the river side, this being a mission far harder to complete without being seen, for in consideration of the fineness of the view many of the Great House's windows faced the water; and there was, moreover, a stone terrace – unusual in those parts – upon which the Saint Hall men were known to stroll and smoke even on the coldest and most shuttered-in evenings, and the story above was balconied.

The house servants, moving as they did between the vari-ous dependencies and the kitchen in performance of their duties, might, if they could be trusted to keep silent, function as cover for the arriving uprisers, for masters rarely paid proper attention to slaves, not unless lust was a factor, and even then one might be substituted for another without much fuss or even notice, an orifice for use being, after all, an orifice for use, whichever body it gave entry to, and the exercise of power the principle gratification. There was, however, the risk of running into white folks entering or emerging from the row of guest cottages that adjoined the Great House, who, seeing a large number of black folks illicitly assembled in the dark, would certainly give the alarm. And even before they reached the house, though it was long past dusk and few boats travelled by night, there was nonetheless the danger of being seen by craft running late on the river – though as those uprising would be carrying neither lamps nor torches it was possible they might stand massed there on the shore and still be passed unseen.

Skin dark as shadow an the night sky. Just close our star eyes, Cyrus thought; and he thought of those other subtle energies sensed more easily in the dark that made cats' fur rise. Still an all, when we moves, we best move fast.

Terrance's team now headed out. Heat an beat of blood, Cyrus thought, salt sweat an night-thrill. He had no skills with a pistol and so did not ask for one. Looking at Abednego, rifle slung across his shoulders, his chest swelled with pride: this man, his man, yes, for he had fought his way to be with him through many perils, a leader, and heeded.

Bed, who was helping load the mule-cart with apple-crates, saw him looking, and shot him a smile both tense and joyous. Realising he himself was doing nothing useful, Cyrus weighed in and helped as well, and soon the job was done, and the mule-cart sent creaking off into the night, the two sitting up front side by side, apples in their bellies and their hands easy on the reins, for there was no reason to hurry; and their spirits no longer retreated from their eyes.

Abednego ordered the lamps in the yard extinguished. More waiting followed. The moon, though immobile when looked upon, and seemingly as fixed in the sky as a vein in a stone, nonetheless slowly moved across it, and once again their energy and courage ebbed, and their formerly wholly-empty and shrivelled stomachs birthed growling discomfort, and some bent over and gasped with cramp, whilst others had quickly to step aside to void their abruptly-reactivated intestines in the shadows, fruit not being a binding form of food but rather the reverse; and Cyrus held the remaining smoked ham in place on one of the white men's platters on the back of the unused mule-cart and Bed sliced into it, handing out slivers to the waiting, and each tiny portion made the man or woman who swallowed it hungrier because more alive, and that reactivation of the body's functions was a powerful painful thing, yet, they knew, good.

After what seemed many hours but the moon's transit revealed to be less than half of one they heard the pounding of hooves, and shortly thereafter a rider, Nathaniel, came galloping into the yard. He pulled up in front of Abednego and, without dismounting, said breathlessly, It done, Bednego: no-one saw us, an we in place. Can't no-one go out that way now.

Abednego nodded. All had been attending, and so he needed give no order as, with Cyrus by his side, he began to lead those who had remained behind out along the river path, and as before they moved in silence, the chuckle of the water swallowing the soft cicada susurrus of cloth against cloth.

The Big House waited as had it not always waited, past an apple orchard and on the other side of a windbreak of tall pines beneath which the uprisers now gathered, its white marble mass, now a mere hundred yards away, intimidating, defeating even, had they not passed beyond choice and so at that moment beyond retreat, beyond surrender, for they were moving towards liberation – in life, or in death; and the corpses of the overseers behind them had, as with any offering, tilted the world in the direction of those who spilt the blood and thereby added to their spirit velocity, and gave them heart of a cold and burning sort; lit lamps within their minds that illuminated as possible acts that before had not seemed possible; or rather revealed to them what they had always known: not that white men could be killed, but that black men – and women – could kill them, and not just one, but many. And if many, why not all?

Peering out from under the pine-branches Cyrus attempted to match what was before him with what he recalled of the layout of the dependencies as he had seen them from the rock-tower in the river. Those extending waterwards beyond the Big House were hard to tell apart in the dark, the lights that showed here and there behind their mostly-shuttered windows offering only a haphazard impression of outlines and proportions. Yet their functions would be the same here as anywhere: there was no profound secret waiting to be revealed, just one – he hoped – final iteration of greed and extinguished compassion. Still he was aware of the beating of his heart, of dread building.

Nearer to, a jetty ran out through a dark, unlit boathouse, and on it no lamps burned, meaning no more arrivals were expected by river that night. A small sailboat was moored next to it, accenting pleasure above toil, and a row of skiffs, turned hull-upwards on the mud of the bank, resembled varnished gourds. At back of the Big House a lawn so well-kept as to appear artificial ran from a stone terrace down to the water and the boats, and on it stood a sundial. Light spilled out across the pallid paving-slabs of the terrace from those of the tall, many-paned windows and doors that were not shuttered, and glinted on the sundial's copper gnomon. At the far end of the lawn there stood on a slight rise a small, ornamental rotunda, its slender stone pillars supporting a dome, colorless in the moonlight and surmounted by a metal weathervane.

On the side of the house that faced the uprisers was neither terrace nor porch, nor any door, only windows. On the first floor a wide veranda ran the building's width, but, though lit by several lamps it was at that hour deserted: this was too cold a night to indolently take the air. Several of the first-floor windows stood unshuttered, and in these lamps burned.

An light inside makes the outside blacker, Cyrus thought: it throws yo reflection back at you like a mirror.

At a signal from Abednego – a soft owl-hoot, given twice – the waiting black folks emerged from beneath the pines, their feet passing from crumbled earth slick with matted needles to smooth hard clay, and between themselves and the many-windowed Big House wall was nothing but a finely-hoed expanse of friable soil, waiting to be seeded with lawn, perhaps, or some other plant doubtless requiring delicate handling and excessive and laborious attention if it were to thrive.

The cold was now intense, and their breaths misted the air, and they side-eyed the lit, unshuttered windows as they hurried forward under the exposing brilliance of the moon, and in the clear air conductive as a tuning-fork their breathing and their footfalls seemed to Cyrus rasp-loud and pounding heavy. Like cattle on a drive, he thought, and he could tell there was, as with a drove, a leaning toward stampede. Within the house a maid in white cap and apron, bearing a salver upon which stood glasses and a decanter, hurried past one of the windows, but she did not pause to look out and they did not slow, and the corner of the house was reached, and there they gathered, panting.

Abednego signaled to a small group of men and women, four of each, to squat and wait there, Cyrus presumed to forestall any attempt at escape by those within via the side-

windows; wordlessly they obeyed. Then Bed led the rest of
them down to the water's edge, hunching over as he went, and
they fell into narrow file behind him, hunching low too, and in
that way they were, as they skirted the back of the house,
shielded from view by the banking of the lawn, from ground
level at least, and the windows on the upper floors were all in
darkness on that side. Past the house was a second windbreak
of pines before which, and almost on the water, the rotunda
stood on its grassy mound; past the pines cottages were
descryable, a serried row of five or six, with screened-in
porches looking out across the gently-curving river. In two of
these lights showed.

As he hurried by, Cyrus glanced at the sparkling windows
on the river side of the Big House, and had an impression of
brocade within, of yellow and gold, and of the crystalline, but
nothing more; there was no sense of movement within, no
sound of talk or music. This absence of life unnerved him. Were
they already betrayed? But he trusted Abednego.

Silently they gathered by the rotunda. On its dais a pair of
mildewed wicker chairs sat sparkling with moonlit frost, and a
metal vase of dead roses stood on a wrought-iron table between
them as if in tableau; symbolic it seemed, though it was not;
and yet they had been drawn here. After a brief aside with a
skinny, wild-haired youth, who nodded and then loped off
along the riverbank, skirting round behind the cottages,
hunching over as he vanished from sight, Abednego ascended
the steps of the rotunda, went to the rail and looked out not
over the river but towards the compound of buildings that
adjoined the Big House on its southern side, and, needing to
see, Cyrus joined him, though the others did not, being content
to be guided, and somehow Cyrus had become their lieutenant.

Past the row of pines he saw a large, well-cultivated and
densely-planted kitchen garden with at its center a covered
well. On its far side was a brick-built kitchen from the chimney
of which smoke rose busily. A covered walkway hung with
lamps ran from the kitchen to a short flight of steps up to a
side-door into the main house; adjoining it on the other side
were a probable larder and then a washhouse; at right angles to
these stood a row of cabins that declared themselves by their
drabness the slave quarters. Smartly turned-out maids and

manservants hurried back and forth along the walkway, bearing in one direction trays piled with plates, soiled napkins, smeared glasses and great tureens, and in the other silver jugs and china cups, snifters, brandy balloons and cut-glass decanters. To witness the orderliness and the opulence, the gleaming plenitude, sensory, optical and conceptual, the touches of ornamentation that graced every building save the quarters of the slaves, a mise-en-scène stylized by moonlight into crystal coal and quicksilver flung with ember-glow, dizzied Cyrus, and his gut twisted and rage flared in him, as, he did not doubt, it flared in Abednego, whose hand he now found and gripped: this was obscenity.

What's back o this, he asked, keeping his voice low, referring to the high brick wall that ran behind kitchen, dependencies and walkway.

Stables an the carriage house, Bed said. A flower garden, a couple big glasshouses kept hot with steam. A fishpond. Privies, pens an stores. Out past all that, a peach orchard.

Okay, Cyrus said. Dogs?

Kept chained.

Where?

In a kennel in the stable-yard.

How many?

Bed shrugged. They chained, he said, then, Look:

Holding a lamp high and glancing behind her, a thin, headscarved young woman with a blanket about her narrow shoulders emerged from the kitchen and commenced to pick her way across the garden. She looked down as she traversed the row she was treading, as if she had been sent out for herbs, or was searching about for something let fall and lost. After a while, however, she stopped her search, stood up straight, and quickly looked about her, and Cyrus could see her chest rising and falling, and the mist of her breath and the wideness in her large eyes; and in her skinniness she trembled in the cold. He wondered if this was Prudence, the girl who had put something in the overseers' supper. Bednego cupped his hands to his mouth and once more made his soft owl-call. She did not look in his direction, but standing stiff as a scarecrow first lowered, then raised her lamp. This action she repeated four times, rhythmically, then, after a studied pause, a fifth. Bednego hooted again and, still without looking in his direction, she turned and hurried back to the kitchen.

Fo crackers, he said. Visitin the fifth.

Where?

The far end cottage.

That all of em?

No.

Whey the rest?

I don't know, Bed said. Out patrollin, maybe.

They gon come back sometime, Cyrus said.

Bed nodded. Come on.

He led Cyrus down to rejoin the others, and as he did so the wild-haired youth he had sent off earlier returned, bright-eyed and breathless. They's two ain't ours in the yard, he announced: a coach an a buggy.

You know em?

The coach is off of Brice, the youth said.

(Neighbors to the south, Bed said to Cyrus.)

The buggy I dint cognize. We gon wait till they goes?

Where the grooms at?

Dint see. Likely in the kitchen. They'll be two, maybe three.

Okay.

She dint trust em, Cyrus said.

Who?

The gal with the lamp. Them in the kitchen, she dint trust em.

Bed looked at him sharply. How you mean?

When she come out, Cyrus said, the way she looked back: dint want to be seen doin what she doin.

Abednego nodded, and for the first time it seemed he might waver. Okay, he said.

You wan wait, the youth asked again.

I reckons we –

From a long way off there came the retort of a rifle, faint yet penetrant, and as one they tensed. In the stable-yard beyond the kitchen-wall the hounds, triggered, began to bark.

At that Bed snapped into focus. You, you – he indicated the wild-haired boy and another youth close by him – go kill them dogs.

Eyes gleaming they sprinted off, pulling their blades out as they went. Bed pointed to a group of four older men: Go catch up with em. Anyone comes out, if they white, kill em. The men nodded and loped off after the youths.

Simeon, run round the front, tell Terrance be ready: it's on. Keep low.

Flashing a smile that was unexpected and yet to Cyrus understandable, a rangy young man wearing a battered straw hat said, I'm gone, and a moment later he was, bare heels flashing like rabbit-tails in the frosty, moonlit grass, heading back the way they had come, and a sudden image of simple freedom and open fields sprang up joyously in Cyrus' mind.

Mary – Bed turned to a short, pretty young woman with a heart-shaped face and eyes made larger and thereby at first glance, but only at first glance, more captivating by malnourishment – go knock up the end cottage; take James an John with you, you know how to do it. Knives is best.

She nodded and the threesome bustled off. Bednego selected four more men to follow along the shore in parallel with them. We know they's five inside, he said. When Mary knocks an one of em answers, the rest o you break in the back windows an the side-door.

Drawing their sickles and corn cutters, the men slipped away into the dark. You wants I go with em, Cyrus asked.

They know what they doin, Bed said. I needs you with me.

The gunshot, a single shot and nothing further, had accelerated their plans and pulse-rates, but in truth only by a little, for they knew it would signify nothing to fright up the white folks inside, not that far off, being as it might be a night hunt for possum or deer; patrollers pursuing some benighted runaway off a neighboring estate; or just the accidental discharge of a firearm by a drunk; and dogs bark at times for no reason that is discernible to men.

Might make em mindful, though, Cyrus thought as the sharp barks continued to chip the air, and he wondered as Abednego had surely wondered why the gun had been fired and what it meant. Durance?

They were now in two groups standing slightly apart, a smaller and a greater. The latter, led by Abednego, was to return to the back of the house and pass in through the terrace-doors; the smaller was to overrun the kitchen yard, sweeping up any house-servants who happened to be there, and force entry through the narrower side-door. Anyone inside the Big House attempting to flee by way of its front entrance would be dealt with by Terrance's people.

Now it was beginning, now they were running, silent as the stormclouds that speed across the sky, though the shouts were rising in their throats like a tide, and every nerve, every cell within them was screaming, a fiddle-note vibrating piercingly, too high for bats, even, but expressive of all the pain of their lives, and this, this would be inscribed as on stone, encoded within them on a microscopic, mitochondrial and nucleic level: feet on earth then grass then hitting the stones of the terrace bruising hard, and the dogs were barking staccato now, and somewhere knuckles were rapping sharply on wood, the sound hard-edged and penetrant in the clear, conductive air, and a young woman's voice was calling, Massa! Massa! Come quick! Mistuh Saint Hall, he tol me come fetch you! – and Cyrus and Abednego, side by side, crashed through the closest terrace door into the sparkling bright beyond, the small panes exploding around them in a storm of glass as the dogs commenced to scream.

Chapter Twenty-Three

W ith one shoulder leading, Cyrus and Abednego staggered side-by-side through the wrecked frames of the French windows, squinting against the stinging skeeters of glass they would later find had finely cut their faces, throwing up their hands like fans to shield their eyes; and then they were in the room, sliding on a rug that humped and travelled forward fast on the waxed parquetry, continuing the momentum of their arrival, and they clutched at each other to keep their balance in a way that to an observer might have appeared comical; might have but did not to the two white men who looked up startled from where they sat at the far end of a dining-table long as a flatboat, one older, one younger, and the air smelt of cigar-smoke and roast meat, and the glint of the chandelier depending overhead was reflected in the polished surface of the table as if it were a brown depth, and the ceiling was high, and in its center was a great white plaster rose, and around it winged cupids were painted, and a sky with clouds, though Cyrus saw this only after all was done.

Now with a groin-straining piston-compression of his thighs he leapt up onto the table and in juddering steps ran its length, kicking aside glasses and decanters, trampling plates, and threw himself upon the white men before they could so much as think to rise, carrying them backwards in the finely-wrought chairs in which they had been sitting, and the slender wood snapped sharply as they hit the rug like three sacks of sand among flung canes.

The older man was directly beneath him, red-faced and bewhiskered and heaving for breath, mottled flesh constricted by an abruptly too-tight collar, and to look into a white man's eyes from above was a new thing to Cyrus, vertiginous almost, and he let his fist continue what his body had begun and punched the man in the face once, then over and over, and it was the same as punching any man and not. Beside him the younger white man twisted round fast and on his hands and knees, backside high, scrambled toward the fireplace, which was large, white-marble-pillar-framed and porticoed, and on the mantlepiece a clock of brass and ormolu began delicately to chime the hour, and Abednego threw himself upon the younger man's back before he could reach what he was aiming for: the poker in its brass bucket, his added weight carrying both of them forward and bringing their heads perilously close to the blazing fire. With both hands Abednego gripped the young white man's scalp, dark fingers in slick blond pomade, and banged his forehead hard on the tombstone-sized marble hearth once, then twice, and the fight went out of him as from a heifer hammer-stunned for slaughter, and when he rolled over in a stupor a red smear was left on the white stone and the skin of his forehead was split and abraded and in the split redness welled.

All this had taken only seconds. Others had followed Cyrus and Abednego in; they now stood there uncertain as to what to do next, and Abednego, getting to his feet, directed that the white men be lain face-down on the floor, each with a black man's knee hard in the small of his back, a black man's weight upon him; and the poker was taken from the bucket and shown them meaningly, to compel their quiescence. His part done, Cyrus also got to his feet. Now he took in something of the room about him; large, whitewashed, high-ceilinged, with close-woven rugs scattered about the polished wooden floor, gilt architraves and dados running round the walls, large vases set on side-tables with gold claw feet – like predators or carrion birds they seemed to Cyrus, who had no notion of lions or gryphons; nor could he have named architraves or dados: gold strips runnin roundabouts he thought them. On the walls were hung paintings like windows onto landscapes in which were figures black and white, at leisure; one appeared to be a view of the Saint Hall estate as pictured from a fancied elevation that did not exist in nature, and around the paintings ophidean gold borders writhed.

The room was getting crowded now. A closed door in the left-hand wall led deeper into the house; beyond it he could hear thudding and raised voices and women screaming. From somewhere outside came several pistol shots: overseers, maybe.

But we got pistols too, an rifles, he thought, an noise don't matter now.

A door to the right of the fireplace that he had not observed, for the dado rail continued unbroken across it and it had no handle, giving the illusion to a casual glance that it was but a continuity of wall, swung open then, and Prudence hurried in, followed by a tall, tobacco-brown man smartly dressed in a brocaded black jacket and white breeches, and other men and women crowded in from the corridor behind him, field-hands and members of the household staff commingling without hierarchy.

This Cornet, Prudence said to Bed, and closer to, Cyrus saw by the angularity of the man's features that he was little better fed than those in the fields, for all that he wore velvet. Cornet, this Abednego. He Diver's right hand tonight.

Cornet nodded, and though Cyrus could not read his face it was evident by his manner that he had at least colluded in the planned uprising. Minnie and Libby run up to the attic when the glass broke, he said. Then over his shoulder he called, Grayson –

Cornet's head butler, Bed said to Cyrus as the man Cornet had called came pushing through the others, younger and rounder-faced than most, and handsome, neatly moustachioed, and smooth in his movements.

Yessir, Mistuh Cornet.

Don't trust him, Cyrus thought, noting the way Grayson's green-brown eyes darted about. Cornet don't neither, I reckons; nor Bed. He got a calculatin air.

You got cord to tie em, Bed asked Prudence. She nodded and hurried back out through the swing-door. The other hands looked about them and looked upon the white men lying facedown on the floor, mazed by the warmth and opulence and sudden easy conquest, wondering: why had they not done this a decade ago?

The others is in the drawin room, Cornet said.

You stay in here with these two, Abednego said. Keep em guessin who in on it.

Cornet nodded, and Cyrus thought Abednego did not wholly trust the head butler either; or perhaps it was that he wanted to keep Grayson out of the other room and under Cornet's eye. Bed was now crossing to a paneled, brass-handled door that led inwards and, leaving the others, Cyrus followed him first into a darkly-paneled hall, then, through an identical door directly opposite, into what was evidently the drawing room, and it was thronged with uprisers.

A hard-faced, snuff-toned man with a shaved head waved a sickle and called, Bednego: come see what we got – and Cyrus followed Bed through the milling crowd.

The room was much the same in scale and proportions as the dining room; was in fact its pair, or mirror; the fireplace carved to match, the detailing identical, though here all was arranged for ease: plumply padded armchairs, sofas and banquettes in dull gold fabric embroidered with glinting thread; rugs so finely-woven as to have no texture; fifteen-foot book-cases flanked the fireplace, by one a ladder on a rail so the upper shelves could easily be reached; scattered here and there small tables, round and rectangular, of inlaid wood or marble, touched with gilt; two wheeled globes the span of a man's arms that Bednego could have told Cyrus were the moon and the earth; a grandfather clock that to Cyrus' mind seemed an upright coffin with for no evident reason a mechanism atop it that clonked second upon second. Before a window stood a gilt harp the height of a man, and by it a grand piano, its propped-up lacquered lid also suggestive to Cyrus of the viewing of the dead; the white dead who were put into the ground in luxury; and above the fireplace was a portrait scaled to life of a haughty, dark-eyed white man in hunting clothes, with by him a white woman in bright green and wearing a hat in which a bird perched amidst a tangle of netting, and the man held a scroll on which there was writing that Cyrus took to be a deed of ownership, and he had one booted foot upon an outcrop, and the mark of rank was upon him, and high, wild clouds had been painted in behind his head, an artifice, Cyrus perceived, for the light that broke between the figures did not illuminate them as it should: a revelation – no doubt accidental – that they were not, in truth, a part of the world; that this was not real.

These he did not doubt were the Saint Halls, but they were not among the white men and women now revealed cowering before the fire: one man and three women, looking up at him and Abednego with eyes at once bright and dull with fear.

Where the Saint Halls, Abednego demanded of the man,

who was young and tousle-haired and scantily mutton-chopped, and Cyrus thought of James Rose, but felt nothing now.

Off visitin, the white man said, his manner surly.

They be back tonight?

The white man flushed, likely at the repeatedly absent suh or massuh, and did not answer, instead lowering his head and hunching his shoulders in a shrug. His hands were tied behind him with a cravat that had been taken from around his neck, and the normally ivory fingers were already red-purpled by the constraining of his circulation. Bed gripped his chin, and his strong brown fingers pressing into the soft pink-gray jaw so confidently was something to see, and he lifted the white man's head up and met his gaze, and Bed's eyes were flat discs as he repeated his question.

Yes.

Bed nodded and let the man's jaw go, and the white man hung his head as though dazed or drunk, and all present understood this was a lie, and for a moment Cyrus thought Bednego would strike him, but he did not, just gave him a look and turned away. Take em up to the attics, he said.

At this the two young white women on the chaise-longue, who had briefly mastered themselves – or had, perhaps more basely, been fixed with dread at what might happen to their failed protector and, consequently, themselves – commenced once more to wail; a third, older, no doubt their chaperone, made no sound, though her blanched face was stiff with fear.

Greta, Eloise, be quiet, the white man said without looking up, then to the older woman: Miss Pruitt, will you calm them.

The older woman murmured something but it made no difference, the wailing continued, and the girls' pale skins mottled with rising hysteria; and there in the glow of the fire Cyrus was struck foremost by their fleshiness, the covering of fat that shaped, that created their femininity: the pushed-up curds of their décolletage, the softness that every black woman on the Saint Hall plantation had been robbed of, both in body through starvation and also, unless fought for in an impossible, paradoxical way, in spirit, for who can fight to be gentle and as a consequence become gentle?

They were not twins, the Misses Brice – Cyrus' mind

flashed to the words of the boy earlier, on returning from the stable-yard: a carriage from Brice – but nearly so, their yellow hair framing their faces in identically elaborate and time-consuming curls set no doubt by deft-fingered and uncomplaining maids, their large, pale blue eyes now red-rimmed with tears, their mouths small and cupid-bowed, chins weak, all traits recessive and, though such a judgment might yet be proved erroneous, markedly unintelligent.

They, the white people, were now, Cyrus thought as he contemplated this tremulous and florid scene, in exactly that situation which all whites feared most; their own especial Judgment Day. Back on Tyler Bed had told him tales from the table of white dread of revolt, and Cyrus knew that now, more than at any other moment in his life – in any of their lives – he – they, the black folks – were not seen by the white; were entirely optically consumed by the projections in the white women's minds, and the realization of that willful blindness from which true sight could in no way be compelled made him sick with rage, for he knew too that they would not see him as himself even as he beat their brains out with a poker; would see only their own nightmare made manifest and mirrored back at them. Nothing would work except perhaps – his stomach lurched in revolt – love. Yet even were that so, and he doubted it in the extreme, such love would not be possible here, if anywhere; nor now, if ever. His knife was light in his hand, as eager to rise and dart as a dragonfly, and as beautiful.

Now the older woman – not in fact so elderly as at first glance he had supposed – demure in indigo to wrists and ankles, her collar buttoned high about her throat, her hair, pulled back hard, and colorless, framing a face that was also colorless, though not without strength of character – stood.

I shall play for us, she said through the sobbing of the girls, and stiffly she moved to the piano-stool, daring any present to stop her, and, glancing at Abednego, none did; but when she sat before the keys he gently closed the lid on them, and she understood, and she lowered her eyes and placed her hands in her lap, and the girls, whose noise-making had for that brief moment subsided into watchfulness, commenced to sobbing again.

Shut up, Bed said without looking at them, and – a small

miracle on this day of many miracles both bright and dreadful – they did; and the black men and women took them by their bare, peach-bruisable arms and led them and the older woman from the room; and the white man was pulled up by the wrists bound behind his back and he cursed as he was shoved forward by three of the men, and attempted to kick out, earning himself a punch to the side of his head as he was thrust from the room after the women, and Cyrus heard the sound of feet clonking on wooden stairs as they went up.

I'ma go speak with Terrance, Bed said, and went out, leaving Cyrus standing looking about him, his curiosity rising as his adrenalin receded, and he felt the tension then between the desire to possess the fine things in that room, in that house, and the need to end the system that gave rise to them, for considering the ugliness of their provenance, was not their beauty a lie, or at the least implicitly degraded?

Perhaps the others felt the same, for they drifted about the room, reaching out hesitantly to touch curtains, ornaments, the spines of books; a youth spun one of the globes, eyes widening neither because he was impressed by its manufactory, nor because he understood the accumulated geographical knowledge it displayed, but simply at his own daring. The tall clock clunked and whirred and struck the quarter-hour, a single chime that meant nothing to most of them.

Struck by the mirrored layout of the rooms, Cyrus crossed to the set of book-cases to the left of the fireplace, looking not at the fine bindings of gilt-stamped leather but at the structure of the casements, and found, folded flat against the edge of one of these, at hip height, a small brass handle. This he pulled out and turned, and within the wall a snib clicked, and a section of the bookcase swung towards him, a door concealed as in the dining room the servants' door had been concealed, cantilevered perhaps, for the movement was light and easy; and the others watched as he passed into the unlit room beyond.

It was not, as it had seemed at first, a secret room, for a paneled door to the right plainly gave onto the main passageway, but it was a private one: a study; and cold, with no fire in the grate, and no lamp burning, though the moonlight spilling in through the unshuttered windows, and the fan of lamplight from the doorway behind him, revealed to Cyrus that the wall opposite was densely spiked with the hung and jutting horns of stags and other animals he did not know, for some were corkscrewed and others queerly proportioned, and their shadows splayed out disconcertingly.

The display of horns was flanked by latticed bookcases; and before them, set at an angle, was a large desk, its upper surface inset with green leather, and behind it a captain's chair, also of green leather, and studded. Next to the door giving onto the hall, and at first glance elegant in a way that suborned their purpose, were displayed fowling pieces, hunting rifles and fancy pistols, their burnished barrels finely filigreed, their stocks gleaming and some inlaid with ivory. On the desk sat a great leatherbound ledger, open, and before it a crystal inkwell and pen set; nearby stood a roll-top desk, closed and, when Cyrus idly attempted to lift its lid, locked; over towards the passage-door was a green baize table, rectangular, on which sat several ivory balls the size of plums, and on one of its raised edges were placed a pair of tapered sticks and a small block of chalk. Yet it was the cabinet immediately to his right that commanded all Cyrus' attention.

This ran two thirds the length of the wall that backed onto the drawing-room and was eight feet in height and four feet deep, had a narrow, varnished wooden frame, and was of glass. Inside, and wired in dramatic poses, were the scoured skeletons of five human beings. The arms of the skeleton nearest to Cyrus were flung upwards as to heaven, exultant, jaws set open wide; its neighbor bowed its skull-head in submission, hands folded across its sternum as a corpse's hands are placed, reverentially; a third knelt, clasping bony fingers in supplication and prayer; a fourth sat upon a stool, chin in hand as if in thought; the fifth leant upon a plinth with one leg crossed before the other at the ankle as a man might lean upon a mantelpiece, the intention evidently counterpointingly comical. All about them, on artfully-arranged branches of oak and cypress and walnut, were placed skeletons of squirrels, possums and raccoons, posed as if frozen in a moment of playful pursuit.

Lightly touching the cold and tremulous glass Cyrus passed along the cabinet, watching the dead within.

Mas Saint Hall calls it nature morte.

Cyrus looked round to see Cornet standing in the doorway: none of the others had followed him into the room. Mort, he echoed, thinking it a person's name, perhaps, maybe with a tale attached.

Some of our people died of the flux, Cornet said. Ten years back. Mistuh Saint Hall made us boil em up. Fo their bones. Fo this.

We should take em out, Cyrus said, his fingertips still on the glass. Bury em someplace.

Cornet nodded. His face was expressionless but there was a glitter in his eyes, a wetness. These was people you knew, Cyrus thought, and something rumbled inside him, as it were subsonically.

My sister, Cornet said thickly, then turned and left.

Beyond the cabinet a display case stood, and inside it pale and wrinkled things in bottles like pickling jars stood on greenglass shelves. In one of these bottles, jugged so close its flesh conformed to the interior curves of the bottle, was a baby with Negro features, eyes screwed shut as though against its imprisonment, nails perfect on its tiny, clenched fingers, and something broke in Cyrus then.

The door giving onto the passageway opened and Abednego came in, followed by another man, and at once he saw Cyrus' pain and, without knowing its source, put aside whatever it was he had been about to say or do and held Cyrus in his arms and let Cyrus bury his face in his shoulder and sob, and Cyrus felt no shame. Afterwards Abednego led him through to the drawing room, to speak to those assembled there, and they were disquieted by Cyrus' tear-reddened eyes, and did not ask what was in that other room.

The man who had come in with Abednego was, it transpired, Terrance. He was tall and wiry and, though starved, strong, and to Cyrus the angularity of his face was striking and amidst soft and curving opulence obscene and even perverse: the skull rising up triumphant through the skin, the deathshead longing to supplant his living features.

Now the house was theirs, hunger rose in them ragingly.

We gon be eatin soon, Bed said, at once alert to their mood, stepping up onto the banquette so as to be seen by all, his muddy black shoes sinking into the yielding yellow satin.

Grayson openin all the stores an cupboards him an Cornet got the keys to; we can bust in the rest. There's preserves an cold meat an such that can be et straight off. We'll rotate the cookin an servin an choppin of wood fo the stove an fires.

Make the white folks do it, someone called out.

Amidst the laughter Bed said, I wouldn't trust no white folks with what I'm gon put in my mouth.

Who knows, one a them might hawk an spit in it, a serving girl said, to more laughter.

Aw, now Retta, Terrance said, who would ever do such a thing?

I ain't givin em no hatchet, an older man said.

We do it our own selves, Abednego said.

Like always, someone added to mm-hms.

The overseers, Cyrus asked quietly, prompting.

The overseers that was in the cottage is dead, Bed said for all to hear. We gots to be on our guard, though: they's several mo skulkin bout the place still. We gots to keep watch.

Who gon watch, someone asked.

We work relays. Go by our teams. Turn patrollin upside-down, catch us some white runaways. Where the Brice grooms?

They here.

Two men in dark-blue livery with gold epaulettes on their shoulders came forward, and for a moment they seemed superior beings simply by reason of the muscle-mass adequate nutrition had permitted them to retain, though of course it was not so, and despite their build their manner was fearful in the extreme, for they had had no part in this, and yet now were inextricably involved.

This Cole an Timothy, Prudence said.

Was you stayin over, Abednego asked, stepping down from the banquette.

Naw, Cole said. We due back on Brice by midnight latest.

Okay then, Bed said. We need a note sayin you gon stay over. Writ by one of them white gals.

Naw, Cyrus said: the ol woman.

Bed nodded. The woman. Then one of you rides back with it to Brice.

The grooms looked at each other in a writhing agony of doubt: to go was to escape a situation that could all too easily turn lethal, but also to abandon a wholly-unexpected chance at freedom, a serious chance to which one need do no more than say yes. Yet the one who rode away might betray the one who stayed behind, out of fear, or through stupidity; for personal advantage, or at the least to avoid retribution of the most savage kind should the revolt fail and he, the bearer of a forged letter, be discovered to have had prior knowledge of it and kept quiet.

Yet it seemed they were true friends, for Cole took Timothy's hand and said, What you reckon? You goes, or me? And Timothy looked down and, shrugging, sighed and said, I'll go. You stay. Jus don't – he cut himself off, reached up and gave Cole's shoulder a squeeze.

We gots to get that note writ, Terrance said.

Can you read, Bed asked.

Well enough.

Take her up ink an paper an make out you can't. See what she puts down. If she tries to tell, an likely she won't be able to help herself, make her do it over. Terrance nodded as Bed continued, Come down after an read Cole what she writ fore you lets her put the wax on it. He'll know if she tries to add in things that ain't true, to try an incite a suspicion in the reader that all ain't right here.

Cole nodded; Terrance went through to the study to find ink and paper and went on upstairs, exiting by the other door.

You reckon Diver reach Amesburg yet, Cyrus asked Abednego.

Twenty miles an mo against the current, Bed said. Three miles an hour'd be good going, so –

A couple hours yet.

An that's just gettin there. Then there's scoutin an executin the raid. Then gettin back.

Thas faster though: downstream.

Even so, best case we gon have to hold this place till the mornin after tomorrow. Though we'll maybe get news befo then, he added, fo better or worse.

His eyes were bright as polished agates, and, ashy and sweaty and drawn-skinned as he was, Bed had never looked so handsome to Cyrus as he did then, and in the warmth of the room he felt desire rise as it had not for the longest time, and he found himself blushing and looking down as if ashamed, though he was not, for desire reciprocated is never shameful, is rather a total liberation of self.

The preparation and distribution of food came next, as a matter of urgency. It was managed by the household staff with the efficiency of decades of experience. Sittings at the long dining-table were held in regular rotation, sixteen at a time, a line of volunteers taking on all tasks in turn, and there was no shortage, for to serve one's fellows was not servitude; and to choose to labor made that labor not a brute extraction but rather the giving of a gift; and it was a pleasure to all to take baskets of edibles out to those watching the avenue, or to flag down the patrolling horsemen and pass them up cold meat and warm bread wrapped in linen napkins, and a stone bottle of cider to warm them against the chill of the night; and Miz Bell the cook was carried in protesting on the shoulders of the two manservants Fredrick and Sugarsnap, and seated flustered and laughing at the head of the table, and there she was waited upon by Cornet and Grayson as if she were Miz Saint Hall herself, and the fires were loaded high with logs and blazed bright and wild.

The sudden consumption of fare far richer than that to which they would have been accustomed even in the days before rations were curtailed was the cause of much subsequent stomach-ache and intestinal distress, and a deal of hurrying to the privies, which soon became foul, but the overall movement that night was towards a restoration of health and spirits, and there was singing, and fiddles were broken out and tunes played not with metronomic enforcement but from the heart and to the heart's beat.

During all this Cyrus and Abednego, who had eaten early, quickly consuming while standing leftover slices of cold mutton and cold roast potatoes, explored the rest of the house, leaving greasy fingerprints on every polished brass doorknob they turned. In one of the upstairs bedrooms, each of which had its own sitting- and dressing-room, they found an elderly, bedbound and grotesquely obese gray-haired white man with rotten teeth and a rotted brain, and breath foul as old blood, who bellowed Niggers! over and over, and as he did so yanked repeatedly on a braided rope depending from the ceiling that was, it transpired, connected to the servants' rooms in the attic, jangling a bell up there – until Cyrus took it from his hand and ripped it down. At that the old man looked at him with a muddled, sclerotic fearfulness, and when Cyrus put a finger to his lips and handed the limp rope back to him the man looked down at it and fell to tremulous and plaintive mumbling. The room was growing cold, and Cyrus and Abednego stoked the fading fire, added logs from the basket, replaced the screen before it, and closed the door on him.

On that floor there was also an internal, building-wide balcony from which twin staircases swept down, overlooking the ballroom that dominated the front third of the house; and set at right-angles to the corridor that led up to it was a narrow stair that a casual glance would not discover, for it seemed the intention of the architect that the reality of the labor that sustained the Big House be at all times concealed. Climbing the uncarpeted, unpolished stair they found in one of six attic rooms the housemaids Minnie and Libby. Young, skinny and fearful, they at first shrank back from two male field-hands coming in with weapons shown openly, but were quickly reassured – and then, when taken to the adjoining room to see the bound and gagged Brice girls; the Saint Hall son and his friend, the older white man; and the older white woman, also tied up – excited. The white girls were shivering with not only fear but also cold, for there were in the attic rooms no fireplaces, nor any other source of warmth.

They say the heat rises so we don't need no grate, Libby said. But it don't.

Cept in summer, Minnie said. Then we stifles.

After sending Minnie and Libby downstairs to join the others, Bed and Cyrus closed the door on the prisoners, turned the lock and returned to the floor below, to continue their exploration of the bedrooms. In the master bedroom they found Miz Saint Hall's personal maid, Hebe, hiding in her mistress's dressing-room, a large pair of scissors ready in her hand. It transpired she had not been trusted with knowledge of the uprising, and when they told her, her eyes flashed. You think I'd side with that creature, she spat.

Well, I don't know you, Bed replied.

Hebe's cheeks colored. Slaps she's gived me, she said. Jabs with her comb. With hat-pins. Sick.

By way of proof she offered the insides of her bare fore-arms, and the skin was marked on the tenderest part with dots darker than the rest.

Put it on Diver, Bed said. Or Cornet.

Cornet? You can tell that fool it's Grayson needs watchin, not me.

Bed nodded slightly. She was lightskinned and haughty, and though her dress was plain and muted in color, it was of watered silk and hung to her ankles. Her hair had been ar-ranged with care, a braided rope about her temples constrain-ing the wavy center in an orderly and decorative way, and her thinness seemed a product of her nature rather than dietary deficiency.

The dressing-room, which was not large and had no win-dow, smelt cloyingly of rosewater and sweet powder, and clothing bulged from a wide wardrobe so overfilled the doors could not properly be closed on what hung within. Next to it were several large chests. Articles of clothing to be adjusted hung from a rail; by the rail stood a small table on which were laid out ribbons, pins in a cushion in the shape of a heart, spools of thread, measuring tape, scissors and scraps of fabric for patching; nearby a pressing-board and iron stood ready, and a small stove; and back of those was a narrow trestle-bed. Opposite the overflowing wardrobe stood another. Idly Cyrus opened it, and found it contained a man's clothing – in the main coats and jackets; shirts and undershirts, he presumed, being stored in the trunk beside it; footwear he supposed the provenance of a boot-black, to be cleaned and maintained elsewhere.

You got his build, Hebe said to Bednego, and her green eyes were gleaming as she studied him and a small smile was rising in her, and Bed met her eyes and her smile and he smiled too, and her urging ran through him like a message down a wire, and he reached in and drew out a jacket of gray watered silk with a black velvet collar, and Cyrus watched, his heart beating, as Abednego slid the jacket on.

Here, said Hebe, and from behind the open door she wheeled a large oval looking glass suspended in a tilting walnut frame, and she pivoted it so Bed could see himself from head to foot, and see himself being seen by Cyrus, and the cut of the jacket and his confidence in wearing it made him somehow more, as clothes that fit well do.

We'll share it all out, he said.

The news spread fast, and there followed then a carnival time when all was turned upside-down, and those who their entire lives had worn abject rags seized silk and lace, satin and fur and velvet, and once the clothing was plundered and disbursed the curtains were torn down and swept round shoulders like the robes of kings and queens and priests; jewelry – rings, brooches, bracelets, cameos, necklaces, tiaras – gemstones that had until that night gleamed against skin that was pale, were now scattered and set anew against skin that was dark, gaining thereby, or so it seemed to their new wearers, in richness and in luster. The butlers and table-maids alone were unchanged in manner and attire, and in that way were the axis around which the household was inverted. The others tore about with a wildness in them, and Cyrus smiled though he was past that now and looking ahead.

It's theirs so let em, he thought. Even if it gets took back, it's theirs.

Oughtta be theirs.

Chapter Twenty-Four

C yrus crossed to one of the windows of the master bedroom and looked out. The moon had set and all was still as a painting in a frame. Behind him Abednego took some small logs from a basket and tossed them on the fire, an oddly soft charcoal sound that was followed by another that made Cyrus look round to see Bed dragging into place before the blaze a warmly-glinting copper bathing tub; and the sight of it made Cyrus' scalp itch, and he at once felt dirty in a way he never would have done when cleanliness was not a possibility. Still, a smile pulled at his lips and he said, Damn. Behind Abednego the bed waited, broad and with a pale blue coverlet on, and posts at each corner, its curtains drawn back receptively.

There came a clonking at the door then, and both men looked round to see struggling in with a large wooden bucket of steaming water the flushed, disheveled Brice girls, their toneless arms at full stretch, small hands reddening round its iron handle: the white folks had been put to work. The girls were accompanied by Sugarsnap, looking handsome in a pale blue velvet jacket and a white shirt that exploded at its front in ruffles, tamed by a crimson neckerchief. Avoiding looking at Cyrus or Bed the girls came forward, clunking and scraping the bucket on the polished boards as they did so, and crying, and both men had to force themselves – as no doubt Sugarsnap had already forced himself – to resist the impulse, ingrained in them from birth so deeply it was twin to nature itself, to hurry forward and offer help to any white person in difficulties. And so they stood there awkwardly, not, after all, enjoying this. Only when it became evident that in their attempt to tip the contents of the bucket into the tub the Brice girls were likely to spill most of it on the floor did Bednego say tersely, You can leave that. Go get us a refill.

The white girls set the bucket down with relief and for the first time looked at him, and their expressions were blank, and perhaps they were surprised, for Cyrus supposed they had doubted they would be allowed to leave the bedroom unmolested, their minds progressing the carnival inversion of the household to its logical end; their violation and, horror above all other horrors, impregnation; and the mere presence of those minds, the fears bleeding out through those pale blue eyes, wearied him, and he said, Yeah: go, and they hurried out, stained silks rustling brisk as a maid's.

Cyrus and Bednego set the bucket close by the fire to keep it warm, and laid on the bed towels they had taken from the chests, and scented soap and face-cloths and nail-brushes, and a soft, curious item somewhat like a mass of tripe that Bed told Cyrus was called a sponge, and was found floating in the South Seas. It was a plant, Bed said, or just possibly an animal of a curious kind, and you rubbed it gently over your body, drawing up the blood and thereby enlivening the skin. Bed moved a folding screen of pale blue silk embroidered with yellow crocuses across the room so it stood between the tub and the door. As he did so the white girls toiled in again, now lugging with considerable difficulty two buckets apiece, overseen by Hebe with a curious expression on her face that was not particularly pleasant to see, their curls tumbled in sweaty disorder. They has to work to keep em tight, Cyrus thought incuriously. The young women labored over to the tub and set the buckets down with clumsy clonks.

Wait, Bed said, and they stood there as he and Cyrus emptied all save one of the buckets into the tub, and the steam rose up, lifting their spirits.

Cyrus stacked the empty buckets and handed them to one of the girls to take back down. Okay, that's us, he said to Hebe.

She nodded, and then her expression softened. You might care fo that, she said, pointing to a small green metal box sitting among fancy bottles and jars on a dressing table that was white and gilt and the shape of an oxbow, and above it three mirrors were set to show a face from all sides. The bottles and jars had been knocked about during the earlier rumpus and ransacking, and the two sets of small drawers pulled open and tipped out, but it seemed no-one had opened the box. Cyrus now went and did so and found its inner surface lined with blue glass and filled with white cream. It feeds the skin, Hebe said. Gives it a glow. Cyrus sniffed the cream, for it was infused with scent. Thas jasmine, Hebe said. Better'n warm bacon grease, ain't it?

Uh-huh, he said. Thank you, Miz Hebe.

She smiled, and he was minded to touch her arm then, to say that all this would turn out for the best, but he could not and so he did not; and after a moment she turned away from him and Bednego and swept out, the white girls trailing after her. Bednego followed and closed the door on them.

Behind the screen and before the dancing fire they removed their clothes, and in their nakedness and arousal they were transfigured, and they kissed hotly, but, anticipating interruption at any moment, went no further, instead standing in the tub and soaping and washing and wiping each other down with the face-towel, wringing the blackened water out into a chamber-pot pulled from under the bed, caressing each other nipple-pricklingly, dick-kickingly with the sponge; then finally holding the saved, fire-warmed bucket up above their heads and, facing each other, tipping the water over themselves with care, and it was like not baptism but an initiation into knowledge of truth, and even their feet were washed clean.

They dried themselves standing before the fire, and their private parts hung loose and heavy, and they moistened each others' skins with the jasmine cream, and to touch and be touched so tenderly electrified them, and they once again became aroused, and breathless and almost tearful they did not dare to meet each others' eyes: only as they worked their fingers out to the tips did they finally glance at each other, then glance again, and each look broke into a smile that was boyish and sweet, that was innocence restored, or rather born anew.

I never thought you'd come, Bed said.

Yeah you did, Cyrus said, and he drew Bed to him for a brief, soft kiss, and their hips joined, and their jousting lances slid hotly over each other and beaded like honeycomb.

But I dint see how, Bed said. It was mo like a dream. I'd tell the others an they'd laugh. Or shrug. Did you know?

Fo real? Naw.

No?

Truth is, I was partway north an then I had to turn.

Had to?

Had to.

Once we was done here I was planning on comin fo you, Abednego said. I was gon sneak back to Tyler, sneak you out. Maybe start another uprisin. Then head north, or fo the territories.

They says war comin, Cyrus said.

They?

White folks.

You heard news?

Saw soldiers. Back in De Bray's Town.

Good.

You reckon Diver gon take the foundry?

Abednego shrugged and looked down. His hands were in Cyrus', and childlike he swung them from side to side, and the smooth egg-shapes of his biceps were pleasing to Cyrus' eyes. I don't know. He looked up. I hope so.

How long we give him?

We don't hear no news by noon day after tomorrow, we scatter an aim fo freedom best as we can. Couple hundred of us, some gon get through, an the rest can trouble the county along the way. They'll be talkin bout the Saint Hall revolt a long time after.

If war don't swallow all.

True.

Cyrus stared into Abednego's eyes and their pupils were dilated, for the fire was all the light in the room, and Cyrus wanted, needed Abednego inside him, and thought how the jasmine cream would ease his entry, and they could draw the curtains round the bed and do it quiet. Quiet enough. To begin with. And later they would not care; and in any case all order here was now turned upside-down, so who among the others would presume to remark on it, and – a log slipped down in the grate with a distracting rustle.

God damn, Cyrus said softly, smiling as with an effort he broke the moment. I reckons we best get dressed.

Bed nodded. Tomorrow be here soon, he said. Down below a fiddle commenced to play something sweet and sad, and a woman's voice joined with it, singing low,

O Canaan
Sweet Canaan

I am bound for the land of Canaan –

Male voices came in gentle on the refrain. Bednego had laid
out clean cotton drawers and undershirts on the bed, and these
they now put on, and over them white, full-sleeved, long-tailed
linen shirts, vests of a hardy weave, lined and satin-backed –
russet-brown for Cyrus and peacock blue for Bednego – and
cream cotton pants that were tight on Cyrus and loose on
Bednego save about the backside, which they hugged to a
degree that drew and delighted Cyrus' eye. Side by side they sat
on the bed to pull on clean cotton socks, and it yielded to them
invitingly, but they did not yield to it; instead they stood back
up and tied matching silk kerchiefs about each others' necks.
After, they wiped their shoes down with the already-dirtied
face-cloth and put them back on, for they were to hand, and in
tolerable repair, and fit their feet. Cyrus retained his hat and
coat, battered in appearance though they were, perhaps out of a
man's habituation to what he wears that overrides a change
even for the better; or from sentiment – a travelling gift from
Bella; or because they matched in coloration the winter woods,
and might later prove vital for concealment. Bednego pulled on
the gray silk jacket he had taken from Saint Hall's wardrobe,
and picked up a black bowler hat he had discovered in a box
atop the wardrobe, half-hidden from sight by its curlicued
front-board. This he now set upon his head at a jaunty angle,
and it fit as if it had been made for him, a small manifestation
of destiny.

Now Cyrus and Abednego stood face to face and surveyed
each other with an eye both loving and critical, and each took
pleasure in allowing the other to make some minor adjustment
to his dress, step back, assess with utmost seriousness, and at
last nod his approval: Damn, yeah. Bed went over to the
dressing-table and, removing his hat, ran Miz Saint Hall's
tortoiseshell comb through his hair till the tight coils were
uniform in their soft springiness and had a gleam to them.

Cyrus joined him at the mirror, though his crop required
no maintenance beyond a moisturization of the scalp. Studying
his reflection in the triple glass, front on and angled left and
right, the mirrors telling him as they told all who looked in
them that he deserved to be seen, and more than that, contemplated, Cyrus for the first time understood the construction of

superiority; its artifice and therefore its claimability, but also its seductive power. They would believe this so easily, the white folks: that what you wore was what you deserved. He thought then of the leatherbound book open on the desk in Saint Hall's study, in which was set down a list – of names, he supposed – and figures; a volume heavy as the gold-bound bible on the pulpit-lectern in the church at Tyler, and each number was preceded by a dollar sign.

Anythin sayin who's owned, we should burn, he said.

Abednego nodded and they went down.

The drawing room they found in silence: the earlier exuberant mood had subsided, and men and women sat about quietly, and there was much watching at windows, for the realization had come upon them that this was but a respite before a far greater and more demanding exertion, and one that might well end in torment and death. And yet they every one of them turned and watched with an intensity as fixed as nails in wood as Bed brought through from the study the book in which their purchases were set down, names, and new names assigned by the master's whim, dates and sums paid; a biblical prophecy in reverse, or so it seemed to those watching as Abednego tore out the first page and placed it in the flames to be consumed. Amen, Libby said as it caught and shriveled black and floated up the flue, and Sugarsnap took a swig from a decanter of plum brandy, and soft amens accompanied each burning that followed, one page at a time.

Once that was done, and it took maybe a half hour, Bed and Cyrus went in search of Prudence. They found her at the table in the kitchen-house, intently listing supplies and provisions, the information she was recording in the main provided by Miz Bell the cook, Grayson and Retta, along with others who came and went in quest of mugs of the cider the kitchen girl Squeak kept steaming in a cauldron on the stove. In her dress Prudence was unchanged, save that she wore pinned to the front of her smock a small brooch of carnelian, the gem's color matching her own; and later Cyrus was told it was a gift from Sugarsnap, for she herself would take nothing of the white folks'.

Leaving the continuation of the list-making to Grayson, who took her place at the table readily enough, and carrying with her a cup of cider, Prudence led Bed and Cyrus back through the house, to go and speak with Terrance out in the avenue. Even to Cyrus, who had never seen the Big House before that night, save remotely from the rock-tower, and had never been in thrall to its particular self-projection, it was strange to pass through that great ballroom as if in ownership; to push open the front doors that were twice the height of a man as if entitled, and pass out through them. The avenue stretched away into the dark, and he saw it now as the architect intended, from a point of elevation. Those tasked with watching it were wholly concealed from sight; only the two black men and one black woman now standing so boldly at the balustrade laid bare the profound disordering within and without.

It's a shame they was away, Prudence said.

We gots tomorrow, Bed said.

They descended the left-hand stair, and found Terrance waiting nearby in the shadow of a cypress. A lady's fox-fur stole was drawn warmingly close around his throat and fastened with a cameo, a tiny painting of a baby, pink and laughing, in an oval. His breath smoked in the cold air but his spirits were lively. I'm prayin on guns fore noon, he said as Prudence handed him the steaming mug of cider. Then we on.

As he was sipping, a rider, a young man in a straw hat, Lexander Cyrus thought his name was, came cantering up the drive, stopped before them and dismounted, and news was exchanged. A patrol had been waylaid by Durance's people on the north road, three white men killed and two dogs, the bodies rolled in a ditch and covered with leaves and dirt. No shots had been fired, and none had escaped.

Still an all, when they don't come home, fo sho there'll be wives with questions, Terrance said, and he tugged at the stole about his neck as though it were a noose tightening, by chance perhaps, but it seemed also a prefiguration, and Bed and Cyrus and Prudence went back inside, disquieted. They made a rapid tour of the house's interior, urging all to be vigilant, and taking those who knew how to fire a rifle and setting them to watch in turn from windows on the upper story. Food and drink and a climax passed had left the uprisers almost dazed and certainly sleepy, but talk of patrollers sharpened their minds, and a goodly proportion rose to their tasks without demur.

You reckons we can last out long as we needs to, Cyrus

asked when he and Abednego were once more alone. Somewhere a clock was ticking.

Can't do more'n try, Bed said. We oughtta go round the outbuildings one mo time.

He looked tired, and when Cyrus gave him a reassuring hug Bed rested his head heavily on Cyrus' shoulder. It's gon be okay, Cyrus said, placing his hand on the back of Bed's neck, giving it a gentle squeeze where the condyles met the base of the skull, and Abednego exhaled muffledly.

In the passage that led to the kitchen garden they ran into Minnie. Should I feed ol Mas Saint Hall, she asked breathlessly.

Why you axin me, Bed said. You free now. Do it or leave it.

She lowered her eyes, almost curtsying, then turned and scurried back toward the kitchen ahead of them.

The incident it seemed recalled to Bednego the need to provide leadership, and to Bed leadership meant sharing with all, rather than, as would have been expedient, deferring to the old hierarchies and passing out information through Cornet, Miz Bell and Elston, the head gardener, for now he went about with Cyrus explaining to everyone who was awake, room by room, when news of the foundry raid would likely reach them, what would happen then, and who would need to do what when morning came. He added, for there had been talk about this, that there was value in holding the white hostages unharmed; and that, while remaining vigilant, all excepting those on watch should now attempt to sleep, since this was likely to be their best chance to rest until all was done.

Sugarsnap, Grayson and Elston were wakeful, yet at that hour had been allotted no duties, and so Bed an Cyrus led them to Saint Hall's study, from the walls of which they took down the fancy sporting guns, carrying them through to the drawing room to examine them away from the Danse Macabre. Some required ammunition of a sort that was not among the boxes found in the gun-cupboard off the main corridor, but most could be pressed into service, and were loaded and set ready by the windows and the French doors, before the broken-in frames of which curtains had been drawn against the intruding draft, though these prudent preparations magnified rather than lessened the tension they felt, being as they were proofs of the reality of imminent attack. That done, there being nothing else to occupy them, inertia set in again, and all fell into inwardliness. Despite the well-stoked fire the room grew chilly: they were immobile, and outside the temperature was sinking fast. The clock on the mantel whirred and chimed twelve. Cyrus, who had fallen into a doze, stirred and became aware that Grayson was watching him intently.

You ever kilt a man, the butler asked.

Cyrus shrugged.

Well, have you?

Come close enough to know I could, Cyrus said grudgingly. You?

Sprawled on the banquette Grayson smiled, raising the pistol he was holding as if born to it, idly drawing a bead on the fireplace and squinting down the length of the barrel. Several golden bangles glinted on his wrist. I reckons I can do what I need to, he said.

Uh-huh, said Cyrus. I reckons you can.

The remainder of the night passed for Bed and Cyrus in brief dozes, stolen on whatever chair or bed or sofa was by rotation temporarily unoccupied; irregular patrolling of the rooms of the Big House; and brief, chilly excursions to the kitchen, slave and guest cabins, stables and other outbuildings, and to the jetty, to check a watch was being kept in all directions, and make sure there was nothing to report. Twice riders came from Durance out on the main road – no further patrols had been seen; and once from the mill-yard, where all was quiet. The Saint Halls did not return; nor Timothy, the Brice groom who had taken the message.

Dawn broke drably, the cocks about the estate crowing as if nothing had changed, and the uprisers stirred and rose, surprised, somehow, and then excited to find they did not have to go to the fields; that this was real, and that for today at least they did not have to fear white violence, or cater to white caprice. Breakfast was their first concern, and as on the night before the work was shared and the portions were generous, for by their reckoning nothing had to last more than two days, and following on hardship it was joyous to be improvident. Once they had eaten, however, the burden of waiting settled upon them once more, and the long day yawned and stretched out, heavy, idle-seeming yet dangerous as a predator. There was little talk, and some bickering, for a number of those who served in the Big House fell back into their habit of assumed superiority – a hierarchy inverted requiring, after all, in order for the inversion to have meaning, a prior hierarchy that was understood and deferred to by all; and any such inversion therefore inclined to relapse.

After breakfasting on fried eggs and ham Cyrus went and wandered the upper rooms, looking out of windows and taking in the view the night had denied him. The fields ran away to north, south and east, and the west bank of the river was under equally extensive cultivation, though he did not know whether the fields on that side were owned by the Saint Halls or some other white folks. In all directions save north the land was flat, the horizons low; to the north was the horseshoe of hills through which he had passed by boat.

It was on the side facing the river that Diver had been most concerned they present a façade of normality once the house was taken, for there was from dawn much traffic on the water, and any non-performance of the day's usual activities would be noticed by many, arousing curiosity and soon enough suspicion; and also, as with the avenue, there was the need to ensure that any who came ashore were not permitted to re-embark.

Since those uprising intended, regardless of what news came, to depart en masse the following day, there were many preparations to make – the butchering and dressing of hogs and sheep, the wrapping of portions of cheese and cured meats and the parceling up of dry supplies; shoes and boots were cobbled and repairs made to leatherwear and outer clothing; the state of the boats was assessed, and the practicality of moving by river, or of taking horses, carts and buggies by road weighed up. Tasks that could be appropriately carried out in the millyard, or before the house in plain view of passing craft, were performed in those locations, and in so orderly a fashion it would have pleased any owner of slaves. Each task completed both relieved and added to the tension they felt, and as they worked they sang, and at times the power in their combined voices terrified them, both in itself, and through the growing certainty that any who chanced to hear their song would surely understand what it signified and respond accordingly, black or white. (Rise up! Rise!) What lay ahead terrified them, but it exalted them too.

Cyrus watched black men on horseback coming and going along the lanes that veined the estate, keeping information flowing between the various parts of it, all of them muffled up in scarves and wearing hats and gloves so no casual eye would detect their race. His chest tensed as a black and yellow landau drawn by two dappled grays appeared on the boundary road, coming from the south, heading north. A mail coach? He did not dare draw breath until it had passed without slowing the pillared entrance to the Saint Hall avenue. He wondered if such passengers as were within would note the absence of hands in the fields, it being the plowing season; whether they would remark upon that absence to each other, and, remarking it, think it in any way consequential. The carriage disappeared into a strip of woodland some way along, in which Cyrus guessed Durance and the others lay concealed, and, fingers drumming on the window-frame, he turned away and crossed the hall and entered another bedroom, a woman's.

Windows facing south looked out on the stable-yard; beyond it was an orchard – plums, he thought – and next to it, set about a fishpond, were four glasshouses, shining single-story structures near twice the size of a slave-dormitory. At the end of each of these were narrow chimney-stacks, and from these smoke issued: evidently Elston and his boys had kept the stoves fuelled, maintaining the warmth and humidity inside and thereby permitting, Cyrus supposed, the continuance of unnatural growth against the inclination of the season; and he wondered what plants were cultivated within, for the transparency of the glass was obscured by condensation and mildew. At that moment Dill, a gangly youth and the youngest of the gardeners at perhaps fifteen years of age, happened to pass by, and Cyrus hailed him, and Dill came in. In that atmosphere of rising tension, beset by nervousness, the youth was pleased to talk.

They called zotics, he said. You goes in there, it's like you someplace else. A jungle. They's bananas – they long an yellow an sweet, come in bunches like crowns, one inside the other – an pineapples, that don't look like you spect by the name. They big as a baby's head an got scales like a pine-cone, an they kinda sour-sweet an bits gets inbetween yo teeth. He smiled and showed large, white and crowded teeth. Course I ain't spose to know that, he added quickly, and his smile twitched and fell on one side.

I ain't gon tell, Cyrus said gently.

Thas right, Dill said, then again more inwardly: thas right. His smile brightened.

Is there animals in there, Cyrus asked, thinking of the carved claws on the feet of the furniture in the Saint Hall drawing room.

Naw – well, rats. Sometimes a cottonmouth or two. Could kill em but the snakes eat the rats so – he shrugged, on the edge of some thought about the nature of things, perhaps, then moved on: They grows flowers in there too. Orchids. Midwinter an they got em on the table.

Huh.

Oh, an them berries Prudence put in the overseers' gravy, they comes from there. Nightshade, it's called. Looks kinda like juniper.

A thudding came from somewhere overhead, as of something pounding repeatedly against a door, and Cyrus and Dill hurried out into the passageway. Up above, muffled, angry words were being exchanged, then a door slammed and a man came down the side-stair fast, almost colliding with Cyrus as he emerged onto the landing. It was Sugarsnap, and there was anger in his eyes as the thudding went on.

He creatin, Sugarsnap said. His hands is tied, but he kickin the door like a horse that won't be shoed.

Who?

Mas Arnold, Sugarsnap said, then corrected himself: Saint Hall's son. Kickin an stampin an demandin he speak with whoever in charge. Whey's Bednego?

Rid over to the mill-yard, Cyrus said. He ain't back yet.

Above their heads the white man pounded his feet on the bare attic floorboards, setting the two small chandeliers jingling and a little plaster dust fell, fine as icing sugar.

They's Prudence, Cyrus said.

I don't reckon he'll listen to no maid, said Sugarsnap. Not one who he –

He don't know you, Mistuh Cyrus, Dill said. You could tell

him how things stand.

Sugarsnap nodded. I reckons he'll take it different from a stranger. Won't know what you is capable of.

Cyrus nodded. Okay. But just till Bed gets back. He ground his jaw. Okay. Less do this.

With Sugarsnap ahead of him and Dill behind, Cyrus ascended. He in a room on his own, Sugarsnap said. We split em up: dint want no conspirations.

Bes be wary, Mistuh Cyrus, Dill said as Sugarsnap took the key and slid it into the lock of a featureless, unpainted plank door.

Wary?

They says the devil can quote Scripture.

He ain't the devil, Cyrus said.

The stamping behind the door stopped.

Chapter Twenty-Five

By the jamb a hoe lent ready, its blade burnished by much use. Bring that, Cyrus said to Sugarsnap as he closed his hand around the doorknob. He acts up, jab him.

The door opened inwards, revealing a small, cold room in which the only furniture was a stool and a narrow cot; the only illumination a small skylight. An attempt had been made by its habitual occupant to introduce color, and express personality, by covering the cot with a throw made of many small scraps of fabric painstakingly stitched together. On this Arnold Saint Hall sat, his hands tied behind his back, and he looked up at them balefully, and his greased hair was tumbled in his eyes so he was compelled at regular intervals to flick it back, and the room smelt of sour sweat and sweet pomade. Saint Hall's son, yet there was nothing in his soft, ruddy features that echoed the portrait in the drawing room below, bone-structure buried, maybe, beneath dissipation and indulgence; or perhaps the painting was inaccurate, a flattery. Wispy mutton chops adorned his cheeks, though he wore neither moustache nor beard, and his lips, full and petulant, were now chapped. His blue-black eyes alone conveyed something of the spirit of the older man as presented by the artist.

Well? Arnold Saint Hall said, his manner presumptive and peremptory, and for a moment it was as though he had summoned Cyrus to account for himself, to account for all of this, and Cyrus was standing as a slave would, and Saint Hall was sitting as a master would; and when Cyrus made no reply, for his mind was at that moment empty, Saint Hall flushed in anger and said, You dumb, nigger? Answer me –

With an open palm Cyrus struck him hard about the face.

God damn you, Saint Hall said.

Cyrus struck him again, this time using the back of the hand, not the palm. The second blow silenced Saint Hall and something in his eyes receded as behind fogged glass, and Cyrus supposed the white man to be calculating if he would now slowly be beaten to death. His stung cheeks reddened, a drop of blood beaded in his left nostril, and he ran his tongue over the crazing of his lips. He was short of breath now, and somehow vulpine. I need to urinate, he said.

Do it, then, Cyrus replied.

God damn, the white man said, but quieter this time. You sho got it in for me, don't you.

I don't know you, Cyrus said. He felt nothing. Had he ever dreamed this dizzying reversal might be achieved? Yet now he found that all he wanted was to be free. Free of what? Whiteness. Saint Hall watched him as through lenses stacked in brass, that is, microscopically, but could not – could no longer – penetrate him; and in that knowledge Cyrus found, perhaps, all the power he needed: He don't know me; he never will.

He turned to Sugarsnap. Gag him, he said. Tie his feet together an hog-tie him. He makes any mo noise put him in a sack.

Now, wait here you –

But Cyrus was already leaving, and had no reason to turn back. Even so, once he was outside the room shudders ran through him and he found his brow was sweaty.

You did good, Mistuh Cyrus, Dill said: he had come out after him.

You reckons?

Uh-huh. Dill smiled lopsidedly. You dint kill him.

Cyrus nodded. It did not feel like much of a triumph, though he supposed it was one. He waited until Sugarsnap came out, the tying and gagging done, asking as he once more locked the door, What about the others?

They tied up an locked in. You wants I put em to work?

Naw. Don't want em seein what we doin today, or hearin talk.

They don't do stuff right anyhow, Dill said. Miz Bel gived one of em a peeler, white gal dint know what it was fo, just kinda jabbed with it.

His remark lightened their mood, and Cyrus was glad of him, and the three of them went down together. They found drawing and dining room unoccupied and, in their disorder, desolate, for the parlor maids had not put them to rights at the day's commencement, and the grates were crowded with ash

that stirred slightly as the draft pulled between the chimney-
vents and the broken-in French doors. Chairs pulled out from
the dining-table stood about the place, but though crocks and
glassware had been taken out, no-one it seemed felt comfortable in those rooms, and Cyrus, Sugarsnap and Dill went on to
the kitchen without pause or discussion. They found Miz Bell
kneading bread and humming. She was a large woman with a
lurching gait, and though robust, as she moved about her small
kingdom that morning Cyrus wondered how she would cope
with hours – days, weeks – of trudging along; with fording
rivers; with running from dogs. Perhaps when it came to it she
would remain behind, but today she was free, and so she was
happy.

You Cyrus, ain't you.

Yes, ma'am.

Well, Cyrus, would you pass me that salt?

He followed where she pointed and fetched a packet down
from an upper shelf and set it by her, and she took a goodly
pinch and added it to the dough. At the back of the kitchen, by
the stove, an older woman dozed in a rocker, and she too was
large, her hips pushing out under the arms of the chair, her
breasts spilling over her folded forearms. Thas Nurse, Miz Bell
said.

That ain't a name.

She raised Mas Arnold an his brother, Miz Bell said. Her
milk built they bones. Twins, they was. The brother died young,
a spider bite turned bad. Now Mas Arnold grown they done put
her here an I feeds her. She spose to work but she mostly
sleeps, so –

So Bell would not go, he knew. She know what's gone on?

Miz Bell shook her head. An I reckons it'd break her heart.
Strange, ain't it?

He shrugged. You wants me to fetch some rosemary fo that
bread?

Thank you. You a gentleman.

He smiled and went out to the garden and hunted about,
guessing rightly the herbs would be planted near the kitchen-
door, and returned with several aromatic sprigs. Finding the
heat of the oven oppressive he left Miz Bell to her work and
came out again, went over to the well, drew up a bucket of

water and drank deep.

Abednego appeared, coming round the side of a row of storage sheds that adjoined the house slaves' cabins. A pistol was slung low on his right hip, and the weight of it in its holster changed the way he walked, giving him somewhat of a rider's roll. Cyrus offered Bednego the bucket, and as he took it their fingers brushed, and as he drank Cyrus watched the rise and fall of his throat, and resisted an impulse to lean in and kiss his Adam's apple. The sky above was dun and dirty, perhaps presaging snow. The temperature, though low, was holding level, and there was no wind.

Come sundown, fo sho they gon be axin whey them Brice gals at, Cyrus said, when Bednego had set the bucket down. Any news from Diver?

Bed shook his head. I ain't expectin none befo noon, he said. But you right, though: them gals is trouble. We gon have to get a second letter writ, send one of our people to go with it, an come back with a reply so we know where we at; chance on there bein nothin they was spose to do tonight. They got they chaperone with em, so.

Cyrus nodded. Bed looked about him and, seeing no-one, stole a kiss, and Cyrus received it and was warmed by its firm, soft fullness.

Prudence came down from the side-door then and, seeing them together, hurried over, looking worried. No-one's seen Grayson or Retta, she said, not since last night.

Maybe they on the avenue.

They ain't: I checked.

The mill-yard?

Them two wouldn't go to the mill-yard; they'd stick close by the house.

Then they run, said Bednego.

Looks that way.

Damn.

If they gets caught –

Less hope they ain't –

But if they is –

I knew he was fo himself.

We all did, Prudence said. But even so I –

Can't tell a man he free then chain him to the spot, Cyrus

said.

Who did that, said Abednego. We stronger together. Damn.

We tell the others, asked Prudence.

What you reckon?

I ain't easy with lyin, said Prudence.

Bed nodded, and his hand found Cyrus' and clasped it, and who knew what meaning Prudence took from that.

There was nothing to do but make their rounds again, urging those on watch to greater vigilance, and those doing tasks to conclude them as speedily as possible. Those of the uprisers minding prisoners were burdened by their inherent kindness, for they permitted those they had tied up and shut in to empty their bladders and bowels in private, and provided them with food and drink, and the white women on being ungagged became hysterical, or pretended hysteria, and their babbling declarations of the many kindnesses they had shown those possessed of darker skins across the years consumed energy better directed elsewhere, as did resisting the impulse to console them. The white men, lacking it seemed all moral capacity, were inclined to see any act of kindness as weakness. Dangerous as bulls, they were best managed as such, though one, an older man named Greenacre, was sly, and, when ungagged so he could drink the water they provided, offered money and the promise of manumission in return for his release. Diver, however, had stipulated from the first that at no time should any person of color be alone with a white person, and that simple stipulation, consistently observed, defeated such attempts at suasion, an onlooker inclined to commonsense and blunt utterances inevitably snapping the delicate threads of deceit before the web grew strong.

Don't let them devils tempt you, Prudence reminded those who had charge of the prisoners. They sweetin now, but member what they done.

Sugarsnap had made a point of coming with Cyrus, Bed and Prudence to Greenacre's cottage. You got my sister Linny pregnant at thirteen, he said to the white man. Baby breached an they both died.

I loved that gal, Greenacre said. It broke my heart when she went. I'da raised that littleun like my own.

Don't let that devil in, Prudence said to Sugarsnap. Speak to that devil like you doin, he start to worm his way in.

You right, Sugarsnap said. His face set, he bent over the kneeling white man and replaced the gag, pulling the corners of Greenacre's mouth back hard as he made the knot tight at the base of his skull, forcing a foxy grin: a real face. Less go, he said.

Dusk was drawing on and still no news had come from the foundry, and all knew it. Miz Pruitt was obliged to write a second letter in her attic room, and Cole, the remaining Saint Hall groom, rode over to Brice, returning an hour later holding a borrowed lantern up before him, for the clouds covered the moon and blinded the night, and he was sweaty as cheese. Though he insisted the letter had been well enough received, and the reply he bore back with him seemed to confirm this in both its sentiment and phrasing, his evident nervousness left none of them easy, nor wholly convinced, and they pored over the text of it repeatedly, seeking hidden meanings, inadvertent disclosures.

The meal that evening was scrappy, disorganized and pro-longed in its arrival, though all were fed eventually.

Around ten o'clock, suddenly uneasy, Abednego decided he must speak with Durance. Though barely adequate as a rider, he took one of the horses from the stable, saddled up with the assistance of Cole; and Cyrus, a croker sack of supplies slung across his back, climbed up behind him and put his arms around his waist. Hats pulled down low on their heads and scarves concealing their faces, bearing a lamp awkwardly aloft they made their way at an unsteady canter to the narrow strip of woodland that bounded the estate to the north-east, and through which the main road ran north. At the boundary fence they tethered the horse and went in on foot, and by means of coded whistles soon enough found Durance, sitting alone in a hollow sufficiently sheltered from the road to permit the lighting of a small fire with little fear of its being observed. She was smoking a pipe and her eyes were red from tobacco and woodsmoke, and still though she sat, she was alert, somehow vital, and the flames threw dancing shadows all about her. Cyrus passed her the crocker sack and she looked inside and rummaged, puffing on her pipe, eventually pulling out a bottle of sloe gin and nodding her approval.

From Mas Saint Hall's cellar, Bed said as Durance filled the cap and took a swallow. She refilled it and passed it to Cyrus, who likewise took a warming gulp, and then poured another for Abednego.

Saint Hall ain't come back then, she said.

No.

Thas a pity. You know when he due?

Cornet says he got senate business up in the county seat, so it could be days. But I'm thinkin more bout patrollers tonight. There gots to be talk goin round bout them as dint come back yesterday.

Durance nodded. I'm surprised we ain't seen em already.

That's why I brung you two mo pistols, Bed said.

You still ain't had no word from Diver?

No, and I'm thinkin we don't even wait till noon tomorrow, Bed said. I'm thinkin we oughtta leave come sun-up. What you reckon, Cyrus? He seemed young then.

I ain't so tied to other folks here, Cyrus said. But I reckons you right. What you think, Miz Durance?

It ain't a easy call, she said, glancing round as two other men appeared and came down into the orange glow of the hollow. One was Strawson, and he briefly shook Cyrus' and Abednego's hands with his unmaimed left, and Durance passed him the bottle. The other man, who Cyrus had not seen before, and who it seemed Abednego did not know, nodded acknowledgment and sat by Strawson, waiting on the gin. He was in rags and barefoot, and, seeing that, Cyrus was guiltily aware of his own clean and well-made clothing, his nourished skin, his protected feet.

Strawson by contrast now wore well-made boots. Patroller boots, he said, seeing Cyrus notice them.

Next patrol I'll get me some, the other man said, though with less conviction in his voice than he might have had the night before.

How many o you out here, Cyrus asked.

Thirty, thirty-five, Strawson said. We lost a few in the night.

We lost two, Bed admitted.

Durance knocked her pipe on the stump on which she was sitting. We don't hear nothin by sun-up we best get goin ourselves, she said.

Either way, come first light someone'll ride out to you, Bed said. He took a handful of bullets from his pocket and handed them to her, and in the firelight they gleamed sitting on her palm. Where's your bow?

String snapped on me.

There was nothing else to be said, and so Cyrus and Abednego came away. It took a little searching about to find where they had tethered the horse. They clambered up into the saddle, Bed first and then Cyrus, and made their slow way back to the Big House. They rode in silence, pensive, and Cyrus lent his face into Bed's wingblade and hugged him close and gently cupped his crotch. Life seed blood warmth pulse –

They found Cole in the stableyard, rubbing down the horses. They restless, he said.

Likely on account of we is, Bed said, handing Cyrus down in a twisting dismount so awkward it came near to pulling Bed off after him.

I hopes that's it, Cole said as the mare he was brushing backed up a few steps, snorted and tossed her mane. A white blaze ran down her nose, and her eyes rolled. A sudden breeze sent the lanterns hung above the stalls swinging and clinking, and Cole, who wore no coat, only a shirt and vest, glanced round and shivered.

We don't hear news by dawn, we movin out, Bed said.

Cole nodded, continuing to move the brush in firm strokes across the mare's glossy chestnut flank. There now, he said, it seemed as much to reassure himself as her, and Bed and Cyrus went round to the side-door and into the house.

Bed's thoughts now turned to the forging of passes, permits and papers of manumission. To have access to ink and paper of good quality was a rare thing, and within the roll-top desk in the study they discovered various stamps and seals that could be pressed into service, an ink-pad and slips of paper, the already-printed elements of which indicated them to be for the making out of receipts and bills of sale. Cornet, the head butler, could not only write, but write elegantly, and had some familiarity with Saint Hall's signature, so he was put to it, and the study fire was lit, and food and drink were brought to him at the green leather desk, to keep him in spirits as he toiled on until his hand cramped up.

Cornet indicated a panel in the study wall that had concealed behind it a small safe, and with much hammering and snapping of chisels and bending of crowbars this was prised from its setting and eventually broken open, though it proved to contain a disappointingly modest quantity of coin – quickly disbursed amongst those nearby – along with various personal papers, one a manuscript. Cornet read aloud the frontispiece of this: A History of My Forebears, Illustrious and Otherwise, by Julius James Covington Saint Hall. With a grunt and a shrug he set it aside, resisting the pull, the lure, the assertion made by the mere setting down of such a record, and validated by the reading of it, that such lives mattered more than theirs; and that forebears unknown or lost had no significance; deserved no acknowledgement.

Meantime the news was passed about that all who could should make ready to leave soon after dawn. This led to a further, though less frenzied, ransacking of the house, in the course of which it was divested of any trifle that might prove of value later on, though there was a wariness concerning any object that too brazenly declared its looted origins – a portrait cameo; a metal item bearing an engraved name or dedication – for to be found in possession of any such would lead the bearer to the gallows without delay, or with only such delay as interrogation and torture necessitated.

The night wore on. Abednego's leadership, in triumvirate with Prudence and Terrance, and with Cyrus at his side, had been sufficient in its firmness of resolve and clarity of purpose to prevent a rash and ill-prepared mass flight in darkness, but all were now feeling the danger in delay, and he as tensely as any of them awaited the coming of the dawn. Some fell to prayer, singly or in small groups. Bednego did not pray, and Cyrus, speaking no words aloud, touched the charm on his breastbone that he had set aside only when they bathed, and that Bed had re-hung around his neck once they had dried themselves and fed their skins: Bird bones for flight.

So Diver dint win through, he said eventually. He and

Abednego had gone out to the colonnaded folly on the lawn and were looking out across the river. In the absence of moon or stars there was little to be seen, but its rippling reached their ears, and the sound was soothing, though also deceptive, for this was above all a landscape of violence, both latent and otherwise.

They inhaled the damp mud smell. Gotta breathe while you can, Cyrus thought. Which way, he said.

North and a sliver to the east, Bed said. We was put to clearin land out there. Ain't no swamp that way, an I know the woods some. We can get through.

Swamp's good fo hidin out in, though.

They says it's rife with gators. An keepin on the move is best, I reckons: go an keep goin. Cyrus nodded as Bed added, What you think bout takin the river?

Rowin gainst the current is tirin an slow, Cyrus said, an even when you ain't looked fo, it's busy: too many eyes pryin. An we lets up any, we gets carried south.

So we goes north.

We goes north, Cyrus agreed.

You got yo supplies made up?

Uh-huh. Got my knapsack. You?

Got my pack.

Somewhere a riverbird cheeped once and then fell silent. It's gettin colder, Cyrus said. Les see how Cornet doin with them passes.

They found him at the master's desk, squinting in the lamplight as he dipped and scratched with the nib. These, he said, indicating a pile of papers by his right elbow, are travel passes made out in all the names I can recall. Whoever gives em out gots to be a readin man or woman, so they can tell whoever gets each one what name to go by, an what the pass says they spose to be doin. These – he indicated a much lower pile of larger sheets of paper – is manumission papers, but they ain't quick to write, on account of no-one never scrawled a black man's freedom: they does it proper. Signed an sealed. Hold on. He then wrote Abednego's name on one of the papers, and Cyrus' on another, though Cyrus had never been Saint Hall's property, appending to each a brief line of description as to age, height, build and complexion, sprinkled fine sand to dry the ink, tipped it into a saucer to use again, then folded each paper neatly in three.

His uncomplaining industriousness moved Cyrus deeply, and as he slipped the paper and its neighbor the travel pass into an inside pocket, he asked the butler, You sorry?

Cornet looked up. Sorry?

That we rose up. You had it better'n most an now thas done.

Cornet shook his head. I look at them – he indicated with the blunt end of the quill the skeletons in the glass case that stood behind Cyrus and Abednego. I look at them, he repeated, and it seemed for a moment he would say more, but did not, and Cyrus nodded and said, We bes let you get on, Mistuh Cornet. You needs anything, you call.

The older man smiled gently. Perhaps some tea, he said, when you has a moment.

They gathered up the passes he had written, and, running into Minnie in the hall, asked her to make up a tray with the best silver teapot, jug of hot water, milk-jug and sugar-bowl. Then they went and divided the passes between the horsemen – by now ten in number – who carried information back and forth between the main house, Durance on the boundary road, the mill-yard, the cabins, the cottages and other, more outlying parts of the estate. Each rider now took with him someone who could read – often holding on for dear life behind him, for by and large they, especially the women, had never so much as sat on a horse before – and so a further four hours passed. It was now eleven o'clock.

We lucky no white folks came visitin today, Cyrus said. He and Abednego were once more at the balustrade of the Big House, looking down the avenue. I seed the mail-coach in the mornin, but it passed by.

It's plowin season, Bed said. They mostly occupied with their own business. Couple flatboats come with deliveries though.

Yeah?

Yeah, but they was mainly run by black folks. They dint say nothin when we brung the receipt in the house an brung it out signed.

Okay.

There was one white man though.

Dint hear bout that.

I reckoned he might be gettin suspicious, so when I come out with the receipt Cornet signed I brought a bottle of whiskey with me, gived it him an said, With the compliments of Mistuh Saint Hall, fo services rendered. He took it.

That work, you reckon?

It hadn't, we'da heard by now.

You sorry they ain't came back?

Who?

Them Saint Halls.

I been here longer, I'd be sorrier, Bed said.

Cyrus nodded. You reckon we oughtta take a horse when we goes?

I'd say we better off on foot: every road gon be watched, that's if they ain't already.

Why ain't no-one come? Cyrus asked, staring out into the restless dark, his chest tightening. I reckons the white folks know. The raid failed, an they know, an they gots a plan. Thas why we ain't seed nothing today.

We gots people watchin from every window, Bed said, an they armed, so. He shrugged.

Uh-huh, said Cyrus. Well, less go in.

They went back in, closing the double-doors, shutting out the night. The ballroom was gloomy, for it was lit only by a single lamp that, earlier on, someone had set on a marble-topped side-table, alongside a glass bell beneath which a stuffed lyre-bird sat; and the room was cold, scarcely warmer than outside, for no spill had been touched to the neatly-laid kindling in the great ormolu fireplace, and the haloed saints looked down from their golden frames, impassive.

When we go we should set fires, Cyrus said.

Smoke'd make people come runnin.

It'd preoccupy em though.

Only the family, Bed said: the rest'd be hard on our tails. Let's try and snatch some sleep. We might hear from Diver yet.

I guess so, Cyrus said; and it was, after all, true: plans changed, contingencies occurred, and sometimes from chaos victory emerged when least expected. A boat might come yet, drawing in at the jetty just before dawn heavy with munitions, and these would be disbursed, and they, the hundreds of Saint Hall, would march out under the morning sun, pistols at their hips, rifles shouldered, their skins their uniforms.

Cyrus and Bed went through to the drawing room. It was unoccupied and smelt strongly of tobacco-smoke, both pipe and cigar. Smeary snifters and tumblers sat about, and several empty wine and brandy bottles were scattered on the floor. Together they sank down onto the yellow silk banquette and lay back, each resting his loosely-held pistol on his chest, ready for use, and in that position Cyrus closed his weary eyes.

Chapter Twenty -Six

C yrus woke from a dream of Old Africa in the darkness of
her hut, closing her warm, bony hands around his, to
find Prudence standing over him, and the bleak beginnings of dawn at the unshuttered windows.

I got a feeling, Prudence said. Her eyes were dark and clear
and wakeful.

Abednego's arm was draped loosely around Cyrus' shoulders, his head tilted back, and his mouth was gaping in seeming
mid-snore, but his eyes snapped open.

You seed anything, Cyrus asked, groping for his pistol,
which had slid down into the armpit of his coat.

She shook her head. Cyrus and Abednego struggled up
from the banquette and adjusted their rucked and rumpled
jackets and vests, then collected their packs from where they
had lent them by the fireplace the night before, and put them
on. Jamming his pistol into its holster, Cyrus crossed to the
north-facing side of the room and, taking up a rifle that had
been set there ready for use, keeping his body to one side,
peeked out of one of the windows. A wind stirring the pine-
break opposite made the line of trees seem, after two days in
which the air had been wholly still, queerly animate. Screwing
up his eyes, Cyrus stared into the shadows beneath them where
watchers might lie concealed, maybe even now be aiming rifles.

Stalkin us.

But he saw no-one, and no sign of anything suspicious.

Bed meantime was at the French doors, holding the curtain
aside and scoping the lawn and the river beyond; Prudence had
gone to rouse the others. The gold threads in the fabric that
covered the furniture, faintly limned with drifting ash, were
dulled, and dust hazed the smeared glassware. This was all past
now.

You see anything, Cyrus asked.

Nothin, Bed said. Yet neither of them doubted Prudence
was right.

Sugarsnap came in then, carrying a rifle loose and muzzle

downward in his hand, looking young and excited. Reckon I seed somethin, he said.

Where, Bed asked.

Out past the overseers' cottages, creepin in by the cabin road. It still too dark to be sho, but it was peoples, an the way they was movin had a purpose.

How you mean?

They was kinda crouched over. Thas what caught my eye.

How many you see?

Fo, five.

White?

Couldn't see.

Armed?

Couldn't see. An it mighta been our own folk movin.

Okay, Bed said. Whoever they is, they ain't gon cross plowed fields. They don't know we seen em, so they gon come slow an stealthy. We still got us time. Go back up. You packed?

Sugarsnap nodded. From other rooms came the sounds of a household rousing: feet moving in passageways, hurrying up and down steps; doors opening and closing. There was little talk: most, it seemed, had made their arrangements the night before; and soon enough, as though by general agreement, they began to gather in the ballroom, it being the largest room in the house, in anticipation of some last, brief sharing of information and offering of guidance before they scattered. Still Diver had not returned.

What you gon say, Cyrus asked Bed quietly, twenty minutes later. Sugarsnap had brought no news of further sightings, and they stood on the lower steps of one of the flights of stairs that swept up from the ballroom floor to the balcony above. All their focus, he knew, had been on becoming an army; there had been no proper plan for flight.

I'm gon lay out the pros an cons square as I can, Bed said. But people got to make their own minds up, make their own choices: I don't know no better than they do.

It seemed that most of those who had been sheltering in the house, and a good many who had been standing guard on the avenue and even over at the millyard, were now assembled there. They hefted packs and sacks and bundles for the journey, and dressed plain: all jewelry and costly clothing was concealed from view, as, in the main, were weapons, though several of the men openly carried rifles. Others of both sexes carried hoes and spades and sickles, chancing that to the unsuspecting eye these would be seen as tools only, and those bearing them not as uprisers fleeing to freedom but as slaves on their plodding way to the fields for the usual long day's work.

Cyrus was struck by the variety of human beings before him, and in that he saw hope, for a patroller anticipating a young buck with a rifle might well overlook an old woman toiling along the field's edge bowed beneath a croker sack; and a white man believing Negroes stupid and cowed might be wrongfooted by a well-written pass or, if that failed, a coolly-drawn pistol. And too, there was this: whatever was happening on the Saint Hall estate, and for all their fear of news of revolt spreading, the other plantation-owners would not want the movement of labor about the district prevented, or not for long, since that would quickly injure their profits. But the hope he felt as he surveyed those before him was not merely pragmatic, but also human: all these men and women, of different colors and complexions, gifts and tempers and inclinations, now had a chance to use their wits and strength, both physical and mental, to bid for freedom. Many would fail – this time – but some would succeed; some would win north. And some of those who failed would achieve, deep within them, a north of the spirit, and would run again, and again. Still, there were a good many children among them, the smaller ones leaning into their mothers' skirts and looking about them with wide eyes, and their littleness, their lack of comprehension troubled him. Yet did they not make flight all the more necessary?

Prudence came up to Bed: it was time. Together the two of them climbed up a few more steps and turned to face those assembled. All were waiting for them to speak, and at once fell silent.

It's time, Abednego said. There's been no news from Diver, an we can't wait no mo: white folks got to know things ain't right here. They comin, maybe already near. But we ready. We prepared. You all got passes – thank you, brother Cornet. The head butler bowed slightly. He wore a short, rust-colored scarf and fingerless gloves of the same brown wool, and a pack was set high on his narrow shoulders. Bed continued, Some of us got other papers too. Use em wisely. Those who got guns, use em wisely. They's small boats if you want to chance the river; if you cross it you can chance west. Or you can head east, hide out in the swamp, or pass through it if you can find a way; or you can head north. The north east boundary's farther off, but it's dry that way, an they's woods fo shelter an concealment. If you of a mind to chance the road they's horses fo those who can ride, an carriages an carts. A pass might see you through. I know everyone been talkin bout they's strength in numbers, or strength in goin alone, or as families. Some o y'all can pass: use that. I can't make no decision fo you; I hope you made em already, fo now is the time to –

At that moment the right-hand front door swung open and Strawson rushed in breathless. They's a white man comin down the avenue on a horse, he announced. We hid but he callin he wants a parlay.

A panicked hubbub broke out. Quiet now, Bed called. Cyrus came up a few stairs to join him as Bed said quietly to Prudence, What you think?

They wants them hostages, she said.

Befo they attacks, Cyrus added.

So they movin in already, Bed said. Then, raising his voice, he announced: They aimin to keep us talkin while they box us in. Now, just in case he got somethin to say, or I can make a delay in whatever the white folks plannin, I'm gon stay an speak with him, but I want all of you to leave right now, go whichever way you goin that ain't the avenue. He gon find a empty room an not know what we doin or where we at. Go fast, go wary, go now an godspeed.

He stepped down to hastily-muttered amens. You too, Prudence, he said. She nodded, shot him a kiss on his cheek, touched Cyrus on the arm, and hurried off, joining the others who, with only a little pushing, were making their way through to the back of the house, thence out onto the lawn and riverbank beyond. Bed spoke quietly with Strawson; Strawson nodded and went out again.

Why we doin this, Cyrus asked, when Bed came back to him. They stood partway up the stairs, so as to be out of the way of those departing.

If they think we holed up in here with a knife to them white gals' throats, they gon hold off rushin in, Bed said. The longer they holds off, the mo chance the rest of us gots to get gone.

Okay, Cyrus said. So we wants him to think we stayin.

Yeah.

But we ain't stayin?

We ain't.

Okay.

Once the room was empty Bed crossed to one of the front windows, made a quick sign, and returned to the staircase. A minute later Terrance and Elston brought the white man in, shoving him as they did so, roughly enough for him to know his skin did not guarantee deference or confer immunity, but not sufficiently to do him harm.

We done searched him, Elston said. He ain't got no pistol.

He was an older man, in his sixties, perhaps, and upright of carriage, his height extended by a gleaming black top-hat at back of which silver hair was visible, and he was dressed in cream pants and a plain black frock-coat of good cut, beneath which a cream, gold-threaded satin vest showed, and he wore cream kid gloves. His skin was threaded red. He had a hawk nose and bright blue eyes, some courage by his bearing, and a mind sharp enough, Cyrus did not doubt, to appreciate the theater of what Bed had contrived for him, beginning with the simple obligation on the white man's part to look up at the black man in order to address him. Terrance and Elston jostled him forward until he stood in the middle of the room, then stepped back, taking up positions on either side of the doors. They drew their pistols and folded their arms across their chests.

My name is Corvelle, the white man said, and his voice was resonant and magnified by the empty room, and his manner was urbane. I am a lawyer, and I represent the interests of both Mister Saint Hall and his neighbor, Mister Brice.

What you want here, Bed asked. His voice was lighter than the white man's, but his manner too was unafraid.

Who am I addressing?

You can call me Abednego.

Firstly, I must inform you of what you must already know: that you have no right to take the actions you have taken.

Right?

Neither under God's law, nor man's.

You spoke with God, Abednego asked.

I am a praying man, and a church-goer.

They ain't no use to this, Cyrus said to Bed. Less end it.

The white man's glittering eyes now locked onto Cyrus. Who is leader here, he asked. Whom should I be addressing?

They ain't no leader, Cyrus said. We free.

It seems to me you are imprisoned.

If we is, then so is you.

A smile twitched at the corners of Corvelle's mouth. I am empowered, he said, to enquire concerning the well-being of the Misses Brice and their governess, Miss Abigail Pruitt.

They safe an well, Abednego said.

And young Mister Saint Hall, and Messers Arbuthnot and Adams?

We ain't animals. They fed an watered.

Might I enquire as to their whereabouts?

You got somethin to trade?

I am empowered to negotiate on my clients' behalf. What are your terms?

Free passage north fo all. Manumission papers fo all. Mas Saint Hall's word he won't neither hinder nor harry us.

The drawing up and proper notarising of such papers is a timely business, Corvelle said smoothly.

We got time.

And in return?

You get the gals, their governess, Mas Saint Hall's son, brother an friend an all the other white folks we got tied up round the place. Mas Saint Hall gets all o this back. Bed indicated with a sweep of his eyes the ballroom, the house. Just not us.

That is audacious, Corvelle said.

Yo forebears fight the British, Bed asked.

They did.

An what they fight fo?

Another faint smile touched Corvelle's mouth. I will return to my clients and inform them of your terms. You will allow me – he produced from a vest-pocket and sprung open a gold pocket-watch – one hour exactly, at which time I shall return with some form of preliminary agreement.

We be waitin right here, Bednego said. During their exchange he had not moved from the step on which he stood, and he did not move now as Corvelle, by the smallest margin possible, inclined his head in acquiescence.

There was a tightness visible in the white man's shoulders as he turned his back on Abednego and Cyrus and crossed to the now-closed front doors, and Elston and Terrance delayed opening them just long enough to make him fear that, after all, they would not let him go; that they might whip him or split his nose or amputate his ears simply because they could. Framed in the pale morning light he turned. Might I speak with the young ladies?

In a hour, Bednego said. When you comes back.

Corvelle nodded, turned, and went out. Beyond him was the balustraded balcony; past that the endless oak-lined avenue, the trees' branches gauzed with milky morning mist, and on the turn before the avenue stood a white horse, with Cole holding its reins. Corvelle went down to it, and Cole suffered the white man to lean heavily on his shoulder while climbing up into the saddle, passed him up the reins, and watched as he rode away.

In a hour we done, Abednego said, as the horse broke into a canter. We leavin now.

Terrance and Elston nodded and, pistols ready, they went out the front way; Bed and Cyrus hurried through to the drawing room, catching up a rifle each as they went.

Out the busted back doors, Bed said. We gon skirt round the way we come in then cut north-east.

As they were crossing to the billowing curtain that covered the French doors there was an explosion of gunfire outside and all the north-facing windows blew in in a cloud of glass. Bed and Cyrus threw themselves to the floor and, heedless of cuts from scattered shards and needles, scrambled forwards flat and fast as gators. More gunfire broke out, but farther off, and from somewhere else there came shouting, then a distant crackling as of fireworks. Now up on their hands and knees, and using their rifle-butts as crutches, like buckled cripples they thrust the French doors open with their heads and, evolving upwards, scuttled hunchbacked across the terrace and onto the frosted and slippery lawn. Before them was the river; to their right the smoke from the massed discharge of rifles beneath the pine-break made an opaque wall through which those now reloading struggled to see, much as Bed and Cyrus struggled to see them and determine their number. A handful of further explosions came from within this gaseous wall, accompanied by brief orange combustion-flares at about breast height, but these seemed to have no particular target beyond the windows in the north wall of the house. Somewhere a woman began to scream and did not let up, a mechanical sound like a kettle left boiling on the stove.

The rising breeze was carrying the gunsmoke in slanting sheets towards the water, leaving Bed and Cyrus only moments before their certain exposure to their assailants' view. Crouching low, they scurried across the frost-slicked lawn and slid down the declivity that led to the river's edge; and there, concealed by its banking, they hunkered, hoping they had managed to break from the house unseen, for there was no shelter for them but the incline: the boat-house was too far off and in any case too elevated, and the water was at their backs, cold and wide and open. The air was icy, the dun sky low and dirty, and the sulfur in the drifting powder-smoke made their eyes and nostrils itch. Cyrus rubbed his face fast as rifle-shots cracked out on the far side of the house. Had everyone left? Cyrus imagined Sugarsnap at an upper window, drawing a bead as the white men came on. Further south there was yelling and the neighing of horses.

Les keep movin long as we can, he said quietly. Bed nodded. Now on all fours, Cyrus, with Bed behind him, crept along the concealing mud slant of the riverbank. They passed on the landward side the row of small, gaily-painted rowboats turned hull-up on the shore, but there could be no question of attempting to escape by water.

They were among reeds and weeds when a shout from the millyard path alarmingly close by made both men throw themselves flat on the ground, and their chests heaved up into their mouths. A pint of whisky an twenty dollars fo every buck you drop, its owner declared.

They brung up that cannon yet, another voice asked. I ain't goin in under grapeshot, not fo gold or glory.

You don't need to worry bout that, the first voice said. The senator don't want no holes blown in his fine fittings.

Yeah, but old man Brice don't want to waste no time.

Don't want his gals bred by niggers.

Only yaller babies he wants is his.

Shut yo mouth, Cobb. That's a lawsuit.

Sprawled flat as a leaf stamped into an icy crust of mud, Cyrus slowly turned his head and saw, through a yellow-brown tangle of weeds, atop the rise of the riverbank, a procession of white men's heads in profile, moving steadily towards the house, and in considerable numbers: dozens at the least; and who knew how many more might be following on. Most held rifles ready, their raised muzzles bobbing repeatedly into Cyrus' line of sight; and their postures were hunched as a man's is when stalking game, and they were wary-eyed, though none looked toward the water, on which as yet no craft was moving. More gunfire broke out: to the south, Cyrus reckoned.

God damn, one of the white men said in a high, cracking voice. By the look of him he was too young to shave, and he wore a slouch hat, and had a protuberant Adam's apple and an overbite. Them niggers got guns. No-one tol us they got guns.

What, you think once they got em they was gon throw em in the river?

I thought they was too dumb to use em.

Only dumb-wit here is you.

Maybe Bolitionists showed em.

Perhaps it was lying on the icy mud that made Cyrus feel it now, but the cindery sky was, he felt sure, presaging snow, and soon; and their breaths misted the air. He looked across the passing white men now, for to study any individual too intently was to risk projecting an optical energy that might draw attention to the onlooker, and the white men's senses were surely attuned to all that was liminal now. Then they were past, and Bed came squirming up alongside him. What you reckon, he murmured.

Give it a minute, Cyrus said, then chance gettin up.

Okay.

A minute passed. They raised their heads like turtles and, seeing no-one on the path, pushed themselves up onto their hands and knees, then squatted on their haunches among the weeds. The white men who had passed by had, it seemed, either gone into the house or were now beyond the further pine-break, the one that screened the kitchen garden and guest cottages from view; or else had gone round to join their fellows out front. Searching the house would no doubt occupy them for some time, as would the discovery of the hostages.

Casting many glances behind them, Bed and Cyrus made their way along the mill-yard path at a fast lope. To their right the fields were wide and flat and as shelterless as the river, and the trees planted at regular intervals to mark the way offered no cover, for they were pruned tall and narrow as serried spearheads, though here and there patches of scrub had been suffered to become established, and there were small copses; and along the water's edge were masses of reeds that stirred and whispered in the breeze, in which a man might lie unseen.

From up ahead, though as yet a good way off, there came more rifle retorts, and yelling carried on the wind. The mill-yard, Abednego said.

They ain't took it yet, then. We gots to go by it?

No: there's a path curves up past the chapel: that's our way. It safe?

No reason I can think of fo the white folks to come along it.

Okay. Looking ahead, Cyrus became aware there was now something on the water, a dark, boxy shape coming towards them faster than the current. He squinted to make it out. They's a boat, he said.

They black folks?

Can't tell.

Quickly Cyrus and Bed concealed themselves amongst the reeds, and squatting watched the boat approach. To Cyrus it seemed impossible that it was Diver; that the foundry raid had, against all evidence, succeeded; and that he was now sending a crew of armed black men back. Yet might not a running battle have been fought there over the course of several days, and might not the white men's attack now be a response to the knowledge they were losing that battle? He craned his neck to see; Bednego sharply pulled him back down.

The vessel, a large flatboat, drew slowly level with their hiding-place. It was strange to Cyrus to see white men at the oars, but there they were. The other white men – thirty or more, and packed in close – were heavily armed, showing rifles, pistols, sabres and farm implements, and they were silent and faced forward like cattle. Three black men lay dead and stripped upon the low roof that covered the front third of the boat, and however they had met their deaths, their bodies were savagely cut about. Cyrus did not seek out their faces, and Abednego too looked across rather than at the funereal scene, and the silence of the white men was like, but was not, the silence of mourners; was more the silence of hunters after they are blooded.

Once the boat had passed on far enough for them to no longer fear being observed, Bed and Cyrus straightened up and clambered back onto the path. They went slower now, knowing for sure their enemies were on all sides, and expending much energy in looking constantly about them. Up ahead the millyard stack rose black and solitary; but they had reached the divide in the path, and took the inland turn. The gunfire from the direction of the mill had ceased, though from that cessation no conclusion was decipherable. The path ran on emptily through the deserted fields, crows wheeled above the cross atop the distant chapel's spire as if prophetic, and to be hurrying toward them seemed ominous to Cyrus. The wind was gusting now, and both men held their hats down on their heads as they lent into it and kept on. Their rifles, still unfamiliar burdens, were heavy in their hands, their thighs burned from so much squatting and crouching, and their packs hindered their movements.

The total absence of human beings from this landscape struck Cyrus as unnatural; as if everyone on the estate had been swallowed by the earth or drawn up into the sky; and he looked back at the Big House then, and the tree-lined avenue that led from it to the main road; and though distance and lack of elevation circumscribed his view he made out what seemed to be small white scraps flitting about beneath the boughs, the aprons worn by women, maybe, and other, darker shapes darting among them; and, though the wind carried the sound of the discharging fire-arms away from him, he saw some of the scraps go down sudden, as if weighted by millstones.

On the main road, to the south, a disorderly body of men, white he did not doubt, had massed, with at its head a troop of cavalry, and as Cyrus watched a bugle was sounded – he caught a glint of brass – and the horsemen and their captain entered the avenue, and the mob came shoving after. Following the line of the road north Cyrus saw, before his view was cut off by the intervening woodland, no-one of either race, on foot or horseback; nor were there visible any carts or buggies. Bed touched his arm and he turned away and they went on, and the wind was rising, and overhead the clouds moved fast.

The untethered shutters of the chapel were banging mindlessly as they drew near, and dead leaves rushed across the graveyard; the branches of the walnut trees creaked, and the grass stirred as if myriad small creatures were hurrying through it guided by a single purpose. Two bodies were lying there, for some reason, or no reason, positioned head to tail: a white man, face-up, and a black man, face down, and the chest of the one, and the back of the other, were a red confusion, and whoever else had been there and survived the encounter had taken with them whatever weapons either man had had in his possession. A glance showed Cyrus the black man was missing fingers from his right hand, an old wound: Strawson; and to Cyrus it seemed strange to know him, even slightly, though there was nothing to be done now, or even thought.

They went round to the south side of the chapel, in search of shelter from the wind, and so as not to be looking upon the dead, and once there took a moment to catch their breaths. The cold air pooled and eddied and spiraled up around them, carrying with it tiny fragments of bark and dirt that obliged them to squint. They shared a swallow of water from Cyrus' flask, and as Cyrus stoppered it their eyes met, and the wind charged up the wildness in them, and overhead the weathercock atop the cross on the spire was spinning, a blur.

They went on, leaving Strawson and the white man behind them, making for the slave cabins, behind which they intended to pass, seeking a track heading nearest to north. Now, here and there, they saw others, some struggling across plowed fields; one on a horse, the rest on foot; singly and in groups, black folk fanning out, beginning their journeys, going as fast as they could, each of them aware that every other black man or woman in sight would divide their pursuers; all knowing the merciless truth: that a gain in freedom for one would be at the cost of a cruel loss for another.

We carryin those we leaves behind inside of us, Cyrus thought. The weight of em, thas a heavy thing –

Shots once more cracked out. Someone fell in a field away to their right and did not get up, and those who were able to, ran, for it seemed they were being fired on from the center of the estate, and that radiate flight was therefore still possible. A glance over his shoulder told Cyrus there were figures rushing toward them with alarming rapidity from the direction of the Big House. As yet all were on foot, and some knelt in order to discharge their rifles and were, therefore, slowed in their advance by having subsequently to stop and laboriously reload. One or two among the fleeing black folks turned and fired back, and Cyrus saw one small figure among their pursuers fall among the furrows and not get up again, and yelled his approval as he ran.

In a short while he and Bed found themselves passing along the now-deserted cabin row. Cyrus wondered where the hands were who had been tied up because considered untrustworthy; whether they had, at the last, been given their own chance at freedom, or had been abandoned, bound and gagged, locked forgotten in one of these comfortless buildings to await the arrival of the overseers and plead their babbling loyalty to massa. Had they been treated as the white captives had been treated, he wondered, given food and drink and permitted to empty their bowels and bladders in private, or, ironically, worse?

Here, Bed said, and they slipped between two cabins and came out on the track that ran behind the row. There's a trail up aways runs out to the land we was clearin.

They found it and hurried on. The double row of cabins, and the copses of trees and thickets along its northern side, screened them from their pursuers' view, and they could for a time advance linearly, without fear of a gunshot in the back.

What's the range o rifles, Cyrus asked, a question he found he could only give voice to once they were not in immediate danger of a lead ball between the shoulderblades.

Bout nine hundred yards, Bed said.

Thas thirty chains.

Bed nodded. Accurate to five hundred, they says, but lead's

lead if it comes yo way.

The trail ran straight, between new-plowed fields. No-one it seemed had followed them in that direction, black or white; and surely the white men would stop to search the cabins when they reached them, both out of fear of ambush, and in order to catch any black folks who might have concealed themselves there in hopes of escaping later, under cover of night.

They went on without pausing at something between a lope and a jog, and after perhaps forty minutes found themselves leaving cultivated land behind them. Here brakes and lone trees were dotted about, and the boundary-line of the forest appeared, a narrow, distant gray strip brushed in thinly between the scumbled white sky and the umber and ocher earth, and all ahead seemed wide and low and panoramic, and a little way on the track fizzled out in tussocky, rutted indeterminacy. It was here that Abednego had spent crippling months clearing the land, reducing nature to desolation prior to its subjugation to commerce; but it was also here that he had come by night to hunt, and so he knew the best and fastest way to cross it.

Nonetheless their going was slow, for they were soon obliged to force their way through much dead growth, and take care to avoid ankle-twisting stumbles among the tussocks – though even as they struggled on, it was in a small way reassuring to know that any pursuer would be in equal difficulties, and that horses could not be ridden here. Still there remained the fear of a bullet in the back, and behind that the possibility of pursuit by dogs, though Cyrus knew of no reason save perversity that would lead to their noses fixing on his and Bed's scents amidst so many others. From far behind them came the occasional crack of a gunshot; up ahead, and now close to, the northern boundary road waited, flat and empty, and a chain beyond it, the wood. The upper branches of the waiting trees stirred visibly and made a rushing sound. Back into the wild places, Cyrus thought. But no longer alone. They kicked their way free of the briary undergrowth and found solid ground once more beneath their feet, and as when he had passed that first fence marking the edge of Tyler, to transgress this boundary, though it was unmarked by any barrier, felt to Cyrus significant and dense in meaning.

Free.

Yet as they stepped onto the road, from a ditch beyond it three previously-concealed figures rose, white men dressed in gray and tan, and they aimed their rifles at Bed and Cyrus level with their chests. Yellow-eyed, drooping-moustachioed, slouch-hatted, patrollers from their dress, which was dirty and much patched, their red-knuckled hands were fitted to their weapons as Cyrus' and Bed's were not, and so the black men had no option but to put up their hands, the left turned palm forward, the right holding the rifle by the forestock, muzzle pointed to the sky.

The oldest white man, their captain it seemed, spat upon the ground. Put them fire-arms down, he said. Slow, now.

Awkwardly Bed and Cyrus did so, sinking in the manner of a curtsy, placing their weapons carefully on the ground so as to avoid an accidental discharge, keeping their eyes on the white man who had spoken as they did so. There was ten feet between them: too far to reach and snatch; too far to jump. Slowly and as one Bed and Cyrus straightened up again.

Now them revolvers. Unbuckle them buckles, let em slide down. Careful now.

Why don't we just blast em, one of the other white men said as Cyrus and Bed moved their hands to their belt-buckles. Though equally moustachioed he was younger, with long, bony hands and bulging blue eyes, the sclera of which were a cheese-rind yellow.

They worth double alive, the older man said, maybe triple. Careful now.

The speeding wind at his back set his hat-brim flapping like a broken wing.

As Bed and Cyrus let the belts fall, dragged down asymetrically by the weight of the pistols in their holsters, a hissing sound came speeding through the trees behind the white men that made the younger two look round, though the older did not; and while their weapons wavered, his did not. Hare, you tie em, he ordered. Here.

The bore of his rifle was a black and lidless eye staring at Cyrus' chest, and he held out a loop of rope to the bony-handed youth, who did not take it, distracted as he was by the sound at his back. This grew rapidly in volume, some force of nature hurtling upon them full-tilt; and all at once hail was pelting down on them all, stinging, blinding, stones big as peas and hard as buckshot, and the wind lurched and shifted abruptly so it was driven first on the slant and then clawed round into the white men's faces, and the force of the gust all but carried Bed and Cyrus forward, and, unable to bear to do otherwise, and caught up in its momentum, they chanced a rush and the old man, vacillating, discharged his rifle between them, the bullet bursting the padded shoulder of Bed's jacket but doing no worse, not even throwing his stride, and they were on him wide-armed and carrying him and the other two back before they could think to take proper aim, and all five of them tumbled into the briar-choked ditch in which the patrollers had lain concealed; but Bed and Cyrus were on top, and in that fury that is charged up in a man whose life is at hazard they tore the rifles from the men beneath them, raised them fast and pounded the stocks in the white men's faces, rapidly reducing them to a concussed state and then, by dint of repetition, bloody unconsciousness, and even then they struck them several blows more, and the hail lashed down and all about them was a disorientating, stinging, shifting storm of marble shot that it seemed could not intensify, but did; and after taking up the white men's rifles and discharging the two that had not yet been fired into their insensate faces, sparing only the man who had not spoken, and had not thereby condemned himself to certain and instant oblivion, Cyrus and Bed threw the weapons down upon bodies already part-buried by hail-stones and staggered back to retrieve their own, picking up and fumblingly rebuckling their belts, looking down as they did so to avoid both the bee-swarm sting of the hail and each others' eyes. But once that was done they did look up, to face at once what they were compelled to face, and they were trembling, with cold and shock and the fast retreat to the heart of blood and adrenalin, but they saw each other, complete, and each saw himself in the other's eyes, complete. And Cyrus reached for Abednego's hand and Bed offered it, and together, hand-in-hand, they ran forward and with a yell jumped the ditch, the bodies, and pelted through the harsh confetti of the hail into the shelter of the waiting wood.

Chapter Twenty-Seven

T hough on its fringes the wood was not dense, the scrub and scattered saplings broke the wind, thereby lessening the force of the still-lashing hail; and a hundred yards further in, the tangle of branches overhead diffused it to a hard white pattering, as of things dropped rather than fired explosively, the small white balls filling their hat-brims and sprinkling the dark earth and fallen leaves at their feet, resting there dry and hard as though made of sugar. And then, as abruptly as it had begun, the storm was over: a wall of hail moving south, the cloud above emptying itself as it went. The hissing died away, the wind subsided, and the wood was still.

Their chests heaving, Bed and Cyrus stood there among the trees, and it was as if they had been transported in an instant to somewhere wholly new. Cyrus looked up at the sky, and though no sun was evident, in consideration of the evenness of the light, he judged the time to be a little past noon.

We best go on, he said. Make the most o the daylight.

Bed nodded, and they cast about for a trail to follow, desiring above all to put a distance between themselves and what lay all too close behind them. Feeling light-headed, for a time Cyrus took in little of his surroundings, which were in any case unfamiliar to him. Bed too seemed dazed, looking about him with a kind of wonder, making as if to speak but finding no words; knuckling away occasionally a suddenly-beading, disconnected tear. Eventually they dawdled to a confused halt, and in what seemed a domed and woven hall of cypresses, through the latticed upper branches of which light fell in faint shafts, they held each other close and cried for what they had had to do, wet cheek hot against hot wet cheek. And after their crying was done, and the rising shudders had passed through them and sunk back into the ground, Bed produced from his pack a bottle of brandy with dust about its shoulders, and they drank a capful each and no more, and ate some slices of cold roast pork, knife to mouth.

Afterwards they turned away from each other to urinate,

and went on, more focused now they had emptied out their grief, though such grief was, they knew, chthonic; a deep spring that would well up again and again, for it was connected to what was primal: the taking of life.

Damn, Cyrus said. Damn.

We got us, Bed said.

Cyrus nodded, though across the years to come the image would rise up before him in unexpected flashes: three bud-pale crocus-faces, with opalescent eyes in which were crystalised, as by the photographer's art, the final moment of life, framed in ditch-dirt, waxy skins blossoming red in the rifle's retort, pollinated by his convulsed finger and the bruise caused by the weapon's recoil against his shoulder, stamened with white bone shards that fruited into what? The nightshade plant in the Saint Hall glasshouse, perhaps, for curiously he dreamed of that too, though he had never been inside.

Zotics.

We got us, he agreed. And who, after all, was pure in this world, and what was of value that was bought with no pain?

Nothin.

I come to do this, an I done it. An we doin it. Together.

Still he felt tremulous, somehow delicate, a mayfly.

They went on, and the ground was dry underfoot, and so their way was the right way. Cyrus wondered how many of the others had gone to the swamp. From his own brief experience he did not envy them, though he had heard of runaways hiding out for years in such places, and knew it to be freedom of a sort, predation by skeeters and gators being preferable to predation by white men. The land began to rise, though at first this was discernible only as an increasing ache in their thighs.

They kept on until dusk was drawing in and the wood about them was sinking into shadow, then made their camp beneath a large oak by a small clear-water stream. This deep in – and through his studying of the bedsheet map Abednego understood enough of the surrounding area to know the wood ran on extensively both north and east, and that they had not, therefore, inadvertently made camp at its farther edge, and thusly put themselves at risk of easy detection and capture – the air, though still, being bitter cold, they risked a fire. There was much dead underbrush available, and many fallen twigs were to hand; and the dryness of the previous weeks' weather made the kindling of it not too tedious a task, and Cyrus' skill with flint and steel had grown considerably in the course of his journeying.

Too tired to cook, they were glad enough simply to be warm, and ate what remained of the cold roast pork. Afterwards, framed by a pair of raised tree-roots that functioned like arm-rests, they leant back against the oak's broad trunk, and Bed set his bowler aside and rested his pomaded head on Cyrus' shoulder, and Cyrus put an arm around him and drew Bed close, and huddled together they stared into the flickering flames as the night fell about them. There were no stars nor moon above, only clouds, unseen. Cyrus thought of bears and wolves, but he was no longer one man, and he and Bed had loaded pistols at their hips, and rifles. He thought vaguely of Durance and Cornet and Prudence, of Sugarsnap and Hebe and Dill, but his thoughts too quickly went to dark places and so he set them aside, attempting to content himself with what was sensory and immediate: Bed's head on his breast, the clean and perfumed scent of his hair, the warmth of the fire, the smell of woodsmoke, the weight of pork in his belly, even the ridged lumpiness of the tree-trunk at his back. Bed turned into him then, sliding his hand across Cyrus' midsection, inside his coat, and Cyrus smiled.

We done it, Bed, he thought. We free, fo now at least, an we alive.

Dotted about in the dark that night there must have been others, thinking the same thoughts as he was, numbering in their hundreds maybe; perhaps only in their dozens, but still it was something, and Cyrus recalled his dream of charcoal figures viewed from a great height, moving north. And if the power of the white man, the slaveholder, could not be wholly overthrown, not all at once, it was nonetheless, he now saw, not everywhere equivalent: here and there the threads dried out and grew brittle, and not all the eggs the spider laid hatched. Following the thought, he recalled hearing that the young of spiders fled the rupturing sack for fear of being devoured by their blindly predating mother, or by each other; and he recalled too that it was said the nearer you came to the free states the less the institution of slavery was venerated, and that there were white folks who wholly repudiated it, who would even fight rather than give a runaway up; and amidst these speculations sleep stole upon him, and Bed slept in his arms.

The following morning was cold and milky. Above their heads, mist tangled in the branches beneath a uniformly pallid sky, and the sun as it rose was a white disc without force and curiously coronaed. Bed and Cyrus got up aching, relieved themselves, splashed their hands and faces in the stream, drank deep and refilled their flasks, kicked over the traces of their fire and went on. The land rose more steeply now, and after several hours' steady going they found themselves clambering over mossy rocks, and then picking their way between the ravines and gorges that fissured a hillside tilting towards verticality. Down some of these gorges water cascaded many hundred feet, and from the pools below spray rose prismatically. This, Bed and Cyrus knew, was or had been Indian land, though which tribe neither could say, but both had heard tales of Indians helping runaway slaves, and that was encouraging; and in any case they felt safer in places that defied cultivation. As they climbed they hummed, then softly sang a song they had learned on Tyler, a simple shucking song, and Tyler felt long ago and far away, and all it meant was falling from them now.

On an outcrop they sat and, legs dangling, ate and drank and looked out across the terrain they had spent the last two days traversing. Their view was framed by the tangled branches of the trees that grew at a cantilever from the fractures in the rock, and they saw they were now high in the crescent of hills through which the Stone River ran, and there, far below them was Saint Hall, and Brice beyond it, and on the river craft were visible as dark drifting dots. That far off neither Cyrus nor Bed could see if there were people in the fields; they did not think so. Past Brice lay other estates, other fields, running on and on, on both sides of the river, and Cyrus did not see how any could evade capture who had gone by road, not even the sharpest-minded, for any paper bearing the Saint Hall name would soon enough be known a likely forgery, and incite, rather than allay, suspicion.

Now they talked of plans, and for the first time these were not plans for many, but only themselves.

The other side o this range, past the woods, there's a railroad, Bed said.

You means real or what they calls underground, Cyrus asked.

Real, Bed said. It runs north east. If we finds it, we can try an figure a way of gettin aboard, or worst, we can follow the tracks. Get to cities. Maybe find us connections to the other railroad. We gots us some money; we gots our wits. Overground or underground, we gon get north.

Cyrus nodded, trying to keep the unease he felt at the prospect of endlessly intimidating novelty hidden from the man whose good opinion he valued above all others'. Okay, he said. Overground or underground.

Abednego was at once alert to his discomfort. It won't be easy, he said, taking Cyrus' hand lightly in his. But we better off hidin in a crowd than a wood. Towns an cities offer possibilities. An the further from Saint Hall we gets, the more use these is – he patted where the forged papers rested in the inside pocket of his jacket.

Cyrus studied Abednego's profile. Where we aimin fo?

A place call New-York to begin with, Bed said. We gets there, we can taste the air, take a view, settle maybe, or maybe keep on goin, up to Canada. Someplace where we won't be fraid of bein drug back. Wouldn't that be somethin, Cyrus? You an me, just livin our lives how we wants, free. He turned to look at Cyrus and he was smiling, and his eyes sparkled, and at that moment he was the most handsome man Cyrus had ever seen. Someplace we can make our lives, Bed went on. Just like the white folks do.

And as Abednego spoke Cyrus felt all he had repressed rise within him like a great choking bolus; everything that those enslaved were in perpetuity denied, a faculty amputated as it were psychically, or cauterised; all that he had continued to deny during his flight, his search, at that time living moment by moment, not daring to look up into the solar disc of the future and risk blinding, burning, consummation in the insanity of black hope. But now, with Bed beside him, he could look up, and to do so was simple and what he saw was real. And they drank whisky to the future, a warming swallow each, and Cyrus offered a libation to the ground and Bed did not demur, nor call it waste, and they stood and went on.

The day was drawing to its close by the time they breasted the hill, and dense woodland was all about them, depriving them of any view of the land ahead. The gradient of the descent, however, was less steep by far than the ascent had been, and therefore easier to manage, and they went on a good way before repeated stumbles over the roots and looped briars that were increasingly hidden by the dusk obliged them to give up and find a place to make camp. The air was damper on this side of the hill, and a fire harder to light, and the heat more quickly drawn from their hands and feet as they sheltered in a thicket of whortleberry. The ground was muddy beneath them and their spirits sank.

Least it ain't rainin, Cyrus said, and he caught Bed's chin between his thumb and forefinger, turned Bed's face to his and kissed him on the lips. The kiss, firm at first, softened, deepened and became probing, and Bed lay back upon the cushioning whortleberry and Cyrus moved on top of him and Bed gasped as Cyrus placed the palm of his hand on Bed's forehead and tilted his head back, stretching out his neck, kissed his Adam's apple and put a hand between his legs. Chill though the air was, both men now needed to feel skin against skin, and rapidly loosened their clothing, unbuttoning vests, pulling up shirts, pushing down pants and then drawers, and moved against each other hotly, and from his knapsack Cyrus produced the box of moisturizing cream from Miz Saint Hall's dressing-table, gift of Hebe, and with its aid their union was made complete, and both gave, and both took, and both were open and opened, and in the deep woods they felt no fear and for the first time gasped and hollered without restraint.

The next morning broke more brightly, and the sky, though pale, was blue, not gray or white, and the sun, when it appeared, was a molten bead glinting bright between the branches, even dazzling. They descended the hill and the woods continued dense and uniform, with oaks predominating. Here and there they were obliged to leap small streams, though had yet to encounter a river requiring fording or the contriving of a raft; or the need somehow to come by a boat. At one of the streams a family of deer had come down to drink, a doe and two fawns, hoof-tipped stick legs splaying, tongues flicking the water delicately as, unobserved, the two men passed them by, and though it was, perhaps, practicality that stayed their hands – the revealing nature of a gunshot; the awkward handling of the carcasses, and the bloody delay dressing them would occasion – compassion played its part too; and the doe, raising her head and seeing them, started, and she and her fawns hobbled off fast into the brake.

The lack of any vantage point from which to survey their surroundings began to weary Cyrus and, no doubt, Abednego, for it made the wood seem endless, and the lack of any trails save the most vestigial made for slow going. Likely made by deer or wild pigs, and therefore indicative of the comparative absence of man, these were reassuring, but ran anything but straight; and while the sun was overhead it was hard to know whether they were still going in at all the right direction. They were now among great gray oaks festooned with pennants of dead moss, as for a jamboree of the departed, and the ground was growing softer underfoot, and they feared finding themselves astray in some unexpected swamp of unknown dimensions.

It was as Bed was pausing at yet another random divide in the trail and looking about him uncertainly, and even ill-temperedly, that Cyrus recalled the compass James Rose had given him, and rummaged for it in his pocket. It was still there, and he drew it out. They's this, he said, offering it to Bednego. I forgot I had it.

Taking it from him, Bed placed the compass level on the palm of his hand. Where you come by it, he asked as they watched the needle shiver then settle on north.

White man gived it to me, Cyrus said.

Gived?

He called it atonement.

For what?

He dint say, Cyrus said, for that was too complex a thing to talk of then.

He a Quaker?

I don't know what that is.

485

White folks who think black slavery goes against what God wants. Say thee an thine stead of you n yourn. Some of em runs waystations fo the underground railway.

He weren't no Quaker. He was – somethin else.

Can I keep hold of it?

Course.

They went forward with greater purpose now they knew they could hold to a course, though for several hours the woods continued uniform about them; then they came to a river that cut across their path, obliging them to pause. It was of considerable width, but shallow, and so greatly silted they found they could cross and keep their feet dry by jumping from one sandbar to another, with only the deeper midpoint requiring a leap of any athleticism, and once Cyrus had made the leap he reached back with his rifle extended, and Bed gripped the stock to steady him as he followed on.

The sun was sinking towards the tangled horizon when they heard the sound: mechanical, yet melancholy and somehow full of yearning: a steam whistle, and beneath it a faint, regular clattering, and sounds as of repeated rapid exhalations of breath. Bed and Cyrus exchanged a glance, for that surely must be a steam-train; this surely must be the railroad; and though there was no sense to it, they at once found themselves stumbling forward, hurrying as to a known and destined station; as if adhering to a timetable. A way off to their left steam pumped up, white, explosive, and the base of the rapidly-slanting column moved rightwards before their eyes, and the speed of its motion, its rushing as it were into the future, sent the steam streaming back behind it towards a sunset that was reddening, dying.

Less run, Cyrus said.

The rapidly-darkening woods broke, revealing a wide pasture, and beyond it in a great curve the rails ran, elevated on sleepers bedded on clinker, and level as nothing in nature is level, and they gleamed with the scouring of them by the repeated procession of iron wheels at speed; and behind the glinting track the wood lay in silhouette, and above the stars were pricking the clear, pale sky, and there was the North Star, brightest of them all, and the train was coming on fast.

It gon slow on the bend: we can get ahead, Cyrus called as he and Abednego ran slantwise across the pasture, the dusk-dewed grass wetting their boots and ankles, and then the train burst from the trees, and he was right: it was slowing, and the iron wheels spun backwards and screamed and slid on the rails, though there was no slackening in the volume of steam that pumped up from the great black bucket of its chimney, and behind it sparks rushed up orange against the deepening dusk, and again the whistle sounded, and Cyrus saw that at its front a great lamp threw out a beam of light cycloptically above a huge grill, sharp, triangular, like a boat's prow but inverted, and set so low it near brushed the ground before it, and on the engine's sides were pumping pistons. And Bed and Cyrus ran on, at a steeper angle now, bent over so as not to catch the attention of the driver, aiming to intercept whatever cars were drawn behind at the point where the curve was most impeding of velocity, and they found themselves crouching down, breathless, concealed in a clump of bushes beside the track just moments before the locomotive reached it.

Sprint, Bed called, jumping up as it thundered past, pistons pumping, and it was huge, tall as three men, and as the cab at back of the engine hurtled by, lamps swinging, Cyrus saw the driver, a white man in goggles, leather gloves and cap and apron, leaning out and staring into the spotlit twilight ahead, and he did not see or hear Cyrus and Bed as they ran alongside him in the gloaming; and next to the driver Cyrus glimpsed a gleaming black man, stripped to the waist and lit orange by an open stove-door into which he was shoveling coal, and he too wore leather gauntlets and a protective apron; and then, though Cyrus was running fast as he could, the engine was past him, and a truck piled with coal followed on, a name written on its side; and then two carriages, in the glazed and curtained windows of which lights showed, and though these had steps between them that might be climbed up onto, and doors for easy access set in both ends, to encounter white folks here was to risk immediate capture, or death.

Then came a closed boxcar with neither doors nor windows, at least not on that side, for the conveyancing of trunks and suchlike, maybe; then what they had hoped for without knowledge that such things existed: three flatcars long as barges on which barrels and crates were piled and tethered under canvas; and Cyrus and Abednego ran faster and faster, for this was the moment when all forces and energies converged; and firstBed and then Cyrus threw his rifle up onto the frontmost flatcar as it drew level and then ahead of them, their commitment by that action made irrevocable; and Bed, who was lighter and so quicker in his movements than Cyrus, accelerated, going all out now, and he caught hold of a protruding handle at back of the iron frame of the second flatcar and, before it could drag his arm from its socket and tumble him under the wheels, pulled himself up, managing as he did so to wedge his left foot into a sort of stirrup set into a crossbar that depended perilously close to the spinning iron wheels, and, after swinging round and out and away from them, he clambered up onto the flatcar.

Sliding a hand under one of the taut, tethering ropes, and hooking it into the crook of his arm, he at once reached back, leaning out so he could lock hands with Cyrus, who was dashing along behind him, panic rising; and once more the whistle sounded, and the train began to accelerate, but just as Cyrus felt his thighs would burst, and his chest would burst, and that he would collapse in a juddering vomiting heap in the pasture and be left behind, alone, their fingers locked around each others' wrists and Bed pulled him up. Arm-socket wrenched and burning, for a terrible thrashing moment as both his feet left the ground Cyrus swung helplessly inwards, towards the lethal, clattering wheels, but then his flailing left foot struck the stirrup and he braced himself against it, then forced the toe of his boot into it; and then he was pivoting, turning as Bed had turned before him, slowly, as if on a spindle, close to, but safe from the devouring wheels, breathless as the darkening woods streamed past him faster and faster; and then he was being hauled up and Bed was falling back and Cyrus fell on top of him and they were laughing.

Epilogue

The bell above the door sounded springily, drawing Mister Reginald Sartain, a white man, through from the back room where his studio was located. It was a sunny morning in May.

What can I do for you gentlemen, he asked of the two Negro men he found standing at his counter. They looked at him warily, unused, he supposed, to being addressed as such by a white man, even a white man in need of their custom, business having been erratic of late, competition increasingly stiff and chemicals, as ever, costly.

We was wantin a photograph took, said the more powerfully-built of the two. Both wore gray frock-coats with silver lapels, gray pants and gray bowler hats with silver bands. Each man carried with him a bulky brown paper package tied neatly with string. The man who had spoken sported a vest of yellow check; the other, one of red velvet. Their dark skins gleamed, and when the larger man removed his hat and set it on the counter alongside the package he had been carrying, Mister Reginald Sartain saw his scalp was shaved glinting cut-throat close.

I'm sure I can oblige you, he said. Here at Sartain's we use the latest in wet collodion-on-glass techniques, as endorsed by the titled heads of Europe. He waited for them to fret about cost; when they did not, he went on, We are pleased to offer a variety of backdrops by which to evoke a mood and setting, and will be pleased to offer you as many prints as you pre-order. (This bait they did not take). A fine British drawing room, perhaps? Or an Arabian harem; or perhaps, yes, a plantation lullaby? When their eyes retreated he hurried on, That backdrop has proved most popular with our Negro clients, particularly those formerly from southern parts. Now the war is over, and such scenes have been consigned to the bonfire of history, we in New-York are free to contemplate them as purely romantic spectacles.

We wants a portrait in our uniforms, the leaner-built of the pair said, and he too placed his parcel on the counter. We brought em with us. You photographed dark skin befo?

Indeed I have; if you would care to peruse – Mister Sartain turned and brought down a particular album from a shelf behind him, flicking through card and tissue-paper until he reached a pleasing image of a bride and groom, twelve inches in height and ten or so wide, he jaunty in a top hat but unsmiling, she smiling uncertainly in high-necked white lace, a circlet of flowers upon her head in place of a tiara.

Cyrus and Abednego looked down at the image. He got an eye, Cyrus said to Bed, who nodded. You got an eye, he said to the white man.

Mister Sartain smiled. May I suggest a front parlor in the contemporary mode, neither ostentatious nor unduly modest?

A pause followed, that was, it transpired, an acquiescence. You gots a place we can change, the bigger man asked.

Will a store-room suffice? Mister Sartain gestured to a small but clean and dry room in which he kept bottles of chemicals, and boxes of plates and photographic paper. As they passed in, and before he went to ready the studio and prepare the plate, he asked, May I inquire as to your names?

Cyrus Tyler an Abednego Tyler, the bigger man said.

Brothers?

Naw.

Mister Sartain nodded and turned away. The way in which Negroes came by their names, and in particular their surnames, was often a complex business, and to delve into it invariably unrewarding, and often awkward in its revealing of the indecency of the fallen white south, though by the darkness of Cyrus' complexion and the Africanness of both men's features he judged neither to be the immediate byproduct of miscegenation.

In the small room Cyrus and Abednego untied the packages containing their uniforms, now clean of dirt and sweat and blood, and patched with minute care, the brass buttons shining; and in with them army boots that had until now never seen polish; that had been for years caked with mud, gleaming glossy as an ebony horse's flanks. Cyrus' cap was not, in fact, his own, but a replacement purchased from a haberdasher in

Five Points; but it fit as well, if not better, than the original. It was two years since the war had ended, and for now, despite its many harshnesses, New York was their home, and the room above the grocer's where they lived their sanctuary. Looking down at the dark blue jacket he felt not so much pride in what they had done as the simple force of necessity.

We come through it, he said to Bednego.

We come through, Bed agreed, unbuttoning and slipping off his coat. Across the line of his neck ran a scar that had been caused by a tiny piece of shrapnel from an exploding cannon; a whisker deeper and he would have bled out. Cyrus had shiny discs and dents scattered about his right forearm from grape-shot. Each knew the other's map as well as his own.

You still handsome though, Cyrus said, and he meant it.

So is you, Bed said. More, even.

Cyrus smiled, suddenly shy before his lover, and dipped his head.

In unison they set their vests aside, unhooked their sus-penders, unknotted and heeled off their shoes and stepped out of them, and then their pants, and changed into their uniforms. From outside there came the sound of the hawkers in the street, the clatter of hooves and creak of carriages. Cyrus placed the cap upon his head and turned to face Abednego. Bed's eyes were dark and brown and liquid-warm, and as Cyrus looked at him Bed darted the tip of his tongue over his full lips in a way that seemed anticipatory. Cyrus smiled, looking him up and down. Each then adjusted the other's cap and brushed out his shoulders as a sergeant would; critically contemplated the result, and nodded.

You ready, Mister Sartain called.

We comin, Bed called back.

In their uniforms and hand in hand like grooms they went through to the studio, a small but unexpectedly high-ceilinged room, with an angled roof made all of skylight. The sky beyond was blue, and puffy white clouds drifted across it. Before Bed and Cyrus the camera stood on its tripod, draped over with black silk and so made priestly or magical, a wood and brass box of transformation, of commemoration, and what the white man had called the set: a chaise-longue placed on an Arabian rug before embroidered curtains pulled across; beside it a

491

bureau on which stood a blue and white vase in which dried sunflowers were arranged, and next to the vase an artfully-placed sheet of music, with lying across it a pen and nearby a bottle of ink; above, a small chandelier hung on a long chain from a roof-beam as it would not in real life, so as to be present in the photographical composition and create thereby a verisimilitude of domesticity.

The white man stood by the camera awaiting them, no particular expression on his face. Self-consciously they came forward, and shyly sat side-by-side on the chaise-longue, at first slightly apart, then closer together; and finally, claiming the moment, Cyrus put his arm around Abednego's back, and Abednego leaned into him, and placed his hand so it curved down into Cyrus' inner thigh, and they looked at each other, deep, and then they looked out at the camera. And this would be found a century later, in a box of faded sepia prints collected together and then forgotten, taken down from a loft and put out for a yard-sale: jumbled stories that could not be claimed but only guessed at, partial proofs.

Still, now, Mister Sartain said as he bent forward and lifted the black silk over his head.

Huh?

For the exposure. You can't move.

Oh.

Still, now.

The End

About the Author

John R Gordon lives and works in London, England. He is a screenwriter, playwright and the author of seven novels, *Black Butterflies*, (GMP 1993), for which he won a New London Writers' Award*; Skin Deep*, (GMP 1997); and *Warriors & Outlaws* (GMP 2001), both of which have been taught on graduate and post-graduate courses on Race & Sexuality in Literature in the United States; *Faggamuffin* (Team Angelica 2012); *Colour Scheme* (Team Angelica 2013); and *Souljah* (Team Angelica 2015). He script-edited and wrote for the world's first black gay television show, Patrik-Ian Polk's *Noah's Arc* (Logo/Viacom, 2005-6). In 2007 he wrote the autobiography of America's most famous black gay porn star from taped interviews he conducted, *My Life in Porn: the Bobby Blake Story*, (Perseus 2008). In 2008 he co-wrote the screenplay for the cult *Noah's Arc* feature-film, *Jumping the Broom* (Logo/Viacom) for which he received an NAACP Image Award nomination; the film won the GLAAD Best (Limited Release) Feature Award. That same year his short film *Souljah* (directed by Rikki Beadle-Blair) won the Soho Rushes Award for Best Film, among others. He is also the creator of the *Yemi & Femi* comic-strip.

As well as mentoring and encouraging young lgbt+ and racially-diverse writers, he also paints, cartoons and does film and theatre design.

www.johnrgordon.com

CPSIA information can be obtained
at www.ICGtesting.com
Printed in the USA
BVHW071459040119
537053BV00002B/185/P